THE RUSH OF STONE

TOR ROXBURGH

CURIOUS CROW BOOKS

IMPRINT PAGE

First published in 2025 by Curious Crow Books

Curious Crow Books

PO Box 433

Ballan Victoria 3342 Australia

Copyright © Tor Roxburgh 2025

ISBN 978-0-9805249-5-6

Cover design by Stuart Bache Design

www.torroxburgh.com

JOIN MY READING COMMUNITY

Welcome to The Rush of Stone. My reading community is always the first to hear about giveaways and new releases. Please stay in touch by joining my email list at www.torroxburgh.com.

THE STONE BODY
To My Precious Ogden
(Upon Your Captaincy)
From Your Mother
N
W
E
S
KOMEY
NEW LYTALIA

PRIMERS

I've prepared two primers to help you enjoy *The Rush of Stone*.
If the events of Book 1 have become a little foggy, there is a useful infographic at the back of the book to refresh your memory about what happened in the story.
And if you'd like a quick and easy refresher on the history of the Stone Body, there's another handy infographic at the back of the book.

1

Fox spent the morning in the Oak House kitchen garden in an old tunic and a worn, short-sleeve shirt. She knew she should change out of her gardening clothes before she visited the city's libraries, but finding anything to fit was a challenge. Her waistline had grown beyond her wardrobe in the three and a half months since she'd allowed her pregnancy to proceed. Evidently, her body relished the idea of accommodating the baby. But acquiring a new wardrobe seemed... Well, it seemed frivolous when the continent's problems were so dire. She'd brought some clothes with her when she'd moved into Mica's tent, but only loose, practical things that accommodated her pregnancy. Working clothes. And they would have to suffice.

She picked up a brush from the open-air potting bench, knocked the dirt off the bristles, and swept the tunic's pleats, dislodging twigs and leaf litter. Luckily, the fabric was dark and didn't show the dirt.

She rock sensed the children approaching before she saw them: her little sister's determined disposition and the impish feel of Mica's orphaned nephew. That sensation of knowing how others were feeling, who they were, was still emerging as her rock skin regrew. She remembered it from her childhood, but remembering it differed from living it.

Saury ran to Fox, linked her fingers with her big sister's, and Doubt came to a halt beside her . 'We've finished pulling the weeds,' Saury said.

'All of them,' Doubt said. The small wiggle in his emotional signature casting doubt on the assertion.

'But did the garden sister say you'd actually finished? Really finished?'

Saury sniffed. 'You can't ask her that. She says garden work never finishes.'

'Yeah,' Doubt said. 'Gives us more to do. All the time.'

Fox hid her smile. 'Go back, both of you. You need to ask her permission to leave. Everyone has to help with growing food, and she's in charge in the kitchen garden, not me.'

Saury gave Doubt a look that made it clear she'd told him so and the two of them headed off, weaving their way between the raised beds.

And then it was Acacia, striding towards Fox from the manor house. It was still a surprise to see her empty-handed. Fox was used to seeing Acacia with a record book and a pencil, but these days she wore the lace cuffs and collar of a senior sewing sister, her lapels bristling with gold and silver needles. It was a clever move, elevating her from house records to the Oak sorority. Fox wasn't sure which Oak companion had the idea, Oria or Talia, but Acacia had always had a gift for diplomacy. Something the city of Komey needed now more than ever.

Acacia smiled, and Fox rock sensed the depth of the other woman's regard. 'Are you ready?'

'Waiting for the children, but yes. And thank you. Thank you for coming with me.'

'It's a relief to get away from the endless lacework.'

'Don't let the sewing circles hear you say that.'

'No chance the sisters will overhear me this far from the house. It's too far for them to walk.'

'Your elevation has lowered the average age.'

'*When God Turned, we were, every one of us, children.*'

'Very pious.'

'I'm practising my theological arguments, trying to come up with justifications for embracing change, supporting the new treaty. Besides, it's true, we're all children in the face of change.'

'Let's find the actual children,' Fox said, 'and then let's see if we can get change moving.'

Acacia linked arms with Fox and Fox felt the other woman's happiness. She'd need to talk to Acacia about shielding her feelings around Berans if Acacia was going to become a successful diplomat. The woman had spent a life in Komey and, like all Companionaris, was adept at managing her feelings, but Fox doubted she understood just how acutely Berans could sense emotions.

'I'm keen to take another look at your map,' Acacia said, 'and I want to hear what stories the wanderers have collected today. The sewing sisters don't like political talk, not unless it's gossip, but they like hearing Beranish stories. They get busy with their hands and they don't always realise their hearts are open when they're listening. Officially, we're all forward-thinking Oaks, committed to the new treaty, but you can't make a new world without stories.'

They walked past the established kitchen garden, out into the parkland that was marked with freshly constructed vegetable beds. No sign now of the stumps of trees that had dotted the place yesterday. The companions had rotted them to humus: Oria was fast and efficient with her newly enhanced talent; Talia had left gaping holes in the landscape and grew more trees than she removed. Oria had sent her back into the house and had to clean up after her. Fox wanted to ask Acacia how Talia was doing, but didn't. Couldn't let go of the feeling Talia deserved to be punished for her part in so many Beranish and rock child deaths. But the girl was trying to make amends. Perhaps she deserved some kindness.

They found the children with the garden sister at the edge of the cleared landscape, standing in front of a grove of cork oaks. The sister had put Saury and Doubt to work and Fox could feel their itchy desire to be done with their duties.

Acacia took the lead, explained to the sister they were walking to the new Beranish camp.

The sister looked uneasy. 'Without an escort? I could look after the children if you want them to stay here.'

Fox felt the weight of everything else the woman wanted to say. That Komey wasn't the city it had been. That the curve of its ornamental paths could hide conservative zealots bent on protecting the old order. That its paths were no place for children. Everyone knew that and more.

'We'll be fine, Sister.' Acacia's light smile returned. 'Don't fret on our account. Fox and the children will sense anyone who is hiding in wait.'

'And then what?' The sister raised an eyebrow.

'Then we'll turn back, take a detour, step off the path. No need for any sort of confrontation.'

The other woman shook her head, but didn't argue.

They made their way through the corks until they reached the first of the many paths that wandered the city's gardens. 'Not too far,' Acacia said, as the children ran ahead.

'And keep your rock sense open,' Fox added.

Saury and Doubt slowed, then took off again.

It was one of those late autumn days that feel like summer, and Fox was thankful for the shade from the trees that crowded the path. Patches of wheat appeared as they crossed into the Wheat Companion's territory, but the oaks persisted. Fox gestured to the timber. 'Has Whilomena complained about this?'

'Does she even know?' Then Acacia clicked her tongue. 'Why am I asking? Of course she knows. The housekeeper's been complaining about the endless stream of visitors to the Oak House cells. They will have told her.'

'I don't know why we're letting them have visitors,' Fox said. 'My father and Whilomena are murderers.'

'I'm not sure anyone is visiting Aikin, but the Wheat Companion still has a lot of supporters. Turning them away would be more trouble than it's worth.' Acacia slowed, stepped off the path to examine a patch of wheat.

'What is it?' Fox asked.

'Not sure. Maybe nothing.'

Fox looked down. The Wheat Companion's bounty was mangy, a struggling fringe pressed between luxurious oak trees and the bald gravel path. She felt rather than saw the children become aware that their elders had halted. They slowed and turned back.

'It's odd that Whilomena hasn't complained about the trees,' Acacia said. 'She's complained about everything else. My sewing circle has heard more than it wants about the quality of our mattresses, the menus from our kitchen, and the want of cupboards and drawers in our cells. I could go on. Why not complain about our trees in her fields?'

'Because Whilomena and Aikin created the problem when they gave Talia her talent. Why would they complain about it being out of control when it's their fault it exists?'

Acacia bent over and broke off a wheat stalk.

Fox looked over her shoulder. 'The colour's nice.'

Acacia rubbed the head between her palms, picked out a grain, bit it.

'Good?' Fox asked.

Acacia shrugged. 'Fine. I think. I'm not an expert.'

'But?'

'Well, I guess I'm surprised the wheat hasn't put up more fight. Trees are trees, but the Wheat Companion's talent is prodigious, and this is her territory. Odd, the wheat hasn't taken root in the bark, overrun Talia's mad, instant forests.'

With the children once again at their side, the four of them moved off. The rest of the walk was uneventful. Fox rock sensed people, Companionaris, but not soldiersisters. She didn't discount the garden sister's fears about the danger of walking unescorted, but it appeared the additional Oak House patrols had worked, at least for now.

When they reached the Beranish camp, they went straight to the portal tent. A misnomer. It should have been called the story tent, because there were plenty of stories but no portals. The only known portal was a seven-day walk from the tent, and it didn't work. Just an empty grave in Oak province that refused to repeat its miracle of turning a rock child into a rock adult, a creature who could flourish plants and animals. Fox tried not to think about how desperately they needed that magic. Worry didn't help.

The tent was full of ordinary men and women sharing obscure fourth stories, fables that hinted at the existence of rock people or doorways in the earth. Storytellers and listeners alike, hoping to find clues about locations.

People sat in tight circles: a Beran or a Companionari sharing a story, a Beranish wanderer searching for clues, a Companionari record keeper taking notes. The latter were members of Acacia's first sisterhood, before her promotion, and several caught sight of her as they entered the tent, smiled and waved. Their greetings offered a moment of cheer in a tent that felt less than cheerful. Fox felt Berans pretending they still had hope and Companionaris full of shame at their culture's role in the death of Obsidian, the world's only rock man.

Fox drew herself up, took a cleansing breath. Worry never helped. Besides, she was here because she had an idea that might work. She spotted Mica and waved. He left off his intense discussion with one of the record keepers and walked over to greet them. Acacia asked him about the progress, oblivious to the bleak emotional signatures surrounding her. He gave her a forced smile. 'Good. Some good stories,' he said. 'It's promising.' He gestured to a scroll nailed to the central pole. 'We've added a bit more advice to the list. We're getting a sense about what is and isn't safe when a wanderer takes a rock child into a portal.'

'But no luck with locations,' Fox said.

He shook his head. 'No. Plenty of stories about what we suspect are portals. Good stories, but no hints about finding them. And we're recording everything: *don't bring new rock children through doorways; don't dance your way into a grave—*'

'A grave?' Fox said. 'That has to be a reference to your portal Mica, yours and Obsidian's, unless all portals are graves. I wonder what dancing has got to do with it. You didn't feel the urge to dance when the portal called you, did you?'

Mica shook his head. 'Just my obsidian rock child pressing me to climb into Promise's empty grave.'

'What happens if you dance?' Doubt asked.

'You could trip,' Saury said. 'Fall into a grave.'

'Not if you were careful,' Doubt said. 'What if you wanted to dance?' He turned to Mica. 'Could you skip? Would skipping count?'

'I don't think it's meant literally,' Mica said. 'It's probably just advice about how to live your life.'

'But you've added it to the list,' Fox said.

'We can't exclude anything when we know so little.'

'Could you hop?' Doubt said.

'Then you'd definitely fall,' Saury said.

Fox didn't shush them. It rarely worked. Instead, she sent them over to memorise the updated list of possible portal rules. For all they knew, the rules could be more of the lies fabricated by the generation of Companionari murderers who'd obliterated portal lore, but everyone hoped there were seeds of truth in the stories. She turned to Mica, asked him for the map. Almost called it *her* map because it felt like hers, but caught herself in time.

'Have you thought of something?'

'We think we should show it to some of the Companionari librarians,' Fox said.

He looked concerned. 'Take the map out of the tent? It's the only real clue we've got.'

She sighed. 'I was going to write letters asking them to come here, but—'

'But some things are best done in person,' Acacia said. 'And this way, we get to look at their collections. It's faster and better, and we might find something or hear something.'

'We've heard plenty and noticed plenty in here,' Mica said. 'Trouble is, we don't have any answers; just questions. Why is the map distorted? Why are the provinces full of little circles and cross stitch symbols? Is the decorative border significant? Why aren't the rusty portal marks in the provinces? Why are they floating in the Komic Sea?'

'But Quartz says you've made some headway with that last question,' Fox said. 'I heard he thinks the mapmakers were protecting the locations of the portals.'

'Yes,' Mica said. 'And we think the mapmaker offset the line of rusty portal marks to give us bearings. We are getting somewhere. But we don't have a scale and we don't know which mark represents Promise's grave. You could spend years walking and digging, walking and digging. Decades. And we'll all be dead of hunger by then.'

'Or be begging for food in Galea,' Acacia said.

'We'll work it out,' Fox said. 'Find more clues.'

Acacia put a hand on Mica's arm. 'Let us take the map and find those clues. Don't disregard Companionari sources because you don't like them. I know it's your right to say no, as a Beran, but all of us will suffer. Berans too.'

'Then take a copy,' Mica said. 'The record keepers have made some.'

Acacia shook her head, let go of his arm. 'That won't do. They're good scribes, but the map is subtle. They won't have caught everything.'

Fox rock sensed Mica's urge to argue, but he nodded and led them deeper into the tent.

Oria had grown a bower from oak trees, shaping it to Beranish specifications, and then petrifying it to shelter the relics: the map, but also the objects found buried with Promise. The part of Fox that had grown up as an adopted Companionari wished she had a pair of gloves before she touched them, but she was Beranish-born. She would be careful, but these were living objects, not an archivist's horde. She glanced at Promise's knife lying in the bower. The handle was smooth and its rough-drawn dragon looked childish. Oria had found it in Promise's scant belongings. Beside the knife lay a scrap of canvas, covered in Old Treaty text. 'Is the translation finished?' She gestured at it.

Mica shook his head. 'Patience and Quartz and some of the other wanderers are working on it, but it doesn't look promising. Some sort of springtime poem. Or maybe a love song.'

'We should take it too,' Fox said.

Mica stiffened, but Acacia spoke before he could object, 'For that, we don't need the original. It's not like the map. It's just words.'

He nodded and waved Acacia away to where the scribes sat working. Then he lifted a hardened canvas tube from the bower and eased out the map, put it into Fox's hands. There was a bit of hope in his signature. He might not like the idea of Companionari librarians touching it, but Fox could feel his longing for their insights.

The mapmaker had drawn the continent in its traditional guise, as a woman running across the sea. Her dress was a patchwork of provinces. In her left arm, she cradled a washing basket that was recognisable as Oak province. Her right arm was thicker than it should have been, and it was missing the canal that joined the Kelp River to the Vagor River. Floating in the Komic Sea, to her right, was the ragged line of dots that Fox had mistaken for rust stains or ghostly transfers from the canvas being folded when damp. A different hand had drawn the border, a wit who'd used images of curved upholstery needles, cotton reels, sewing needles and threads to outline preposterous chimeric creatures.

Fox turned the map upside down, examined it from every direction, but it didn't offer any new insights despite her sense there was something she was missing. Not the figure; not the border. She clicked her tongue and frowned, rolled the map, slipped it back into its protective tube under Mica's worried gaze. 'I'll be careful.'

'I know.' He looked her up and down, frowned, gestured at her tunic. 'But maybe you should get changed. You've enough soil on you to grow a crop.'

Fox looked down, saw she'd missed much of the dirt when she'd cleaned herself off.

Mica looked over Fox's shoulder and waved. 'What do you think Acacia? Should Fox be visiting Komey's libraries in her gardening clothes?'

Acacia gave Fox an apologetic look. 'We *do* need to look our best. I think Oria has some Companionari clothes in her tent. You could ask to borrow something. I heard her talking about not trusting the dress sister with her favourite things, never mind they no longer fit her. Let's go see her and then head to Mallow House.'

Fox stiffened, remembering her last visit to Lark Mallow.

'Come on,' Acacia said. 'It won't be that bad. You need to build a relationship with Lark.'

'She made it clear she doesn't want or need my help.'

'But perhaps we need hers,' Acacia said. 'Help with the Mallow House library and with the other adoptees. Don't be proud Fox.' Then she pointed at Mica. 'And you... You should come with us. Let's see how Lark reacts to a visit from a wanderer.'

2

Mica was grateful for Acacia's invitation. He'd been planning to accompany the women on their mission, but he was under no illusion that Fox would welcome his protective presence. She was prickly about accepting help. She always had been. It was as though she feared acts of kindness could undo her. He understood. She'd needed that attitude growing up surrounded by Companionaris, but he'd thought it would change now she was free.

It hadn't changed. If anything, it was worse.

He'd made a clumsy attempt that morning to ask her what was wrong. Why, when they loved each other, trusted each other? Why was she refusing his efforts to take care of her and their unborn daughter?

She'd rolled away from him, told him she didn't need anyone's help.

I can look after myself.

I never said you couldn't. But you won't let me do anything for you.

I need to be free.

Komey is a dangerous place.

I lived here all my life. I know it better than you do.

Doubt tugged at Mica's sleeve, gestured at Oria's tent door. 'Here they come.'

Acacia emerged first. She'd looked immaculate when she'd arrived in the portal tent, but evidently Oria had persuaded her to change into a more elaborate silk suit. The gold and silver needles of her office glinted on the suit's wide lapels. Fox came next, in a clean tunic, but more humbly dressed than Acacia. She'd even kept the shirt from her morning in the garden. The combination wasn't as impressive, but to Mica's mind her beauty made up for it, her golden eyes outdoing the glint of Acacia's needles.

Oria followed. As usual, she was wearing Promise's antique hunting costume, but now her arms were full of gossamer fabric. It was still a shock seeing the Oak Companion in a youthful form, almost impossible to believe there was a ninety-four-year-old within. Promise had been smaller than modern Berans, darker. As soon as Oria spoke, belief became easier. Her words were full of the old woman's autocratic habits.

'Fox True! Not another step.'

'I'm fine like this. This is enough.'

'This isn't about you though, is it? You have a duty to present yourself well.'

Mica felt Fox draw herself up, then she took a breath. 'You're right. Thank you. Give me a scarf.'

Oria sorted through her bundle, choosing a brilliant red scarf with braided gold edges. She swept it over Fox's shoulders and smiled. Then, strangely, almost mechanically, Oria's left hand moved, caught hold of the scarf and drew it over Fox's hair. Mica felt Oria react, fear burning bright in her signature, and yet her face remained calm, controlled. Whatever was wrong, she didn't want anyone to know. She stepped back, rubbed her hand. Then she used that Companionari habit of tucking away her emotions and he lost the shape of her feelings. She reached up with her right hand, pulled the scarf back down from Fox's hair, resettling it over her shoulders, pinned a broach to fasten it. Then she stood back and tilted her head. 'Better.'

Doubt had sidled over to stand beside the Oak Companion. 'Are you coming with us, Huntress?'

The old woman's signature softened. 'Next time.' Then she glanced over at Saury. 'Perhaps the three of us could visit some of the great houses together. You two could be useful. Representatives of the future. But not today. I'm expected in the portal tent. I promised Quartz I'd listen to some of the more outlandish stories. See if I can make sense of them from a Companionari perspective. Go with Fox and Acacia. Remember your manners.'

The walk to Mallow House took longer than expected. Twice, they stepped off the path and kept out of sight while groups of soldiersisters from hostile houses marched by. Acacia had argued that they didn't need to hide, but Mica didn't trust Komey's militia and he could feel Fox agreed. Supposedly, the city's military sisters were aligned to the new peace, supported the ambitions of the new treaty. But it wasn't true. Komey was full of trouble. Rogue houses where companion mothers hid mercenaries, zealots roaming free, and the rest: desperate, hungry people fleeing failed provinces.

The security arrangements at Mallow House were a reminder of the changes. House guards stood in strategic positions around the building and Mica rock sensed a sharp edge in their emotional signatures. Inside, the housekeeper escorted them to a public sewing room. He was expecting Lark to be austere, but it was the tail end of laughter that met them as they entered the room. Three women sat companionably, working at lace cards and Mica didn't need to be told which of them had been born a Beran. As soon as the women looked up, he saw Lark's heritage. Eyes darker than most Berans', but alive with golden hues, making a lie of her bare arms. She registered Fox and Acacia and the genial expression fell away, replaced by the austere character he'd heard about. She did nothing to hide the frosty chill of her signature.

'Another *welfare check*, is it?'

'No,' Acacia said. 'Far from it. We're after your help.'

Lark looked at Fox, her gaze sharp. Doubt and Saury edged closer to Mica. 'I got your letter,' Lark said to Fox. 'A nice apology for your rudeness. But I see you still don't know how to dress when making a house call.' She looked Fox up and down, 'And I thought you said we talents should live like Berans.'

'That's not exactly what I said. But yes, I'm living as a Beran, but—'

'But you're wearing Companionari clothing: a Companionari tunic and that grubby shirt is Oak-ish. Dressed badly, but dressed as a daughter of the house.'

Fox looked down at herself and frowned. It was obvious to Mica she hadn't realised she'd clung to old habits. Nor had he. In all the years he'd known her, she'd dressed as an Oak House daughter because she was an Oak House daughter. And when she'd moved into his tent, she'd brought her Companionari belongings with her.

Fox spoke, wrong-footed. 'I don't... It's not...'

Lark shrugged. 'Well, it is what it is. You are an Oak even if you pretend otherwise. But I am surprised to see you here. You asked for my advice. I gave it. I believe I suggested you spend your time helping the Berans and Companionaris who need your help instead of bothering people like me. And the people who need your help are not in Mallow House.'

Fox opened her mouth to argue and then closed it again. There was a pause, and when she spoke, her words were careful. Mica suspected Acacia had schooled her. 'You're right, Lark, and it was good advice. I'm afraid most of their needs are beyond me. We're doing what we can.' The shift in attention from herself to the situation in Komey loosened Fox's tongue. She talked about the efforts to expand various kitchen gardens, the demolition of Whilomena's mill house, the treaty negotiations. The more she explained, the less it seemed to please Lark. Lark interrupted Fox with a query that surprised Mica. 'And what about the Beranish slaves? I hear nothing about you trying to save them.'

Fox fell silent, looked at Mica, but he could offer little comfort. 'We've been searching for them,' he said. 'We haven't found them.'

The younger of Lark's two sewing sisters sniffed. 'If you ask me, that shows the entire slavery story is just baseless gossip. If you can't find them, they don't exist.'

Lark glared at the woman. 'That's where you're wrong,' she said. 'Anyone who knows Whilomena knows she's capable.'

'We sent a delegation to New Lytalia,' Acacia said.

'And?' Lark asked.

Acacia shook her head. 'Our people searched the port. They heard talk of a ship lost at sea. We think those might be the first refugees that Whilomena spirited away. We don't know about the others, the later ones who disappeared. There are rumours of Berans in the port, hidden against their will. But our delegation couldn't find anyone. And the Pike Companion refused our request for a widespread search.'

'That's politics,' Lark said. 'Don't take it personally. Probably nothing to do with the missing Berans. Lucia Pike is careful of her status. She'll take any chance to remind you New Lytalia is a borough, not a province.' She turned to Mica. 'And because your people ceded land to her family, she can do what she wants. She likes to say no to remind us. If you want her permission, you're going to have to cater to her interests.'

'We haven't given up,' Acacia said. 'But it's possible the missing Berans have already left the Stone Body for Galea.'

Lark nodded. 'Very well. Keep at it. I hear Lucia has arrived in Komey for a visit. You might try sending her some ostentatious gifts before you attempt another request.' She gestured to the empty chairs in the sewing circle. 'Sit.' Then she turned to the children. 'And you two keep your fingers off the upholstery and away from the sewing baskets. You're both filthy.'

'We've been gardening,' Saury said, sitting on the edge of the nearest seat.

Doubt squeezed in beside her. 'Planting vegetables.'

Lark sniffed, but her signature was full of approval. 'Still, don't think about touching anything in this room. Keep your hands in your laps. And you,' she turned to Acacia, 'I see congratulations are in order. They've elevated you since I last saw you. A sewing sister and suddenly senior by the look of your needles. You said you needed help. What brings you to Mallow House?'

Fox opened the canvas tube, unfurled the map and held it out. Lark and the other two sewing sisters set aside their lacework and leant forward.

'It's pre-treaty?' Lark asked.

'We think so,' Mica said. 'Or just after.' He pointed out the map's features: the rusty portal marks, the symbols, and the strange border. 'We're not sure what's decorative and what's meaningful. We're hoping to find some clues in your library if you'll let us look.'

Lark took the map onto her lap and put on her glasses. Then she smiled, brushed her fingers over the map woman's right boot, the location of Mallow province. 'It's been a while since I've seen this.'

At first, Mica thought she was admiring Mallow's place on the map. Then he realised her fingers were stroking the jumble of circles and crosses. He held still. 'You know what they mean?'

'When I was a girl, I was a novitiate in the Mallow trading room in Komey. I worked in house records.' She glanced at Acacia, acknowledging their shared background. 'Teaches you a bit about everything, record keeping.'

Fox went to speak, but Mica gestured for her to wait.

'I wasn't always well behaved,' Lark said. 'In fact, I was no stranger to my sorority's long list of punishments for wilful girls. One time, my senior sister gave me a year-long, pointless task to teach me obedience. I had to create modern records from the early trading room ledgers.' She tapped the cluster of circles and crosses in Mallow province. 'The old records used this numbering system. It's based on buttons. Can you see?'

Mica looked at the jumble of symbols and started smiling, felt the other emotional signatures in the room lifting. Lark was right.

The little circles looked like stylised buttons. Some were blank, empty circles. Some looked like a buttons stitched with two holes, others like buttons stitched with four holes.

'This,' Lark pointed to a small empty circle, 'is the symbol for one. The button with a single horizontal line is a five. If it's a vertical line, it's a ten. Two horizontal lines is the number fifty, and a circle with two verticals represents one hundred. A cross inside the circle stands for five hundred. If it's an *x* instead of a cross, the number is one thousand. And if the circle is a solid circle, that's a zero.'

Fox leant over the map and began counting the button symbols in Oak province. 'Five, no... Six thousand... one hundred and... sixty-two. No, sixty-one!'

Lark clicked her tongue. 'You're not being observant, girl.' She pointed to a mark between the symbols. 'If you were paying more attention, you would have noticed this. A vertical line on its own, without a surrounding circle, is like a full stop. There are two different numbers in Oak: two thousand, seven hundred and thirty-seven; and three thousand, four hundred and twenty-four.'

Mica sat back, some of his excitement fading with the realisation they were still missing crucial information. '*Two thousand, seven hundred and thirty-seven* what? Footsteps? Strides? It could be the distance between portals, but where is the scale?'

Acacia turned to him, sitting back in her chair. 'But Lark has given us something. Because of her, we know the map is trying to tell us about the distances.' Mica felt the pleasure in Lark's signature.

Fox was leaning over the map again. 'They decorated most of the provinces with solid circles. Zeros. Most of the provinces aren't in the portal chain.'

Mica nodded. 'Which is what we'd expect. There are only a few rust marks...' he broke off. 'I mean, portal marks,' he corrected himself. 'Once we know what measure we're counting, the off-set between each mark, the bearings, should give us exact locations.'

Fox stood. 'So let's go search the library.'

Lark glared at her. 'Far be it from me to teach a guest, sewing circle manners, but you might like to sit down. I haven't put my sewing away and I believe I'm the senior Mallow sister in the room.'

Fox sat back down. Frowned. Then she seemed to realise protocol wasn't the only thing she'd forgotten. None of them had retrieved the map. It was still open on Lark's lap. Mica felt Fox compose herself. She held out her hands and Lark handed it back. Then Lark put away her lace card, and stood, signalling the end of the session.

An hour later, everyone's hopes had plummeted. An extensive search of the Mallow House library revealed nothing. They found two maps of the Stone Body. Neither offered any insights, but Lark signed out the maps in the loan book. As they left, she reminded Fox to present herself with more care if she wanted to use the front door when she next visited.

They were on the path outside the gate when a junior sister caught up with them. She slowed to a halt, took a breath, composed herself and bowed. Then she presented Fox with a small parcel that, she assured them, came with Lark's compliments. They stood as Fox unwrapped it. Inside were two lace collars and a poem lauding good deportment. Fox snorted and then looked up at the windows of Mallow House. 'As though deportment matters at a time like this.'

Acacia reached out and smoothed the collars. 'But they're lovely. The lacework is extraordinary. I'm not familiar with this pattern. The sewing circles have all been crazy about antique cards since summer. It's a generous gift. Something from her own hand. I believe she cares for you.'

Fox looked unconvinced. 'She's not being nice, Acacia. She's judging me. But I'll make use of them.' Fox held out the open parcel for Acacia to hold and then picked up a collar. She turned to Saury, took hold of her little sister's shoulders and turned her about. She lifted her sister's hair and used the collar to tie it back. 'There. Perfect. Something useful.' She turned Saury back again, smiled at her. 'And we'll match.' Fox picked up the other collar and tied back her own hair. 'See? Now that's a good use for lace.'

Mica was too far from the house to feel Lark's reaction, but he could imagine it. Fox would need to write yet another letter of apology if they ever needed the woman's help again.

The rest of the day was as disappointing. They visited several other collections and signed out ten more, likely useless, versions of the map of the Stone Body as a woman; two letters about early settler treks across the Stone Body; and a couple of rough translations that added weight to the theory that Promise's Old Treaty text was a song, not a poem.

Walking back, no one felt satisfied. And Lark's questions about the slaves troubled Mica. It was all he could do to stop himself walking off in search of a horse that could carry him to New Lytalia to resume the search in person. They needed to do something more. It wasn't right to focus on the portals and leave their brothers and sisters to their fate. 'We should send someone to New Lytalia to have another look.'

Fox rubbed a weary hand over the back of her neck. 'Another delegation?'

Saury looked up, following the conversation and Doubt drifted closer.

'I'm tempted to go myself,' Mica said.

'We could all go,' Saury said. 'Together. All of us. As a family.'

'No,' Acacia said to Mica. 'We need you and Fox in Komey. You're the ones Komey identifies with the new treaty. You're witnesses to Aikin and Whilomena's crimes. You can persuade...'

'Doubt and I were there too,' Saury pointed out. 'We're the ones who died and got brought back.'

'But you don't need all of us,' Doubt said to Acacia, 'do you? You could spare me. The Huntress and I could go together. She said I can use El Embaucador if I ask first and she could ride Canción.'

'We stay together,' Mica said, 'and that means we stay here for as long as Komey needs us. But we should send someone. Maybe a single person would do better than a delegation. Someone who could poke about without being noticed by the Pike Companion's people.' They'd reached a fork in the path and as though a decision needed to be made, everyone came to a halt. The camp was to their left; Oak House to their right. Mica turned to Acacia. 'The Oak Embassy in the port… It's still closed, isn't it?'

Acacia nodded. 'Oria never appointed a new ambassador to the borough when the old one died.'

'Then we need to visit Oak House,' Mica said. 'Because I've got an idea.'

Fox nodded. 'And while we're there, we should ask Aikin about any maps and documents in the Oak House library.' Mica made a face at the sound of Aikin's name, but Fox pressed on. 'We'd be stupid not to. He knows every book and every manuscript it holds. He might help.'

'Why would he?' Mica asked. 'He's our enemy.'

Fox looked uncomfortable. 'Aikin's not just the man who killed people. He's more complicated than that. He might help if he thought he was doing good. He thought he was doing good when he killed people.'

Mica snorted, but he didn't argue. She was wrong, but he understood Fox's feelings. She'd loved her adopted father after a fashion. It wasn't easy to accept he was nothing but a monster.

○ ○ ○

3

A ikin had been awake for several minutes, the soft sound of the Whilomena's sleep accompanying his thoughts, the bars of their cells no barrier to that communion, at least. He woke like this each day: no light to signal the dawn, but his body knowing it was time to get up. There had been some natural light in the Wheat House cells, but the Oak House cells were dark until the guard lit lamps and light until she extinguished them at night. He doubted there was anyone alive who would thrive in such circumstances, but he had done well enough, using the enforced leisure to refine his thinking. He wasn't without rancour. His efforts to save everyone from starvation and the chaos that would bring had been rejected. Worse, punished. But there was still time to save everyone, if he wanted to. And he wasn't sure which direction he would take.

There was a sharp and unbridgeable gap between what was right and how he felt. He was aware of a churlish, even petulant, desire to be done with the Companionaris and the Berans, leave the Stone Body and make a new life in Galea. The notion brought a smile because he knew himself too well. Those scales would never come close to balancing. The fire that drove him was duty. He would save the Stone Body even if it made him the most hated man on the continent.

'If you must wake at such a pointless hour,' Whilomena yawned, 'you should at least refrain from staring at me.'

'But you're beautiful when you sleep.'

She swung her legs out of bed and sat up. 'That's true. Now turn around. I'm going to get dressed.'

'You didn't make me turn around yesterday.'

'Yesterday, you recited a poem that pleased me. What have you got for me today?'

He did his best to look stricken, hit his forehead in mock forgetfulness. When she looked sufficiently disappointed, he laughed. 'Beloved, I wouldn't let a day go past without reminding you of why I asked you to marry me.'

'I think it was the other way around.'

She walked over to the door of her cell, held onto the bars. 'Go on, then. What have you got for me?'

This time he sang for her. He had a pleasant voice. He'd sung in the Oak House choir when he was younger and the poem he'd composed upon waking suited a Beranish tune that had been a favourite this year.

She looked delighted. When she moved away from the bars of her cell, she took off her nightclothes and dressed. Her movements were quick, but unhurried, with no coquettish flourishes. It was this: these ordinary, unadorned domestic moments that signalled their intimacy. With Aikin, Whilomena didn't need to perform. The Wheat Companion could be herself.

Whilomena had five visitors that morning, Aikin none; a state of affairs that described most of their mornings over the past three and a half months. Even incarcerated, the Wheat Mother mattered. She even had her own social secretary on the jail house staff. Not one of her own women, a clever junior named Cerris Cork had been provided by Oria. Whilomena thought it was a sign of respect, one companion to another, but Aikin understood. Oria would have stripped Whilomena of all comforts if she could have done so without alienating half of Komey.

Cerris reserved Whilomena's afternoons for important visitors. Today, it was three sisters from the Eden sorority and baby Sorrel, the infant Edenic Companion.

They sat on spindly chairs in the corridor between the cells and Sorrel grizzled as they explained their visit.

'The old Mother was very fond of Berans,' one said.

'Aren't we all,' Whilomena said.

'And, well... Well, several sisters are persuaded that a new treaty is not such a bad idea, given all our difficulties.'

Whilomena stilled, just a flare of nostrils signalled her displeasure. The sisters leaned back at the sight. Sorrel chewed her bonnet strap.

'We feel.... Well, what with the crop problems and the like,' another sister ventured.

Aikin had seen this scenario before. It didn't end well. He cleared his throat. 'Sisters, how right you are. A new treaty is a noble ambition, but I ask you: is now the time?' Two of the women looked over their shoulders to stare at him. The sister holding Sorrel, bent over the baby, suddenly busy. 'Our leading companion, the Mother of Komey, Whilomena, sits in front of you, locked in a cell. How could any house sign a new treaty when Wheat House and its companion are being intimidated?'

One sister frowned. 'Intimidated?'

'Oh yes.' Aikin nodded. 'Allegations, but no due process, no formal charges, no trial. How else can we can describe it?'

Whilomena's nostrils flared. 'I am not intimidated.'

'Let me rephrase that,' Aikin said, *'an attempted intimidation.'*

The same sister spoke again, 'The thing is, in a province like ours, with fields that are worked daily, by Berans... The relationship needs to be good. And we have some crop problems that these new stone creatures might solve. A new treaty would—'

'Traitors!' Whilomena hissed. 'Mealy mouthed, cowardly—'

'Mother Wheat,' Aikin spoke a warning.

'Get out!' Whilomena yelled at the women. 'Out!'

The Edenic sisters stood up, stepped back. The woman holding Sorrel, clutched the baby to her chest.

Whilomena jabbed her finger through the bars. 'No more wheat for you. See how you like that.'

'Mother Wheat,' Aikin said, pleading now. 'Please. Contain yourself. Eden is a great house, leading a noble province. Sorrel's bounty is vital.'

For a moment, it looked as though Whilomena saw his point because she nodded. Then she resumed her furious admonishment. 'And if Sorrel were old enough to do anything more than grow tainted vegetables and drool, she'd start a brand new sorority. She'd get rid of the lot of you.'

After they had gone, Aikin tried to give Whilomena some perspective, some insight into the basic principles of human behaviour, what worked, what didn't. He shared some quotes on the matter, but it only seemed to make things worse. A readiness to accept new information had never been a strength.

The next two delegations arrived full of support for Wheat House, if a little wary about recent events, but they left recalled to all of Whilomena's shortcomings. Aikin waved Cerris over, told her to cancel the rest of Whilomena's appointments.

Whilomena glared at him. 'I'll thank you not to interfere in my administrative duties. Cerris, I'll be keeping those appointments.'

Cerris opened her mouth to answer, but Aikin spoke before she could get a word in. 'Darling Whilomena, you're not in a fit state to meet with anyone. You're out of sorts. Surely, you can see that.'

'What I can see is that you're in no position to tell me what to do.'

Cerris lifted a hand and Whilomena turned on her. 'What?'

'There aren't any more callers today. Yesterday you told me to leave the late afternoon free. You wanted to rest.'

Whilomena's brow cleared. 'How wise of me.'

After Cerris left, they returned to their beds. Aikin lay down flat, stared at the decorative paintwork on the ceiling. He couldn't see Whilomena without turning to face her, but her mutterings were loud enough, full of outrage about the cheek of the Edenic sisters. As the afternoon wore on her mutterings lengthened and became even louder. 'They talk to me as though I haven't just spent months trying to solve the food crisis. To save their stupid lives. They act as though I made a mistake and we should all be grovelling to the Berans. By the Back! This city is full of brainless women. They want every beggar to eat my bread as they sit on their hands, watching our companionships fail. I have to get out of here, Aikin.'

He turned and looked at her. She was sitting on the edge of her bed, her chin in her hand, the picture of thought. But he didn't believe she was thinking. She'd been saying the same thing every day: that she had to get out. Lecturing him about how Komey should be run. Which set his teeth on edge. He agreed with her, of course. One leading parley was the best way forward, but it had become difficult to listen to.

Then he noticed something different because she'd fallen silent. The usual lecture didn't seem to be forthcoming. She stared at the empty audience chairs in the corridor. After a while she looked up. 'I believe I've endured this for long enough. There are things I need to do.'

'We both have better things to do.'

'For me, it's different. You'd like to get out. I have to get out. For everyone's sake.'

'How so?'

She gave him a smile, the sort of dismissive smile she reserved for children and annoying sisters. 'Don't worry about it. It's nothing to do with you. Let's talk about something else. Something more cheerful.'

'Like what?'

She tapped her chin in thought. 'Well, let's see.' She gave him another bright smile. 'I know just the thing. Why don't you tell me everything about your triumph. I want to hear about Glory and Talia. I know I said the details of your experiments were boring, but I see now I was wrong. You did something extraordinary.'

He wasn't convinced, but it was preferable to listening to her complain, so he explained. It was gratifying really. In the past, she'd been too impatient to listen. Then, in the middle of a description about how much crushed rock child he'd rubbed into each cut to create the new companionships, he hesitated.

'Go on. I'm listening. Keep going.'

'Why do you want to know? You never wanted to before.'

'I told you. I'm proud of you. Besides, I should know how to do it. What if you're not around?' She patted her hair, reassuring herself that every strand was in place. 'What if I got out of here and you didn't? I might need to know all this. For all our sakes.'

'You could always visit me and ask. What's going on?'

She gave him a look of exasperation and lay back down. 'You get so fixed on the small things in life. It's not attractive. I was just being nice, but by all means, let's sit here in silence.'

It didn't take long for that silence to grow heavy, and she sat up again. 'Call Cerris for me. I need something.' Aikin told her to call Cerris herself. 'No, you call her,' she said. 'I can't yell when I want something. It wouldn't do. And there's no bell pull in this dreadful place.'

He sighed, but she had a point. If either of them were going to get out, they needed to maintain Whilomena's power. He lifted his voice, didn't yell, but when he called out, he put some strength behind his words. Cerris appeared moments later and Whilomena asked her to fetch the Oak Companion. Aikin waited until Cerris had left before asking why.

'I told you. I can't stay here.'

And that's all she would say. They waited for more than an hour. Aikin had more or less decided Oria was going to ignore Whilomena, but she came.

'This better be good,' the Oak Companion said. 'I'm busy.'

'Let me out right now or I'll rot all the wheat in the silos.'

Akin couldn't quite stop the gasp that escaped his lips. He hadn't seen this, hadn't even thought it. But of course. It was the obvious power play. A clever, clever move. He hadn't credited Whilomena with this sort of strategic thinking.

Oria stilled. 'If you did, you'd spend the rest of your life behind bars.'

'But half of Komey would die and, if the city got hungry enough, someone would let me out. Let's save everyone the time and the pain.'

'We could kill you, trigger a crossover.'

'I don't think you would. You don't have the stomach for that sort of thing. Besides, the crossover might fail and, once again, half the city would die. Because I hear you haven't found any new portals and the one you have isn't working. So no more magical stone people.'

Oria looked as though she'd bitten a lemon, but he could see that Whilomena had won. He glanced at her in admiration, but she wouldn't meet his gaze. 'Whilomena? Tell me you're not leaving me here?'

She sighed, a quiet little sigh, a sigh bordering on irritation.

'*Whilomena?*'

'What?' she snapped. 'I can't do everything for everybody all the time. I have a house to look after, a sorority, a province. I have duties, Aikin. This is not about you. Besides, Oria's your aunt. She should free you.'

'But Whilomena...' He could hear the neediness in his voice, hated himself for it. He took a breath. 'Think about what you're doing.'

'I know what I'm doing. This is best. You should stay here. Once I know my house is in order, I'll fetch you.'

He stood there like a fool, hands wrapped around the decorative cast iron bars as Oria called the warden, ordered Whilomena's door unlocked. Then Whilomena walked out of her cell. She avoided his eye the entire time, wouldn't answer his questions, didn't even offer an apologetic look. It made sense, but then again it didn't. She could have freed him. Oria would have capitulated.

Watching her receding back, he felt a rage he'd never felt before. The words of Gideon Aries, reflecting upon his own failed marriage to the Aries Companion, flooded Aikin's mind. He shouted:

I will not be the flapping shoe that slaps the path, lamenting you. I will not speak of you again. I have loved in error. I will not repeat my mistake. You live, you walk about, but you will walk yourself into corners. I will ascend the stairs.

'You hear me, Whilomena?' he yelled. 'You'll regret this. I'll ascend those stairs. Without you. And your life will be a series of small, dirty corners.'

When he'd calmed himself, he sat on his bed, his thoughts returning to their earlier conversation. She'd shown an odd interest in his treatment of Talia and Glory. *What if I get out and you don't?* she'd asked. *I might need to know,* she'd said. He wondered why she might need to know and he didn't like the answer. Somehow, Whilomena had got hold of a rock child and she intended to use it. He was sure she hadn't gained one since they'd returned to Komey. Separating rock children from their wanderers was difficult. She must have come upon one earlier on, and the only place that could have happened was in New Lytalia.

It was Whilomena who had organised for the shipload of Berans to be killed. His people had collected their wanderers' stones, but it was her endeavour. It was as clear as day now that he thought about it. She had turned one of his people, stolen from him. She wasn't a disappointment. The woman was a traitor.

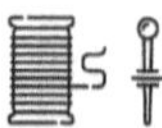

The stone walls of Oak House made life bearable, but Talia couldn't relax, and it showed. Her hands shook. There was a flicker in one of her eyelids. She'd lost weight. The other companions said it got easier as you came to terms with your talent, but they were wrong and she didn't like to think about why. Didn't want to, but couldn't stop thinking about it. The way she'd gained her talent was corrupt, and she was corrupt. Deserved to suffer.

She took a sip of water, wedged herself deeper into the nook between the ovens, and closed her eyes. It was an awful place to be. It had been impossibly hot in the summer. Even now, in late autumn, it was too warm and too close, but having a wall at her back and double walls on either side dampened her talent. And today, like every other day, she needed the nook to retreat and rest. It had been three and a half months since Aikin involved her in his murderous alchemy, three and a half months since she became an oak companion. Surplus to need because Oria lived. No, it was worse than that. She wasn't just surplus to need. Her effect on the landscape was destructive.

Being indoors, deep in the nook, slowed things down, but nothing halted the trees. When she slept, her talent ran riot. She grew nightmarish groves of cork, white oak and, more recently, giant date palms. All tangled together, growing in the wrong places, ripping up paths, damaging kitchen gardens. She spent her mornings rotting trees and stumps, undoing the work of her dreams. And the rest of her days weren't much better: holding acorns back, stopping date seeds germinating, steadying saplings, taking breaks in the nook to restore her energy. But she made amends, or hoped she did, with the energy she had left. She used her minor talents to rush crops of onions and olives. And there was her other significant talent: growing rice. Less destructive than trees, easier to control, and it was doing some good because she was feeding people.

She finished her water and leant forward, set the glass on a bench. Growing rice was the only bit of happiness she had. Oria didn't share a talent for it. No one did. Rice hadn't been grown for over ten years, but there must have been a grain or two in the room when Aikin treated her because she had a gift for it. In the afternoons, she took herself off, walked through the abandoned ornamental gardens of Rice House. The remnant Rice sorority called her Little Mother Rice. She had half a mind to leave Komey, go live in the abandoned province. In the middle of a landscape of paddies the talent might grow even stronger. She might do something really good on the Stone Body. She might be forgiven.

She was half asleep when she registered there were fresh voices in the kitchen. Opening her eyes, she saw the people she'd been avoiding: Mica and Fox. Looking thin and worn, they threaded their way through the room. Acacia and the two children followed. Talia shrank back. They hadn't seen her yet, and she needed a moment to prepare.

Willie came into view, pulling off his apron, a huge smile on his face. 'My favourite people. You must be hungry. We have two different dishes: vegetable stew or broccoli and cheese pie.' He held up a finger, paused in thought. 'But why not have both?'

'Thank you, Willie, but this isn't a social visit,' Mica said. 'And we don't need that much. It wouldn't be right.'

'But you must have something.'

Mica looked at Fox, who frowned but nodded. He turned back to Willie. 'You're right. A piece of pie would be lovely.'

'How are you managing?' Fox asked Willie. 'How is the kitchen faring with all the extra Berans to feed?'

Willie shrugged as he waved at the room. The place was overflowing, full of Companionari staff and Beranish cooks. 'We're a four-cook kitchen now. The menu has narrowed with the shortages, but we're doing our best.'

'Could I have pie *and* stew?' Saury asked. 'Just a bite of each. I promise I won't take too much.'

'Me too,' Doubt said.

Willie looked pleased. He snapped his fingers at a passing kitchen hand, waved at the ovens.

The visitors followed his gesture and Talia felt herself caught in their gaze. She eased out of the nook and stood up. Mica waved. Fox and Acacia smiled. It was kind, but their kindness brought a rush of shame. The cost of her awful talent rose in her gullet like an overeaten meal. She forced her emotions back. Didn't manage it neatly and gently like a true Companionari. She did her best to dissolve her emotions, but ended up pushing them to the edges of her body, which was a temporary solution. They would sit there and fester, before creeping back to haunt her, worsening her dreams.

Talia forced herself to move. She walked over and joined Fox and the others. Whatever need had brought them to the kitchen, she would try to help.

The children sat at one of the kitchen benches and Willie ushered the adults into the staff dining room with Talia following. The cook was about to leave them to their meal when Acacia invited him to sit. 'Join us.'

'Please,' Fox said.

Willie sat down, issuing a small sigh of satisfaction to be off his feet. Acacia resumed speaking, 'I'm glad to hear that you're getting enough help, Willie.'

'More than I need.'

'Because it makes this easier. We need someone in New Lytalia. We want to re-open the embassy and its kitchen needs a cook.'

'Ah, I see. Yes, of course. I have several junior cooks who would make us proud. Has Oria settled on a new ambassador?'

Talia felt her cheeks redden, and once again had to stifle her shame, shove it away. Choosing an ambassador would have been her decision if her companionship were legitimate. Fox must have rock sensed her emotions because the other woman began explaining that there hadn't been time to speak to Talia, that they hadn't even spoken to Oria.

'It's fine. You don't need to tell me anything. I'm not deciding anything in Oak House.'

'You should,' Acacia said.

Mica turned his attention back to Willie. 'The thing is, we need a spy in the port and we want you to be that spy.'

The cook laughed. 'I doubt I'm cut out for that sort of thing.'

'On the contrary.' Fox reached forward, covered his hand with hers. 'You'd be perfect. Think about it. As the embassy cook, you'd have a reason to get out and about, talk to people. You'd have to source supplies. You'd have to speak to people on the docks. And you'd have to visit the Briar Embassy for flowers and the Winter Embassy for brassicas and Eden for summer foods, and so on and so on.'

'And what am I meant to be finding out?'

'Where Whilomena has hidden the refugees,' Mica said. 'So we can free them.'

Willie sat back in his seat. 'Of course. It makes sense. But do you really think I'm the right person for the job?'

Acacia took up the pitch, insisting that the cover was perfect. When Oria had gotten old, had been dying, she'd ignored her provincial obligations, hadn't replaced the ambassador. Now that Oria was renewed, now that there were two companions, the embassy could re-open. Appointing a cook would be the natural first step. Unremarkable. 'Normally, we'd also send a housekeeper,' Acacia said, 'but only if you know someone who is an ally, someone who can keep their mouth shut.'

'Not our housekeeper,' Willie said, 'that's for sure.'

The idea of leaving made Talia bold, and she spoke up. 'I could go. If it would help.'

Fox hesitated. 'It's not a bad idea, but I'd be worried you'd attract too much attention. You'd be a novelty in the port. Everyone would talk about you.'

'But that might be useful, me being a distraction.'

The others sat back, thought for a moment, but Mica shook his head. 'The simplest plan is the best plan. You can be more useful here.' He gave a nod towards the kitchen gardens as though she were a proper companion, not someone whose talent did more harm than good.

Then Fox spoke up again, 'And we could use your help with Aikin. We need his knowledge of the library. We're searching for clues to the portals.'

Aikin, the one person Talia never wanted to see again. But she smiled, said yes. And after they'd finished eating, she followed them down to the cells.

The others were full of outrage and shock when they discovered Whilomena's release, but Talia couldn't feel anything. The sight of Aikin was too overwhelming. It was all she could do to stop trees erupting through the floor and walls to crush him, never mind the dampening effect of the stone.

'I don't see why you're asking me,' Aikin said to Fox when she had explained what she wanted. 'Go upstairs and ask the librarian for help.'

'We will if we have to,' Fox said, 'but you know the collection better than the librarian. We have to find more portals. If you care about the Stone Body, now is the moment to show it.'

Aikin stepped back from the bars of his cell, crossed his arms. Somehow, he still looked elegant, despite the months behind bars. It was a reminder, if Talia needed one, that he had friends in the house. He looked down his nose at Fox. 'You need portals because you refuse to use the method that works. It's your fault people are still hungry. There are thirty-seven provinces. Only thirty-seven stones need to be sacrificed to secure another thousand years of plenty. It's repugnant, yes. I admit that. It's lamentable, but so is making promises you can't keep, which is what you've done.'

Fox shook her head. 'You weren't like this when I was growing up.'

'Like what?'

'You used to tell me that ideals mattered.'

For the first time, Aikin looked uncomfortable, but he shook his head. 'Never said they don't.'

Fox put her hands on the bars of his cell, and Talia flinched. It felt reckless, risky. She wanted to tell the other woman to be careful, keep clear of Aikin. Fox was speaking, 'You know as well as any of us, this business about sacrificing stones is... Well, wrong. Just wrong. The portals work, but because you didn't find them, because they weren't your discovery, you won't help. And that's the truth.'

Aikin snorted, but Talia could see Fox's words had affected him. 'Maybe, maybe, but you want me to sit here for the rest of my days. I'm idealistic. I am. But I want my life back. Let me out and let's see where that takes us.'

Acacia joined Fox at the bars. 'We'll let you out under guard,' Acacia said. 'Come upstairs, look at Fox's map and at Promise's text and show us what the Oak House library has to offer.'

Talia felt the trees' hunger as a prickle under her skin. So eager, so capable of crushing him. It took all her effort to control herself and she didn't have room to spare, to argue against Acacia's plan.

Aikin gave Acacia a sceptical look. 'And what then? You bring me back down here? Lock me up again? No thank you.'

'We might negotiate something.'

Fox and Mica protested, but Acacia held up her hand, turned to Fox. 'You criticised him for caring more about winning than helping the Stone Body. Aren't you doing the same if you refuse to negotiate?'

Talia stayed in the shadows, holding back the trees as the argument continued, but she already knew, all of them knew, Acacia was right. If Aikin could help, they had to negotiate with him. Talia closed her eyes, steadied herself, wishing she were brave and strong like Acacia and Fox.

Upstairs in the library, there was no way to avoid Aikin's attention. He smiled at Talia as though they were allies, and she almost lost her grip on the trees. She was relieved when he sat down and began examining the relics. He didn't linger over the song, but he took his time with the map.

Talia felt it when he caught sight of something, almost as though she were Beranish and had rock covered arms. If she needed confirmation, she only needed to look at Mica and Fox. They'd felt something shift too because they turned to each other, a mixture of hope and worry on their faces.

Aikin sat back, smiled. 'Well. I think it's time to get down to business.'

Fox gestured at the map. 'You've seen something. What is it?'

Acacia took a seat opposite Aikin, drew in her chair, put her elbows on the table. 'Don't expect us to give you your freedom when you haven't given us anything.'

Aikin opened his arms. 'Despite what my daughter alleges, I am who I always was: an idealist, a romantic, a believer in trust. I won't make you write up a contract and put your signatures to it. If you give me your word that you'll free me, I'll tell you what I think I've found.'

'Not an enticing offer,' Acacia said.

'You might have found something trivial,' Fox said.

Aikin spoke scornfully, 'You know me better than that.' He tapped the map, returned his attention to Acacia. 'Tell you what. I'm a generous man. If you think my insights offer the key to this map, or part of the key, if you value them, you will let me go. And,' he held up a finger, 'I'll even give you something for nothing. There's a map. Another map of the Stone Body in the library. Nothing special about the artistic aspect, but it's accurate. Most of the known versions aren't. It could be useful to you.'

Acacia looked up at Mica. He nodded.

No, no, no. Talia wished she could voice the words, but she couldn't. She knew her reasons were too personal, too selfish. Aikin had ruined her life. Acacia looked at Fox and Fox nodded, agreeing to the deal. Then she turned to Talia, called her Mother Oak, reminded her she had the right to release Aikin. What could Talia say? No? No, when the people who had the right to say no, had said yes? She nodded and it was done.

Aikin stood up and walked over to a desk, lifted the lid, rummaged around, and returned with a device, a small loupe for close work. Not the long glass that Talia had seen people use outdoors. This was a squat, bulging piece of glass, its straight sides set in a brass cylinder. Aikin placed it on the map, right on top of the marks Fox had once believed were rust spots. He put his eye close to the glass and chuckled. He said nothing, just slid the map and glass across the table to Acacia. She looked at Mica and Fox for permission and, receiving it, put her eye to the glass.

'What is it?' Talia asked.

'A tiny image of a tree,' Acacia said, 'and I think the next one is a seed.'

'A tree?' Fox said. 'That must be the Oak portal! The first rust mark is the Oak portal.'

Acacia shook her head, a strand of her dark hair coming loose. She tucked it behind her ear. 'No, I don't think so. It doesn't look like an oak.' She moved the glass and let out a sigh of relief. 'Oh, here we are. Yes. The third mark looks like an oak.' She looked up at Mica. 'So this mark must represent your portal, Promise's grave.'

'We've Lark's numbering system,' Mica sounded excited, 'and the bearings suggested by the off-sets. We're nearly there. I know I said we should stay in Komey, visit all the libraries, but we should go to Oak. Use the bearings from the line of the rust marks to work our way from Oak's portal to the next one. If we're methodical about it, careful, we'll find something.' He reached over the table, turned the map around to face him. 'There are two marks above Oak, so they must be north of Promise's grave. The rest are below, probably to the south. See how the portal mark, the rust mark, above Oak's is kind of close?' He put his finger on the mark in question. 'Maybe we should focus on finding this one?'

Acacia turned the map back to face her and bit her lip.

Fox looked unconvinced. 'But the proximity of one rust mark to another might mean nothing. When you fold the map, they're equidistant. Don't forget that.'

'But it might mean something,' Mica said.

'Okay,' Fox said, 'but the next portal could be anywhere along the bearing. We have numbers but we still don't have a key to the measure.'

Acacia had her eye to the glass again, and she held up her hand for their attention. 'I think that closer mark is a grain of wheat so that limits the distance. The portal will be on a line between Promise's grave and the far edge of Wheat province. It will be somewhere along that line. We can search. We can find it.'

'That's a very long way to dig,' Fox said.

Aikin cleared his throat. 'So I'm free?'

Talia hesitated. She couldn't go back on the agreement but perhaps she could adjust it? 'Yes, but only if you leave the Stone Body. I banish you.'

Aikin turned, shocked, looked her full in the face. 'What are you talking about? We agreed.'

'If it's my authority freeing you. I'm giving it on condition that you travel from here to New Lytalia and from there to Galea, never to return. That doesn't break the agreement.'

He started to argue then stopped. She saw competing emotions in his expression. Then something changed. His gaze didn't waver, but a smile touched his lips. He actually looked pleased. Talia didn't know what had occurred to him. She couldn't see any holes in her plan. He would leave the Stone Body. He'd be gone forever. He might write letters, might still attempt to peddle his influence, but he wouldn't be here. It would limit any damage he could do.

Then he nodded, said he accepted. 'Mind you, I don't appreciate Talia's underhanded dealings.' He turned to Fox. 'She broke the spirit of our deal. And in return, I'm not inclined to be generous. If you want the library's accurate map of the Stone Body, you can find it yourselves.' He crossed his arms. 'I hope it takes you a long time.'

As night descended and Talia settled back into her nook between the ovens, she realised her eyelid had stopped flickering. Her struggle with the trees hadn't lessened. She'd spent the late afternoon rotting down errant groves. And she had to live with her decision to release Aikin, but her heart felt lighter. Perhaps it was the knowledge that Aikin would soon be gone, gone forever from the Stone Body.

4

Fox stood at the lip of Promise's grave and looked down. The warmer days had dried the soil and the earth had lost its loamy scent. The place no longer felt magic. There was no sign of the power that had triggered Oria's transformation into Promise, had compelled Mica, and had transformed his rock child into a man. It was disappointingly ordinary and Fox had to remind herself there was reason to hope they would find the other fresher portals. The distance was unknown, but the route was clear. It was a difficult plan, but at least they had a plan: they would dig a very long furrow.

Mica stood beside her, their hands almost touching. There was grief in his signature as he frowned at the grave. 'It feels empty. I can't help thinking of Obsidian.'

'I know,' she said. 'Hard to believe this hole in the ground created him; hard to believe he's gone.'

'And the grave feels exhausted,' he said. 'Or broken. There's nothing here. Maybe we should fill it in. I've been thinking that it might need to be closed before it can work again.'

Oria turned away, spoke over her shoulder, 'Leave it be. We

haven't time to muck about. We're here to plough our way to the next portal. There's enough earth to move without filling in holes.'

Mica stiffened. Fox reached out and touched his arm, and he sighed.

They followed Oria to where Quartz and Acacia stood, watching Patience and Sousette, the Caballo Companion and her wanderer, prepare two enormous working horses for the plough. Patience held their leads as Sousette checked over the harness in the back of the handcart.

The animals had stood quietly since Patience had walked them to the graveside from the station. They'd hardly moved other than an occasional shake of a head or a whicker, and the repositioning of a dinner plate-sized hoof. They were unlike any of the riding horses Fox had known. Disciplined and practised, they were unfazed by Saury and Doubt's quick movements and high-pitched voices as the two children played in the surrounding trees.

Sousette signalled to Patience that she was ready, and to Fox's surprise, Patience turned and called Doubt and Saury to his side. He handed one horse's lead to Doubt and the other to Fox's sister. 'Stand still and don't bother them. These horses know what they're about. This is a chance for you to watch and learn, so pay attention.' He left the children and walked over to the handcart where Sousette handed him two heavy-looking collars. Patience motioned for help. 'A hand here.'

Quartz and Mica both moved, but Oria reached out and held Mica back. 'Let Quartz do it. He's been too long in the portal tent.'

'I know the feeling,' Mica said.

'It's harder on him. You've been visiting libraries, helping Fox. He's been sitting in the tent day after day, not finding any answers, not being able to sort Companionari fabrications from genuine Beranish fourth stories.' She smiled as Quartz hefted the collar onto his shoulder. 'This will do him good.'

Patience and Quartz carried the collars to the horses and the Caballo wanderer explained their purpose to the children. Acacia had found the harness and plough in the Aries House museum. Antiques, but there had not been time to locate something else. '... a beautiful bit of kit,' the wanderer told the children. 'Not as lightweight as modern collars, but the Wheat Companion doesn't plough, so there was nothing else in the city. But we shouldn't have any trouble working out this old-fashioned system. The horses are kind. They won't mind us fumbling our way through.'

Sousette sighed, sniffed, wiped a tear from her weathered cheek. 'The darlings are so generous, so patient with us, so good. If only they knew how I've failed them.' She took a jagged breath. 'They are the last generation.'

Oria huffed, 'Self-indulgent twaddle. Unbecoming of your station.' Then the Oak Companion waved a hand at the plough. 'We're doing this for you too, for your horses' future. Pull yourself together.'

'Forgive me.' Sousette smiled. 'Pay no attention. I'm just an old sentimental mother.'

Patience stood in front of Doubt, at the head of the more distant horse; Quartz was mirroring Patience, standing in front of Saury and her horse.

Patience motioned for Doubt to thread the end of the horse's lead through the oval-shaped collar. Saury followed the boy's example. Patience turned to Quartz. 'Now, watch me. Do what I do and say what I say. Mimic my tone.' Patience took Doubt's place at his horse's head, reins threaded through the collar. 'Down,' he said, and the horse lowered its head. The Caballo wanderer lifted the collar onto his horse's neck and Quartz followed his example.

Then Patience led Quartz back to the handcart for the rest of the gear. Sousette handed each man a bundle: leather straps, tangles of long chains and something resembling a belt that was worked with decorative studs. Fox's arms tingled, and she felt something quicken as though a part of her could sense the way each piece should sit on a horse, but she couldn't quite catch the whole. She had to stop herself from walking over and joining in.

After carrying the gear over to the horses, Patience disappeared between them and Quartz stood at his animal's head, watching what Fox couldn't see, glancing from his own gear to Patience and then back again. Then he walked to the near side of his own horse and eased the belt-like part of the harness onto its back, dropping the chains to the ground on either side.

Fox found she'd moved closer without realising, itching to help.

Now, the two wanderers were at their horses' rears, lifting their tails, each fitting a strap beneath. Fox edged closer still, found herself standing near her sister. She took another step or two, reached out and stroked the horse's satin nose as she watched Quartz unhook a bit of chain and draw it to one of several hooks on the horse's collar. She couldn't help herself. 'The lower hook. It needs to be lower down. The collar will tip if you put it up there.' She moved closer, ran a hand down the horse's neck. It turned its head to nuzzle her. Deep inside her, like the touch of a feather, Fox felt the baby move, startling her. As one, Mica and the other Berans turned to her. Even Oria, who was still adjusting to her rock skin, reacted.

Fox closed her eyes, dropped within. She found her daughter, resting upright, eyes closed. Then the baby shifted again, and Fox felt that same flutter. She laughed, opened her eyes.

'You should sit down,' Mica said.

'Don't be silly,' Fox said.

'Don't fuss,' Patience told the younger wanderer. 'Our women work the horses right the way through. Some labour with the horses.'

Acacia looked confused. 'What's going on?'

Fox explained, and then Patience was beside her, holding out the two long ropes that were the reins. 'I think you need to show your young man how capable you are. Besides, I think you might have a feel for this. Come walk beside me. We'll hitch the chains to the plough and you can be the first to turn the furrow.'

Fox walked beside the plough for more than an hour, then she and the children returned to camp, leaving the others to the work.

The canvas was quiet as they walked between the Oak camp's tents. Oria's presence in the province after such a long absence meant the Berans were deep in the groves, milling timber. Even the cook's apprentices were labouring. Fox and Saury and Doubt leant the cook a hand with the vegetables. Afterwards, with a meagre lunch some hours away, the children left to find playmates and Fox went to Mica's tent to write letters.

She sat on Mica's wooden bench and set out her materials on his table. Took her time with the task. First, she unscrewed the ink jar and placed it to her right, turned it about until it aligned with the table's edge. Next, she opened her leather folio and sorted her paper stock. Then she filled her pen, careful to clean the nib with a soft piece of linen. The time it took Fox to get ready would have earned her praise during her novitiate. But it wasn't praiseworthy. She was avoiding the task. She'd told Acacia she would write to the other adoptees. Acacia said Fox's time would have been better spent if she'd stayed in Komey and continued visiting the women in person. But Fox had insisted on coming to Oak. She'd told Acacia she was needed here, that letters would suffice, but it wasn't true. There were plenty of people to plough the furrow and letters were unlikely to bend those complicated hearts. Truth was, Fox wasn't brave enough to keep visiting people who didn't want to hear what she had to say.

She sighed, looked at the blank paper in front of her. She was tired. It might all feel better after a rest.

Fox packed away her folio and her ink, and lay down. She woke about an hour later, groggy from sleep, splashed a little water on her face, tied her hair back with Lark's collar, and headed out to look for the children. She found Doubt and Saury in the wild flax field with a group of youngsters. A boy was chanting a song about chopping wood and the other children had formed a circle and were dancing: leaping, spinning, clapping hands, laughing.

Fox felt a familiar tingle in her arms as she watched them. Like it always did, the sensation faded the moment she tried to catch hold of it. There was a pattern, if she could only look at it correctly. Like knowing when Quartz had been about to connect the end of the chain to the wrong part of the horse's collar. Or folding the map to align the portal marks after she'd retrieved it from the hiding spot behind her bedhead in Oak House. And there'd been other times when she'd felt something, known how something should be.

She steadied herself, closed her eyes, used her Companionari training to clear her mind and settle her emotions. She opened her eyes again and just watched without trying to force any understanding.

The boy was singing the chorus. The lyrics told of the axe's whistle and the wood chopper's swing. Half of the dancers became wood choppers and the other half played at being axes. The wood choppers knelt to allow the other children to jump over their shoulders, mimicking the path of a swinging axe, whistling the sound. Then the children re-formed a line and danced forward, arms crossed, as the lyrics told of carrying the kindling home. They sang and laughed, oblivious to the damage their feet were doing to the flax. Bent knees had crushed seed heads into the earth. Dancing footfalls had flattened stems. It almost looked as though a sewing sister had embroidered the landscape using a mad woman's pattern of tangled flax threads.

Then Fox had it. It wasn't mad. The pattern was perfect. The children had danced, and the dance had marked its own notation on the earth and on the flax. Her rock skin felt electric with the truth: a dance made a pattern and a pattern could describe a dance. And while the children had drawn their dance unintentionally, the anonymous hand that had added the decorative border around Fox's map of the Stone Body had drawn hers knowingly. Fox hadn't recognised the border as a notation until just now. Not surprising. The artist had hidden her purpose, disguised her pattern beneath a whimsical drawing of cotton reels and threads and curved needles. She'd been skilled enough to make the whole appear as nothing more than an illustration of chimeric beasts. To hide a dance? And why would a dance need to be hidden?

Fox frowned.

The children continued dancing. Their line moved sideways and Fox saw how she would draw such a move if she were an artist trying to capture it. The step reminded Fox of a bargello stitch. The children broke apart, turning on their heels, clapping hands. How would Fox represent those movements using images from an ordinary sewing basket? She smiled. A bobbin for the little circles created by the heels, knots for the toe marks. And what of leaps? How would one draw a leap? A long stitch? And what about two dancers passing one another, swaying past each other like the children in front of her? Fox would draw two curved upholstery needles.

But why? What did the dance on her map's border signify? Then she had it. Dances moved across floors and landscapes. They had lengths; they offered measures; took up space... A scale!

Fox turned and ran, calling out for Mica.

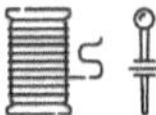

Mica heard a shout from the camp, felt the horses' shivered response, saw the plough falter.

'Whoa, there,' Patience said. 'Easy, lads. Easy.'

Sousette reached for the horses, glancing over her shoulder, looking for the source of the trouble. Mica and the others turned, scanned the landscape, their gazes narrowing in on the plantation. Mica felt a moment of fear, then rock sensed Fox just beyond view, rushing between the trees. Not frightened. Excited. And there was a crowd of children on her heels.

'What's wrong?' Acacia asked.

'Nothing. It's fine.' He put a reassuring hand on the woman's arm. 'It's just Fox coming back with a bunch of camp children.'

As Fox burst into the clearing, Mica called out, 'Careful. The ground is uneven.'

She looked down but didn't stop. If anything, she ran faster. 'The border's a dance!'

The horses shifted, nervous at the commotion. Their ears flicked backwards and forwards, tracking the threat. They tossed their heads, edged sideways, and Patience had to let go of the plough to get a better grip on the ropes. He began walking towards the horses' heads. The abandoned plough dug into the earth, anchoring them.

'Whoa, whoa,' Patience crooned, pulling on the ropes. He called out to Fox, keeping his voice low. 'Don't run! Keep the children back!'

Fox pulled up short, waved at the children, bent over to catch her breath. Most of the children halted beside her, but a few kept running. Acacia, Oria, Quartz and Mica intercepted them, herded them back to Fox.

Fox was smiling, almost laughing. 'The border. I think it's dance notation. All we need to do is work out the matching dance. Then we'll have the scale for the distance between the portals. And with Lark's numbers... We can multiply the dance length and we'll locate the nearest portal.' She looked at Mica. 'Where's the map? I want to see if I recognise the dance.'

Mica gestured to the handcart where he'd left the canvas tube. Fox hurried over to the cart and fished it out. He called out after her, careful to keep his voice low so as not to scare the horses. 'What do you mean, the border is a dance?'

She was already hurrying back. She pointed at the children. 'They'll show you.' Fox turned her attention to them. 'Show Mica the wood chopper's dance.'

Sousette and Patience objected. 'Not here,' Patience said.

So, Mica and the others followed Fox and the children through the grove of cork oaks to the wild flax field. Mica felt Oria's displeasure when she saw the state of her crop, but Fox waved her anger away with an explanation about the hidden meaning in the bent stalks. Then Fox unfurled the map, and the adults crowded around, looking from the image on the canvas to the imprint of the children's footsteps on the flax. Mica followed Fox's finger as she pointed to marks on the field and compared them to marks on the map.

'The woodcutter's dance isn't the border's dance, but you can see what I mean, can't you?' she pointed at the field. 'I mean look. Footsteps make marks.' She tapped the map. 'The border is a dance, but hidden from those who shouldn't know about it.'

Fox passed the map to Quartz, who squinted at it and then passed it to Acacia. 'I think you're right,' Acacia said, her finger hovering above the canvas. Mica could feel her hesitation about touching the relic. Oria had no such hesitation. She reached over and took the map from Acacia's hands without asking. The old woman traced the border's path from the bottom left-hand corner of the map to the bottom right-hand corner. She frowned, tapped her lip, then her expression cleared. 'Yes, I see. It's possible. I think you're onto something, Fox. The border's linear, directional. I think that's significant.'

Saury had come closer, was standing near Oria. 'Let me see,' she said, standing on her toes.

'You're holding it too high,' Doubt complained.

'Can I see?' a girl asked.

'Me too!' another girl said.

'I want to dance,' a boy said. 'Can we dance? The horses can't see us here.'

'Let's dance!' another child shouted, jumping up and down.

Oria handed the map to Mica and then turned to the children, waving them away. 'Off. Go play somewhere else and don't go near the horses.'

'But I thought you wanted us to dance,' the boy complained.

'Not now,' Oria said. She turned back to the adults. 'The point is, there isn't a loop in that border pattern: no return, no arrows showing when to halt and come back.' She reached over Mica, tracing the border from beginning to end. 'See? All the lines, all four chimeric creatures, are heading in one direction. A normal dance doesn't work like that. You don't go dancing off into the distance in a straight line. I've seen a lot of dance cards in my time and there's always a return.' She bent down and picked up a stick. 'Follow me. I'll show you what I mean, what a return looks like.' She looked around her. 'Can someone see a bare patch of dirt I can draw on? I need a big, long patch.'

The camp children had lingered, ignoring the Oak Companion's insistence they should leave, and they jumped at the task, disappearing in all directions, looking for a cleared space for Oria to use her stick. Soon, everyone crowded around a patch of loose dirt and Oria began making marks.

She drew quickly and confidently: lines and dots and sweeping curves and arrows turning in on themselves. The image on the ground looked like the outline of a flower. She threw the stick out of the way and gestured for Acacia to join her.

'You recognise it?' she asked the other woman.

'*The Tulip.*' Acacia nodded. 'The opening of *The Florist's Reel.*'

The two of them took their places at the base of the flower's head: Acacia tall and lovely; Oria, an old woman in a young woman's body. They smiled, bowed, took each other's hands, and danced. They danced up the centre of the pattern, released each other, put their hands on their hips and danced back along the curved outline of the tulip. Then they turned and danced back again, joining hands at the tulip's peak, before dancing down the middle of the flower to halt at its base.

'You see?' Oria gestured to the scuffed lines, her arm moving up and down the pattern. 'You don't go dancing off into the distance and yet the border on the map has no returns. There are curves, yes, deviations and quick turns, but the drawing moves forward, only forward, never backwards.'

'But can we dance it?' Mica asked. 'Measure the length it gives us.'

Oria sighed, shook her head. 'We could if we knew the dance. Dance notation isn't like musical notation. We won't get an exact measure unless we find someone familiar with this dance.'

'And you're not,' Fox said.

Oria shook her head again.

Acacia frowned. 'It doesn't look like a Companionari dance. Companionaris may have drawn it, but I suspect it's Beranish.'

'Then we must ask our people,' Mica said. 'And we can begin here, with everyone in the Oak camp.'

Mica had never regretted offering the Bass refugees a home in Oak province. He'd only ever regretted the cost: the loss of his personal freedom; the deaths when he'd fought to change Oak's fate. Now, more than ever, he felt grateful that his impetuous nature had invited strangers to his provincial home. More people meant more possibilities that someone would recognise the map's dance. And there weren't just Berans from Bass camping in Oak. There were Berans from Canis, a wanderer from Taurine and another from Mouflon.

In the end, they gathered the entire camp in the field and the camp's children performed the wood cutter's dance. The Berans didn't have a tradition of drawing dances, so the concept of notation was best understood as Fox had seen it: impressed upon the Stone Body. Once again, Fox pointed to the marks the children left behind them, explained the connection with the map's border.

Then Fox and Mica walked from person to person; Mica holding out the map, Fox speaking about the decorative artwork. As each person looked, each one shook their head and Mica's heart sank. They might ride across the Stone Body, asking every person in every province, and never find the answer.

Then everything changed.

Patience and Sousette returned from tending the horses. They'd seen the map many times, had heard Fox shouting about the border being a dance, but they'd not looked at the relic with a dance pattern in mind.

Mica held out the map.

'There are four decorative chimera,' Fox said, 'and Oria thinks the notation is for a quadrille.'

Sousette's face lit up, but it was Patience who spoke. 'In Caballo, we call a quadrille, a quadriga. We think of the dance as the chariot and the dancers as the chariot's four horses.'

Mica tapped the map. 'And this quadriga? Do you know it?'

Patience turned to Sousette, who nodded. 'It's *The Flying Change*,' she said. 'The mad-looking beasts are wrong, though. The mapmaker should have used images of fillies because it's a dance for young women, a progress across a meadow, something danced outdoors.'

Oria stepped closer, unable to hide her excitement. 'You're saying it traces a line across a meadow?'

Sousette gestured at the field. 'A grassy meadow like this, yes. It's a coming of age dance. A girl dances it on her twentieth birthday with three of her peers. The straight line is her life as a woman, start to finish, but the dance's path involves several flourishes along that path, hence the name.'

Mica frowned, and Patience explained. 'A flying change, a horse leading with one leg and then switching to the other, a subtle shift that can make a horse appear to dance.'

Oria waved the explanation away. 'Never mind that. Can we recreate the dance? Will it give us a measurement?'

Patience nodded. 'We'll need four twenty-year-old women. Actually, we'll need as many twenty-year-old women as we can find. They'll differ in height and stride, but if we have enough of them, the differences might average out.'

Mica agreed. It wouldn't be anything exact, not like a timber merchant's measure, but perhaps it would be close enough.

They rehearsed and danced for the next six days: in the meadow, beside the camp, on the lawns of the manor house, and on the slate plains between the forest and the crater where Doubt and Oria had first struck up their friendship. Then they calculated and recalculated until they found the measure. They no longer needed the horses and the plough. The measure meant the portal could be located on paper. All they would need was the accurate map in the Oak House Library.

On the train trip back to Komey, Fox rested her head against Mica's shoulder. He stroked her hair. He couldn't help noticing how thin she'd become. They all were. Careful with their supplies, worried about how long the Stone Body's food stores would last. The knowledge made his heart clench. He feared being called to the new portal, leaving her; he feared not being called; feared the famine growing; and worst of all, feared a portal calling Fox, wrenching her away from him. 'When we get back and we've located the portal...'

'Umm?' she said, sounding sleepy.

'It's just if you're called, I don't think you should go.'

She lifted her head from his shoulder, stared at him, eyes narrowing.

'I mean it,' he said. 'You're pregnant. You and Oria both. You mustn't go.'

Her expression softened, but the determination in her gaze didn't. She patted his hand. 'You can't do that, Mica. You mustn't. Neither Oria nor I would risk people starving for the sake of our daughters. If I'm called into a grave, I mean to answer.'

5

Aikin stood up. Being confined to the Oak barracks while awaiting deportation was disadvantage enough without being caught sitting down, and he could hear footsteps. He recognised the sound of his guard's footfalls entering the long corridor, but not the person accompanying her. Someone with a light step. His departure from his confinement in Komey was imminent, but the second set of footsteps didn't have the clomp and heft he associated with a military escort. A visitor? Unlikely. Visitors had been outlawed. No, this must be the river captain herself. It made sense. Leary about transporting such a rogue, unwilling to take a contract without inspecting the merchandise.

He felt a tingle of excitement.

The barge captain, if it was she, was about to make her first mistake. This visit to inspect him would allow him to inspect her. Then he hesitated. Mistakes could cut both ways. He recalled the advice from *The Book of Kinesis*:

We see a play when we see another: the speech, the costume, the actions. When dealing with the other, do not deceive yourself. You do not see within. All you may do is turn things about: cast your own character aright.

How he missed his beloved book.

Aikin glanced at himself in the mirror above his basin. What would the barge captain see? The pale face of a man too long indoors and, below that face, the lapels of a coat that looked too warm for the season's last gasp of heat before winter. The coat suggested placing pride above comfort. Was that the right impression? Too much pride might hint at a willingness to fight his fate. That wouldn't do. A little bitterness was acceptable, but it would need to be combined with an impression that Aikin was making the best of a bad lot. Above all, he should not look dangerous. He pulled off his coat, kicked it under the bed, ruffled his hair.

The door opened and the guard ushered in a woman in white canvas trews stitched with images of winding rivers.

The guard gestured towards Aikin. 'Master Aikin. Not charged with a crime, but ordered off the Stone Body by Mother Talia—'

Aikin held up a hand. 'Yes. All right. Thank you,' he said, allowing bitterness to addle his voice. 'I'm sure the captain and everyone else on the Stone Body knows my circumstances.'

The captain nodded her wind-weathered face. 'I do. Wanted to meet you before accepting the contract.'

'Here I am. The fallen man.' Aikin shook his head, let his shoulders sag a little. Bitter but defeated; no threat to anyone.

The barge captain looked him up and down, but didn't speak. Aikin turned to the guard. Now was the moment for a touch of pride. 'Well? Introduce me. Whom do I have the pleasure of meeting?'

The guard pursed her lips, but spoke politely enough, 'This is Captain Yavo Tribute, Mistress of *The Laughing Waters*.'

'A pleasure to meet you,' Aikin said, bowing.

The woman grunted, but acknowledged Aikin's words with a nod. 'And I don't need to ask how you feel about this banishment. I want to know whether you accept it.'

'It doesn't matter whether he accepts it,' the guard said.

'It matters to Captain Tribute,' Aikin said. 'She is the one who must decide whether I'm a problem for *The Laughing Waters*.'

'Not a fool, then,' the bargewoman said.

'I hope not,' Aikin said, drawing himself up.

'And the answer to my question?'

He spoke truthfully, 'I can't change Talia Oak's decree so what choice do I have but to make the best of what is in front of me? I'm heartbroken at the prospect of leaving the Stone Body to a future of famine and unrest. I have the knowledge to save it. But will anyone listen?' Aikin let the bitterness return. 'No. They won't.'

The bargewoman raised an eyebrow. 'And what of your new life?'

He would answer with the truth again, but dress his feelings to suit his purpose. 'I've always wanted to visit Galea.' He squared his shoulders. 'I'm told there is room for a man who can solve problems. They respect outcomes in Galea. I've written and received letters. I have secured a position...' He willed himself to blush and felt a gratifying heat in his face. He cleared his throat. '... as a shipping clerk. It's a step down—'

The captain frowned.

Damn! He'd spoken thoughtlessly. Of course his words would cause offence to someone connected to shipping. 'Being a clerk, that is. Working in shipping will be fascinating.' The captain looked mollified and Aikin spoke again to make up for his lack of insight, turn things around. 'It's just... Well, having run a department, I had hoped for a senior position. No doubt my fall from grace, my tarnished reputation, worked against me.'

'Then you are resigned to leaving the Stone Body?'

Aikin shook his head. 'Who could be happy to leave the place of their heart? I hope the young Oak Companion may yet rescind her order. If not, if I live out a year or two in Galea, she may allow me to return. If things become grim on the Stone Body, if she realises she needs me.'

'A pragmatist, then. Do you swim?'

Aikin guessed at the cause of the woman's interest. A lack of swimming ability would make him easier to manage. 'No. Sadly, I never learnt.' It was a lie. He could swim well enough.

'Excellent. Any sign of trouble and we will drop you in the water.' Captain Yavo turned to the guard. 'Tell your captain I accept the contract.'

'And when will we depart?' Aikin asked.

'This afternoon, so ready yourself.' The woman looked around the barracks, saw the paucity of Aikin's belongings. 'I guess you don't need much time to pack.'

Aikin spoke to the guard. 'If I may, I'll send for my houseboy. Have him fetch my personal effects and some clothing.'

'Mother Talia forbade visitors.'

'Very well. Letters will have to suffice although it will be cold on the water, will it not Captain?'

The woman frowned but nodded. She turned to the guard. 'No harm in a man organising his personal effects and a little warm clothing. Let the houseboy come. We can't have him dying from a chill.'

The guard looked doubtful.

'Once I've taken the contract, the man is my responsibility,' Yavo said, 'and I don't see the harm in it.'

Aikin almost crowed with delight. The houseboy was young, naïve, not to be trusted with confidential messages, but he would send the boy to Captain Birch with a letter and a message. Each on their own, innocuous. Together, Aikin trusted Birch would make sense of what Aikin wanted: to be liberated from *The Laughing Waters* just before the barge reached New Lytalia. He would be free to work his magic on the Stone Body. Lie low for a time, until he judged the circumstance had ripened, and then he would emerge. He would triumph!

After his visitors left, Aikin sat down at his desk and pulled a bit of paper towards him, doing his best to ignore the unsatisfactory nature of the furniture. Ridiculous campaign furniture. As though Oak's military sorority had recently returned from a taxing war when there hadn't been a war in more than a thousand years.

He closed his eyes. He couldn't stand much more of this confinement. He needed to get out of this place, free himself. He dropped his consciousness down into his body, settled his emotions. When he opened his eyes, he took up his pen.

Dear Birch, my old friend,

And he certainly hoped she was. Still, even if Birch had been suborned by Whilomena that didn't mean the soldiersister would refuse him help. Not when there was money in the offer.

How it pains me to say farewell. Know that I value all you have done for me, your good sense, your ability to know when to act and when to be patient. It seems we must be patient once more. Komey is not ready to save itself, so we must accept the suffering that the city faces. Take heart. Think of the future.

I do not expect to see your kind face at the quay when I depart this afternoon. Do not trouble yourself to wave me off. I only hope that we will meet again some day. Perhaps you will travel. I'd like to think so.

I must admit I am nervous about all that is ahead of me. Is it selfish of me to dread entering New Lytalia in custody? I confess, I had hoped Mother Talia might spare me that indignity...

The rest was nothing. Just platitudes. It might be enough. Birch would know to act before Aikin reached New Lytalia, but not to act until Aikin had left Komey. He wrote five more letters to various Oak House acquaintances. It would stop the important letter standing out.

He sat back, stared at the ceiling. He wondered what message to send with the houseboy. Some warning about the formidable nature of the barge captain? But Birch would know to be careful. Some suggestion about the number of mercenaries Birch might need to hire? Aikin shook his head. Birch knew her business well enough. Perhaps a reminder that she would need to hasten? That was important. She'd have to overtake the barge. If nothing else, the warning would ease Aikin's anxiety. Yes, that would do.

When the guard reappeared with Aikin's houseboy, Aikin waved the boy over to the desk. He handed him a list of clothes and keepsakes to pack and went over the list in careful detail. Then he gave the boy the letters to deliver, unsealed. 'These five,' Aikin tapped the decoy correspondence, 'you must give to the housekeeper in Oak, but I'm afraid you'll need to go to Birch's house to deliver this last one. You know where she lives?' The boy nodded. 'Tell her I looked forward to entertaining her once I set up my new life. That she shouldn't wait too long before she visits me.' Aikin turned to his guard. 'Read them if you need to, but don't delay my boy. I don't want to start my new life looking dishevelled.'

The guard gave Aikin a look of dislike, but she waved the houseboy to her side and scanned the letters. 'Nothing for the Wheat Mother? I am surprised. Rumour was, you two were engaged. Sick of you, I'd say.'

Aikin gave the woman a bland look. 'Just those five. Thank you.'

'I hear she's going on a spiritual quest.'

'A spiritual quest?' Aikin couldn't keep the surprise from his voice.

'I know,' the guard smirked. 'Must be disappointing for you, her going off to attend to her soul while you're locked up here.'

Aikin said nothing, just waited. It wasn't long before the guard continued, unable to resist the pleasure of showing she knew more than her captive. 'I wouldn't have taken her for a religious type, me, but she's sent her sorority walking—'

'Whilomena? Walking?'

'Not her, the sorority. Mind you, they're all going to New Lytalia. The Wheat Mother will travel on *The Meandering Queen*. I've heard she's in a hurry to start her retreat,' the guard giggled at the shocking image of a companion rushing. 'Her sisters are walking down to be there when she's finished.'

'How odd?' Aikin couldn't keep the confusion from his voice. 'But that makes no sense. Whilomena would never hurry. What reason has she given?'

'A lot of reasons, apparently. You, first and foremost.'

'Me?'

'Mistakes in her personal life have taken a dreadful spiritual toll, so they say. She's asked the Pike Mother to look after the Wheat sorority, walk them down, while she gets on with cleansing herself.'

Aikin was incredulous. 'And the Pike Companion? She's leaving Komey because Whilomena asked her to? Just like that? Doesn't make sense. What's her interest in this?'

'That one? She's mad for punishment. Old fashioned. Jumped at the chance to make her own sisters walk back to their home borough. That and the fun of lording it over the Wheat sorority. It's a horrid long distance from Komey to the port when you're on foot.'

For a fleeting moment, Aikin wondered whether Whilomena's antics represented some plan to save him when he arrived in New Lytalia, then he recalled his earlier realisation that she'd squirrelled away one of his rock children. That was it then. The reason for her hurry.

The guard was still speaking, the smirk still on her face as though the best was yet to come, 'So, you've caused a spiritual emergency. The poor woman has to cleanse herself, which I can believe. They say she's going to take the Komic Silence on her mother's old sailboat. She'll contemplate the Turning while she imbibes the majesty and glory of the Komic Sea.'

And suddenly Aikin understood. Whilomena planned to treat herself while she was oh-so-conveniently on her own during a retreat at sea. Her talent must be failing. She should have told him. He would have helped. Of course he would. Aikin found he was smiling, an awful rigid smile. It hurt. He'd get over it. Still, he had to admit it hurt. He consoled himself that he was heading in Whilomena's direction. If he got there in time, he might be merciful. Might even help her. But should he? Would he? And what about the misplaced love Gideon Aries had warned of? The lesson that Aikin told himself he'd taken to heart? Maybe he'd just stop Whilomena, take back the rock child she'd stolen from him, and leave her in the dusty corner of failure. He shook his head, uncertain which path his heart would have him take: saviour or punisher.

The guard must have misunderstood Aikin's silence for scepticism. 'It's true! Everyone is talking about it.'

Aikin didn't answer, just turned to the houseboy and told him to hurry.

Talia was up early. She was always up early now that she slept in the kitchen. The first shift of kitchen hands started at five in the morning and she woke to the sound of their work. When she'd first moved into the nook, the kitchen hands had done their best to keep quiet, but they were used to her presence now, and the benches rattled with boards and bowls and knives, and chatter filled the air.

She eased herself out of the nook, stood, stretched the kinks from her bones, and looked out the window. No, that wasn't right. She looked at the window. The glass was dark. Neither the light of the fading moon nor the approaching dawn were strong enough to penetrate the leaves that pressed against the glass. As it did each morning, her heart sank. On good mornings, she could make out the tangle of trees beyond the glass. This morning, it was as though the world outside didn't exist. Layer upon layer of leaves shuttered the kitchen.

One of the kitchen hands brought over a bowl of warm water, placed it on the nearest bench. He offered her a bar of soap and a new cloth. 'Here Mother,' he said, his voice more gentle than she felt she deserved. 'And when you've finished, we have a fresh brew and a bit of bread and jam ready for you.' Talia gestured to the windows, reminded him she needed to get outside, but he pressed the soap and the cloth into her hands. 'Breakfast first.'

As little as she deserved it, she accepted the kindness and the good sense behind it. She stepped up to the basin, talking as she went, 'They're thick today. I'm worried it will take longer than usual. I want to clear the trees before the house wakes.'

'Yes, but eat,' the kitchen hand said. 'There's time enough.'

Outside, after her modest breakfast, Talia stood at the edge of the tangled grove and felt exhausted. The beginnings and endings of days were losing their meaning. It was getting hard to keep track of the mundane.

She rubbed her temples, tried to recall what this day held, caught the memory after a moment of thought. She'd scheduled a visit to the Oak House dress room. The sorority had been pressing her to choose a wardrobe. As if that mattered. But she would do it. And later on, Indica Rice, daughter of the late, failed Rice Companion, had invited Talia to join the first sewing circle to meet since the province had failed. Talia would do that too. Would they be her last engagements in Komey? Would she leave the city today? She was considering it. She didn't know why she hadn't already left. The tangle in front of her was evidence enough that she needed to get away from people.

She stared at the trees, concentrated, used a part of her talent to hold back all the acorns and seeds that longed to grow. She spent the larger part of it rushing last night's trees to the sharp end of their life. As they always did, leaves fell, boughs cracked and thudded to the ground, and the earth moved and writhed with the unexpected pace of decomposition.

A scream ripped the pre-dawn air, a sharp animal sound. Talia gasped, and the trees' destruction shivered to a halt. In the silence the screams continued, louder now. For a moment, she thought, hoped, it was an animal, but knew it wasn't. A person hurt. Someone young. Her heart fell as she made out the word uttered between the wails: *Mumma!*

She moved, wishing she were dead, her heart breaking. This was her doing. Even as she ran, she knew this would be her last day in Komey, that she'd lingered too long, wanting company and comfort. Selfish!

She found the boy beneath a cork tree, under a bough, arm trapped. Broken, clearly broken. Thank the Back it wasn't worse. She bent down, hefted the bough, threw it off him. She picked him up and carried him back to the house, to the nursing sister. Even now, amid the boy's need, she had to work to suppress the acorns and seeds that hungered to surround her. Talia watched from the doorway as the sister tended to the boy. She didn't know whether the child was Companionari or Beranish, or which was worse. Then, with a groan, she saw her stupidity. She was staring at a bare, broken arm. An Oak House child, harmed by an inept and corrupt Oak House Mother.

The nursing sister gave her a sharp look. 'I don't need you moaning and groaning in my doorway, Mother Talia. You're making things worse for the boy. Off you go. Get about your business.'

Talia turned and walked away. The woman was right. Talia had business to attend to. Instead of turning towards the front door and her duty with the trees, Talia headed upstairs, her body knowing better than her head that the only important business today was her departure. The realisation that she would leave, the unconscious decision, lifted her spirits. Now, the day's pointless tasks had a meaning. She needed a new wardrobe because she would need travelling clothes for a journey and working clothes for a new life. And she needed to keep her appointment with the sewing circle in Rice House because she had to tell Indica and the others about her decision to make a new life in their abandoned province. Rice was the only place where the world would be safe from her. She'd camp in the manor on her own. She wouldn't let anyone near her until she'd worked out how to control her talent. And the Oaks? She shook her head. She didn't need to worry about them. The Oaks had Oria. They'd manage fine without Talia, be better off without her.

The dress sister stood with her back to Talia, working at a long table, bent over an antique parley dress. She turned at the sound of the door.

'Mother Oak!' the young woman gave Talia a welcoming smile.

'I've been hoping you would keep our appointment today. The sisters said you might.' She put down her needle and walked over, running a dressmaker's eye up and down Talia's figure. 'I have your measurements, of course, but I think the last time you were measured was a year ago, and I can see that you've grown taller since then. You're almost eighteen, yes?'

Talia nodded. 'But I'm not here for a Komey wardrobe. I... I'm leaving Komey. For work.' She did her best to keep her explanation vague, 'I need clothes for a journey and some everyday provincial clothes.'

The woman's expression cleared. 'To Oak. Of course. I had heard Oria might return there, but it makes sense to send you to our province, what with the strength of your talent.'

There was no reason not to tell the dress sister the truth, but somehow it didn't feel right, not when Talia was yet to speak to Indica and the other Rice sisters. So she lied, 'I'm going on a tour of the provinces.'

The dress sister clapped her hands. 'How lovely. A formal tour. The sixteenth Oak Companion undertook a ceremonial progress. We have her travelling clothes but they are in the dress room archive. We'd need several weeks to air them and alter them.'

'No, nothing like that. I just want some practical clothes and I need them in a hurry.'

The dress sister frowned, a hint of alarm creeping into her expression. But there were advantages to being a companion. 'Well,' Talia tightened her tone. 'You know what to do. Take my measurements.'

The dress sister didn't argue, but the worry didn't leave her face. She confirmed Talia's measurements and then walked her through the enormous room, stopping by each outfit that might fit and might be suitable. Everything was ornamental and cumbersome. In the end Talia choose a military uniform as her travelling outfit. The twenty-first Oak Companion had worn it as a tribute to her birthmother who had been a soldiersister. It was a little loose, and the dress sister wanted to take it in, but Talia insisted on wearing it.

'Right now? But you're not leaving today?'

Talia tightened her belt.

'Well, I suppose if your sorority thinks it's important, if Oria thinks this is a good idea.'

'Believe me, it's a good idea,' Talia said. 'I'm a liability in Komey.'

'I'm sure that's not true.'

It was hard to resist the urge to apologise and explain, to let the tears that threatened to fall, fall. The urge plagued Talia. It would be a relief when there was no longer any need to hold back, when she was alone. Last night, she'd wanted to apologise to the viander of rooms when he'd tripped over Talia's feet in the kitchen. This morning, when she'd brought the boy into the house, she'd had to stop herself making a weeping apology to the door mistress for all the leaves the wind blew into the foyer. Talia straightened her jacket and looked at her reflection in the mirror. The style was more ornamental than a real soldiersister's uniform and more colourful but the cut was sensible. She eyed the boots. If they didn't fit, she wouldn't take them. Surely there would be other boots in the house.

'Those are good leather. Not for walking long distances, mind. But you'll be on a train most of the time, won't you?' The woman still looked troubled. 'And you won't be alone.' It was a statement, but Talia could feel it contained a question. She said nothing, just nodded and then asked about working clothes.

'Working clothes?' The dress sister's voice rose a notch. 'Whatever for?'

'Things to wear in the provinces, in the gardens. Pants. A tunic or two.'

'Dress like a garden sister?' the woman's voice rose even higher. 'No, no. Of course not. What am I saying? Obviously you're wanting an ornamental version of work clothes.'

'Real clothes. Not ornamental.'

'Then... I think, maybe, I should fetch your sorority. For some useful advice about what you'll need.'

Talia's voice was sharper than she intended, 'Just get me what I've asked for.'

The dress sister look troubled, but she led Talia out of the dress room, down the stairs to a series of rooms tucked away at the tail end of the house: linen presses, stock rooms, and a room full of clothes for house staff and gardening staff. Talia found what she wanted, stuffed the two work outfits into a laundry bag, and left by the back door. The dress sister didn't call for help, but from the look on the woman's face, it wouldn't be long before someone heard about the new Mother's madness. So, Talia hurried. She kept to a walk but moved quickly, passing the remains of the nightmarish grove. Then she left the path, cut across country, heading for Rice House. She let trees grow behind her. Just enough of them to obscure her path. She laughed, realising how foolish she was. The trees wouldn't hide her. Their presence would highlight her passage. Still, it was a relief to loosen the grip. As she passed from the Oak gardens into the gardens of Rice House, her talent refocused as she began flourishing grain.

6

Despite her abrupt departure from Oak House, Talia was late to the Rice House sewing circle, and she made herself even later because she stopped to hide her laundry bag between the rice stalks.

Indica and the other women were already sitting in the public sewing room when she walked in. The room smelt of disuse. Two of the sewing sisters held delicate handkerchiefs to their noses, their sewing idle in their laps. Three others were stitching and knotting, but their expressions spoke volumes. It was clear no one could enjoy the transcendent potential of handwork under such conditions, and Talia knew her tardiness was testing everyone's good intentions. Indica and her cousin Oryza worked their pieces with expressions of false cheer on their faces.

Talia apologised for being late and walked over to the only empty seat, the companion's chair. She wished she could defer. Doubtless the last thing anyone wanted was a protracted discussion about who should sit where, so she sat. A little too quickly because the dust on the upholstery lifted into the air. She coughed, apologised again, shook her head. Her nose itched, but she busied herself opening the companion's sewing basket, determined not to make a spectacle. She wondered how long she needed to wait before bringing up her move to Rice.

Oryza waved a finger at Indica. 'There, see! Even the Little Rice Mother is finding this room impossible. Surely we can go upstairs now. I mean, we've made our point. We've opened the door, we've sat in the chairs, we've put the room to use. Enough is enough. This place needs to be cleaned.'

'Knocked down,' said another woman under her breath.

Indica gave the circle a furious look. 'Don't be dim. People will pass by, notice us sewing, hear us talking. But yes Oryza,' she waved a hand at the glass doors that overlooked the gardens, 'please *do* open those doors. Let in some air.'

Oryza looked scandalised. 'Me? There are lesser sisters in the room.'

'You were the first to complain.'

With a great sigh, Oryza got up and made much of throwing open the doors.

'There,' Indica said. 'All the room needs is a bit of fresh air. You've all grown soft. I remember my mother talking about working in the paddies. Dawn to dusk.'

'Would that we could,' said one sister.

'We will again,' Indica said. 'That's the point.'

One of the younger sisters looked confused. 'The Rice Companion worked in the fields? Worked with her own hands?'

'No, you idiot,' Indica said. 'Worked with her talent. I remember Mother standing beside the water channels, calling up the rice. What a sight!' She closed her eyes and inhaled as though the memory was a scent. When she opened her eyes again, she was smiling.

Outside, a group of children ran past the open glass doors, giving the sisters a wide-eyed look. The sight brought the morning back to Talia, the broken arm, the need for her departure. She went to speak, to explain, but Indica was talking again.

'It would be nice if this room smelt sweeter, but it's good to be back in here. We haven't been in this room since Mother died and everything fell apart. Now we're a House again. My son and Talia will marry and Komey will—'

Talia flinched. 'Marry? Marry Nuka?'

'Well, of course,' Indica said, shaking out a piece of embroidery that looked like a stomacher for a ball dress. 'You must marry. All the early companions married within their own houses, so if you marry Nuka, Komey will realise you've made your choice to be the Rice Companion, not a second companion to the Oaks. Oak House doesn't need you.' She stared at Talia. 'Make no mistake, Oak will make things difficult but the marriage will help.'

'I don't think Oria would make things difficult. She wants what's best for the Stone Body.'

Indica laughed, shook her head, and several of the other sisters looked amused. 'So innocent, so charming.'

There were footsteps in the corridor. A man looked into the sewing room and exclaimed to the person he was with. Talia couldn't make out the words, but his excitement was meaning enough. Indica's plan was working, the sewing circle would cause a stir. 'The point is,' Talia said. 'What I want to say... The thing is, I need to live in Rice province.'

Indica nodded. 'Well, of course. After you're married to Nuka, after you've conceived. That's when you'll take up your provincial duties. That's the way it must be done.'

'No. I need to go today,' Talia said. 'Go by myself and start growing rice. I could help with the famine. My talent wouldn't cause trouble for anyone like it does now. If I was on my own.'

'On your own in the province?' someone tittered.

Talia looked around the circle. The sisters were behaving as though she'd said something foolish. They hid smiles, looked away. One lifted her handkerchief, hiding her face. In Oak House she was treated as though her every word deserved respect. That didn't feel right. It was part of the reason Rice House had felt like home. But she'd never sat in a sewing circle with them, hadn't asked for anything until now, had never been laughed at. She just grew rice where they asked her to grow it, listened when they told her she was useful.

Indica shook her head, but it was Oryza who spoke, 'A companion's never alone.' She picked up her lace card, began knotting. 'It wouldn't be right.' The other women chorused agreement. 'A companion's sorority accompanies her.'

'Always,' Indica said. 'And we'll help you choose the right women. We'll draw up a list.'

Talia tried to explain. She told them about waking in the kitchen; the trees pressing against the glass, the boy's awful screams. None of her words seemed to land quite right. Indica's expression became stiff. Oryza frowned. Each word Talia added seemed to make things worse, as though she were speaking into an abyss. Outside the open windows, the rice rustled, stretched, Talia's anxiety spurring its growth. She clenched her fists around the bit of embroidery she'd pulled from the basket. There was a buzzing in her head, light but uncomfortable. She'd felt it, on and off, for days. The Oak House nursing sister said it was stress, that Talia should relax, stop sleeping in the kitchen, lie down on a proper bed like a normal person. Just the thought of the woman's impossible advice started Talia's heart racing. 'I thought I might go today,' Talia said.

For a moment, no one responded. The sewing sisters looked at Indica, who gave Talia a pitying look. 'You're tired, Little Mother. Anyone can see that. Perhaps you should go upstairs and rest. This circle is important, but we mustn't risk your health. I've the perfect room for you in my suite where no one will bother you. A lovely view of the rice you've grown for us. You should let us take care of you. We all love you so.'

Talia didn't need rock skin to feel the falseness. Not just in Indica's words, there was something about Indica's languid movements: too studied, too controlled. The woman's smile felt like a prelude to an attack. A thready feeling of panic rose within Talia. She needed to get out, leave before they caught her in their web, trapped her in a small room in Komey. They thought her naïve, but they didn't understand the danger they were in.

Talia relaxed her hands. She kept her eyes open as she dropped her consciousness into her body, settled her feelings, pressed them back. 'How kind,' she said, her voice soft, doing her best to sound compliant. 'It's something to think about for the future, but I should be going. I have an appointment I need to keep.'

Indica lifted a hand as though she would stop Talia.

Talia lifted her own, waved away the woman's objections. 'It's so good of you to make room for me. I relish the thought of being in Rice House, but I need to sleep in the Oak House kitchen, for now. It helps.'

Indica smiled. 'Dear, sweet Little Mother, what a treasure you are. If you need a nook, we'll build you one and I think we can do better than a nook in a kitchen.' The other women all nodded. 'It's the least we can do. But I don't think we should delay. Let me send a sister to accompany you to your appointment. I know you don't have a handmaid, but please let Oryza go with you. I can see the Oaks aren't looking after you.'

Talia smiled, didn't argue. She didn't trust herself not to make things worse. Instead, she focused on her sewing to give herself time to think. She had a strong feeling, a dread. They would lock her up. If they let her leave the house, they'd chaperone her to ensure her return. She poked her needle through the delicate fabric of the handkerchief in her lap, drew it out again. If she stood, if she tried to walk out the door, they would grab her. And in this house, with the numbers on their side, she was vulnerable. Outside, it would be different. Talia was powerful in the landscape, dangerous.

She glanced up at the glass doors that led to the garden, then returned her attention to her stitching. She would leave that way, step out, run off. The buzzing in her head stopped as she calmed herself. She completed the flower on the handkerchief and selected a different colour thread. How to get to the glass doors without being grabbed first? How to get herself over there? Then she had an idea.

Talia pretended to be unhappy with her choice of thread. She looked in her basket and then mimed surprise. She pulled out a half completed handkerchief and spread it on her knee, looked at it. 'Was the late Rice Companion fond of sewing? This piece from her basket is glorious. I'm not sure I would be equal to it.'

'Mother loved to sew,' Indica said. 'I remember how beautifully she stitched. But she was more of a collector than a maker.'

Talia's heart leapt. This was what she needed: an excuse to stand, a reason to move. She made a show of looking around the sewing room at the ornamental tapestries and weavings. 'And which pieces are from her collection?'

Indica put her sewing in her lap and gazed at the walls. She pointed to two large tapestries. That they were on the wrong side of the room didn't help, but Talia drew Indica out, asked about how and when her mother acquired them. Talia stood up, walked over to admire them. As she'd suspected they would, Indica and Oryza followed her, and the other sewing sisters followed them. Talia wished they'd remained in their chairs and just watched her wander around the room, but that was too much to ask. She moved on, walked over to a painting on the next wall, asked about it.

'Ah,' Indica said, 'now that's a lovely work. Before Mother's time, but I remember she liked it. It's Rice Manor, of course.' Indica moved closer, pointing out several features of the house and the landscape. '… and you can just make out the Kelp River behind the manor.'

'Is the manor quite close to Kelp, then?'

'We share the river, but Kelp Manor is a fair walk.'

Talia moved to the next piece. It was a large weaving, and it was as close as she was going to get to the nearest glass door. She felt for her courage, took hold of it. 'This is nice,' she said, but she didn't stop when she reached the far side of the weaving. She kept walking, stepped outside, over the threshold.

'Talia?' Indica sounded puzzled.

'Where are you going?' Oryza said. 'Wait.'

Talia turned, smiled at them, tried to look reassuring, but she kept walking, quickening her pace.

'Stop!' Indica said. She turned to the other women. 'Stop her.'

First one, then all the sisters moved. Talia started running and, as she ran, she unleashed her talent. She pulled at the ground, didn't trouble herself about discerning acorns from seeds or seeds from grains. At first, the sound was like the splatter of rain on flagstones and then the air in her wake was full of pops and bangs and booms. Someone screamed, and Talia almost halted. She didn't want to hurt anyone, not the sewing sisters, not even Indica, who wanted to trap her. But she didn't stop. She kept running. She only looked back when the sound of their pursuit disappeared.

Then Talia stood still. She looked back at the crazy landscape between her and the house she'd fled. She listened for screams. Nothing. Just shouts of outrage and people calling her home. She smiled, turned, and ran. She'd lost her laundry bag, only had the clothes on her back, but she knew what to do. The first stop on the train to Rice was Oak province. She'd go there first, get clothes and supplies and then continue her journey.

The grass path to the station was dusty and worn, and as Talia approached the station, it was full of foot traffic. There were traders and workers, heading in the same direction as she was, all bound for the provinces. In the other direction walked hungry-looking Berans on the last part of their long journey in the hope of help. Almost everyone stared at her. She made a spectacle, rice flourishing around her, trees in her wake. She was concentrating hard, doing her best to keep the trees at bay and the path clear. Several people waved at her, called out greetings and she forced herself to respond: a wave, a smile, but no words. Too busy concentrating on keeping the landscape in check.

By the time she reached the station, her eyelid was twitching and the light buzz in her head had returned. It was a relief to sit on the platform, her back to a stone building, to wait for her train. She almost didn't notice when someone familiar sat down beside her.

Willie said hello and this time her smile was genuine.

'I don't know about you,' he said, glancing at his watch, 'but I'm hungry. Not quite lunchtime, but close enough. And better here than on the train.' He bent and opened a small picnic basket and offered her a delicious-looking sandwich. 'You look as though you need this as much as I do.' He handed her the sandwich. 'And where are you off to?'

She didn't answer, but took a bite to give herself time to think. The taste brought the familiar comfort of the Oak House kitchen. 'You first,' she said, playing for time. 'What are *you* doing here? I thought you were going to the port. Wouldn't a barge be quicker?'

He looked uncomfortable. 'Still going to New Lytalia, but I'm taking the train.'

'Lots of stops. A barge would be more direct.'

The cook looked even more uncomfortable. Instead of answering, he reached into his picnic basket and pulled out a flask and a cup. 'You'll have something to drink? I made a nice fruit cordial this morning.'

Talia accepted the cup, took a sip. It was clear he didn't want to answer her question, but her curiosity won out. 'I don't mean to be rude. I know you're not time poor.' She frowned, lowered her voice. 'I mean, you wouldn't be in a hurry if it weren't for your mission. I thought Acacia and the others wanted you to get to the port with all speed.'

Willie looked even more uncomfortable. 'No offence taken. I've never been troubled about admitting the need to hurry. I work in a kitchen, don't forget. But, well, you see, it's possible I insulted one of the riverhood captains when I asked about the food on their barge.'

'And there wasn't another barge you could take?' she asked.

Willie made a face. 'They're a prickly lot. Here,' he pressed a second sandwich into Talia's hands, 'eat another. You don't look quite yourself.'

Talia laughed, took the sandwich. She hesitated a moment and then decided she'd tell Willie the truth. He'd been open with her, and she doubted he'd interfere with her plans. 'You're right. I'm not myself.' And she told him about her morning.

'I don't like the idea of you being alone in that province.'

'You sound like them, the Rice women.'

'No,' he said. 'It's not that. I agree with you. You can't stay in Komey if people are getting hurt. But someone else from Oak, one of your friends, should go with you.'

Talia didn't want to talk about her lack of friends. She asked him how he was going to manage in New Lytalia, where diplomacy would be essential to his mission. 'You'll have to do better than you did with the riverhood captain. You can't go insulting people about their produce or their cooking.'

He looked embarrassed. 'I've learnt my lesson. And Acacia's given me a book on diplomacy for new companions, which I crammed this morning.'

He pulled it out of his bag and handed it to her. It was a small, pocket-sized edition, what one would find in a companion's library or bedside table. It surprised her no one had given her one.

'Keep it,' he said.

'I don't need it. I'm going to be on my own. No need for tips on diplomacy when there's no one to talk to.' She held it out, but he shook his head.

'No. You keep it. There's lots in there about being a new companion. You might find something that will help with your...' he looked embarrassed again, 'your unexpected talents.'

She smiled, nodded, slipped it into her pocket. Then her train arrived, and she hugged the cook, the farewell harder than expected because it was the only one she'd been able to make.

Talia walked past the wagon with the horses, past the doors of the two passenger carriages, and only stopped when she reached the front of the train. She knocked on the driver's door, ready and determined to persuade her way inside. Because she would need to see the tracks if she was going to keep them clear of trees.

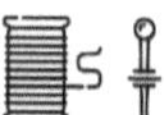

Aikin dressed in the clothes his houseboy delivered: pressed trousers, comfortable shoes that wouldn't slip on the deck of a barge, a loose shirt, and a thick coat against the inevitable turn in the season. He shaved in the small campaign mirror and then returned his razor to his bag. Should he use his razor today for a more violent purpose? Pull it out en route to the barge? Try to dispatch his escort? Much as he longed to be free, he wouldn't. He'd made a plan and would stick to it. Besides, the numbers wouldn't favour him, and freeing himself in Komey would be a temporary solution. Better to keep to his plan, wait for Birch to act before *The Laughing Waters* entered the port. And if Birch failed to appear? Well, he could jump the barge, swim for shore. He'd have plenty of time to lull Captain Yavo into complacency. Still, he'd keep the razor handy. If all went awry, he wouldn't be powerless. He tucked the shaving pouch into his bag and looked through the rest of his personal effects, the gold coins, the clothing, and his toiletries.

That made him smile.

The boy had packed his jars of hand salves, perfumes and tonics, none of which Aikin cared about. The purpose of asking for his toiletries was to get his hands on the near-empty jar with the crushed remains of the talc chip. Birch had found it in a wanderer's pouch when she'd sourced Aikin's first few rock children. The chip was such a tiny, misshapen thing, Aikin hadn't been confident of its status, so he hadn't used it on his cousins.

He had half a mind to use the chip powder on himself. The volume would scarcely cover the tip of a woman's fingernail so it wouldn't be difficult. He'd nicked himself shaving. He could rub the dust into the cut and the deed would be done. Might kill him; might not. There'd been no mention in *The Book of Kinesis* of men making use of wanderer stones, only women.

He held up the jar, looked at the powder. Was it a rock child? Would it kill him if it was? He sighed. He wouldn't do it. Better to be prudent. He discarded the rest of his toiletries and put the jar with the rock child powder back in the bag.

He stood up straight, taking stock of his assets. Birch, a razor, a bit of what might be magical dust, a mind full of ideas... Nothing was certain, but he wasn't powerless.

Beyond his door, he heard the footsteps he'd been waiting for. How many guards would escort him to the docks? It sounded like three, maybe four people. He closed his bag, then re-opened it, stared at the lonely jar. The words of *The Book of Kinesis* filled him.

The Author of the Future must avoid death. That much is certain, for death ends the story. But the Author who fears death ends the story before it can begin. For how can one write the Future, when one is consumed with fear for one's future? Be aware of the Ifs, Buts, and Maybes, but be sanguine. Bold sanguinity is the Author's friend.

Aikin lifted the jar from the bag, twisted open the lid, licked his finger. He swept up the powdered talc chip and rubbed it into the cut on his cheek.

The sensation of burning was immediate, but insignificant. The same sort of sting as a shaving cut. He sighed, closed his bag, faced the door. He adjusted his posture, relaxed slightly. No need to look like a child ready for the first day of school. His cheek itched, but he ignored it. The door opened and Yavo Tribute entered, along with one of her riverhood sisters and two soldiersisters.

The walk to the docks was as humiliating as Aikin had expected. People staring, commenting. He stared right back, ignored the jeers. But he didn't seem able to tuck away the feelings that flushed his face. Irritating because he wasn't ashamed of all he'd done. He felt confident he'd done the right thing by crushing those rock children, poisoning those wanderers. What did he care about the opinions of ignorant idiots? He didn't. He couldn't care less, but his face was hot under the public's gaze. Then he stumbled.

The soldiersisters mistook it for an attempt to escape, grabbed hold of him. He shook them off, but stumbled again. Aikin righted himself, but they took hold of him more firmly, cursing him. He wondered if it was the talc powder affecting him. Talia and Glory hadn't complained of fatigue or unsteadiness, only pain. But he felt odd, decidedly odd.

Aikin kept walking, but he was relieved to see *The Laughing Waters* docked on the far side of the river. Not long now. His escort turned towards the bridge. His feet felt leaden, and his face itched. He desperately wanted to get to his cabin, take off his coat, and lie down. He stumbled.

The soldier on his left tightened her grip, her fingers biting into his upper arm. 'Behave yourself,' she hissed.

'I-yam,' Aikin slurred.

The woman hesitated, frowned, stared at him, called out to the rest of the escort that the prisoner looked sick.

'If he's sick, that's even more reason to get him onto the boat,' the soldier to his right said. 'Come on!' She pulled Aikin forward, but Captain Yavo called a halt.

'I'm not taking illness onto *The Laughing Waters*,' she said. She stepped in front of him, took hold of his chin, turned his head, peered at the shaving nick. 'Looks infected.'

Aikin had trouble focusing on Yavo's face. It was too close, too warm. He looked away, peered over her shoulder at Birch. Birch? Was that Birch standing under the bridge? With some others. Aikin closed an eye, as though it might help clarify the situation. Not Birch. He must have been confused. It was just a group of thugs. Layabouts. Dock workers, maybe.

The soldier to Aikin's left tried to pull him forward. 'The man's feigning illness to escape banishment.'

Yavo shook her head, her proximity still too warm and close. 'No. This looks nasty. Maybe an infected bite?'

'Might be a lesion,' someone said. 'A plague lesion.'

The captain stepped back. 'Could be...? Not sure, but I can't take any chances. A nursing sister needs to see him, clear him.'

The soldier on Aikin's left let go and the one on his right loosened her grip. Aikin stumbled but stayed on his feet. 'We're not taking him back to the barracks,' one soldier complained. 'You can't expect us to.'

Yavo ignored the woman, told her crew member to fetch a nursing sister.

Aikin closed one eye. He could see Birch again. It was Birch, and she was with the dockworkers. Or maybe they were thugs because Birch waved them forward. Aikin swayed on his feet, opened both eyes. Birch was still there and getting closer. 'Is swrong momen, Birsh,' Aikin called out, the words slippery whispers. 'Non now. Too zoon. Jus befror Neuu Lytaliyya. Bether.'

Then he gave up, fell over, lay with his sore face in the dirt. Afraid he would die like the women he'd first experimented on.

Stupid, stupid, stupid. Experimenting on himself when there was no one around who knew what was wrong and how to look after him.

He tried to keep his head, think what to do. Instead, his mind filled with the Ifs, the Buts, the Maybes of a man afraid of death. And with one other pressing realisation: he was no better than Whilomena. She stole a rock child from him; he hid the existence of the talc chip from her. They were the same. Ruthless. He missed her. If he lived, he would consider forgiving her.

Shouts surrounded him. Grunts. Someone lifted him. A soldier cried out. Someone carried him.

'Get him to the station,' he heard Birch say. 'There's a nursing sister at the train station.'

The station? A train? He wanted to tell them to get help, not trains, but even his slippery whispers had abandoned him. He was a voiceless package without the correct address.

7

F ox looked at the Komey crowd, shielded her eyes from the sun, seeking the people she knew and the wanderers she hoped the new portal would call. Quartz, because he was sensible and knew as much as anyone could about rock children. Likewise Patience. But not Mica. Never mind, he was the only person who'd travelled through a portal, Fox didn't want him to go. Nor Saury, who was far too young. And not Oria, nor Fox herself. She wouldn't admit it to Mica, but she was worried about their unborn babies and the impact of the transformation. Selfish, but she hoped neither she nor Oria would feel the call. Course, she would step into the portal if called, but it wasn't a welcome thought.

She found Mica in the crowd and felt the warmth of his emotional signature when he spotted her, full of hope, full of love. She and Saury joined him, and the three of them stood waiting. Fox looked around for Doubt. As usual, he'd found a spot near Oria. He was half-hidden, holding onto the back of her coat, a look of determination on his face. Fox didn't think the companion had noticed him. Fox would need to warn Oria before they got any closer to the portal trench. It wouldn't do to pull the boy into it by accident.

Almost every Beran in the city seemed to be present at the edge of the gardens surrounding the Lacuna bell, along with some fifty Companionaris. Fox widened her rock sense, reaching for the signatures she'd been seeking and dreading since they'd disappeared: Aikin and Talia. Hard to know whether it was a relief or a worry not to find them.

Fox hated the truth of their ongoing betrayals, but it had to be faced: they'd obviously colluded. They'd left on the same day, fled Komey together on the same train, headed to Oak or Aries or Rice or Kelp. Please, not Kelp. Fox couldn't bear the thought of the harm they might do in her home, the place of her birth. The thought of Aikin loose anywhere on the Stone body, killing wanderers, was frightening enough, but it was the knowledge of Talia's treachery that was especially painful. Just thinking about it, hurt. And the reports from Rice House were damning. Indica said Talia had used her talent against people, against an innocent group of sewing sisters, who'd tried to help her, tried to rehabilitate her.

Quartz stepped forward, faced the crowd, drawing Fox's attention back to the present. 'We'll walk together to the Lacuna bell. Walk as a group. But I need the wanderers in front. If there is a call, we need to feel it with no one in the way.'

Mica and Patience were the first to step forward. Then there was movement in the crowd as the rest of the wanderers re-positioned themselves. Fox settled her emotions and followed their example, drawing Saury with her, ignoring the urge to push her sister back into the crowd. The Stone Body needed everyone to play a part, even someone as young as Saury. Fox glanced along the line and saw several wanderers from Persica, a couple from Caballo, another from the Winter province, and yet another from Salix. And more. People she'd never even seen before; men and several women. Last of all was Oria, moving hesitantly, careful of her right to be there. Fox caught her eye and nodded. They both had an obligation. Neither their pregnancies nor their complex origins excused them from this.

Fox glanced at Mica. His face tight with worry. He looked from Fox to Oria, then turned to Quartz, started arguing they should be sent back to the camp. 'We don't know what the transformation will do to their daughters.'

Quartz pinched his bottom lip, looked at Fox and Oria, cleared his throat. 'Well?' he asked. 'What do you say? Mica has a point—'

'If I'm called, I'm going,' Oria said. 'I don't claim to have the right... But, well, my body might want this.'

Quartz turned to Fox. 'And you? Are you sure?'

Mica raised his hand, but she spoke before he could, before her own fear could stop her, 'I'm not sure, but I trust the Stone Body.'

'All right then.' Quartz pushed a lock of hair out of his eyes and scanned the assembled wanderers. 'But everyone is going to stick to the rules. Truth be told, the *rules* might not be rules, but they are all we have. Some are probably nonsense, but remember this...' He began reciting the list: 'If you're called, move slowly, don't make any moves that look or feel like a dance. Don't talk when you're in the portal. If more than one person is called at a time, hold hands if you want to arrive together. Or hold onto clothing. And remember to grip your rock child. Now the hard part. As all of you know, there were hints new stones could birth rock people who are difficult to manage. Some stories suggest a wanderer's bond with a stone matters. We don't know why, so you'll have to make your own decisions about that. The main thing we know from Mica's successful transformation is that rock people are both childlike and powerful. Try to make their birth gentle and loving. Name them well. Welcome them.' Quartz smiled. 'Good luck. To all of us.'

For a moment all was still, then there was movement: wanderers opening pouches, lifting out their rock children, cradling them. Most, including Mica, carried four or five stones. Fox and Saury each had three. Oria just one: the stone that had accompanied Promise into the grave. Fox could read the hope and fear in everyone's signature. If there was a call to be heard, it seemed they were not yet close enough to hear it. Then Quartz started towards the bell, walking carefully, his five stones riding in his open hands. The rest of the wanderers followed; the crowd of Berans and Companionaris walked a few steps behind.

The bell hung in the open air, beneath intersecting stone arches. Colonnaded paths stretched, star-like, in all directions. At first, Fox couldn't see the portal beneath the bell, but as they came closer, the lip came into focus and she spied the earthen walls. Volunteers had worked day and night to excavate the trench. Companionaris all. No Beran wanted to risk being called to an unearthed stone they'd never met before.

'I feel something,' one of the Persica wanderers spoke up.

'Me too,' his compatriot agreed.

Quartz held up his hand and everyone halted. For a moment or two, no one moved, waiting in case another wanderer was called. Then the two Persicans started forward, stepping as one.

'Stop,' Saury called out. 'Quartz said you shouldn't dance. You're almost dancing.'

'She's right,' Quartz said. 'Watch what you're doing.'

The men stopped, but Fox could see it wasn't easy. They swayed like trees in the wind, listed in the portal's direction.

'Does it feel as though you're thirsty?' Mica asked.

One nodded, steadied himself, stood upright again.

The other spoke with some difficulty. 'Breathless.' He had one stone in his right hand and he used his left to lower his other stones to the ground. His companion did the same. Quartz came forward, collected the stones that hadn't called. Then the two Persicans were moving again, out of sync at first, then stepping in tandem.

Quartz spoke before Fox could open her mouth to warn them. 'You're doing it again,' Quartz said. 'One of you should take a step, then another. Hold hands but keep the pattern uneven.'

'It's hard,' the first man gasped, but he tried. He took a step, keeping a careful eye on his compatriot, who took the next. Now that their timing was uneven, they seemed more comfortable, less strained.

Even though it was a little late, Mica called out the question Quartz hadn't asked. 'Do you know your stones well enough?'

'I do,' the first man said.

'Probably. Maybe,' the second Persica wanderer glanced back, looking troubled, 'but I don't think I can stop. If someone else is called, ask earlier.'

'Then you need to come back,' Quartz said. 'We can't take any risks.'

The Persican wanderer gave Quartz a pained looked, shook his head in some sort of apology and kept moving.

Quartz glanced at Mica, and the two of them moved as one. They dropped their rock children and ran towards the man. But they were too slow. The Persicans jumped into the trench and disappeared from sight.

Mica reached the edge of the hole and pulled up short. He turned to Quartz, a bleak look on his face. 'I... They look dead. Is that how it was? With me? When you found me?' he sighed. 'At least they're still holding hands.'

'Yes,' Quartz said. 'Let's hope it helps.'

Fox realised she was gripping Saury's hand, had pulled her close as though it was she and her sister who were in danger, not the wanderers who'd disappeared into the portal. She loosened her grip, but Saury didn't and Fox could feel the girl's distress. And Doubt's too. Oria must have noticed because she reached back and put an arm around him, drew him close.

Quartz was speaking again. 'Well, what's done is done. We need to move the bodies they've left behind, but I don't think it's a task for Berans.' He put a hand on Mica's shoulder, drew him away from the edge of the portal. When they reached the crowd, they collected the abandoned rock children. Then Quartz asked for volunteers to empty the portal. 'And our people need to move back until it's done.'

Saury kept hold of Fox's hand as they moved away. When they'd put a bit more distance between themselves and the portal, the Berans halted. When everyone began talking at once, Fox realised they'd been walking in silence. Soon, talking became arguing. Some Berans were in favour of returning to camp, waiting on news from the Persicans before any other wanderers approached the portal. Others wanted to try again immediately. Still others argued about methods for assessing wanderer-rock child bonds. When Patience called for a story cycle, some shook their heads as though they didn't believe there was time for such niceties, or anything to be gained. That in itself worried Fox.

'Listen!' Patience said. 'We are nothing without our stories and our stones. Who are we if we abandon the Beranish path?' That quietened them, yet no one felt relaxed, and their signatures bristled in Fox's arms: fear and uncertainty. Patience was speaking again, beginning the cycle. He introduced himself, spoke of his own state. The distress surrounding Fox diminished as the familiar pattern played out.

Patience called on Mica for the second story and Mica spoke about his experience being called by his obsidian rock child to climb into Promise's grave in Oak. Fox had heard the story many times, but today it carried new meaning. She held her breath as Mica described the feel of the call, the longing to press his body against the earth, how his breathlessness eased and felt like love as he succumbed to his stone's desires.

Fox thought Patience would tell a third story about the taboo that had kept Berans from digging graves for their dead, the lie that had hidden the portals. He didn't. He retold what they'd all just witnessed: the story of the Persican wanderers. As he spoke, Fox realised the Persicans' path into the Lacuna bell portal differed from Mica's. They'd been nothing of the dance in Mica's story. And Mica's story had been full of the tone of his trust in his rock child.

'And now, we need a the fourth story,' Patience said.

Oria shook her head. 'Have we not heard enough of them in the portal tent?'

Quartz glared at her, and she had the good grace to fall silent. He turned to Patience. 'You have one in mind?'

Patience nodded and began speaking, 'On an ordinary day, in an ordinary camp, an ordinary girl opened an ordinary tent flap onto an extraordinary tent. She licked her ordinary lips and lifted her ordinary foot...'

Fox felt goose bumps flutter across her rock skin. She'd heard this story. It had been told in the portal tent. She opened her rock sense, widened it.

Patience continued speaking. 'The ordinary girl's mother shouted, called her away. The wind pushed and pulled at the ordinary girl, pushed and pulled her towards the extraordinary tent. And the sun burnt so bright, the grass at the girl's heels burst into flame. Still the ordinary girl's mother cried, calling her back. But the ordinary girl put her hands over her ordinary ears. She bent her ordinary body forward, let the wind push and pull her. Her ordinary feet ran ahead of the flames. Then the ordinary girl stepped inside the extraordinary tent and was gone from sight. With a snap, the wind blew out the fire. With a crack, it held the tent flap open. With a cry, the mother ran after her daughter. On an ordinary day, an ordinary mother saw the end of an ordinary story: an ordinary girl lay dead on the ground.'

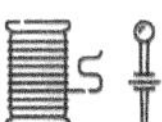

Some two hours later, when the Companionari volunteers had finished removing the bodies and carrying them to the Beranish camp, Fox, Oria and the other wanderers walked back to the Lacuna bell. Fox was nervous. The fourth story still rattled about in her head. Not the endless arguments among the Berans about whether to wait for news from the Persicans or approach the portal again. It was the story that troubled her. It felt like her story or Saury's story: ordinary girls swept away, leaving dead, soulless shells behind.

A compromise had been reached between the arguing factions. The wanderers would approach the bell again, en mass, but they would take precautions. Each wanderer would judge their own rock children, assess the strength of their personal connection to the stones they carried. Those rock children who were less closely bonded would remain in the camp, guarded by Berans with the help of Oak House's most trusted soldiersisters. It was no small matter. Not when Whilomena's rogue militias were still hunting for stones. None of the wanderers felt easy. Some refused to participate altogether, but most agreed, despite the feeling that leaving their rock children anywhere in Komey was reckless.

For Fox, Saury and Oria, the choice about which stone to carry back to the bell was easy. Oria only had one stone, the rock child that had followed Promise into her grave and re-emerged when Oria inhabited Promise's body. Saury had her pebble. And Fox had chosen Mica's blue stone child. She hadn't carried it for long, but she'd known it for most of her life, which felt close enough. For the other wanderers, the choice had been more difficult. Even Mica and Quartz had fretted over the decision.

Fox looked up, caught sight of the bell. The Companionaris kept its clapper tied up so that it couldn't ring in the wind and call a false crossover. *False.* All crossovers were. She hoped the clapper would stay tied up forever. It symbolised the lies that had led to Fox's wasted years in Komey.

Saury slipped her hand into Fox's and spoke, 'If we're called together, maybe the Stone Body will take us home. I'd like to go home,' she glanced at Fox, her forehead creased, 'But I guess we shouldn't? Should we? Do you think we still have to stay away from Kelp? Father said he'd kill any wanderer who stepped foot in the province and we're both wanderers. But maybe he's heard the news and he's changed his mind.'

'We're not going to Kelp. He won't change. You know that. If we're called, we must think about New Lytalia, not Kelp. That's what everyone agreed. That's where we can be of most use; helping Willie find the missing Berans before Whilomena finds a way to ship them out and sell them in Galea.'

Mica caught up with them, took up a position on Fox's other side, slid his hand into hers. They'd fought earlier, argued about whether Fox should obey the call, but he'd given way. Had to. The story of the ordinary girl implied a universal obligation to obey a portal's call. But it was good to feel his hand in hers, feel the calluses from his life outdoors, know the warmth of his signature.

'Still,' Saury said, 'I'd like to see Grandma again. And the ocean. I miss the ocean.'

'Maybe next time,' Mica said. 'When all this is over, we could try and speak with your father, negotiate something.'

Fox couldn't help the memories that assailed her. She could almost hear the slap of waves against the wooden boats, hear her father's autocratic tones, smell the kelp fires burning on the sand. She pushed the memory aside, focused on Patience and Quartz.

'Are we clear about what to do?' Quartz asked everyone. There was a general murmur of assent. 'Good. Then put your rock children into your open palms.'

Most of the wanderers were already holding their chosen stones, but the rest took a moment to open their pouches. Fox tied up her hair with Lark's lace and then fixed Saury's hair. She thought about what would be left behind if she was called: her body, her clothing, her objects. Mica had been dressed when he arrived with Obsidian in Komey, dressed as he had been, but with empty pockets. She didn't like the thought of being unarmed in a strange place so she slid her knife from her pocket, undid her hair, sheathed the knife in lace and then tied it back into place. A brutal hair pin that would ruin Lark's lacework. Would the Stone Body count her improvised hair tie as clothing? She hoped so.

Quartz waved them forward, gesturing for them to form a line. The wanders shifted about, spilling over the edge of the flagstone path onto the grass. Quartz and Patience took up positions at either end and they started forward. Step by slow step, the wanderers approached the portal.

Saury tightened her grip on Fox's hand, her breathing shallow, and Fox could feel how frightened she was. Saury wasn't the only one. Fear roiled Fox's arms from all directions. And Fox shared their terror. Her mouth was dry, her stomach clenched. She rolled her shoulders, dropped a finger of consciousness down and settled her emotions.

'I'm called,' Patience said. He stopped walking, and the line of wanderers followed suit.

'Me too,' Saury said. 'Like a rope is pulling me.'

'And me,' Fox said. For a moment, she wondered whether she was telling the truth. Perhaps the pull she felt was a need to protect her sister, mixed up with the fearful signatures surrounding her. Her head felt hot, her mouth dry, her heart was a bird fluttering against glass.

Mica's grip tightened. He whispered, urging her to stay.

She ignored him. Had to because Saury was right. The call was a rope, reeling her in. She pulled her hand from Mica's and held tighter to Saury's. The two of them walked toward the bell. Ahead of them, with visible effort, Patience halted. Then, when Fox reached him, he held out his hand and she grabbed it. Then they were moving again. It was all she could do not to run to the portal. Instead, the three of them walked, haltingly, keeping their rhythm uneven, careful of every step. She tried to listen to Quartz and Mica and Oria, all calling out instructions.

Think of New Lytalia. Think of the port.

Imagine the barges coming and going.

Think of the embassy, of Willie.

Somewhat clumsily, they sat, three abreast, on the portal's lip, then eased themselves over, lowered themselves, got their feet onto the raw earth. Then they were kneeling, then lying hand-in-hand, enveloped by the scents of the Stone Body.

Think of Willie. Think of the sounds of the sea. The smell of fish…

Fox recalled the slap of waves against the wooden boats, the sound of her father's autocratic tones, the stink of fish and smoke. She tried to push the memory aside, but it wouldn't go. She felt as though she was choking, took a shuddering breath, tightened her grip on Saury and Patience. Then the hungry ground claimed them, and all thought disappeared.

8

Mica was dreaming about Fox and the Beranish slaves. In the dream, the missing Berans had persuaded her to climb down into Promise's grave. He tried to stop her, warn her to be careful, but she ignored him. He could feel her fear. It inched up his arms, twining with his own alarm. Then she turned to him, called for him. But in a man's voice, *Mica! Mica!*

'... wake up.' It was Quartz, not Fox. Mica opened his eyes and found the senior wanderer standing over him. 'Good. We're needed. Get dressed. Oria's sent for us. Someone's arrived.'

'Fox is back already?'

Quartz shook his head. 'Oria would have said.'

Mica sat up and reached for his shirt. 'Who then?' But the question was too slow. Quartz had already left, the tent door flapping behind him, reminding Mica of the ordinary girl and the extraordinary tent. He shivered, pushed away his worry. He pulled on his pants and shoes and grabbed a coat, hurrying after Quartz. He crossed the chilly camp fire clearing and entered the close air of Oria's tent.

There was an unexpected collection of people inside and despite Quartz's assurance that Oria would have said if Fox had returned, he realised he'd been hoping she would be there. Instead, Oria stood, hands on hips, frowning at her visitors. Two ancient Companionaris in ill-fitting coats and knitted caps. Someone had draped blankets over their shoulders. Probably Acacia, because she was busy serving them teas and fussing over them. They shivered despite the close warmth of the tent and their hands shook. It was cold enough outside to make anyone shiver, but Mica suspected their shaking limbs were signs of the palsy of old age. The camp cook was there too, standing near Acacia, holding a teapot. And Sousette and Doubt. Those two sat side-by side on a cushioned bench, a quilt wrapped around their shoulders.

Mica noticed Acacia's boots. Wet, and the hem of her cloak was wet as well. He looked down at the two blanketed women's feet. Wet like Acacia's. So they had just arrived. Walked from Oak House to the camp? Or from somewhere else? He looked at Oria's feet. Slippers. Then at Sousette and Doubt's feet. Likewise. He made a note to talk to Doubt about coming home, giving Oria a bit of peace. He knew Oria was more troubled by Sousette than Doubt, but the boy was Mica's responsibility and he should sleep in his own bed.

One of the old women leant forward, put down her mug of tea, her dowager's hump straining against the blanket. 'I don't blame you for not recognising us,' she said to Oria. 'And I wouldn't have recognised you either. On any other occasion, I'd challenge your claim that you're the reincarnated Oak Companion, but tonight… Who am I to doubt Acacia's story about your transformation when I look like this?'

Oria stared at the visitors. Mica could feel the Oak Companion trying to place them. She picked up the lamp, moved it a little closer, to see their faces.

'I'll save you the guesswork,' the stranger said. 'I'm Hazel.' The name meant nothing to Mica, and it meant nothing to Oria because she continued peering at the stranger. 'Hazel!' the woman replied. 'Your third cousin. From Persica.'

Oria laughed, put down the lamp. 'I don't think so. That would make you Alder's daughter. I haven't seen Hazel since she joined Persica's provincial sorority, but she'd be twenty-nine at most.' Oria gestured at the visitor. 'And you must be, what? Eighty? Ninety?'

The old woman didn't answer, but the shake in her hands worsened and she tucked them under her arms to steady them. 'Twenty-seven. I was twenty-seven when I woke this morning. Who knows what I am now?'

Mica could feel the horror underlying her words, but Oria seemed oblivious for all that she had her own rock skin. She gave Hazel an irritated look. 'You're not making any sense.' Oria turned to Acacia, her irritation unabated, 'Where did you find these two and what possessed you to bring them here?'

The second visitor started crying. Acacia handed her a handkerchief, then turned to Oria. 'Stop lecturing and listen! They arrived on the Persican train. Drove it themselves. Demanded help. Our soldiers were on rotation at the station, so they brought them to me. I thought it was worth waking you. It was worth waking you.'

The second woman had broken into great jagged sobs. Mica could scarcely follow her when she spoke, 'It's, it's, it's tru-u. And I— I, I. I am six-ah, six, sixteen.' Mica felt a horrible weight in his chest as he listened. 'I... We—' She took a deep breath and tried again, 'We ran. Hazel and I, we ran.'

'Cerise is the only reason we're still alive,' Hazel said, turning to the stuttering woman beside her. 'We ran to the station. We only got away because we were young enough to run.'

Oria was shaking her head. 'You're not making sense. Something's happened in Persica, yes? All right. Start at the beginning. Who was chasing you?'

'No one,' Hazel said. 'Death. I don't know.' Both the visitors were crying now. After a moment or two, Hazel tried again. Her explanation veered from something about over-ripened fruit and a book she'd been holding, to running out of the manor house, to the smell in the air. 'We should have stayed to help the others, but it was too quick.'

'But what was it?' Mica said. 'What was too quick?'

Hazel looked around, noticing the other people in the tent. She blinked, took a breath, brought her hands back into her lap. 'I don't know. I don't understand it myself.'

'Tell them again about the fruit,' Cerise said.

'The fruit, yes. I heard fruit dropping to the ground.'

'We always hear it,' Cerise said, 'but not like today.'

'I was reading,' Hazel said. 'The falling fruit sounded as though it was banging on the ground, like hail. I thought of hail.'

Cerise waved an arthritic hand, 'I was inside too. And I looked out the window. Boughs were falling, and the fruit was ripening and falling, but not like normal. Everything was going too fast. I smelt rot. In the beginning, I thought it was Mother Persica.'

Hazel nodded. 'Sometimes it sounds like thunder when Mother Persica walks in the orchard, if she's in a hurry or if she's angry.'

Cerise continued the explanation, 'But it wasn't her. It wasn't normal.'

'We all ran outside to see it,' Hazel said. 'I thought Mother Persica's gravity had surged.'

'The Persican wanderers and their twins,' Quartz said. 'They must have emerged in their home province,'

The comment seemed to confuse the visitors. 'I don't know about any twins,' Cerise said, 'but everyone was happy in the first few moments.' She turned to Hazel. 'Do you think it could have been Mother Persica's talent going wrong? Maybe she was ill.'

Hazel rolled her ancient eyes like the young woman she was. 'I told you in the train. It wasn't her. I saw the Mother die, and it didn't stop when she was dead. It was chaos.' Hazel turned to Oria as though the Oak Companion might not have been paying attention. 'The sorority shrivelled up like the fruit.'

'What about the camp?' Quartz asked, his voice urgent. 'The Berans?'

'I don't know. We ran.' Hazel looked ashamed. 'We just grabbed each other's hands and ran because we were the only two left who could. I wasn't even sure it was Cerise whose hand I was holding. I thought she was some visiting sister, some old woman I didn't know.' She turned to Cerise. 'Because you looked so different.'

'We ran through the orchards together,' Cerise agreed. 'I held onto Hazel's hand and when she started getting too old, I pulled her along. Because I didn't want to be left on my own.'

Quartz looked at Oria. 'It's got to be the Persican wanderers with their twins. There must be something wrong with the Lacuna bell portal.'

'No,' Mica said, 'Don't even think it. Fox went into that portal.'

'And Saury,' Doubt sounded frightened. 'Will Saury be all right?'

'Patience will look after them,' Sousette said. She dropped the quilt from her shoulders and stood up, began gathering her clothes. 'But we should head out, look for them. Just in case they need us.'

'I'll come with you,' Mica said.

The Caballo Companion shook out her cloak, sending a waft of horsey air in Mica's direction. 'Excellent. We'll ride out together.'

Doubt left the bench and came over to stand beside Mica. The wanderer expected the boy to begin his usual boasts about his riding abilities and his potential usefulness on any expedition. Instead, he slipped his hand into Mica's, held on tight. 'Don't leave me here,' he whispered. 'Please.'

Quartz was pacing, shaking his head, but when he spoke it was to agree with the idea of a search party, 'Yes. Maybe you should ride out, but we have to close the portal. We should close it tonight. We don't understand what's happened. That's reason enough to close it.'

'Wait.' Oria held up a hand. 'Let's think this through. Closing the portal means closing off any chance of ending the famine.'

Her words recalled Mica to the state of his own body. Lean didn't describe it. And some others in the tent looked worse. Quartz was gaunt and he could see the bones in Acacia's wrist as she returned the Persican's empty cups to the cook's tray. And Komey's death toll was rising. Yet, it wasn't the famine that made him want to argue with Quartz. If Mica entered the portal, if he was called, the Stone

Body might take him to Fox. She and the others had focused on reaching New Lytalia. He could do the same. 'We should leave it open, but guard it,' he said. 'Only wanderers who know what they're doing should answer the call. I'll go if I'm called.'

'Stay,' Doubt said. 'Please. Don't go. You mustn't.'

Mica looked down at his nephew. 'We'll ride out to look for Fox and the others. But if I'm called, you need to stay here in the camp.'

Oria nodded. 'You can stay with me in my tent or with Quartz or Acacia.' She turned her attention to Mica. 'But we should take a moment before we act, think this through. The portal rules are even more important than we thought. Remember what that Persican said when we asked him whether he knew his rock child?'

It was Quartz who answered: 'The man seemed uncertain. What did he say? *Probably. Maybe.*'

Mica shivered. 'I still can't believe it, though. Obsidian wouldn't have hurt anyone and I can't believe a rock child, even a child that was new to its wanderer, would harm us.'

Acacia nodded. 'You're right. But a child transformed, without a trusted wanderer, in a difficult and unfamiliar situation...'

Mica shook his head. 'Obsidian was loving.'

Quartz reached out and gripped his arm, silenced him. The senior wanderer gestured for Acacia to continue.

Acacia frowned, bit her lip. Mica felt her searching for an idea at the edge of her mind. When she spoke, her words were uncertain, 'The power to rush life. That's what the talent is. Think about Talia and her trouble.' Several people in the tent nodded, Oria included, but Mica could feel their mixed emotions. Talia was a difficult subject. 'I mean it,' Acacia insisted. 'Think about her for a minute. She knew this world; she was among familiar people; yet she couldn't control her talent. How much harder to be transformed from stone to twin? Is it any surprise a twin might cause havoc, be unable to distinguish what to hurry along and what to keep steady?'

Her words made sense. 'Then we should all be vigilant,' Mica said. 'Not let anyone into the portal who isn't bonded to their rock child, tightly bonded. And I don't want to leave the portal untended until morning.'

'Nor I.' Oria was already moving.

Each of them must have felt the need to look down on the trench once more, because they all followed her as she crossed the tent. Only the camp cook and the poor Persicans remained seated, none in any hurry to risk themselves.

Dawn was closing in as they left the camp, but the stars were still visible overhead. Doubt seemed to have regained some of his confidence and soon he was skipping between Mica and Oria, giving a running commentary on his horsemanship and the possible expedition to find Saury and Fox and Patience. When they caught sight of the bell, the sun was yet to rise, but the stars had faded and pre-dawn light banded the eastern edge of the sky.

Mica realised he felt a call well before they reached the portal. A sudden pinch, a stitch, an urge to cough. He said nothing. Just slipped his hand into his pocket and fingered his rock children, feeling for the child that was pulling at him. His blue stone chip had left him for Fox, but he had four others: two long-term friends; two new to his pouch and pocket. He felt his way across their various shapes. No, not his flint child or his schist. They hadn't called. Then his fingers touched the smooth surface of his turquoise rock child. It had left another wanderer a year ago to be with him. Was that long enough? He felt warmly towards it, but he felt a tenderness towards all his rock children.

He frowned, tried to calculate the risks. Fox and Saury might need him... But Patience was with them. So, that implied he shouldn't answer the call? But what if the three of them faced more trouble than they could manage? His reticence might kill them. Because if they were in trouble, he could probably help. He was an experienced wanderer. He knew his way around the Stone Body. Not just that. He had travelled where few others had ventured before. So, he should answer the call. Of course he should.

Beneath his fingers, his turquoise seemed to agree. It pulsed with burning need. He made a bargain. If no one else was called, he would go. His risk. When he arrived, when he and his new twin arrived, he would run if he found himself among people. Because his new rock twin would follow him; he felt sure of that. He'd grab his twin's hand as soon as he landed. He knew something of the port; enough to know what part of the beach was usually empty. He would picture that, think on that.

He realised he was walking ahead, and that Quartz speaking, 'Can you hear me, Mica? Stop! Stop for a moment.'

Mica forced himself to slow and then, with enormous effort, he stopped, made himself turn to face the others. They were watching him and he realised he was the only one who'd been called. Better that way. He'd land on an empty beach. He'd be alone. He found he was smiling. He would help Fox and the others. It was the right thing to do.

'Which stone?' Quartz asked.

Mica lied. He hadn't planned to lie, but the word *schist* left his lips.

Quartz's stance eased, and he nodded. 'Leave the other children on the ground.' Then Oria spoke up, reciting the rules, all of which felt redundant. Quartz interrupted, reminding him to empty his pockets. Mica ignored him, just waved some sort of acknowledgement with his free hand, and turned back to the portal. He was closer to the trench than he'd realised. He knew he should stop and pass his other rock children to the others, but then Quartz would know he'd lied. Instead, he hurried, ran. He heard footsteps, but wasn't sure whether Quartz was chasing him or whether the sound was just the beat of the turquoise's call.

Someone shouted for him to wait. Then Oria said something about her hand, but he'd already jumped into the trench and the turquoise was out of his pocket and in his fist.

He landed awkwardly, flat on his face. It didn't matter. It was all right. All that mattered was being on the ground, face in the earth. Only, his hand was empty, and that was wrong. He ignored the odd feeling in his arms that Oria and some others were climbing into the trench behind him. Trying to stop him? But he wouldn't let them. He just needed to find his turquoise. He groped for it, got a mouthful of dirt but found it, touched its silky face with the tip of his finger. It was enough. He lost the ordinary world as the grandeur of the Stone Body filled his senses, too late for hands to hold him back.

9

For a moment, Fox was confused, didn't realise she was in the sea. She flayed about, tried to stand, then realised she was in a huge body of water, floating on her back. No. Had been floating on her back. In her panic and confusion, she seemed to have lost her balance, and now she was sinking. She kicked, got her head above water, used her arms to stabilise herself. Not swimming, the taboo meant none of the Berans in fishing provinces were good at that, but she could tread water, could splash about, keep afloat. If only there weren't so many waves.

She steadied herself again, did her best to stay calm. She looked around, seeking Saury, Patience, and the three new twins. There was a boat nearby, a fishing boat, sails flapping. It was daytime and the day felt full, noon-ish. She could smell fish on the boat, a catch. The people on board were shouting, leaning over the wooden edge of the bow with their backs to her, pointing at the water beyond. They must have spotted the others, which was some comfort. She hadn't expected this: landing in the water and then finding a fishing boat in the middle of the Komic Sea. And where was her twin? When Mica had transformed, he'd arrived with Obsidian at his side, but Mica and Obsidian hadn't faced undercurrents.

She turned herself about, searching for the others, turned full circle to face the boat again. No sign of anyone. She called out, but no one heard her. The fishers were too busy leaning over the bow, arguing, shouting, upset about something.

She caught a scent on the salty breeze: burning kelp. They didn't burn kelp on New Lytalia's beaches. She didn't have time to parse its obvious meaning because something or someone yanked her, dragged her down. She fought back and rose to the surface again. A moment later, her sister's face broke the waves, water streaming from her hair. 'Don't pull me down!' Fox said. 'We've got to try to stay afloat.'

Saury let go, and Fox realised her sister looked terrified. The girl put a finger to her lips and made a desperate gesture for Fox to follow, for them to dive. It was only then that Fox realised what she should have recognised upon waking: kelp was burning on the Kelp beach and a Kelp fishing boat was floating in front of her. Wrong place, wrong body of water. They were in the Kelp Ocean, not the Komic Sea, a place forbidden to her by treaty and to Saury by their father's edict.

Then Saury had hold of her tunic again and she pulled Fox down, ignored Fox's instinctive efforts to fight her off. Fox had just enough time to take a breath before she was underwater. And Saury didn't let go, just pulled her deeper. It took Fox a moment to realise what was missing: the burning sensation, the feeling her lungs would burst. She wasn't drowning! She forced herself to stop fighting. It took all of her Companionari training, but she managed it. When they were deep below, Saury stopped. She floated in front of Fox, golden eyes a deep purple in the underwater light. The girl nodded at Fox, then pointed from her own arms to Fox's arms.

Fox looked down. The journey through the Stone Body had transformed her beyond what Mica had experienced. For a start, there were gills on her upper arms, opening and closing as though they'd always been there, always known what to do. And it wasn't just the gills. Her newly regrown rock skin was completely different now. Underwater, it was hard to see whether the colour changes were real or just a trick of the attenuated light, but everything else had altered. In places, her bare arms seemed to have reemerged, but she hadn't lost her rock skin altogether. Pearlescent patches capped her shoulders and elbows, looking like armour plates, and thick dark bands surrounded her wrists. She looked at Saury. Her rock skin matched. If Fox hadn't been so worried about Patience and the twins, she would have stopped to examine everything more closely. Instead, she nodded, acknowledged their shared transformation. Then, as her sister turned away and moved towards the boat, Fox followed, her skill treading water translating into something resembling swimming. It wasn't until the curve of the wooden hull hid them that they rose to the surface.

Fox looked up at the boat. She couldn't see her father, but now she knew where she was, she could feel Pace among the fishers.

Saury pulled Fox close, put her lips to Fox's ear. 'Don't make a sound.' Saury must have felt the doubt in Fox's emotional signature because she pressed her lips even closer, gripped Fox's arm as though she was the elder of the two. 'I heard him call for the harpoon.'

Fox glanced back up at the boat again. 'Where are the twins? Where's Patience?' she whispered.

Saury pressed her lips against Fox's ear again, and Fox felt the heat of her breath as she spoke, 'Forward. Patience is in trouble. I had to choose. I came for you.'

'And the twins?'

'Out of range and drifting away.' Saury turned and began moving in the hull's shadow, heading for the bow.

Fox kicked and caught up with her, pulled her close, whispered in her ear. 'Let's dive down. Safer. We'll pull Patience down like you did me.' Saury nodded, and they dropped below the surface.

Fox felt for their father as she swam. Found him again, despite the muffling effect of the water. Saury was right to be scared. Pace was blistering and resolute. The fishers surrounding him felt like tea candles to their father's bonfire, but the fishers' emotions were angry and hostile too. Pace wasn't alone in wanting them dead. Everyone aboard would have recognised their signatures. The banished and the forbidden. But in Fox's case, the terms of the old treaty meant her return threatened everyone's life, and there was no way to let them know how things had changed.

Fox came abreast with Saury as they cleared the bow, in front of them, she saw a bubbly churn that was Patience. Surely, he had gills? The Stone Body would have reworked him, matched him and his twin, prepared them for the ocean. She hoped. But he mustn't have realised. Impossible to see what was obvious when you were terrified of drowning. She couldn't hear him, but she rock sensed that Patience was shouting for help. Then he forgot to kick and sank below the surface.

She felt for the twins, found them, but they were retreating. The distance and the waves made it hard to keep hold of their signatures.

Patience rose again and then sank again, oblivious to their approach. Then he rallied, kicked himself up. As his head broke the surface, there was a sudden intrusion, a white diagonal line of bubbles in the water, followed by a ruddy cloud that blossomed around the wanderer. Patience's signature blinked out. Fox screamed, but the sea gulped the sound. The poor wanderer wasn't still in death. The waves shifted him about, diluting his blood, playing with him as though he was nothing more than an odd-shaped piece of kelp.

Then Saury was in Fox's arms, burying her head, her hair a sudden halo.

Ahead of Fox, something changed. Patience jerked. Not life. One of the fishers was reeling in the harpoon line.

It was impossible. Fox couldn't let it happen, couldn't let Pace and the fishers treat him like that. She pushed Saury away and swam over to the dead wanderer. She pulled her knife from her hair. The bit of lace that had acted as its hilt floated away and, from the corner of her eye, she saw Saury catch it.

Fox gripped the harpoon line. It was hard to see because something floated around her hands, looking like a bit of dark kelp. Above her, the fishers doubled down against the sudden resistance on the line. Fox wished she could brace herself against something, anything, but was wary of using the hull. Instead, she swam against them, knowing she needed to hurry, finding herself stronger than expected. Even so, the fishers would win in a tug of war. At the very least, the line would bite her hands. They didn't; it didn't. She held her own, and even though it was hard to see what she was doing, she sawed at the line, ignoring the floating kelp and the churning water. Then Patience was free. She pulled the dead man down into the deep, away from the boat.

It was only when she and Saury and the dead wanderer had reached the seabed that she realised she could no longer feel their twins. The rock people were gone.

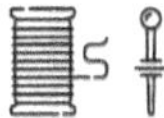

Saury spoke, but it was just bubbles. Fox would have laughed if circumstances were different, if it wasn't for Patience and the missing twins. Then Saury nodded at the place where Fox gripped the Caballo wanderer and Fox looked down. What she saw made little sense. She'd thought it was the bit of kelp that had entangled her hand, but it wasn't. Her hand was covered in writhing tentacles that extended beyond her fingers to clutch the wanderer's shirt. A sea creature, but ... helping? No. Using her as an anchor? She bent, looked closer, reeled back, swallowed a scream. The tentacles were rooted in her wrist.

She looked at her other hand and saw that what she'd thought of as a rock skin band was loose and writhing. So, tentacles. She would have tried taking a steadying breath if she could have. She turned to Saury and saw her sister staring at her own hands. Saury's tentacles weren't extended, but she had them too. Fox shivered, then used her Companionari training to settle her fears. This wasn't monstrous. This was natural. This must be part of the Stone Body's plan. The water was getting rougher, threatening to wrench Patience away. She gripped him with both hands. Now she was aware of the change in her rock skin, she could feel it … feel them. She could feel where her tentacles touched Patience's belt and shirt, a touch that wasn't the same as hands or fingers. Almost flavoursome, as though she could taste the wet leather and cotton.

Not just gills then. A completely new version of rock skin, adapted for life in the water. She looked at Saury and smiled, and Saury grinned back. Only the sadness in her little sister's eyes and signature told the true state of her heart.

Another wave rocked them. They were both struggling to keep their footing on the seabed, but Saury was using her tentacles to manage the ocean's shifts. Fox turned back to Patience, wondering what they should do next. He was limp and lifeless, only the waves brought movement.

And the waves were getting worse, like gusts of underwater wind in an ocean storm, billowing, shifting direction. Fox didn't dare breach the surface to assess the weather, but from where they were, it didn't feel promising. And the light had changed. The afternoon was winding down, but it felt like the darkness of a squall. Fox gestured for Saury to follow and she led them, half swimming, half walking, to the anchor's chain. They held on, taking turns holding onto the dead wanderer with their tentacles. Fox was waiting. They both were waiting for surely their father would see the change in the weather and set his boat for home. Only he didn't. The signatures above them began to shift from anger to worry, and Fox realised it was she and Saury who were keeping the boat in place. If they could feel Pace and his crew, the people above them could feel Fox and Saury.

Now Fox regretted her decision to wait, hoping for the twins return. Her hands ached, she was cold and her unborn daughter was unsettled. The baby was curled tight as a nut in a hard shell. Fox didn't know whether it meant anything. Perhaps it meant nothing, but she was uneasy. The world didn't feel right above or below. They needed to leave.

The water billowed again, slamming the hull above them. It pulled Fox from the anchor chain, ripped the wanderer's body from her fingers. She caught Patience and signalled Saury to follow her, and she swam away, pulling the wanderer's body in her wake.

They left the dead wanderer in an underwater cave, unable to say any words over him, unable to distinguish their tears from the salty water of Kelp's ocean. Fox hoped she'd be able to find him again. The Caballos would want to return his body to the land. She shivered. Likely there would be nothing left to claim. The sea would have it, but they owed it to Patience to do what they could.

Back in the open water, the temperature had dropped even further. Fox turned towards the beach, caught Saury's hand, urged her sister forward. Saury was sluggish with the cold now, but she followed Fox, kicking the water, clinging to Fox's hand. As they neared the shore, Fox couldn't help wondering how long the two of them could survive, whether she'd left their escape too late. They'd not be able to start a fire out in the open, and they couldn't look to the camp for shelter. The only other option was Kelp's manor house. The companion wasn't a cruel woman, but she'd side with Pace so there would be no sanctuary there, but at least the Kelp sorority lacked rock skin. If she and Saury were careful, they might creep into the house. A place by a fire was too much to hope for, but they might find blankets, they might survive. And when Fox felt warm, she'd be able to think.

With the decision made, Fox bypassed the beach and swam directly into the mouth of the Kelp River. It was even colder than the sea, what warmth there was, rested near the surface. She hurried, pulling Saury with her.

By the time they reached the manor's jetty, Fox had to take hold of her semi-conscious sister and push her up the jetty's ladder. Even with tentacles, the climb was going to be impossible. The only other option was to make use of the nearest boat. With a leg wound around a lower rung of the sturdy ladder, one tentacular re-enforced hand on the boat's lip, and an arm around Saury, Fox heaved. She got Saury's head and shoulders over the edge of the boat, but no further. Fox made a silent plea to the Stone Body and let go of the ladder, pulling herself onto the boat. Saury began slipping back into the water. Fox grabbed her hair, got a hand under her arm, got hold of her belt, and pulled. For a moment, the task seemed impossible, then Saury was beside Fox. Fox only rested for a moment. Saury was still breathing so Fox half dragged and half pulled her into the tiny cabin. Then Fox stripped off their wet clothes and wrapped them both in blankets.

It was still dark when Fox woke and rock sensed something was wrong. She thought it was her baby, but when she checked, her daughter was fine. It was Saury. Her sister was asleep, but feverish and the confusion in her signature told Fox they wouldn't be able to swim upriver. And yet, they couldn't stay. The sorority would find them. And they couldn't use the boat to search for the twins. The fishers would see them. And it would only be a matter of time before they were captured or killed.

She knew the answer but hated it. She needed to sail upriver, get them both out of Kelp province, seek help, and trust that the twins would be all right on their own. There was no choice. If they left before dawn, they might escape unseen. She'd sail to New Lytalia. Willie would be there. Perhaps there would be others there by now. Mica might be there.

But first they needed to survive and that meant food and dry clothes, and something for Saury's fever, and maybe a weapon for Fox. She'd take what they needed from the manor and apologise later. She dressed in her damp tunic and tucked the blanket around Saury and left.

The manor's interior was full of shadows. The only light in the building came from the moon and the banked fires in the common areas. Fox wrinkled her nose at the smell of overcooked fish.

Concentrate.

All that mattered was the state of the signatures in the building. She felt for them. Found them, every one of them above her, filled with whispering sleep. She wouldn't stay long. Knowing the manor layout helped, but being in the building felt wrong. It was dangerous, and it felt dishonest. Fox had to force herself to concentrate on what she needed, not the endless letters of apology she was already composing in her head.

She'd entered through the front door. It wasn't the obvious choice, but she had childhood memories of the manor cook sleeping in the disused mudroom during the winter months. Likely, the woman had retired by now, but Fox wasn't about to take any chances.

She moved through the small foyer, using her rock sense, careful to remain silent. She passed the formal sitting room, passed the small ballroom, then entered the hallway behind the stairs. She stopped outside the closed door of the guardroom. The manor hadn't seen soldiersisters for generations, but there could be weapons inside and she wanted arms.

Fox opened her rock sense, felt the space beyond the door. The room was empty. She turned the handle, opened the door. A slither of dusty, disused air met her nose. Then the door stuck fast, wouldn't budge. She lifted it and pushed it open. Glancing down, she saw her tentacles had gloved her hands, bolstered her strength. With the tentacular flavour of the brass handle flooding her senses, she stepped inside.

There were racks of swords and long, rusty lances, but she didn't know how to use those weapons and doubted they'd be helpful on a small sailboat. Then her heart lifted as she spotted a bow on a shelf. She reached up and lifted it down, slung it across her back. Bows, she knew. But finding arrows proved difficult. There was a quiver on the floor behind the door, but it only held two arrows. She searched the room again, but there was nothing else. Deciding two arrows were better than none, she buckled the quiver to her belt. A knife and two arrows: it would have to be enough. Aikin and Whilomena's soldiersisters were still roaming the Stone Body. Travel wasn't safe, so securing more arrows would be a priority. She left the guardroom and moved on.

The kitchen was silent; the floor was clean; stools upturned. Fox felt nervous being so close to the mudroom, but couldn't feel the cook. Still, the suspicion that the cook might be nearby, set her on edge. She took a breath, calmed herself, unwound her fear and walked into the pantry. She found a satchel and filled it with travel tack. Then she left the kitchen and crossed the hall to the nursing sister's room.

She found an odd assortment of clothes in the cupboards. Not perfect by any means, but dry. There were shoes too, but she didn't take them. Saury had grown up in a camp and preferred bare feet; Fox was still getting used to Beranish life, but would follow Saury's lead. Besides, she and Saury might need to dive into the water in a hurry and shoes wouldn't help. She found some fever powders in the sister's medicine cabinet and put them into her satchel.

It was a relief to leave the building and Fox almost missed the sense of footsteps approaching from the river. Her first thought was Saury, but it wasn't Saury. The person was a Beran, an older woman. Anywhere else, in any other province, Fox would have waved, asked for help, but not in Kelp. She was near the edge of the kitchen garden, still some way from the jetty, and there wasn't any cover. But stupid to think cover would help. The woman's preoccupation was the only reason she hadn't noticed Fox already. But she would.

The woman entered the kitchen garden and began walking up the central path. A cook. A new one, bound up with worry, which was probably connected with the night's events on the ocean.

Fox dropped, crouched and used the only defence left to her. She slipped her consciousness down and tried something she'd never tried before: dispelling all her emotions. She unravelled everything and anything she could find until there was no feeling left, just a small living creature, crouching in a garden. The stranger passed by and entered the back door without sensing her. Fox stood up. It was past time she and Saury were gone.

She hurried now. Fox ran down the jetty and jumped onto the boat. She only stopped to check on Saury, and shake a little fever powder into her mouth, before casting off. She hoisted the sails, grateful that wind meant she didn't have to row. It might come to that, but the tide and the wind were both in her favour. The boat moved upriver. Above it, a noisy flock of parley gulls shouted something that felt like encouragement.

For the first time since she'd found herself in the sea, Fox had time to think. Her heart was heavy with the loss of the twins, but she could do nothing for them if she and Saury were dead. She thought of Obsidian. He'd sensed the Berans dying in Whilomena's mill house. He'd known where to go, where he needed to be. She just hoped that these twins had the same ability. Mica had told her to name her twin, but it felt impossible. Instead, she thanked the Stone Body for the wind and tide. Then she focused on what mattered, putting as much distance as she could between the two of them and Kelp province.

10

Talia hadn't burnt her bridges, fled Komey, lost her position in Oak House, only to be trapped in another one of Aikin's plots. But that's what happened; was still happening.

She'd been sitting next to the driver, waiting for the train to pull out of the station. She'd been thinking about Willie and the book he'd given her, about her future in Rice Manor. What little attention she had left was focused on the kindness of the driver for letting her sit beside him. And the trees, of course: the press of the acorns and dates in the landscape. When the thug pulled open the cabin door and climbed in, she'd barely reacted. It wasn't until he put a knife to the driver's throat she realised what was happening.

Talia could still hear the sibilant sound of his instructions: 'Move! Drive! And don't stop.'

She frowned at the memory, picked up her cup of tea. Not sorry that one was dead. Her stomach rumbled. It was well past dinner-time, and her body was oblivious to the impossibility of a meal being served. She took a sip of tea. It was too hot, but she knew it would dampen her appetite.

At first, she'd been too frightened for the safety of the train driver to do anything at all. She sat beside the driver, watched the knife, held the trees at bay, but didn't act. Even when they were well underway and the soldiersister insisted the driver ignore the scheduled stop at Oak station, Talia hadn't acted. It was the driver who'd had the courage to do something, and it cost him his life. An hour beyond Oak station, the driver took his foot off the pedal.

Talia didn't want to think about what happened next. Better to think about the present. But it was all intertwined. When the driver died, there was mayhem, and Talia's body had reacted predictably. It grew a forest around the train, and one of her boughs crushed the killer. She gave a bitter laugh, upsetting her cup. She sighed, tipped the spilt tea from her saucer onto the floor of the already damaged first carriage. What a mess. Not the spilt tea. It was the forest. Talia's trees had pierced the carriage windows, ripped the leather seats, and scattered broken glass and splintered wood all over the floor. The kitchenette was intact. Well stocked with tea. No food, but an abundance of tea.

She'd been glad about the trees at first. They hemmed in the train, giving her an illusion of control. But no one was in control. Not her; not the thugs who'd survived; not the marshal they held hostage in the last carriage. And as for Aikin, he was with Talia in the first carriage. She'd found him there when she'd fled the engine. Better than sitting with the dead driver, but not much better because Aikin wouldn't wake. Another factor that had seemed fortuitous in the beginning. But now, they were all prisoners in Talia's little locomotive kingdom and the good fortune felt like a stalemate.

She'd considered using the tree branches to help the marshal in the last carriage, but it was impossible because she couldn't see who was where. So now she was trying to wake Aikin. Her enemy. The source of the trouble. Because everyone was hungry and tired, and a solution had to be found.

Only Aikin wouldn't wake, even though the welt on his face had almost healed.

She set down her cup and stared at him. Her plan, if you could call it a plan, had been to wake him and then tie him up in branches and twigs. Squeeze him. Just enough to show she was serious, make him order his people to back off. It was still her plan, if she could only get him to open his eyes.

She walked over to his side. He lay across several seats, his head near a broken window, his feet hanging over the aisle. The thought of touching him revolted her, but she reached down and felt his forehead. He wasn't hot, but his face glistened as though he had a fever. She bent lower, sniffed him. He smelt perfumed, like the earth after rain. It disturbed her to smell something wholesome on someone so corrupt. Not sick then. Perhaps he'd taken a blow to his head? Reluctantly, she felt for injuries, but found nothing.

She'd already spoken to the thugs through the closed doors between the two carriages. They had no account for Aikin's condition. They claimed he was unsteady, possibly drunk, when they liberated him from his guards. Even then, she'd known what was really going on. She'd seen the cut on his face, watched it healing moment by moment. She wasn't stupid. Aikin wasn't sick. The fool had treated himself with rock powder, probably trying for leverage in a world that had discarded him. Well, it had backfired. Men weren't supposed to be treated. He was lucky to be alive.

Talia shook his shoulder. 'Wake up!'

He didn't react.

She picked up his hand, careful to avoid touching the hoary warts on the back of his fingers. Again, no prizes for guessing what the warts were. It was disturbing to see rock skin emerging on a Companionari, but she knew what she was looking at. She'd seen Fox change from bare-armed to Beran. And yet neither Talia nor Glory Bass had rock skin. Perhaps it was a side effect of a man being treated? Maybe that was why her ancestors had reserved the treatment to women. In which case, he should wake up.

The sound of the forest surrounding the train alerted Talia to the fact her attention had wavered. That and the deepening shadows in the carriage. She walked to the windows and rotted down the new branches, readmitting the last bit of sunlight.

This couldn't go on. She needed Aikin to wake. If he woke, he'd leave, take his thugs with him. Then she and the marshal could walk back to Oak Manor. Talia would tell the Oak sorority about Aikin and they could decide what to do: chase him or pass the problem on to Komey. A memory intruded, Talia releasing the sorority from the basement, telling them she was their companion, their leader. She pushed it away. Not her role to lead anyone. Oria was their companion. Talia's future was a lonely life in Rice province, doing her best not to hurt anyone. Talia would let the Oaks know what had happened, but that was all.

The plan refused to rest peacefully in her psyche. Was she prepared to release Aikin and let him wander the Stone Body, creating havoc? But the alternative was abhorrent. Short of killing him, she would have to bring him back to Komey herself or shepherd him to New Lytalia and see him banished.

The memory of her misguided marriage proposal surfaced, the time she thought Aikin was some sort of saviour. The trees surrounding the train rattled and creaked. In the wagon coupled to the end of the train, a horse whinnied. She settled her emotions, calmed the trees and walked back to Aikin's side, knowing she would do it: try to take him to the port and see him banished. But it was clear he wasn't going anywhere in his current state. She felt confident that once he was awake, it would be easier to decide how she would get him to New Lytalia. And then she realised she had the inkling of an idea about how to rouse him.

Obsidian.

Talia hadn't been with Mica when Obsidian woke the dead and dying, but it occurred to her, her talent was simply an echo of a rock person's talent. Perhaps she could use it to rouse Aikin. If she concentrated, thought about him, focused her generative powers on him instead of the trees?

Talia sat down on the seat facing Aikin and picked up his hand. She closed her eyes, blew out a breath. She'd need to keep her eyes closed, avoid the provocation of looking at him, if she was going to think wholesome, healing thoughts about a man like Aikin. Eyes open, she might end up rotting him down to humus. She laughed and then chided herself for laughing. He was her enemy, yes, but she needed to think of him with compassion. But how?

Talia made herself recall his care when he'd treated her. Aikin had been kind, idealistic about his purpose in life. He'd said he wanted to help the Berans and the Companionaris and, even now, she believed that was true. He'd killed rock children, but had he known they were alive? Maybe not.

Talia sighed, fidgeted, but kept hold of Aikin's hand. None of these thoughts seemed to be helping. He wasn't stirring. She kept her eyes closed, used her training to settle herself, banished her chatter. She focused on the feeling of Aikin's fingers in hers. It was a risk to think of trees and rice, but that's all she had. And what were trees and rice but living shapes? Not so different from a person. In fact, everything on the Stone Body was simply a shape. Some shapes were mostly immobile, like cliffs and dirt; others were quick, like people and animals. Plants had to be somewhere in between. So Aikin might need less pull than a tree, but not as much as a cliff.

Talia's lips twitched at the notion and she reminded herself to attend to what was in front of her, a man, a person, an entity in difficulty. She wouldn't think of him as Aikin. He was a shape that was quicker than a plant.

She could feel his pulse. Blood. Blood was like sap. And life? Life was like the wiggle of germination. That wasn't the problem. His pulse was as sharp and crisp as a pocket watch, a tiny *tick-tick, tick-tick* in his fingers, a louder beat in his palms, a deeper throb in his wrists. The rhythm felt right. And he was alive, just quiescent.

He felt dormant. He was an acorn in cold ground, a sapling without enough light, a grain of rice on a hard stone flag. She called him body to body, coaxed him towards her with a hint of sunshine and a promise of help as rich and moist and full as good soil. And he came. Fast. Avid. Hungry. Grabbing. She pulled away, opened her eyes.

For a moment, nothing seemed to have changed. Then he stirred. He opened his eyes, stared at her. He didn't look like the wild energy that had grabbed her, hungry for everything on offer. Just someone who was confused. 'Talia? What are you doing here? Are we in New Lytalia?'

'We're somewhere between Oak and Aries.'

He frowned, pulled his hand from hers, touched his face. 'Then things have gone wrong.'

'You could say that. The train driver is dead and your thugs are threatening to kill the marshal.'

'Who?'

'Your thugs, soldiersisters, whatever… They are yours. Don't try and claim this isn't because of you.'

He sighed, his expression settling into a weariness she suspected had little to do with his health, '*Ware the well-intentioned plans of the stupidly loyal. The calamities they create will be of your own making.*'

Talia glared at him. 'That's as may be, but you need to fix things or I'll rot you down to a stump of a man.'

He peered at her, a slight smile on his face. 'You can do that? I'd like to see it. Not on me, of course.' He scratched the welt on his face. 'But what makes you so confident that your talents extend to people? Have you been killing people?'

'No!'

'Ha! A weak boast then, an empty threat. Unimpressive, Talia.' He frowned. 'Well … impressive that you've grown enough spine to threaten me. I guess that's something.'

The man was infuriating. 'I revived you, you idiot! I'm pretty sure I can put you back under. Even if I can't, I can crush you with my forest.' It was true. And crushing the carriage would be a relief, even if she ended up killing herself. He must have recognised the honesty in her words, because his gaze moved from her face to the wreckage surrounding them. There was a tiny flicker of something: fear, but quickly hidden.

His expression relaxed. He smiled. 'Tell me everything.' He sat up, ran his hands through his hair. The warty shapes on the back of his fingers had already changed. Though still confined to his hands, they no longer appeared deformed. Instead, they looked like tiny patches of rock skin. She glanced down, caught sight of her own hands, and gasped. She shoved her hands into her tunic pockets, stood up.

Turned God, please no.

She looked away, not wanting him to see her expression. It was unbearable. She'd welcome rock skin in any other circumstance, but rock skin that matched his? Talia wouldn't, couldn't, be linked to Aikin. She had to be rid of him. She took a step back, already knowing this was the cost of linking to him when she'd roused him.

The trees surrounding the train cracked and rattled. In the wagon, the horses reacted, hooves clattering, and the train rocked. Talia took a breath, schooled herself to do the right thing. And she would. She'd tolerate him, escort him to the port. She just needed a moment. She stepped back, widening the gap between them.

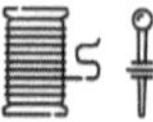

I t was maddening. The silly girl had described the impasse they faced, and by the Back, Aikin wanted to sort it out, but almost immediately Talia had begun behaving strangely. The woman who had talked about crushing him disappeared. In her place was a girl who jumped up and then fled to the far end of the carriage. For no reason. He checked. He looked over his shoulder, looking for a threat, but there wasn't one.

And now she stood with her hands behind her back, meeting each of his quite reasonable requests with silence. Worse, she seemed to have lost control of her talents. A rice paddy had sprouted between them, and the desperate whinnying sounds from the back of the train hadn't wavered. And the wreckage in the carriage was worse. The last two intact windows had shattered under the press of her trees. Then the idiot grew a tree between the connecting doors, cutting him off from the next carriage and whoever was in there. Birch? He hoped it was Birch, and that Birch had a plan. But only a fool would count on being rescued.

He waved at the rice, which was now chest high, amazed she'd found so much grain to work with. 'Can you at least rot some of this down?'

She didn't speak, only shook her head.

He spread his hands. 'What's wrong?'

She glanced at the nearest window as though she might leap through it.

'Go on,' he said. 'If you want to go, go. I don't care. I'll have a hard time getting out on my own, but I'm not incapable of climbing trees. Besides, there's sure to be an axe. Trains always have axes.'

She took another breath, blinked, didn't move, didn't speak. It was infuriating, and not even the genius of *The Book of Kinesis* had any wisdom to offer. It hadn't dealt with fools in trains. 'Look, you said you were worried about the marshal in the other carriage. Are you still worried about the marshal?' Her gaze didn't waver, but she nodded. 'Okay, then. Can you clear that tree that's between the connecting doors? It will help me talk to the...' He wasn't sure what to call Birch, if it was Birch and not some idiot flunky.

'The thugs?'

'Yes, but let's call them soldiers.'

'Just send them away.'

He kept his expression neutral. '... I could do that. If that is important to you. Or I could just leave with them. Leave you and the marsh—'

'No! I'm not letting you leave. You are not leaving. You and I are staying together.'

He spread his hands again. 'Okay. Then what? What's your plan?'

She didn't answer.

Aikin wanted to sigh. He wanted to stamp his feet or yell. He wanted to get the Back off the train, leave her to whatever malaise had gripped her. But she might kill him if he tried, and he couldn't have that. It wasn't just his own life in the balance. The welfare of everyone on the Stone Body might rest on his shoulders: if the portals didn't work; if the twins were not all they promised to be.

He stopped, forced himself to think. Talia was a silly, innocent, pliable girl, but not lacking in courage. Something had startled her. Perhaps it was his presence. There was a time when she'd seemed half in love with him. Later, she'd behaved as though she loathed him. The girl's feelings were complex. But the impasse on the train had to be broken, so she'd need to set her feelings for him aside. He thought of Gideon Aries. Course, Aries was talking about his daughters, but the reflection was no less apt:

A man might come at a conversation boots first and fall flat on his face. Better for a man to begin sideways, test the ground beneath his feet.

Aikin had commented on the rice in the carriage. Perhaps the subject of rice was a good place to start. Neutral. Safe-ish. Unlikely to set her off. He fingered the nearest plant, broke off its head. 'I was wondering about this,' he said, careful not to look up, 'how you grew all this. But it's simple, isn't it? One grain is enough. One stray grain and then you have a plant. How many new grains can a plant produce?' He let his question sink into the carriage. Didn't rush to fill the silence, didn't look at her.

'I don't count them,' her voice sounded rusty. 'Maybe hundreds.'

'Close to making something out of nothing.'

'There must always be something to work with.'

Not friendly, but he nodded. He was careful not to look up. He gave a gentle sigh. Smiled at the ground. Half shrugged. He wondered where his bag was, longed for his razor, wondered whether he could kill her before she killed him. He pushed the thought aside. Best wait. He looked at the connecting doors between the carriages, made a show of contemplating them. 'I'm going to have to shout, which isn't ideal.'

'I'm not getting rid of the tree. It's keeping you where I can see you.'

'Quite right. Shouting it is, then.' He walked over to the doors and raised his voice, 'This is Aikin Oak speaking. I want you to stand down! Leave the marshal where she is. I don't want her hurt. You need to walk over to your nearest exit. If a path opens between the trees, leave. Go to Aries. Don't try to find me. Stay in Aries!'

'Yes,' Talia said. 'And tell them they mustn't take the horses from the wagon. We'll need the horses.'

He chanced a look at Talia and nodded. She was a little wide-eyed, but there was a slight easing of tension now that negotiations had begun and he'd voiced a way out of the impasse. He turned back to the door and told the soldiersisters to rap on the side of the train when they were ready for Talia to open a path through her forest and to leave the horses where they were.

There was a moment or two and then he heard it: three knocks. He looked at the floor when he spoke, not wanting to spook Talia, 'It's up to you now. Let them out or not.'

He imagined he felt something shift within her, but perhaps it was just the change in the density and stillness of the forest air. And then there was a cacophony as she broke down the trees. In the aftermath, the train shifted beneath their feet and the soldiers clambered down.

Aikin turned his attention back to the connecting doors and called out to the marshal, suggested she might want to leave on foot and head back to Oak's station. At first, nothing happened. After a goodly while, there was movement. Lighter this time, but the unmistakable shifting that told him the marshal had climbed out of the carriage.

They were alone now. Awkward. He could almost feel Talia becoming unsettled again. Not a good time for questions. Asking her what was next wouldn't help. He would wait. Aikin was nothing if not a patient man. He walked to the nearest row of seats and lay down. 'Wake me when you decide what we're doing.' He poked his head above the seat to look at her. Her hands were behind her back.

The wide-eyed look hadn't left her face. He dropped his head back down and closed his eyes.

'I was going to Rice Manor,' she said. He didn't answer. 'Before this happened,' she said. 'Now I'm going to New Lytalia, taking you there.'

'Fine,' he said. 'You'll get no argument from me. I didn't attack my escort or put myself on this train. I was ready to go to the port. Still am. Once you clear the tracks, I can drive the train.'

'The tracks are broken,' she said.

That explained her interest in the horses. Not his favourite mode of transport, but it would be better than walking.

'We'll stop at Rice Manor for supplies,' she said.

That made him laugh. If ever there was proof that Komey's young women needed more provincial experience, it was this. 'Up to you, obviously. But there's nothing in Rice, just dust and wind and even the parley gulls don't go there. We're better off stopping at Kelp Manor. We might even get a boat.' He thought she was going to argue, but she didn't.

'Kelp?' she said, and there was a slight lift in her voice. 'Yes. That's a good idea. Let's start with Kelp.'

11

After his journey through the portal, Mica regained consciousness with a throbbing head, uncomfortable rock skin, and the smell of waste filling his nose. Waste and ... unwashed bodies?

He opened his eyes and for a second it felt as though he hadn't opened them at all. The world was dark and confusing, but the smell was real. He could feel people, wooden walls, and water beyond. And the world rocked, dipped and rose, worrying the tangle of bodies and signatures surrounding him. People full of pain and fatigue, sorrow and dismay. And suddenly it was obvious where he was: Whilomena's slave ship. Where else would the Stone Body send him? The ships had plagued him since he and Obsidian had first overheard Whilomena talking about her schemes. He stretched his rock sense, feeling for Fox, knowing she wouldn't be on the ship, but wanting her. And she wasn't. Nor was Saury, nor was Patience. And that made sense. This was Mica's imperative. It was his worry that had called him here. Called him? Or called for him and his twin?

Mica turned his head and relief swept through him. There was indeed a twin beside him, nose wrinkled, the tiniest touch of a frown on his almost identical face. Mica smiled. 'Hello there, brother. Welcome. I'm so glad you're here.'

The rock man met his gaze without an answering smile, as though he wasn't sure he agreed. And he did look different. Obsidian had been fuller, softer. This twin was thinner, ragged and wild, his expression shifting with each rise and dip of the ship, filling Mica's rock skin with a rushing sensation. Mica glanced down. His rock skin had changed. It was flat now, and oddly ridged. He ran his hand down his forearm. The skin was cool and smooth, but when he tried to run his hand back up again, he had to pull his hand away. There were barbs at the base of each segment. Scales. He had scales.

'Who's there?' someone called out. 'You! You there! Who are you? Where did you come from?'

'Stop yelling!' someone else said. 'People are trying to sleep.'

'There's someone here. Look. Two of them. New people here. Can't you feel them?' The questioner clambered towards Mica, his questions continuing, voice lower now, but no less urgent, 'Strangers! Who are you? How did you get in? The hatch didn't open. Is there a way out? Or have you been hiding all this time?' The questioner, a man, squeezed past a barrel, coming closer. 'But you can't have been here. I'd have felt you. We all would. You've come from the outside, somewhere on deck. So there *is* another way out. There is, isn't there? You've found one.' A wave rocked the ship and the man struggled to remain standing up, slipped, knock his head with an awful thwacking sound. He stumbled forward, landed beside Mica, and started shouting about there being a way to escape. The hold came alive.

Mica's twin shifted, frightened. Mica made a soothing sound and it almost worked, but the people in the hull were responding to the news, hurrying forward, calling out. There was a strange sharp edge to the air, a horrid feeling of urgency. Mica's heart began racing and his twin's answered, and together they spiralled, rushing faster and faster. No, no, no, no. Not another Persica. Because they couldn't run away. They were stuck in the hold. 'Shush...' Mica said. He reached out, grabbed the questioner to stop him from shouting, had to squeeze his arm to get his attention. 'Don't yell! Just don't yell or we'll all die! Please.'

The man fell silent, stared at Mica, the whites of his eyes loud as any emotional signature. But the rest of the hold didn't stop. Everyone was talking now, and moving, and Mica's twin moaned. Mica didn't want to add to the noise, but he had to. He lifted his voice, 'Stop! Be quiet or we all die!' The space inside the hull fell silent. Only the creaking and rocking remained. Mica dropped his voice to a whisper, 'Thank you, thank you. I'll explain, but I have to... I have to do something first.'

He turned to his twin, reached out, took the rock man's hands. It was like holding sparks, like throwing a log onto embers. 'Shush,' he crooned, ignoring the pain of the touch, wishing he could steady himself like a Companionari, shut his feelings down. Because he and his twin were spiralling again, hearts racing. 'Shush,' he lullabied the words. 'Shush now...' But there was no quietening, no lessening of the rushing sensation. Mica could almost feel himself ageing or growing younger; it was too dark to know which. He spoke the welcome, desperate now:

'Welcome to this life on the Stone Body, Cerulean. I name you for the colour of your childhood as a living stone. We'll look for the second part of your name as we come to know you. You will know it when it's spoken. For now, you are Cerulean.' The rushing sensation continued unabated. Mica heard someone groan, someone scream. He felt something uncomfortable in his mouth, something odd. A tooth. No, not one tooth, several teeth. Falling out! He'd failed. They were all going to die. He couldn't run, so he did the only other thing he could think of doing. He reached out and pulled the rock man closer, embraced him. 'I love you. I love you. We love you. Don't kill us. Please... Darling Cerulean. Precious one, please stop.' The heat that felt like sparks burnt where they touched, chest to chest, arm to arm. Mica ran his tongue over his teeth. They were back. Cerulean had turned time back, rewound things. Mica didn't let go. He finished the welcome, whispering in Cerulean's ear, 'Welcome to your body; welcome to your life. We have longed for you; waited for you. Your existence is precious.'

He stopped speaking, but still held on. The hull was silent. He could feel the terror in the surrounding signatures. But no one uttered a word. Every signature fearful; every Beran holding their breath. Fear was a painful flavour, but death was absolute.

Mica spoke without letting go of his twin, careful to keep his tone even and calm. He explained. Did his best. If the Berans surrounding him hadn't just experienced the rush of stone, they would have disbelieved him, but they had and they did.

The man who'd first noticed them cleared his throat, 'I don't know what this means, whether your presence will save us or kill us, but you got one thing wrong. You told your twin we're on the Stone Body. We're not. We're on *The Crested Wave.* And I think I speak for everyone when I say, I hope you've not made a desperate situation worse.'

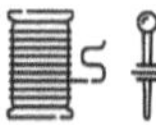

Mica watched as mugs of fish stew passed hand to hand. The food moved from a pot on the deck to a Beran at the top of a ladder, then down a few rungs to the next Beran, and down a few more. From there, the mugs spread throughout the hull until everyone had food. The count didn't seem precise, else the Komic oceanhood would have worked out the hold contained two extra guests. And that mattered. Not because Mica had some brilliant plan for their escape that required their existence to remain secret. It mattered because anything, any change, any disturbance, could unnerve Cerulean and kill them all. Mica didn't want to think about what would happen if the Companionari soldiersisters climbed down the ladder to investigate who was supposed to be in the hold and who wasn't.

His current plan, his only plan, was to stay in the shadows between the barrels at the rear of the hold until *The Crested Wave* docked in Galea. Then he'd flee with Cerulean before Cerulean aged anyone to dust.

The only comfort was Lupe, a Beranish woman from Canis. She carried over their dinner, moving slowly and carefully. Like all the Berans from the province that had once been home to the Stone Body's dogs and wolves, she exuded calm. Right now, she stood side on, handing Mica the mugs. Somehow she seemed to know facing Cerulean would be too confronting. And she was right. Mica's rock skin prickled with Cerulean's fear. His twin didn't like her being so close. The air shivered, almost crackled. In the depths of the hold, someone cried. People started spilling their stew as they scrambled closer to the base of the ladder.

'Settle down everyone,' Lupe said. 'Everything's fine. You won't hurt anyone, will you, lad?' She spoke without attempting to meet the rock man's eyes. She looked at him, but kept her gaze low.

'You should step back,' Mica whispered.

'No,' she said, and her voice warm and easy. 'Your man here... Your brother. What did you say his name was?'

'Cerulean,' Mica said.

'Well, Cerulean needs to get used to me and everyone else, because we're not going anywhere. Stuck in here, we are. So he has to trust us. He's like the wild dogs in Canis,' there was a catch in her throat. 'They were always terrified when we first introduced them to the camp.'

'What if he's a wolf?' Mica said. 'I heard you can't tame them.'

'Ah now... This one's no wolf,' her voice was warm. 'This one's a big, nervous pup. And you're almost as frightened as he is. Anxiety is all. No different from any of the young dogs I've trained, and I've trained my fair share.'

In the background, Mica heard the other Berans from Canis

doing much the same, reassuring the people that Cerulean wouldn't hurt anyone, urging them to return to their places. Mica spoke, gesturing at the people with his chin, 'Maybe they should keep their distance. Rock twins can kill people, have killed ... when frightened.'

'Dogs can kill too. Cerulean isn't the first danger any of us have faced and he'll not be the last. At least with a wild creature, there's no malice.' Lupe smiled, but Mica felt the sadness in her signature. 'But fear is a flavour that spreads from tongue to tongue, armpit to armpit. All of us need to call a halt to it. Show Cerulean we're confident and trustworthy.' One of her compatriots had come forward and held out a mug of stew to Lupe. She thanked the woman. Then she sat down and began eating. 'Eat up, Wanderer. Show him it's safe to relax.'

But Mica couldn't do it. He stood rooted to the spot; the air surrounding him seemed even tighter and sharper. Fear looped between Mica and the huddled Berans and Cerulean. He ran his tongue over his teeth. Not loose. Yet. But his hand shook as he gripped the mug, slopping his dinner. It felt like the palsy of age. 'You should move back a bit,' he spoke to Lupe without turning his head. 'Further away.'

'And if I do, he'll never learn that we are friends. I told you to relax, Wanderer. And that's an order. Trust me. I know what I'm doing. Help me show him you and I are friends. That's the first step. He's almost comfortable with you, he's relying on you. He'll never be safe around people if you don't show him you feel safe.'

Not for the first time, Mica wished he had some of Fox's skill with managing emotions. He did his best. He focused on the warmth and comfort of Lupe's emotional signature, dropped his shoulders, took several deep breaths. The air gentled; Cerulean relaxed; the huddled Berans began talking again, creeping back to their places in the hold.

Lupe looked at Mica and smiled, nodded her approval, but when she spoke, she directed her words at the rock man. 'That's better, isn't it? Your brother and I are great friends. And you're such a good boy. We're going to eat our dinner and you'll not frighten me off by making the air rattle and hiss. And why would you when we're going to be such good friends?'

So, they ate, and Lupe's warm chatter surrounded them and when she moved, gathering their mugs and handing them over to a compatriot, her movements were solid, comfortable, safe. There was so much about her that reminded Mica of life on the Stone Body. He missed his homeland. He missed Fox and couldn't help worrying about her. What if her twin was wild, too? But no. He wouldn't think of it. He would stay happy and relaxed, the way Lupe wanted him to be.

Lupe glanced back at him. 'That's right. Keep things steady and even. Cerulean's counting on you. A wild thing like your rock brother? He needs to have faith in his pack. And until he accepts me, his pack comprises you. How about we all sit back, and you soothe all of us with a story cycle?'

'You're looking for knowledge?'

'I'm looking for a story.'

'Which one?'

'The only story that matters right now, the one we all need. Tell us the story of rock twins.'

Mica had told the imprisoned Berans about rock people when he introduced Cerulean, but that had been a short, quick, desperate account. What Lupe was asking for was different. And he would need to move to tell the story properly. He and Cerulean had been almost stationary since they arrived, but a cycle demanded a wanderer claim a larger footprint, be more like the pack leader like Lupe had wanted. Mica smiled at Cerulean and, for the first time since they'd arrived, he turned away from his twin. He walked over to the nearest barrel, jumped up, and sat on it. His twin moaned and the air tightened. Mica waved Cerulean over. The rock man moved cautiously, wide-eyed, but he came and stood beside Mica. The sharpness in the air receded.

Mica touched Cerulean's shoulder, rested his hand there, and began. He told the Berans about himself, explained his hopes and dreams and needs. He projected warmth and certainty into his voice, used all his skill and training, all his years of storytelling. Mica chose Obsidian's tale as the second story. He felt Obsidian come back to life under his tongue: the rock man's goodness, his talents, his quirks, and the revelations about the Companionaris' lies. Technically, the account of Persica should have been the third story in the cycle. It was the contrasting account. But the Berans were frightened enough, so he spoke instead of Cerulean. He told them about Cerulean as a rock child. He recalled their first touch, how smooth and warm the stone had felt in his hand. Then he talked about their year together, and about being called together to enter the portal. Mica concluded with their arrival on the ship, holding up his arms, pointing to his rock skin and explaining that his transformation was a natural part of the process.

A man called out a question: 'This skin Cerulean's given you? It's odd. I mean, I can't see it well, too dark for that, but I've been feeling the shape of it. There's not much there, is there? Is it real rock skin? Can you still rock sense?'

Mica lowered his arms. He opened his mouth to speak, and hesitated. It *was* working, but in truth it was more like scales than rock. And when he'd first examined it, he'd noticed ladder-like slits on his upper arms.

'What is it?' the man asked. 'You're holding something back.'

'My rock skin's working...' he hesitated.

'But?' the man prompted. 'You owe us your thoughts, Wanderer.'

Mica looked at Cerulean and frowned. 'Just that... Well, there are some differences between my skin and Cerulean's. Obsidian's skin was identical to mine.'

'Feels identical to me,' the man said. 'When I rock sense it.'

'It is, almost. But my scales are slightly bigger, rounder, bumpier—'

Lupe spoke up, 'You talked about bonding, but this lad hasn't bonded... Not truly. If he had, he wouldn't be so skittish.'

Mica felt his heart sink. They had warned him. Quartz and Oria had told him not to go into the portal with a new rock child. This was his fault. He shouldn't have risked the portal with a stone he'd only carried for a year. And to make matters worse, he'd lost his grip on it when he was in the trench. He'd only had a finger on his rock child when the Stone Body had moved them. The only comfort was he hadn't created another Persica. Everyone in the hold was alive.

'Not much separating the two of you, though,' someone said.

Mica withdrew his hand from Cerulean's shoulder and ran his finger down his twin's scales, counted the ladder-like slits that marked his brother's arms. 'We both got horizontal lines on our arms, seven of them. I think they might be gills. But I'd have to get in the water to know for sure.' And voicing it got him thinking. If he and Cerulean could slip off the ship, they might survive in the water. If they could get off soon, they could avoid hurting anyone and they might make it back to the Stone Body, raise the alarm. 'How many days did you say the ship's been at sea?'

It was Lupe who answered. 'Five, but we haven't gone far. Becalmed.'

'Eh, Wanderer,' an elderly voice called out. 'All very interesting, I'm sure, but you owe us a fourth story.'

Mica took a breath, 'Okay. Yes. The fourth story. I have one that wants to be heard. I dismissed it when it first came to mind. It seemed too small and childish for such momentous times, but it's pressing me, wants to be told. You probably know it. It's the story of the lonely mouse.'

There were mummers of agreement at the mention of the childhood favourite.

Mica clapped his hands and began, 'One day Mouse woke up in her hole in the banks of the Cava River and decided she needed a family. A husband would help her collect seeds, clean the house, cook the dinner. He might even hold her hand in the evenings when she sat on the threshold enjoying the sunset. Mouse was a careful bride. She didn't want to choose the first groom she came across, so she prepared for a long journey. She packed seeds and other delicacies into the pocket of her apron, and she took a sharp stone for throwing in case of bandits. Thus she set out and thus she continued.

'The first groom Mouse met was industrious, but he smelt of blue cheese, of which she had little liking, so she kept walking. The next groom she came across was amusing, but his fur stood up on end, so she kept on walking. Mouse soon discovered that the world contained any number of mousy grooms, but every one of them had shortcomings. One had long toenails that curled over his feet. Another had a runny nose. One had dirty hands. Another had dirty ears. By the time she had rejected the sixteenth groom, she was sad and hungry and there was nothing left in her pocket but the sharp stone. She knew she had to return home by the quickest route or starve, so she pinched her nose and dived into the Cava, pleased to let the current do its work.

'And so it did.

'That year, the Cava was full of spring rains and the strength of it took Mouse by surprise. It sucked her down and turned her about. When she got her head above water, it was all she could do to drag herself up the nearest bank.

'As fortune would have it, the Cava had brought her level with her mouse hole. As fortune would also have it, the Cava had carried her to the wrong side of the river. And as fortune would further have it, she'd lost her sharp little stone.'

Mica paused. He'd forgotten this part of the story. The part about a stone being lost after a journey. He started speaking again and found he was also listening, 'As the afternoon sun dried Mouse's fur, it tilted west and its rays hit something that caught her eye, turned her head. Across the river, sitting beside Mouse's front door, was Mouse's twin sister and all of Mouse's loneliness disappeared.

'The sisters waved. They called out. They even danced and sang at the sight of one another, but they could not cross the Cava. Soon, their dance brought frustrated tears.

'The salt of the sisters' tears flowed into the Cava and the Stone

Body noticed the taste of it, and it took pity on the sisters. It webbed their feet to make them better swimmers. And just in case webbed feet weren't quite enough, it grew them wings. And just in case webbed feet and wings weren't enough to keep them together, it fashioned them gills. Soon it didn't matter where the sisters were, they could always come together to clean and cook and hold hands in the evenings.'

Mica felt astonished by the story. Of its own accord, his scales had lifted like armoured goosebumps and so had Cerulean's. 'I had forgotten about Mouse and her sister. The details of it. I don't know why I hesitated. It's about rock twins. I should have given that story to the portal tent when I was still in Komey.'

The Berans were silent, but Mica knew the silence for what it was. They were thinking, feeling, each heart making knowledge.

'We're still close to home,' one man spoke up. 'Like Mouse being close to her hole.'

'Are you going to grow wings and save us?' a child asked.

'I wish I could,' Mica said.

The older voice, the one who had urged Mica to get on with the fourth story, spoke up again, 'Them up top, the oceanhood, them up on the deck... Not the soldiers; the sailors. They're careful like Mouse. Everything was shipshape before we left. But they're no different from Mouse. They don't know what will happen next. They might end up under water or be blown back home. Right now, they're waiting on the wind. And maybe the rest of you aren't rock sensing right, but they're nervous. We're becalmed and they don't like it. They'll do something if the wind won't blow. I don't know what that something is, but I can feel them turning over something awful in their hearts. I can rock sense they've stopped looking at the sky and watching for storm gulls. We'd best be ready lest it's us that's paying some superstitious price.'

O O O

12

Fox watched the river, watched the scenery on its banks shift as she made headway. But it wasn't fast, and it wasn't easy. She didn't have Saury's help to keep the boat moving, so she sailed when she could and rowed when she couldn't sail. The rowing would have been impossible without her strange new rock skin, but her tentacles were astounding. She found she could call on them when she needed them. She could stretch them down to glove her hands when she wanted all her strength to row and then fold them away when she was sailing. Even so, she longed to drop anchor and rest.

Fox needed time: to think; to care for Saury. Her sister was comfortable enough. Fox had seen to that. She'd given Saury water and more fever powders. She'd wrapped her in warm covers and her sister was soon asleep again, but leaving her sister alone in the cabin didn't feel right. And then there was the problem of the twins. Fox wished she could drop anchor to give them a chance to catch up. There were so many reasons to stop, but there was a bigger reason to flee. Her father was vengeful. She couldn't feel him following, but she suspected he'd come after them. She was glad she'd suppressed her pregnancy while there was so much danger surrounding them.

Fox steadied her stroke, shifting direction slightly. She could read the colours of the river, understood its shapes and depths. The talent for patterns had already helped her avoid sandbars and submerged hazards, and her regrown rock skin had only strengthened her understanding of the river.

Saury's voice interrupted her thoughts. Fox lifted the oars from the water and listened to her sister's question about whether they were safe. 'All's well,' Fox spoke without thinking, but when she opened her rock sense to check, she felt glad it was the truth. They were still alone. Fox stowed the oars and hesitated as the boat began turning about. No choice, she'd have to drop the anchor if she wanted to talk to Saury. The chain rattled out as she made her way to the cabin. She knelt down, kept her voice low, 'How are you feeling?'

'Better. I think I was too cold.'

'And now?'

'Still a bit cold, but it's okay. Where are we?'

'On the Kelp River. On our way to the port.'

'The twins?'

'Still missing. I'm hoping they'll come and find us. Are you hungry?' Saury nodded. Fox brushed a lock of hair from Saury's face and then stood up. Anxiety at the risk she was taking still ate at her, but surely they could afford a brief rest. She fetched a little water from the river and the cheese and hardtack from the leather satchel she'd taken from the manor. They ate quickly and spoke in whispers. The river and its surrounds still felt empty, but their fear kept them quiet.

'Do you think he'll follow us?' Saury asked.

'Yes, but we're a long way ahead of him.'

'Maybe. But he'll catch up. He'll have more people to help.'

Fox looked at her sister and thought about lying. Instead, she nodded. 'But I don't think our father will cross the border into Eden. So we'll cross before he catches us.'

Saury mustered a shallow smile. 'And if we can't reach Eden in time?'

'We will.' Fox resisted the urge to glance downriver.

'But if? I can feel you're scared,' Saury said.

Fox stood up. 'I am. We both know him. Yes, I'm scared, so it's time to go.'

Saury tried to get up too, but Fox shook her head. 'No. Don't. Sleep. Rest while you can. Recover. I'll need your help soon enough. Better that you're rested.'

There was nothing more to say. Everything that could be said, could be rock sensed. They loved each other, dreaded the thought of their father's pursuit, would defend each other to the death if they had to.

The wind had dropped again, so Fox went back to her oars. It was well into the evening when she admitted defeat, called in a croaky whisper for Saury's help. 'Are you awake?' There was silence for a moment and Fox tried again, 'Saury?'

'I'm awake,' Saury's voice was full of sleep. 'Is it my turn?'

'For a bit. Just while I eat something and close my eyes for ten minutes.'

Saury was already standing before Fox finished speaking, her movements stronger now, the frailty gone from her signature as suddenly as it had arrived. Fox leant on her oars, lifted the blades from the water.

Saury came over, crouched down, readied herself to take over. 'You can let go.'

Fox tried to obey. 'I can't. My fingers are cramped.' She laughed, a sound laced with fatigue and worry. Saury had to pry Fox's fingers from the oars. Then she helped her to the cabin, helped Fox lie down, covered her as the boat drifted. 'Quick!' Fox croaked. 'Get back to the oars.' Saury left the cabin, but instead of the sound of the oars, Fox heard the rattle of the anchor chain. She thought about protesting that they should keep going but didn't have the energy. She only roused herself when Saury returned to the cabin and tried to light the stove to make tea. The smoke would travel, and they mustn't alert anyone to their presence. Their father wasn't the only threat.

Aikin and Whilomena had sent soldiersisters to kill wanderers for their rock children.

Leaving the stove, Saury resettled Fox, tucked the blankets around her, fussed over her. Soon the anchor lifted, and they were moving again. Fox fell asleep to the cadence of her sister's oars.

Fox woke just before dawn to the boat drifting downriver and the awareness of the approach of their father's triumphant signature. She stood up, hit her head, but not before she saw Saury was asleep at the oars.

The girl woke with a gasp and began rowing, apologising with every stroke, 'Sorry, sorry. I only closed my eyes for a moment.' Then her emotional signature stilled for long enough to feel the signatures behind them. Saury gasped, and the oars faltered.

'Keep going!' Fox hurried over as Saury resumed rowing, got down on her hands and knees, fumbled about, groping for the second set of oars but couldn't find them. For a moment, all Fox could feel were the cold, wet bottom boards and the planks and ribs of the hull. She steadied herself, fought her panic, reminded herself to use her regrown rock skin. And there the oars were! Exactly where they were meant to be. She pulled them free, fitted them into the oarlocks and began rowing.

At first, she and Saury were at odds, then Fox took charge, remembering the sounds of her childhood, how to commence and how to continue. 'Weighenough!' she shouted, and they both stopped rowing. 'All Kelp ready!' Fox felt Saury fall into line with the familiar commands, like a fisher obeying a captain in a storm. 'Annnd.... Kelp pull! Kelp pull!' The boat's drift ceased, and they began moving upriver. Fox kept up the call and the boat gained speed. She could have stopped calling, but didn't. Somehow, the sound blocked out the gleeful hatred that hunted them. 'Kelp pull. Kelp pull. Kelp pull—'

'I'm sorry,' Saury whispered. 'It's all my fault. I'm so sorry.'

Fox stopped the call, but kept most of her attention on her oars.

She did her best to put some confidence in her voice, 'It's okay. It's not your fault.'

'But they'll catch us.'

'If they do, they won't keep us. We have our new rock skin.' They were beginning to put a bit of distance between their boat and their pursuers. It was true their rock skin would help them if they were caught, but it wouldn't be enough. There were at least six men on their father's boat. Fox needed to think of something else.

'Should we...? Maybe we should get off the river?' Saury asked.

Fox shook her head. 'They'd catch us on land. We wouldn't be fast enough. Give me a minute. I'll think of something.'

They were silent, surrounded by the feeling of gleeful pursuit and the sound of the men's voices and the quiet noise of their own oars working the water. Fox renewed her efforts to turn her fear aside, clear her head, save them.

They could dive off the boat and swim upriver, but she didn't feel confident they could out-swim their pursuers. Perhaps they could hide in the water and wait for the fishers to pass them by? Fox could because she could disappear into nothing, hide her emotions, but Saury didn't have any Companionari training. Their father would sense Saury's position underwater. Fox didn't know what equipment Pace had on board the riverboat, but if he'd moved the harpoon onto it, the channel wouldn't be deep enough to protect them.

What then? Go on the attack?

Fox pulled on the oars, and her rock skin prickled as she turned over the question. There was something, an edge, a pattern she wasn't quite catching.

Saury had taken over the call now, and they were maintaining their steady stroke. The gap between the boats was stable. But time was against them.

Fox played with an image, a vision of them swimming back, attacking the boat. She saw herself piercing Pace's hull, sinking the boat. She had her two arrows, but they'd probably snap. Her knife might be strong enough. And with her tentacles supporting her arms and hands, she could wield it. But she shook her head. The crew would drown in the river's current. She might not care about her father, but the fishers were her camp kin.

Fox realised Saury had stopped calling, was speaking. 'If we hang on long enough, the twins might help. They must know we're in trouble.'

Fox shook her head, took up the call in Saury's stead, 'Kelp pull. Kelp pull...'

'Then he'll catch us,' Saury's voice broke, and she started to cry, 'I can feel it. He'll catch us and kill us!'

Then Fox stopped the call as the pattern took shape, becoming an idea. 'I have it. We'll disable them. But I can't do it alone. I'll need your help.'

'Disable them? How?'

'I'll set their sails on fire with an arrow and then we'll send their oars downriver.'

'What?'

'I'll light the arrow on the stove and set the sails alight.'

'And they'd keep rowing,' Saury said.

'Yes, but they'll stop first because they'll have to put out the fire.'

'And how are we going to send their oars downriver?'

'We start by increasing our lead so I can get everything ready. Then we drop anchor, let them come into view, come close enough. I loose the arrows. Hopefully just one, but I have the second ready if I need it.'

'Can you do it?'

Fox smiled. 'Oh yes! I'm good with a bow.'

'And then?'

'The hard part. We both go into the river. Straight away. You head to their starboard. Feel everything: fear, hope, terror, whatever... Let them to sense your approach, but don't get too close. You mustn't let them spear you or harpoon you.'

'No,' Saury laughed and, for the first time in hours, Fox felt a glimpse of confidence in her sister's signature. 'Thank you for reminding me. Because otherwise I might just let them—'

'I'm serious.'

'Okay, but what will you do?'

'I'll hide my emotions like a Companionari. I'll disappear from their rock skin. We want them to think I've left the river and you're surrendering. And while they're all focused on looking at you, focusing on you and the fire, on catching you and putting it out, I'm going to lift their port-side oars out of the oarlocks and drop them into the water.'

Understanding dawned on Saury's face. 'Because there are no gates on Kelp's riverboats. The oarlocks are unlocked.'

'Exactly. The collars stop the oars from falling into the water, but there's no gate to stop someone from lifting them out. And I've got the strength and the grip with my tentacles.'

'And so have I! So, I do the starboard oars?'

'Yes, when the moment is right. Distract them first. Feel for what I'm doing and wait until I've finished. Then I'll dive under, and we'll work together to grab the second lot of oars.'

'So, when do we do it?'

'Now. No point waiting until we're more exhausted. But first, we need to widen our lead a little to give me time to prepare.'

For the next half hour, Fox and Saury focused on rowing, using their rock skin to aid their efforts. Soon, their pursuers disappeared from sight. A little later, when the gap had increased, Fox told Saury to keep rowing while she prepared her bow and arrows and lit the stove.

It took Fox two tries to start the stove, but she managed. Then she tore off her sleeves and used them to wrap the head of each arrow, tying them tight. The fletch on one arrow was motheaten. She would loose the better one first.

'They're gaining on us,' Saury called out.

'Nearly ready,' Fox said. She took a jug of fish oil from the small larder and pulled out the stopper. She tipped oil over both arrows, and the excess splashed onto the cabin floor.

'What's happening in there?' Saury called out in a panicked whisper. 'Because I can see them.'

'I'm ready. Just getting in position.'

'Hurry!'

Fox stepped out of the cabin, but stayed close enough to the stove to reach back with her arrow. Her heel slipped on the spilled oil, but she righted herself. She dropped the motheaten arrow back into the quiver and lifted the bow from her shoulders. She held the bow in her left hand and the better arrow in the other. 'Okay, Saury. Now. Drop anchor and then keep out of my line of sight. Be ready to dive into the water as soon as the arrow hits the sail.'

Saury moved quickly and Fox kept her eye on the other boat as the anchor chain rattled out. For a moment, their boat continued drifting, then stopped abruptly. Fox lost her balance, slipped, and then righted herself. She held the bow low now, kept it out of sight.

'I warned you!' her father called out, his signature gleeful. 'Can't say I didn't. I told you...'

Fox stopped listening. She swivelled and reached back, held the arrowhead to the hot plate. The swaddled head smoked and blackened and then caught. She brought it to the bow. She wanted to correct her stance, but didn't dare. Instead, she positioned her upper body as best she could, nocked the flaming arrow, aimed, loosed, and then lost her footing, falling on her face.

She banged her jaw, bit her cheek, and sat up to the sound of yells and cries. She looked over the gunwale, a grin on her face. The sails on the other boat were on fire.

She felt Saury's hands helping her up. 'Are you all right?'

'Get in the water.'

'Not without you.'

Saury was right. They had to act together to make this work. Fox dropped her bow into the bottom of the boat and unbuckled the quiver, readied herself. They stood, looking at each other, pretending to look as though they were at odds. 'Now?' Fox said.

'Now!' Saury said. Then Saury started yelling that she surrendered, imploring their father to forgive her. For a second Fox felt the words as though they were true, then steadied herself, recalling their plan. Now Saury turned to Fox, shouted at her, as though there really was an argument between them, 'Go if you want to! I don't care. I'm giving up!' Then Saury dived off the stern.

Fox yelled out that Saury was a fool, and then she too dived. Off the side of the boat and into the water, for all intents and purposes heading for the riverbank.

The river felt icy, and Fox had to fight the urge to return to the surface. Then her gills opened, and she pressed on, tucking away her feelings, heading for Pace's boat. She shredded her emotions, scattered them, dissolved them. She'd scarcely begun and hardly finished when she found herself facing the first oar. Fox opened her senses to the physical world above her. She could feel every detail of the boat. She felt Saury's ruckus and the chaos in the crew's attention: their alarm at the sight of the burning sails, their confusion over Saury's pleas.

Fox braced herself against the hull, using the suckers on her tentacles for purchase. The oarsmen were still in position, but the nearest one had let go of his oar. Fox reached up with one hand and took hold of it. She kept her fingers below the surface, used her muscular tentacles to lift the oar clear of the oarlock. Gently, she lowered it into the water without a splash and moved to the next oar.

She wasn't as lucky this time. This crew member was standing, beating at the burning sails, but he'd clamped his oars between his legs. She would have to be fast and brutal. She shoved the oar up, hit him with it, and then wrenched it away, threw it into the water. There were shouts above her. The oarsman called out a warning. Fishers yelling at each other, telling one another to save the oars and the sails. She moved on.

The last port-side oar was being used to catch hold of the closest of the lost oars. Easy. She yanked it from the fisher's hands and then dived to avoid a spear.

It was just as chaotic on the starboard side. Fox didn't know whether to be pleased or dismayed that Saury had ignored her and was already stealing oars. There were two left, and Saury was busy fighting for control of one of them. Fox didn't go to her sister's aid because the oar in front of her was lifting out of the water. Fox grabbed the tip of the blade just before it disappeared, used her tentacles, ripped it from the fisher's grip. She turned her attention to Saury. Her sister was fighting a losing battle for the middle oar. Outnumbered, she risked being hauled into the boat. And a one-oared boat was no threat. Fox swam to Saury's side, pulled her away, and the two of them sank down into the deepest part of the channel.

A single spear dug into the riverbed, missing them by a wide margin, and then they were free as their father's boat drifted downriver.

Fox and Saury gave at each other water smiles and then turned towards their own boat, still anchored upriver. For the first time since her abrupt awakening, Fox relaxed. They would rest and dry off, and since the stove was already lit, Fox would boil the kettle and they would enjoy a warm cup of tea.

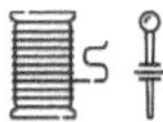

Fox woke in comfort and warmth. In a bed. There was a distinct and not unpleasant earthy scent in the air. Out of place for a moment, but then she remembered. Safe. They were safe. The canal lock keeper had welcomed them into her cottage on Eden's side of the border.

Fox smiled. *Welcomed* was an exaggeration. The Companionari woman was wary and gruff to the point of rudeness, but the riverhood code took precedence. That or Saury's age or the sisters' exhaustion or the riverhood's dislike of Kelp's keeper. Probably the latter because the woman had grumbled about the riverhood's difficult dealings with Kelp when she told them they might stay. Neither Fox nor Saury mentioned their parentage.

Fox rolled over, looked outside, relishing the thick covers on her bed and the sunshine streaming through the window. It was raining, but the sky was blue: a sun shower. Rain dripped from the pumpkin tendrils fringing the window, pooled and poured from the lantern-like gourds. A magical beginning to the day. She felt for her unborn daughter. Suppressed: alive, but not quick. Fox almost released her but resisted the urge. The morning felt safe and wonderful, but they were still a long way from the port. It might have been different if Mica was with them. The thought triggered a powerful longing that she couldn't afford to indulge.

She sat up, taking in the full view of Eden's landscape. She'd felt its fecundity last night, the tangle of its quick-growing summer plants, but her arms hadn't prepared her for the sight of it. The world was awash with greens and reds and yellows and everything in between. Huge tomato plants dominated, but there were aubergines and peppers and capsicums. And the ground was a riot of cucumbers and pumpkins. Evidently, the infant Edenic Companion's talents weren't faltering, which made Fox wonder about the hunger in Komey. Surely, there was enough here for everyone?

She would ask the lock keeper and she would visit Eden's camp to see what could be done about getting some produce into the city. She might need to stop in at the manor house, find out what was wrong. Food couldn't be withheld when people were starving.

Saury's bed was rumpled but empty. Fox opened her senses and frowned. Her sister wasn't in the cottage and wasn't in the garden. Fox told herself not to panic. She put on her pants, pulled her tunic over her head, buckled her belt and quiver, all the while searching for Saury. She found the lock keeper's signature at the edge of her range. The woman was standing on the canal bank, concentrating, but there was no sign of Saury. Fox slung her bow over her shoulders and hurried outside.

The lock keeper turned towards her as she approached, a fishing line in her hands.

'Where's my sister?' Fox asked. 'Have you seen her? I can't feel her.'

'No *Good morning*? No *Hello*? By the Back manners aren't what they used to be! And no doubt you've helped yourself to breakfast. Which you're welcome to, of course. Riverhood code: feed folk no matter who they are.'

Fox's stomach grumbled, but she didn't argue. It wasn't important. She clambered up the last bit of bank, reaching the lock keeper's side. 'I'm sorry. I'm just worried about Saury,' she told the woman.

'Don't be. Your girl got up early. Up before dawn and off she went.'

'By herself?!' Fox turned around, scanning the thick green landscape. 'But she's too young to be out on her own. What possessed her?'

'Said she was called. I told her to wake you and take you with her. The cottage isn't a hotel. I can't look after guests when I have work to do.'

Fox looked at the lock keeper, at the fishing rod, at the empty canal, but calmed her emotions. A polite approach was needed. 'I'm very grateful for the riverhood's hospitality and it is time I took my leave. If you could tell me exactly what she said and point me in the right direction, I'll be gone and you have my deepest gratitude.'

The lock keeper looked mollified. 'Your sister left because a stone called her. Walking her own path, that one. As we all should. Said you'd rowed all day yesterday and needed sleep. Said to tell you she was walking in the right direction. You're to walk along the towpath and you'll find her waiting.'

So, Saury hadn't taken the boat. Fox wondered whether she should take it, but she doubted she'd be faster rowing than walking.

In the end, she left the boat in the lock keeper's care and followed Saury on foot.

Two hours later, Fox felt the edge of her sister's signature, a line of worry threading through it. There was someone with Saury, a Companionari. Fear gripped Fox, and yet Saury didn't seem to be alarmed. Fox widened her rock sense. There were others too, but further away: all of them Companionaris bar one. And the Beran seemed upset, not panicked, but unhappy. And familiar. Hard to tell what was going on, but Fox didn't like any of it. Just because Saury wasn't alarmed didn't mean her sister was safe.

Fox tightened the lace tie concealing her knife. Then she lifted her bow from her shoulders. She cursed herself for not remembering to ask the lock keeper for arrows. One motheaten arrow and one knife. It wasn't much, but it would have to do. Fox didn't run, but she moved efficiently, rock sensing the best path. She would travel on the open territory of the towpath while she could, but she could use Eden's plants to hide her presence if she needed to. She reached into the quiver and pulled out her arrow.

Then Saury's signature shifted. It was undercut with worry now, and a bit of belligerence. The belligerence would have been reassuring to Fox, but for the hungry need that was building within the Companionari beside her.

Fox's heart sank as the picture came together. The woman wanted something from Saury; Saury, who had left to claim a rock child. The conclusion was obvious. These were some of Aikin and Whilomena's soldiersisters. Fox's fear redoubled as everything shifted.

The soldier's voice reached Fox's ears. 'I said, who are you?! Answer me!'

Fox bent low, crept forward. Saury and the Companionari soldier came into view. Fox's heart clenched as she watched the Companionari lift her sword, put the tip to Saury's throat. Saury's arms came up in surrender, but her tentacles were reaching for the hilt.

'Stop that! I'm not about to hurt you, lass.' It was a lie. Fox felt it and Saury must have felt it too, because the girl began backing away. The soldier followed her until the pillar of a small stone bridge halted the girl's retreat. The Companionari continued speaking, 'I just asked you to come with me. A nice, polite request.'

Fox moved closer to the canal. A more exposed position, but she needed a better angle. The soldier was still talking, 'What are you doing out here on your own, a young girl like you? Because you're not Edenic. Not with that weird rock skin.'

A bead of blood appeared beneath the sword at Saury's throat and the girl shrank back. 'Leave me alone!' Saury's voice was unsteady.

'This doesn't have to end badly,' the soldier said. 'We've another Beran with us. Why don't you come and meet him? He wouldn't be with us if we weren't all friends, now, would he? Just give me your word you'll keep those tentacles lashed and I can lower my sword.'

Fox notched her arrow, cursing the fact she still didn't have a clean line to her target. Almost, but Saury was too close to the soldier for Fox to take the shot.

Fox took a step closer to the water to improve her line of sight, keeping her bow raised. Saury's signature shifted, flooded with relief, registering Fox's presence.

The girl lifted her chin, glared at the soldier. Fox hoped her sister wouldn't say anything. There was only one chance to end this without a knife fight, and Fox needed the soldier to keep still.

'If you were a friend,' Saury said, 'you wouldn't have cut me with your sword.'

The soldier's signature flared, and she took a step forward. 'You're coming with me, or you'll get more than a graze.'

Fox loosed the arrow, and Saury ducked, rock sensing Fox's intention. The soldier fell where she stood. Soundless other than the thump when she hit the ground.

Fox hoped she hadn't killed the woman, but didn't regret acting. She ran to Saury. The relief of holding her sister released Fox's narrow focus. The altercation between Saury and the soldier hadn't gone unnoticed. The other Companionaris must have heard because they were moving. Not running yet, but heading towards the sisters, signatures sharp with aggression. Further away, the Beran was motionless. Unable to move? And there was something familiar about him. Fox didn't have time to tease out his identity. All she knew was his signature was full of frustration and alarm.

'I think it's Peri,' Saury said. 'I know him. I think he's a prisoner. His stones must have called me. I didn't know about him until I got here and then the soldiersister saw me. I thought it was just some stones calling. And Mica said you have to listen when they—'

'Not now!' Fox said. She glanced at the water. Her instinct urged her to take Saury and jump into the canal while they could. Swimming, they'd outpace the soldiersisters. But Fox couldn't abandon Perigean Tide. She'd remembered him. Peri. She hadn't seen him since childhood and they couldn't leave without helping him.

Fox grabbed Saury's hand and led her around the stone pillar and then turned away from the waterway, diving headlong into the tangle of crops. She pulled her knife from its lace holster and when they couldn't push their way forward, she slashed at the plants. They had the advantage of rock skin and they moved in silence, circling the soldiers. There was an angry cry as the Companionaris came upon their companion. Fox and Saury made the most of the moment and ran.

They found Peri in a rough-cut clearing. He whistled a quick bird call in greeting and his smile widened, giving them both a crooked grin of recognition. His gaze dropped to Fox's hands, saw her knife, and then he held up his bound hands.

Fox ran over, crouched down, and cut the ropes. Ignoring Peri and Fox, Saury ran over and scooped up the wanderer's pouch that lay among the soldiersisters' belonging.

Fox felt a shift in the soldiersisters' signatures. They were full of revenge now. Their attention, tight with listening and looking. Their footsteps were hunters' footsteps: quick padding sensations heading in the Berans' direction. There wasn't much time.

There was only one place where the Berans would have an advantage: the canal. Fox explained as much as she could to Peri in a quick whisper. The bow and the empty quiver would be nothing but a nuisance, so she dumped them on the ground. The knife was precious. She sheathed it in its lace holster and double knotted it into her hair. Peri watched her and frowned. She felt grateful that he didn't argue. And then they ran, angling towards the water.

There were no shouts behind them, but Fox felt the soldiersisters closing in. She shivered but kept running, racing to the edge of the towpath. 'Hold your breath!' she yelled at Peri, and she grabbed him. Saury was a streak as she dived in first, disappearing under the water. Fox pulled Peri off the path and together they fell headlong into the water.

13

Talia looked down to where the Kelp River met the ocean. She was exhausted and cold, but the view lifted her spirits. Kelp province was even more beautiful than she'd imagined. She'd thought being in this place would bring Fox and Saury to mind, but it was hard to relate the province to anything or anyone in Komey. Komey was orderly. Kelp was vast and wild. The wind bit her skin and battered the open water, casting white frills onto the beach. The parley gulls flocked above her head, their long wings clapping the air like a hundred Mothers on a hundred parley beds calling for attention.

'Talia!' Aikin said. 'Watch it! Pay attention to your trees!'

Talia started, looked around. A semi-circle of swaying date palms had sprung up where moments before coastal grasses had bent under the wild weather. She looked at Aikin face on, acknowledged the warning, but didn't thank him.

'So,' he said, 'are we going into the camp or straight to the manor?'

Talia turned her horse towards the manor, too tired to bother answering him. She hoped they'd built the place from stone. She needed some sleep.

'You should let me do the talking,' Aikin said.

She rode on, shook her head. 'As if I would.'

'Listen to me,' he said. 'If you start yapping about what's happened, you might make yourself feel better, but they'll turn us away. The Kelp Companion's infamous. She only cares about Kelp. She'll see you as a risk so she won't let you rest in her manor.'

'Maybe, but she'll like you even less when she hears what you've done.'

'Listen to me, Talia. I know what I'm talking about.'

Talia had a headache, and it was getting worse, and the argument wasn't helping. 'I'm not lying about you, Aikin. You're my prisoner.'

'Perhaps, but I'm intent on going to New Lytalia and I accept my banishment, so I think that also makes us travelling companions on a shared mission.'

Talia sighed. His talk was making her head worse, and she needed to concentrate on keeping the landscape in check. The acorns and seeds felt stronger here, more real. She could feel the press of the surrounding landscape. She wanted to ask Aikin if he felt it too, if it was their shared rock skin that made things worse, but she couldn't bear the intimacy the conversation suggested. Talia didn't want them to be joined in anything other than a journey that would banish him.

'And I'm better suited to explaining our travels,' he said. 'I've had a lifetime dealing with companions. Please let me do the talking.'

Talia rubbed her right eye where the ache bit hardest. 'Just keep it simple. No flourishes.'

'I'll keep it charming. That's what I do best.'

'If you try to escape, I'll kill you.'

'You've already made that clear. And I told you. I want to reach the port. Why would I try to escape?'

Talia rubbed the back of her neck, probing the knot of tension that was driving her suffering. 'All right! But right now I need you to stop talking.'

They found the Kelp Companion and her sisters in the manor garden, planting daisies in the black sandy soil, oblivious to the weather. When the women caught sight of them, they got off their knees. The companion stood out. She was tall and gaunt, middle-aged and ugly, but not ordinary. She positioned herself a pace in front of her sisters, impatient as though having to pause anything, even daisy planting, took enormous energy. Talia wanted to ask her whether it was the fish that gave her that demeanour: was she holding them back? was it a struggle? how did she cope with her companionship? Aikin saved Talia from blurting out her questions. 'We've ridden direct from Oak House,' he said, 'on house business. We're on our way to New Lytalia.'

The Kelp Companion didn't speak, but Talia could feel her waiting, suspending judgement, her wariness as sharp and real as the smell of salt in the air. As if Talia didn't have enough to cope with, with the rush of the river and the clamouring plants, now she had the swirling emotions of the women in front of them.

Aikin was still talking, his voice smiley and full of patter. 'I know. Who would want to go to New Lytalia? Dreadful place. I said to the Oak Companion, "Oria, I'm not going there unless it's absolutely necessary."' He gave a laugh, shrugged, 'Apparently, it is. The port is being difficult. Tariffs, duties, outrageous demands... I'm sure you're aware how impossible the Pike family can be?' Talia was still trying to find the right words to stop him going too far when she felt the Kelp Companion's reaction to his words. Excitement so sharp it made her hands prickle. '... and, well, Oria said she needed a new Master of Trade,' Aikin continued, 'and gave me the commission.'

Talia flinched at the lie, but the Kelp Companion reacted with a thirst for it. The woman's expression remained unchanged and she chose her words carefully, made them casual, 'The Pike Companion, you say? Now there's someone I haven't heard news of in a while. The Borough of New Lytalia has such a fascinating history. Deeply meaningful, of course, but in some ways it is just a place where a river touches a sea.' She paused and they all heard it, the sound of

Kelp's own river rushing past the manor. 'Not so different to this place.'

'Quite,' Aikin agreed.

The Kelp Companion smiled at Aikin, and Talia could feel the effort it took. Aikin had been right. Pleasantries didn't come easily to the woman. The companion gestured downriver, and Talia turned in her saddle, gazed at the river's mouth, the outline of the camp, and the waves thundering on the beach. She turned back again as the Kelp Companion continued speaking, 'We don't have a bay, but the Kelp's delta is as wide as a mother's arms and as strong as a companion's sense of duty.' She laughed. It felt even less natural than her smile. The province must desperately need trade for the companion to debase herself like this.

'Tell Oria we can move her timber for her if she'd like.' The Kelp Companion passed her trowel to one of her sisters and wiped her hands on her gardening tunic. She stepped forward and gave them both a long look. 'But I think you know that already? Or you wouldn't be in my garden. I mean, why take this route?'

Talia was uncomfortable. It wasn't just the trees pushing her or the pain behind her eye; it was the cruelty of Aikin's false promise. This woman needed Oak's trade. Perhaps Talia might make the lie real? She was an Oak companion, after all. She might do something. Grow trees here. It would be a relief to let loose a few stands. She felt the wriggle of several acorns and pushed them back to dormancy. She rubbed her eye for the umpteenth time. It didn't help. She dropped her hand back to her reins.

Aikin was smiling. 'Just so. I'd hoped we might stay a day or two.' He gave the bleak stone building behind them an admiring look. 'Such a charming manor.'

The Kelp Companion looked sceptical. 'You'd be the first to think so. My ancestral Mother was no architect. But you're welcome.' She lifted an eyebrow. 'Perhaps you'd like to introduce yourself, and your chaperone.'

'I'm not...' Talia said. 'I mean, yes I am chaperoning him, but it's not—'

Aikin interrupted before she could say more, 'It's just that my chaperone is stations above me. Oria sent the second Mother with me. May I present Companion Talia Oak?'

Then everyone was speaking at once.

'A second Mother?' the companion asked. 'That doesn't make sense.'

'Aikin!' Talia protested. 'Stop it!'

At the sound of Aikin's name, the Kelp Companion drew in a sharp breath and her long face flushed. She looked at Aikin. 'Not Aikin Oak? the man who adopted the talent from our camp?'

Aikin blinked, a half-smile on his face, which answered Talia's earlier question. His rock skin wasn't working or he would have known the Kelp Companion was brimming with outrage. 'Fox? I... Well, yes.'

The companion took a step towards him as though she might pull him off his horse and slap him. 'Well, you have a lot to answer for. The very least of which is the theft of my boat and compensation for the trouble she's caused out on the ocean and in the river. But what I want is an explanation for the dreadful job you did parenting her.' She took another step toward him. Her sorority shifted uneasily. 'You let her come here,' the companion hissed. 'Here! Didn't you tell her, the treaty forbids it?'

'I—' Aikin started.

'And bringing her poor little sister with her when Pace, my admittedly difficult keeper, gave express instructions that Saury was never to set foot—'

Talia interrupted. 'But they're here? Are they all right? Where are they? And what about Patience and the twins?'

The companion frowned at Talia. 'I don't know what you're talking about.' She turned back to Aikin, arms loose but hands clenched. The woman's indignation, her outrage, pressed against Talia's being. Cold, burning cold. Talia felt it as though she were the one full of emotion, not the companion. It was like slipping on ice, like tripping, like losing her footing on stairs. Then Talia's grip on her talent slipped. 'Help!' she said, but it was only a whisper. Life crackled around her and she forced herself to try again, 'Help! Please. I need to get inside.'

But it was too late. Trees and rice burst from the soil, sending the horses skittering and the sorority running for shelter.

The Kelp Companion turned to face Talia. 'What are you doing? Stop it!' The woman stood her ground and shook off the sister who tried to pull her away. Then she reached out and grabbed the reins of Talia's horse. She didn't drop her gaze. 'Control yourself Mother Oak,' she hissed. 'By the Back! There's no need for a show of force.'

The trees surrounding them continued popping and cracking.

'She can't help it,' Aikin shouted.

Talia closed her eyes, calmed herself and forced the growth and decay to still. She opened her eyes to silence, to devastation, to chaos.

'The garden!' one of the Kelp sisters cried. 'Mother, look what she's done to our garden.'

There were trees everywhere and the grasses beneath the horses' hooves were torn up and tangled with rice. 'I need to sleep,' Talia said. 'Behind stone. Please.'

For a second, the companion stood stock still, aghast, then she shook her head and sighed. She walked over and reached up, helped Talia from her saddle. 'You should have said you didn't have control!' She waved over one of her sister's and gave her the reins of Talia's snorting horse, told her to take the animal to the stable. Then she got her shoulder under Talia's arm, began walking her to the manor. 'And you,' she called to Aikin over her shoulder. 'Follow me. I won't have you roaming around.'

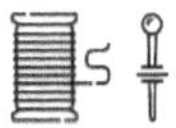

'Will you take a little sole, Master Oak?' Aikin looked over the platter held by the woman to his left. The fish was fresh caught and succulent and there was a hint of citrus in the air as he looked over the platter. But it was obvious from the plate and from the state of the women at the table there wasn't enough to go around and there hadn't been enough for some time. He reached for the silver servers and helped himself to an ostentatiously small portion and then returned for an equally frugal serve of potatoes. Then he took the platter and held it for the sister on his right, a young woman dressed in a beautiful tunic embroidered with patterns of kelp fronds. She took a tiny serve and passed the platter to the next sister. Then she turned back and smiled at him, held his gaze a little too long.

'I think I saw you walking in the garden this morning. Are you enjoying our sea air?'

Aikin recalled the feeling of the wind whipping his hair into a horrible mess and the needle-like splatter of rain on his face. 'Delightfully bracing. Perhaps a little chilly. But one can never complain about being outdoors.'

'Speaking of which,' the Kelp Companion waved her fork at him, 'You're not to go beyond the garden gate on your own. I heard you were seen lingering there. We won't have you wandering down to the camp.'

'I can chaperone him,' the young sister offered. 'It would be my pleasure.'

Aikin blushed. It wasn't the young sister's interest that embarrassed him. It was the companion's humiliating comments. The suggestion that he wasn't to be trusted around Beranish women. Not an insult. Technically, she was just reminding him of the terms of the treaty. But it felt insulting. He squared his shoulders and let a little chill enter his voice, 'Don't worry. I have no intention of visiting the camp. I'm quite delighted by your manor.'

The young sister beside him leant closer, put a hand on his arm. 'Oh, but you must see the camp. Our Beranish tent paintings are thought to be the best on the Stone Body. It would be such a shame for you to miss them.'

She was right, of course. He should see them. There was no one better versed in Beranish art than Aikin. But these people knew nothing of his interests or education, his true value. He felt like telling them, had to remind himself that he had plans to keep and their isolation, their lack of knowledge about him and events in Komey, was to his advantage. Better to suffer humiliation than be thwarted. He loosened his shoulders and concentrated on the last morsel of fish on his plate.

The Kelp Companion sighed and Aikin glimpsed the shake of her head as she gave the sister beside him a lingering look. 'Please excuse Trevalla, Master Oak. She's not yet suppressing and Companionari men are a rare commodity in the provinces. I'd send her to the city to catch a baby but she has a minor talent for sea urchins and we need her here. Although no one's catching much at the moment. Still, it would be a kindness if you could accommodate her. I'd offer you a fee, but as you owe me money a fee might be waived...?' She gazed at him, eyebrow raised.

Aikin realised he was blushing again. Another humiliation. And he had a ridiculous urge to scratch the back of his hands. The rough rock skin covering his knuckles itched. He hated it. His beautiful, beautiful hands ruined and for nothing. Then again, perhaps it was a blessing that his rock skin didn't work. He wouldn't want to feel this conversation more deeply. From now on, he would leave off experimenting on himself. If he found another rock child on his travels, he'd save it to buy gratitude from a woman. He touched his cheek, feeling for the blemish. It was gone. That was something. He smoothed his shirt and the sensation of the quality of the fabric eased the discomfort of being at the table. He was glad he had grabbed his necessities from the train. It cost nothing to take care of oneself even if it sometimes came with unwelcome attention.

He cleared his throat and met the companion's eye. 'One thing at a time. Let's stick to our existing, more modest, arrangement. Once I get to New Lytalia, I will send you compensation for the trouble Fox caused. You have my word. As to the other matter, I'm full of regret that I can't help. Talia is planning for us to leave in the morning.'

'I'd say that's plenty of time,' someone laughed.

'Good luck getting that new Oak Mother out of the kitchen,' another sister said.

Yet another sister giggled, 'She's quite taken by our bread oven. Lucky we're out of wheat and can't bake or we'd have a real problem.'

The Kelp Companion silenced the table with a hard look. 'I'll thank all of you to keep a respectful tongue in your head. The second Oak Mother may be uninvited, but she's a companion and she has shown us great kindness by remaining in our kitchen, in our stone oven. Her affliction shouldn't be a source of amusement.' The Kelp Companion turned her attention back to Aikin. 'Very well. Your debt stands. I expect you to send me the money you owe me as promised. And don't forget the camp's oars must be paid for too.'

'As agreed.'

'And the harpoon that was lost.'

'Of course,' Aikin found he had regained his composure. His voice was light and pleasant, belying his feelings. When the table broke up, the sisters invited him to watch the evening's sewing circle but he excused himself with more charm and finesse than the sorority deserved. He even kissed the companion's gnarly hand.

'I will withdraw to the library. With some reluctance.' He gave her an insipid smile and then stepped back, his eye on the door.

Trevalla started towards him, another offer on her lips, but the Kelp Companion waved her away and reached for Aikin herself. She took his arm and steered him towards the door. 'Not quite so fast. There's a volume I want to show you. You must take it when you go. Give it to Talia. It might be useful to her. It's a rather over-wrought poem by the first Kelp Companion. I seem to recall that she speaks of her talent as a wild horse. I think reading it will help Talia.'

'That is a kindness,' Aikin said.

'I don't imagine it will offer any magical answers. Are there truly no explanations for her sudden talent?'

'None,' Aikin lied. The Kelp Companion would find out eventually, but he wasn't fool enough to tell her. 'All I can say is that Talia will be grateful for the gift of the poem. It's surprising what one can learn from the past.'

The Kelp Companion opened the library door and ushered him in. 'You are not a man to my taste,' she said, much as someone might comment on the weather. Aikin didn't quite manage to contain his surprise at her lack of diplomacy. It was an odd thing to say. He hoped this wouldn't be another proposition. Surely not. It was possible she was still young enough to make a daughter, but she had to be close to the end of her fertility.

She released his arm and led him to a bookshelf. 'You're too prickly and too quick with your charm, but I can see you are clever. Talia needs someone, but I don't know if she needs someone clever.' She lifted a thin book from the shelf, brought it down, but didn't hand it over. She gave him a questioning look. 'A sorority should include a couple of brilliant women and several kind women. And yet, Talia's travelling without a sorority…'

'As I explained, Oria sent Talia on a sensitive trade mission—'

'*The fewer people the better.* Yes, I haven't forgotten your explanation. And yet, I am not convinced I have the actual story. Are you and Talia enamoured? Have you run off together? Is that why you turned down Trevalla this evening?'

He shook his head. 'No. On the contrary. You're not the only one who doesn't like me. Talia can't stand me.' He shrugged. 'But my house insisted. And she sees our journey as a duty.'

The Kelp Companion's lips thinned, but she nodded, sensing a truth. 'I don't like all this secrecy,' she handed him the thin, linen bound volume, 'but I accept all companions have secrets. Evidently, you are one of Talia's. I'm glad you're leaving. I will welcome Oria's trade, but I won't be sorry to see the back of you.'

Aikin didn't smile, but he gave her a tiny nod. He looked down at the book in his hands. The gold lettering spelt out: *Natal Elegy*. A nostalgic poem about the woman's birth as a companion or a lament? Or both? The back of Aikin's hands itched with the certainty that it was both. Likely this first Mother knew her talent had cost a wanderer's life and a stone's life. If the title was anything to go by, she lamented it. But he would enjoy reading it. His instinct was to keep it for himself, but Talia's trees were a nuisance and if the poem helped? 'Thank you, I'll give it to her in the morning.'

'I hope it brings relief.' The Kelp Companion brushed the dust off her hands. 'Much as I distrust you, I regret your unwillingness to help Trevalla. Are you sure?'

Aikin opened the cover. 'Absolutely. Not if she was the last sister on the Stone Body.'

The companion stiffened and then sighed. 'Very well, I'll leave you. Make sure you close the door when you've finished.'

It was a relief to be alone. He closed the door and didn't relax until her footsteps had faded to silence. He needed this: the quiet of a library. This library was a fraction of the size of the Oak House library, but there was a wonderful, familiar comfort to be standing in front of shelves. He took full advantage and was rewarded with a glorious little memoir by a son of the house and two boxes of well-written letters between Komey and Kelp, written in the third century.

He lingered longer than he should and as he turned to leave, he realised he would be tired in the morning. Then something caught his eye. A book squeezed into the last space on a top shelf. Not disguised this time, just ignored. The title worked onto the spine for anyone to see. It was the two *K*s in the name, the *k* in *Book* and the larger *K* in *Kinesis*, that caught his attention.

His whole body tingled. He realised he had tears in his eyes. He took a deep breath. How wonderful! How blessed! For several minutes, he just stood there and let the tears fall. There was no need to rush. For the first time in his life he understood the Companionari way: the reverence for the slow, savoured moment. He stood in front of the greatest work in Companionari history in reverence. The book he lost had returned in new form. He reached up and took it down. He had the urge to slip it into his jacket and hurry out of the room, but he resisted. Instead, he stroked the cover. He leant against the bookshelf and opened the book. And it *was* different. Goosebumps fluttered over his arms, and his rock skin prickled. He would read every word. Tonight and again and again.

14

It was hot in the hold of *The Crested Wave*, a damp heat made thicker and horribly present by the dark, and by the emotional signatures above the Berans' head. The Berans were quieter than they had been when Mica arrived, each man and woman and child stretching their rock sense, trying to understand the mood on deck. Mica and Cerulean were no longer the focus. Cerulean was still restless and fearful, and the air still sharpened when anyone moved too quickly, but he no longer held the refugees' attention. No, it was the sailors and the body of water surrounding the ship that worried them.

Mica squatted, his back against the hull, half hidden behind the barrels. He was trying to rest. Cerulean was busy with some sort of game. His twin was tracing the boards that lined the hold. He touched one plank at a time, moved forward and back along the grain, as though he could read the ship with his fingers. Not for the first time, Mica lamented the absence of a shared language.

Mica looked up. He too was oppressed by the feeling of the soldiersisters and the sailors. The soldiersisters were frustrated and bored as they drilled, but they weren't the source of everyone's unease. They felt uncomfortable and strained, like an over-tight lace on a tent flap. They weren't happy, but they weren't wrong. It was the oceanhood sailors who felt wrong. On the surface, all was normal. They went about their shipshape chores with a brittle efficiency. Beneath the surface, their signatures were full of furtiveness and fleeting spikes of fear and shame. The scales of Mica's rock skin lifted, prickled like a child hearing a frightening fourth story.

'They keep whispering to one another,' a man spoke. 'What are they saying?'

'As I pointed out last time you asked the same question,' another man said, 'we don't know. We can't hear any words from down here.'

'Shush,' a woman said. 'I'm concentrating on the sea.'

'Waste of time,' another woman said. 'You'll get nowhere with that. The sea speaks its own language and our arms don't have the dictionary.'

'We should ask the cook what the sailors are planning,' the first man said. 'When she doles out the stew, we should ask what's going on.'

'The cook won't tell you,' Lupe said. 'Can't you feel her? She's just like the others.'

Someone told Lupe she was wrong because cooks always talked. 'It's in their nature. Besides, we don't even know for sure the crew has a secret.'

Cerulean stopped tracing the hull with his fingers and edged closer to Mica. He came and stood beside the wanderer, full of need. His twin didn't like the uneasiness that was growing within the hold and he wanted Mica's reassurance.

'But they have a secret,' Lupe said. 'The hunger to keep things quiet? That's what we're feeling.'

Beyond the hold, the Komic Sea was silent, and almost louder for its silence. None of these Berans had ever lived near the sea, let alone travelled on it. Mica had checked. There were people from Canis, from flax-growing Linum, from Rice, and from Murasia with its failed fig trees. All inland provinces.

'And the sea?' he said, unable to help himself from seeking reassurance he knew he couldn't get. 'Is it all right? To me, it feels … heavy, full. Like a cook about to tip water into a pot.'

'Well it would, wouldn't it?' Lupe said, not unkindly. 'I don't think we should read too much into it. It's natural. Longing to fill up the hold. It's troubling us because we're not used to it, because the sailors are making us jumpy.'

Zizania, a young mother from a Rice province family, nodded, jiggled her baby on her knee. Mica could feel her desperation for a reassuring story. Her son, Dust, grizzled. 'That's right,' she said. 'It's nothing. We're going to be fine. There's nothing going on.'

'Let's hope,' Mica said, 'But I think it's time we talked about a plan.' When he'd first arrived, Mica had argued for patience. Now, patience felt dangerous.

'The only thing we need to plan is how to get out,' a young woman from Linum said.

Zizania spoke up, 'We shouldn't do anything rash. We'll get out when we get to Galea. It's too dangerous to try anything while we're at sea.'

Mica felt for her, but fear could make a person too cautious. He chose his words with care, 'I think we have to talk about what the oceanhood could be planning. We need knowledge. We need a cycle. Does anyone know any stories about sailors using violence at sea? Stories about becalming? Stories about sacrifi—'

'Don't say it!' Zizania said. 'We should keep still and be quiet. Stay in the hold. Everything will be all right when we get to Galea.'

Mica felt Cerulean's uneasiness and reached behind his back, took his twin's hand, and drew him closer.

'Mica's right to speak it,' Lupe said. 'If there are stories of sacrifice we need to hear them because it might come to that. And I know some.' Lupe didn't bother rendering her tales like a storyteller or wait for Mica to take the lead. She shared the sharp outlines. The first story was a violent lullaby where the oceanhood's cook cut the cords holding Baby's hammock, and Baby flew out over the waves.

Zizania whimpered. Mica rock sensed Lupe moving closer to the young woman, felt her lean over to stroke Zizania's hair. Beside Mica, Cerulean edged from foot to foot, but the air wasn't fracturing. Mica ran his tongue over his teeth to be sure, but they were still firm.

'Awful,' Lupe said, 'I know. But we need to understand what the sailors might be contemplating.' Lupe's second story was about a boy, a lookout. He climbed into the crow's nest and found a family of ravens inside. He tied the birds to the ship's empty, windless sails. The ravens spread their wings and dragged the ship across the waves, only to drop dead from exhaustion when the ship docked.

Then a woman from Linum told a story about a crop of bad flax mistakenly made into sailcloth. When the sails failed, a sailor had to sacrifice her thick black hair to fix the weave.

Five more stories came in quick succession. Then Zizania spoke up, 'I ... don't want to tell it, but... It wouldn't happen in real life.'

'What wouldn't happen?' someone asked.

'Just a stupid story,' Zizania said.

'Stupid or not, we need to hear it,' Lupe said. Mica felt the shape of Lupe's hand giving Zizania's shoulder a reassuring squeeze. 'Please. Tell us what you know.'

'I was living with my family in Aries, in a refugee camp. It was when I was a girl. There was an old Companionari woman visiting, distributing alms. She heard my father was a wanderer. She gave this story to my father because it's about Rice and she knew we were Rice Berans. It's a story about the first Rice settlers and the sea.'

Zizania hesitated and then began, 'The first Rice Mother was lonely. She was by herself in the province, so she wrote to her cousin in Galea, inviting the rest of her family to join her on the Stone Body. They took passage on a boat called *Joy of the Wind*, only there was no wind and no joy. The crew killed all the passengers when the ship was becalmed.'

'How?' Mica asked. 'How did they do it?'

'It's a rhyme.' She said, and her voice was unsteady as she spoke:

They stood in a line

> Tied together with twine
> As the crew sought the spine
> To dispatch them.
>
> The crew made them wait
> Lest the sky change their fate
> But the sea was the plate
> To receive them.
>
> The mate pushed just one
> Then the second one spun
> As the twine had begun
> To tangle them.
>
> They fell to the sea
> Sacrificed as the fee
> And the ocean felt free
> To consume them.

Someone gasped. 'And you didn't think to tell us this earlier?'

'Don't,' Mica said. 'Blaming doesn't help.'

For a few minutes, the hold was full of worried shouts and urgent conversations, and the twisting feeling of Cerulean pacing, shaking the air. Mica stood up, took hold of his twin again, held him close, chest to chest, spoke reassuringly. The rock man stilled, and the Berans fell silent.

'I think I have an idea,' Mica said, letting Cerulean go. 'Well, the beginning of an idea.'

'Go on,' a woman called out. 'We could use one.'

'Cerulean and I could be the sacrifice. We wouldn't drown. We've got gills. Probably. Yes, I'm sure they're gills.'

'They'd tie you up,' Zizania said.

Mica shook his head. 'Even if they tied our hands, we'd be all right. We can find a sharp rock on the seabed or something like it. It won't matter how long it takes to free ourselves because we'll breathe underwater.'

'Assuming those slits are gills,' someone said.

'Right,' Mica said. 'But I'm sure they are. They must be.'

A man sitting near Zizania pointed at her. 'But she said they killed everyone, all their passengers, and we haven't got gills.'

Mica was only half listening because his idea was growing. A beautiful, neat, clever shape of an idea. Cerulean hooted, and the air felt fluid and hot, the opposite of the rock man's usual sharp rattle. Mica calmed himself. They'd be even worse off if Cerulean reversed things and rushed them into a second childhood. When the air had steadied, he spoke again, 'All you have to do is turn us over to the oceanhood. We're stowaways. We caused the becalming. Tell them we're not quite right. Tell them that. Demand they punish us for stowing away and pretending to be Berans.'

'But you *are* Berans. Anyone can see that.'

'And yet, our rock skin doesn't look right, does it? We don't look like real Berans. They'll jump at the chance to drown strangers, people who've wronged them, people they don't have to feel guilty about.'

'But how will it help?' Zizania asked. 'Unless the wind blows when they push you overboard, it will only be a matter of time before they come for us.'

Mica sighed. She had a point. He paced, worrying at the problem, getting nowhere. Cerulean followed him, unsettled by Mica's fretful emotional signature. Mica forced himself to calm down. 'I don't know,' he said to Zizania, 'but it's an opportunity for something to happen, for us to do something new. We just have to work out what that something is.'

'Take over the ship,' a man suggested. 'Do something to the hatch as they're dragging you and Cerulean out.'

'Use Cerulean to turn them to dust,' another man said.

'And us at the same time?' Zizania said. 'If they drag Cerulean out, we'll all die because he'll panic.'

Mica halted, rubbed his face, thinking. 'Yes, yes, but Cerulean and I could go peacefully. Just having us would distract them. And when we're in the water, when they think we've drowned, we could rap on the hull to make them think we're vengeful ghosts. They might flee in the lifeboats.'

'*Might* isn't good enough,' Lupe said. 'We must think through every outcome. Let's assume they don't flee in the lifeboats. What then?'

Mica shrugged. 'Maybe you *do* break the hatch. There are enough of you with good strong rock skin. You could do it.'

'We would have done that already if it was a good idea,' a woman said. 'The soldiersisters are armed.'

'That's true,' Lupe said, 'but Mica's right, we could break out while he and Cerulean bang on the hull. It will still be dangerous, but there's a chance. Better than a chance. The sailors and the soldiersisters would lean over the rail, trying to see what's wrong. That would give us the advantage.'

Zizania spoke up, asked Mica the real question. 'What about your twin? How will you stop him from rushing everyone when all this is going on?'

Mica stood looking into the dark of the hold, unable to think of a solution.

'Perhaps we could train him,' Lupe suggested. 'Harness, voice, treats, body language and practice. It works with dogs.'

'Cerulean isn't a dog,' Mica said, 'and it wouldn't be right to put him in a harness.'

'Why not?'

'He's not an animal.'

'Don't be silly. We're all animals.'

'He's a man,' Mica insisted.

'Of a sort, maybe. But you must admit he's a wild creature. Half wild at the very least.'

Mica started pacing again, rubbed his forehead, trying to think things through. 'But even if I agreed, there wouldn't be time to train him properly and we don't have a harness.'

'Time is a problem,' Lupe said. 'But we're from Canis. We know how to work with half wild creatures so you're lucky. We'll socialise him. Cerulean is clever. He'll learn in a hurry. And we have you. He trusts you, and that's a solid beginning. As for the harness, Linum's Berans can fashion a rope to tie you together. If they've got a little flax fibre. And if they haven't they could use rags.' A couple of people from Linum called out their readiness to help, and then Lupe continued outlining her thoughts, 'And we can explain how to make a Canis halter, which is what we use…' she broke off, emotion in her voice. 'Which is what we used to use to teach our dogs to walk through crowded trading rooms.'

'But would it be right?' Mica asked. 'He's a magical creature. He shouldn't be in a harness.'

'Then I'll halter both of you. If it makes you feel better.'

Mica stopped pacing. 'It would, yes. Teach us together. Tie us together.'

'I can do that,' Lupe said.

'It might work,' one of the other Canis Berans called out. 'But how long do we have?'

Lupe looked at Mica. 'How long do you think we've got until they come for us?'

Mica looked up into the dark reaches of the hold, felt the ocean-hood above them, felt the ship and the seascape beyond. He felt the flat water, the slack sails and the sailors. 'I think… I think we have the rest of the day.'

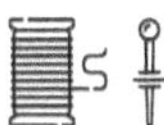

Mica held the rope that joined him to Cerulean and started walking. Small steps that inched him nearer the knot of deliberately noisy Berans. He felt Cerulean's fear, his reluctance, but the rock man took a tentative step. The Berans in front of him waved their arms and stamped their feet. One sang a drinking song for added effect.

The texture of the rope felt soft in Mica's nervous hands. Linum's Berans had ripped the flax padding from their jackets. They'd spun it between their palms and then plaited it into a rope, but they'd made the Canis harnesses from strips of donated clothing. There hadn't been enough flax left for flax harnesses, but Mica liked the feel of the old clothes. He patted his chest. It was reassuring. He could almost rock sense the echo of the people who'd ruined their shirts and rendered their hems to provide the material.

'Voice,' Lupe reminded him.

That's right. He had to keep speaking to Cerulean. Lupe said he had to be encouraging. 'Come on, Cerulean,' he kept his voice low and warm. 'Come on, Brother. It's just a few more steps and we'll be through to the other side. They won't hurt us. We've done this twice already. You know this.' Mica took another step and then another and, for a moment, it appeared his coaxing had worked. Then Cerulean reared back, pulled on the rope. The air felt tight and dangerous.

'Voice and harness,' Lupe said. 'Use your torso. Don't pull him, but don't release the tension until he stops fighting you.' She held up her hand to stop Mica moving, as though Mica might not have understood that he had to stand still. 'Good,' she said. 'Stand your ground. You're both feeling the constraint of the harness and, if you hold steady Mica, Cerulean will give in. Because you're showing him you know what's best.'

Mica stood his ground, felt the harness tightening.

'You're not standing solid,' Lupe said. 'Anchor him.'

Mica set his feet more firmly on the boards. Like a rock. Be like a rock. You're a boulder. You're unmovable.

Ahead of him, the Berans continued their noisy pantomime; behind him, Cerulean pulled, and the air felt sharp and hurried. For a moment, he thought he could feel the rush of stone. It was too dark to see Lupe, but he worried her hair might be turning white. He ran his tongue over his teeth.

'Concentrate,' Lupe said. 'You've stopped talking. Don't stop vocalising. You need to use your voice. Reassure him.'

Mica took a breath and spoke encouragingly to Cerulean. At first, the rope remained strained, the harnesses tight on both their chests, but after a few moments, Cerulean shifted. He didn't give in, but he stopped pulling back. The rope eased, the harnesses relaxed. Not loose, but not taut. Mica smiled. 'Good.'

'Really?' one of the younger Canis Berans said. 'That's all you've got? Praise him.'

'Use your tone,' Lupe said. 'Project joy. He needs joy.'

At first, Mica couldn't find any joy, couldn't remember what it felt like. Then he thought of Fox. He remembered their clandestine meetings near the Oak House kitchen garden, the way her hair shone and the spark of her golden gaze. His heart lifted. 'Brilliant Cerulean. You're doing wonderfully well.' He glanced back. The rock man smiled. His first smile. Mica found he was grinning too.

'Keep talking,' Lupe said.

And Mica kept talking. He talked them through the crowd and back again.

There was no lunch served to prisoners on *The Crested Wave*, ever, but Mica felt lunchtime come and go. A while later, someone shared a piece of dried fruit they'd been saving for emergencies. Mica used a quarter of it to reward Cerulean when they passed through the noisy knot of Berans for the eighth time. He gave himself a quarter too. They were a team; not master, not beast. They would share what they had.

They repeated the lesson again and again with Lupe calling out instructions and variations. She told the Berans to grab hold of Mica and Cerulean, jostle them. She made Mica and Cerulean hurry and stumble. Above all, she told the knot of Berans to be angrier, noisier. It never went smoothly. Mica lost teeth and regained them; lost years and then found them. The atmosphere in the hold was hot and liquid and then cold and brittle, but he didn't die. No one died.

Mica wasn't sure Cerulean was ready when Lupe announced they'd run out of time. Course, she was right. They'd agreed they couldn't wait another day and everyone could rock sense the sun beginning to set. Any earlier, and they wouldn't have the advantage of the dark; any later, and the crew might leave them in the hold until morning.

Lupe knocked on the hatch, banged it with the back of her right hand and held the end of the Mica and Cerulean's rope with her other. Mica felt the crew's reaction. They were full of alarm and hungry shameful desire. Not the soldiersisters. A soldier ambled over and opened the hatch, her head and torso a silhouette against the darkening sky.

'What?'

'The captain,' Lupe said. 'I need the captain. Tell her we know why the wind stopped and the sky is empty of storm gulls.'

15

Fox knew she and Saury looked alarming with their bizarre new rock skin, but the skipper's reluctance to let them board the barge surprised her. The riverhood had a duty to those in distress and anyone could see Peri was exhausted and half-drowned. They'd kept to the water for most of the journey, reluctant to risk another encounter with the soldiersisters. They swam upriver and along the canal and only ventured back onto land to bypass the canal locks, worried the soldiersisters could have ridden ahead and poisoned their welcome. Fox was almost certain she'd felt the soldiers tracking the three of them. Beyond the upper lock, they'd entered the Vagor River and then somehow survived the rough and tumble of its flow into the Cava. Peri only just.

The skipper leant over the barge's railing. 'We're going to the port, yes,' she agreed. 'Headed there, but we're hired out. Not taking passengers. Can't.'

'But we need help!' Fox said. 'Please.'

Peri was shivering beside her. He held onto Fox's upper arm with both hands as Fox hung from the rope ladder. The barge rumbled, and the ladder vibrated under her hands. They were slowly being pulled past the point where the Vagor met the Cava. In the right direction, but it was preposterous that they were being denied succour. She lifted herself a little higher, up another rung, drawing Peri with her, her muscular tentacles managing the feat. She could force the issue. With a bit of effort, she'd be able to pull Peri up with her, and Saury could manage on her own. They could continue the argument on deck.

Peri spoke to her, teeth chattering, 'Maybe we sh... sh... should swim back to the riverbank.'

Fox shook her head, kept her eye on the skipper. She could feel the soldiersisters. They *had* followed, and they were close. Fox was running out of options. 'Please,' she searched the skipper's face for some sign of compassion, 'we need help.'

'Not here, you don't,' the skipper insisted, and Fox felt something akin to regret in the woman's words. 'Best not. We have a passenger. We're not able to help.'

Saury had been treading water a little further along the side of the barge, one hand anchored to the barge with her tentacular rock skin. Fox felt her sister move. The girl reached up and began heaving herself out of the water. She used her suckers to grip the slick planks, her feet scrabbling for purchase. The skipper leant over the rail to see what was going on and gasped, reeling back. Saury's rock skin looked extraordinary, muscular tentacles reaching up to lip the edge of the deck.

'Back and Path,' the skipper's voice bounced off the water as her face reappeared. Then she took another backward step. She called for the mate to fetch a couple of oars.

Fox was still trying to work out why she wanted them when the skipper returned. She leant over the rail and wielded an oar, halting Saury's progress. 'Go,' she said, her voice urgent. 'You can't come up here.' The mate stood above Fox's head, a second oar in her hands.

'I ca... can't hold on much longer,' Peri said.

Overhead and out of sight, someone called out a question. Fox was still thinking about why the voice sounded familiar when an unwelcome face joined the skipper at the rail.

'What's going on?' Whilomena said. 'Fox Oak?' She leant further over the rail, narrowed her eyes. 'It's you.' Fox rock sensed the woman's excitement. The companion felt like greed, like danger. 'And where's your father? Is he with you?' Whilomena peered over Fox's shoulder, searching for Aikin.

'They want to come aboard,' the skipper said.

'Then help them up, Ogden. We're old friends.'

The skipper gave a slight shake of her head and withdrew her oar, signalled for the mate to do the same. Fox could feel the woman's worry and her dislike of Whilomena. It put a different perspective on her reluctance to let them board. Fox decided to flee, but then Peri's fingers slipped from her arm and she had to drop one of her hands from the ladder to save him. Whilomena was dangerous, yes, but Peri wouldn't last much longer and Ogden felt true. Besides, they needed to board, escape their pursuers. So, Fox called Saury to help her with Peri. Together they half-heaved, half-pushed him up the ladder, anchoring themselves on either side. Even to Fox, their climb felt spider-like and unnatural, and the mate stood at a noticeable distance when they landed on deck.

Whilomena stood before them, dressed in a ridiculous striped outfit, and she gripped a folded parasol as though it were a weapon. Fox might have felt comforted at the thought that the companion was frightened of them, but the woman stepped closer, squinted at Fox. She gave a pleased little laugh and bent down to look at the tentacles covering Fox's hands. 'Interesting,' Whilomena said. 'Ugly, but interesting. What brought this on?'

Fox retracted her tentacles, wrapped them around her wrists.

'By the Back!' Ogden exclaimed.

'Yes.' Whilomena nodded. 'I'm as curious as you, Skipper.'

'It's just rock skin,' Peri said. 'They travelled through a portal. It changed them.'

'Then where are their twins?' Whilomena asked him.

'Never heard of rock skin that moved,' the mate said. 'Heard about those portals. You saying they can breathe life into rock skin?'

'You're asking for the stories?' Peri said.

'Perhaps when you're rested, Wanderer,' Whilomena said. She stepped back from Fox and gave Peri a smile. 'Let's get you into a cabin and some warm clothes. Dry off, eat something, and then you can tell your stories.'

'We'll stay here,' Fox said, 'on deck.'

Whilomena smiled, but her signature was hard and greedy. She snapped her fingers, and several soldiersisters appeared. Fox backed away, found herself hard up against the rail, but Saury and Peri were slower. Before she had time to shout a warning or unsheathe her knife, the soldiersisters had them. Saury might have fought free, but Peri didn't have the energy to do anything but sink to the deck. And they couldn't leave him; a wanderer with stones. They couldn't. Saury looked at Fox and Fox shook her head.

Ogden drew herself up, glared at the Wheat Companion. 'This is my barge. Tell your soldiersisters to stand down.'

Whilomena didn't bother answering. She turned to the soldiers. 'Take them below. Tie them up. Strip them of any fetish stones. And make sure you tie them up, well.'

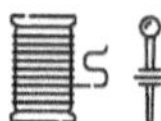

As soon as the door of the hold slammed shut, before the barge weighed anchor, Fox moved. She shuffled past Peri on her knees and positioned herself behind Saury. Their hands were bound tight behind their backs, but Fox had an idea. She lowered the top of her head. 'Get my knife, Saury. It's still there, in the lace, in my hair.' Fox shifted about, crouching down even lower. The barge rumbled, idling still. So close to the floor, the smell of wheat and dust and dirt filled her nose.

'Okay, but you need to get lower still,' Saury said.

Grunting, Fox inched closer and bent even lower. It was

awkward, manoeuvring in the dark, with her own hands tied behind her back. Then, finally, she felt the tips of Saury's fingers on her head. 'Can you feel it? Can you get the knife?'

'I can't find it,' Saury complained. 'I can feel the lace collar, but I can't find the knife. Are you sure it hasn't fallen out?'

'It's there,' Fox said. 'I can feel the weight of it.'

'Let me try,' Peri said.

'Wait,' Saury said. 'Give me a chance.' The girl walked her fingers over Fox's scalp, trying to locate the lace-wrapped knife. It wasn't a simple task. The soldiers had not only bound their hands behind their backs, they'd wound the ropes over the Berans' rock skin, blunting their rock sense and trapping the sisters' tentacles. Fox just hoped the lace was worse for wear, and could be ripped apart, because Saury was in no position to untie knots.

'I've got it! I've got it!' Saury tugged at the sheath and Fox bit her lip to stop from crying out as her sister pulled her hair. For a few minutes, Saury wriggled the knife, but it didn't come free. 'It's all tangled,' Saury sounded tearful. 'I can't get it.'

'Let me try,' Peri said. 'My hands are stronger.'

'One more try,' Saury said.

Keeping her head at the level of Saury's hands was hurting Fox's back. 'Just rip the lace. If you can, get a grip on the hilt.'

'Let me try,' Peri repeated. 'We need to get out of here. My rock children are calling me. I need to find them.'

'They're safe for now,' Fox said. 'We're not in port yet and I doubt Whilomena has the equipment aboard to do them much harm. We'll get to them as soon as we can.'

'I've got an idea,' Saury said.

Fox heard Saury moving. Then the shuffling stopped and then Saury's breath was in Fox's hair.

'I can't see what you're doing,' Peri said.

'I'm biting the lace,' Saury said, voice muffled.

Peri sighed but seemed to have given up trying to take over the task because he didn't complain. Moments later, the knife clattered to the wooden floor of the barge's cargo hold.

'Bravo Saury!' Fox said. She sat up. She was still on her knees, but it was a relief to straighten her back.

'Now, you can help,' Saury said to Peri. 'Your hands are the strongest, so you should hold the knife.'

Fox shifted back to give Peri more room. He swivelled about and began feeling for the knife, constrained by the ropes that bound his hands behind his back. Now he was the one grunting from the effort. The barge's cargo hold was dark, but Fox could just make out the glint of the blade.

'More to the left,' Fox said. Peri shuffled to the right. 'Sorry,' Fox said. 'My left; your right. Move to your right.'

'That's it!' Saury said. 'I think you're almost there.'

Peri's fingers touched the knife, and he grabbed it, cut himself, dropped it. The second time, he was more careful. He walked his fingers up and down the blade until he knew its position, and then he closed his fist on the hilt.

'Me first,' Saury said. She turned her back to Peri's back. 'Ready Peri?'

'I'm ready. The knife's blade is pointed to the ceiling of the cargo hold.'

'Just be careful,' Fox told Saury. 'Don't cut yourself. Don't cut a tentacle.'

'Then guide her,' Peri said.

Fox struggled up, getting higher onto her knees so she could see. She leant over the place where Saury was attempting to match the rope to the blade's edge. It was hard to see anything. Their prison had no portholes, and all they had to work with was a shaft of daylight from a poorly patched crack, high up between two boards. The light barely penetrated the gloom and Fox had to be careful to avoid blocking it out completely.

She called out instructions: now telling Saury to rub harder; now telling Peri to hold the knife steady. Finally, the rope separated and

Saury staggered to her feet. Then she shimmied about, shook her arms. Her movement sent clouds of dust into the air and Peri sneezed.

'It's the wheat dust,' Fox said.

'I don't care what sort of dust it is,' Peri said. 'It's awful.'

'But it matters,' Fox said. 'It tells us something about the skipper. She sympathised with us, but she carries Whilomena's bounty. She might not be a friend.'

Peri rapped the knife against the floor to get Saury's attention. 'Stop dancing about. Cut me loose.'

Saury stopped twirling. She took the knife and cut Peri free. Then Peri took it and freed Fox. For a moment, the three of them stood rubbing their wrists. Then the sound surrounding them shifted as the barge started moving. Fox bent down and picked up the tattered lace. It was ruined and would never again adorn a tunic, but Lark's gift had proved itself again and again, and she wouldn't abandon it.

Peri returned the knife to Fox and she wrapped her thickest tentacle around its hilt and tucked the broken lace into her pocket with her other hand. Something to give her daughter when she was born; something to show Mica.

Peri walked over to the base of a wooden ladder fixed to the wall. The only exit was the door above it.

'How do we get out?' Saury asked.

Peri stared at the door, head back. It wasn't easy to make out in the dark, but they could all feel its shape now their rock skin was free. There was a stout oak beam on the outside keeping it barred. 'If we can't get out now,' Peri said, 'we'll get out when someone comes to fetch us. And then we'll free the rock children.'

Fox came to stand beside him at the ladder's base, Saury at her heels. 'They might not come until we reach the port.'

Peri scratched his head. 'At least it's not locked, but it may as well be with that bar on the outside.'

'Just enough to keep us inside,' Fox said.

'I don't want to die again,' Saury whispered.

It was understandable that Saury was afraid after all she'd been through, but it wasn't the murderous events in Whilomena's mill house folly that filled Fox's mind. It was the memory of a story. She turned to Peri. 'Do you know the tale about Bride dying three times?'

She felt the wanderer's hesitation, didn't need to see his expression to understand his concern. It was a gruesome tale, and Saury was scared enough already. 'I don't think any of us need to hear that one,' he said. 'Not when we can't get out.'

But the more Fox thought about it, the more she thought he was wrong. It was short enough, and it was the right story. She smoothed her still-damp and wrinkled tunic, prepared herself for the telling.

'Granny used to whisper this to me when Father was angry,' Fox said. 'She said it would make me stronger. *Better to know*, she said.' Fox licked her lips and looked from Peri to her sister and back again. 'Bride died once by Husband's hand and it was a shock. The second time he killed her, it was so familiar it felt ordinary. And then Bride returned to Husband so he could kill her for the third time.' Fox looked up, trying to recall her grandmother's exact words. The story was nuanced and the message would be in the nuance. What had Bride's ghost lamented? Then Fox had it. She nodded. '*For the want of a harder face to warn me; the want of a bigger dream to call me; the want of two faster feet beneath me; the want of a kinder hand to aid me; the want of freedom's cloak to warm me.*'

'Awful,' Peri said.

'But what do you think it's telling us?' Fox asked him.

'It's your story. You'll know the answer.'

But it was Saury who spoke, 'Before they killed me, Whilomena and Aikin seemed so kind. I lacked the harder face to warn me. And my next death, if we can't get out of here, it's going to be familiar because I've died before. I think... I can already feel it getting nearer.'

Fox put her arm around her sister, drew her close. 'But Saury, remember this: we have a bigger dream to call us,' she spoke into her sister's hair, 'and kind hands to aid us.'

Peri shook his head. 'We're locked up and alone. Ogden may not be a friend. No one's going to aid us.'

Fox felt something spark in Saury's emotional signature. She stepped away from Fox, looked up at the door. 'I think we'll be all right. I think the part about *freedom's cloak* is about me because I was the one who said we had to get free and I was the one who said we'd be able to get the knife. So, perhaps there is a way to escape if we keep looking.'

'We'd need an axe,' Peri said.

'We have what we have,' Fox said, 'Which is a knife and our hands and a broken bit of lace.'

'But we have tentacles,' Saury said.

Fox looked at Saury. Her sister's rock skin had uncoiled from her wrists. It wasn't gloving the girl's hands. Instead, it bloomed around them as though her tentacles were ready for whatever action the girl needed to take. Fox hesitated, feeling for a pattern. 'When we needed to get on the barge, I saw you reach for the deck.' Saury nodded, but Fox rock sensed her sister's puzzlement. Fox bit her lip. 'I think ... your tentacles flattened when you reached up.' Fox looked from Saury's hands with their halo of tentacles to the door.

She turned to Peri. 'Climb up and feel if there's any movement of air around the door's edges.'

'And if there is?' Saury asked.

Fox licked her lips. She unravelled her rock skin from her wrists. She reached out with one long suckered arm, flattened it until it was so thin it could have been a precious ribbon in a Companionari sister's sewing basket. 'I think... I think Saury and I can reach between the door and the jamb and lift the bar. We might open the door.'

Peri reached for the ladder, and she could feel his excitement growing. He spoke over his shoulder as he ascended, 'Then all we need is a plan for what to do once we're out. How to save the rock children. I can feel them. They aren't on deck.'

'They'll be in Whilomena's cabin,' Fox said. 'We go there and then we get off this barge and into the river. The barge will have outpaced the soldiersisters who were chasing us so we can head for shore, walk to the port.'

Fox could no longer see Peri clearly, but she felt his movement as he ran his hand along the edge of the door, felt his joy.

'There's a breeze.'

'We're coming up,' Fox said.

'Can we all fit on the ladder?' Peri asked.

'Suckers,' Saury said. 'Easy.'

Saury and Fox positioned themselves on either side of the door: one foot on a rung, one hand free and the other hand's tentacles anchoring them to the wall. Peri stood in the middle, ready to push the door open.

Fox didn't need to nod at Saury. They used their rock sense to synchronise their movement. Together, they flattened several tentacles and reached between the door and its frame. They felt for the bar, gripped it: Saury on the hinged side of the door; Fox on the other. They gave the bar a jiggle and then Fox spoke, 'If I slide it towards you, can you hold it until Peri can get out and lower it to the floor? There isn't enough room on my side.'

'Do you want to swap sides?' Peri said.

'Let's not wait,' Saury said. 'Fast feet because I don't want to die.'

'Then, let's do it,' Peri said. 'Because I can't feel anyone in the corridor. Let's not wait for that to change.'

'Agreed,' Fox said.

'Then let's go.'

Fox slid the oak bar towards Saury. It moved, bit by bit, until it was past the metal bracket on Fox's side. Fox had to stretch her tentacle to keep hold of it, shift it to her sister without dropping it or making a sound. Her rock skin felt the strain and her suckers were close to their limit.

'I've got it,' Saury whispered.

Fox withdrew her tentacles, tightened her grip on her knife. She waited as Saury eased the bar down and then she too withdrew her tentacles.

'I'll open the door a crack and try to slip through,' Peri said. 'Everyone clear? I don't want to pinch anyone's skin.'

'Just hurry!' Saury said.

Fox reached above Peri's head to steady the door, used her suckers to counter the swing as he pushed it. Then he slipped through the opening like a dancer and Fox felt him checking in both directions, felt the relief in his signature.

And then they were out, standing alone in the empty corridor.

16

Talia woke to a gentle touch on her arm. She rolled over and met the Kelp Companion's gaze. The province's Mother was leaning into the disused oven. She gave Talia's hand a pat before backing out. 'It's morning. I wanted to speak to you before you left, before everyone comes down for breakfast.' The companion had the same intensity that Talia had sensed on the day they met. It wasn't just her manner and voice. She gave Talia goosebumps. The woman felt like a gust of wind against Talia's rock skin.

Talia sat up and ran her fingers through her hair, wondering whether she could ask the companion what the feeling meant, but the Kelp Mother was already out of sight, clattering about in the kitchen. Talia heard water pouring into a kettle and a kettle landing on a stove. From where she sat, she could see out the kitchen windows to the surprisingly empty landscape. No tangle of nightmarish trees. The rest had done her good. That and the relative absence of people bothering her. Kelp's landscape sparkled in the morning light and the replanted daisies embroidered the world with every colour a dedicated sewing sister could wish for.

'I gave your Master of Trade a book for you,' the Kelp Companion called out. 'There's a poem in it I want you to read. Make sure he gives it to you. I would have given it to you myself, but I wasn't sure you'd recover in time. Can you read Old Treaty?'

'A little.' Talia eased herself out of the oven and dropped to her feet. The floor was cold after the warmth of her bedding. She pulled on her boots and put her coat over her tunic.

The Kelp Companion was still talking, 'Well, a little is better than none. My sisters told me you'd regained your senses so I thought I'd come down and fix a farewell treat for you.' She began pounding at something in a mortar. 'We're out of wheat, but there's a grass in my talent that makes a lovely flour. Damn seeds are tiny though.' She thumped the pestle against the mortar for emphasis. 'You can't get much of it, but it makes excellent pancakes.' Then she gestured behind Talia. 'There's a basin and pitcher over there. Wash your hands and face and then you can take over the pestle while I make us tea.'

Talia obeyed. She could feel the landscape calling, pressing, demanding, but it was still manageable. She helped the companion mix and fry a sticky batter. Then they sat at the table and ate, smearing the pancakes with a fresh lemony paste. 'I'm sorry about your garden and your boat.'

The Kelp Companion looked up, her gaze intense and probing. Then she returned her attention to her food. 'I believe there are more important things for us to speak about.' She looked up again, expectantly. Talia said nothing, uncertain what the woman wanted. The Kelp Companion frowned but nodded. 'There's something beneficial about sitting for an hour or two in a sewing circle, talking things over with your sisters. Last night I spoke with mine and I realised I'd been ignoring my instincts. So, *hooks on lines*. That's what we say around here when we get down to business. I've watched your Master of Trade and my sisters have told me about you, how burdened you are, how full of regret, how you weep when you think you're alone.' She cut a slice of her pancake. Talia waited, her new rock sense telling her there was a purpose, a big question the woman was working towards. Then the Kelp Companion was speaking again, 'I'm a literalist in terms of faith. I've tried to emulate the Turned God in everything I do. So I value people who honour the Turned God by taking their own path, always have. I've not looked to Komey. I've only looked at Kelp.' She gave a slight frown. 'But it seems my preferences have split us off from the rest of the Stone Body. I see that I've become parochial.'

'Surely not, you can't—'

The companion held up her hand, shook her head. 'No need to be polite. I lost a boat, the camp lost a set of oars and a harpoon, and that's all I was worried about. Small things. But you've changed that. You've brought secrets and lies and unease into the manor.' Talia blushed and opened her mouth to speak, unsure what to say. 'No. Say nothing. Bad enough listening to your Master of Trade with all his contorted stories. Let's just say you've done me a perverse favour. You and Aikin reminded me that the rest of the world matters.' The woman set down her fork. 'So I'm sending Trevalla to Komey. She can find someone to father a baby and she'll open up Kelp House and establish a new city-focused sorority. We haven't used our Komey house for a decade... More. I thought we had all we needed here. We did for a while, but life is getting hard with so many hungry refugees seeking asylum, and now you've arrived full of lies and half-truths,' she paused. 'Well, yes, I do want to know what you've got to say for yourself. Tell me why you're really here. I'd ask Aikin, but it would be hard to believe his answer. A nasty greedy man.'

Talia smiled. 'He considers himself charming.'

'Oh, he's that. But charm wears thin. So, the truth now, *hooks on lines*. You owe me that.'

So Talia told her everything and felt lighter for it.

Afterwards, the Kelp Companion sat back, stared out the window for a good few minutes. 'He's even more dangerous than I thought.'

'I know,' Talia said.

'Do you? Do you, really? And yet you're travelling with him. On your own.'

'Not by choice,' Talia pointed out.

'You need to be careful. He wouldn't hesitate to kill you if it suited him.'

'I have my trees. He's my prisoner.'

'I don't think so. You've been down here in the kitchen for days, unaware of your surrounds. He could have left and you wouldn't have known. Could have done anything.'

'I know, but he wants to go to New Lytalia.'

'So you are travelling companions.'

'He's my prisoner, but it helps that he wants to go where I'm taking him.'

The Kelp Companion held Talia's gaze, shook her head. 'Until he doesn't. That's what you need to be careful about. He's an opportunist. Still, I admire his conviction and I can't say he was completely wrong to do what he did.'

'What! It was dreadful, monstrous,' Talia couldn't keep the shock from her voice.

'Crushing the stones made sense.'

'And the deaths? You don't think that's wrong? Killing children? Murdering wanderers? Killing Berans who were guests?'

'Oh, it is, yes. The murders were wrong, but letting people die from starvation is wrong too. If you don't like it, Talia, you must find an alternative.' The Kelp Companion pushed her plate away. 'Stop running around after Aikin. Find out whether these portals can save us.'

'I have to take Aikin to New Lytalia. I have to see him banished.'

The companion lifted her empty cup and turned it over, upending it on its saucer. 'Very worthy, I'm sure.' She righted the cup and stared at the leaves.

'You don't think so?'

The companion frowned at the cup. 'I think you should have kept him in jail in Komey. Banishment won't last. You probably need to kill him.'

'What?'

'You won't. Of course. But it would be best. Then you could get on with saving the Stone Body and afterwards you could grow rice, do some good in the world. And I wouldn't mind you as a neighbour.' The companion inclined her head towards the view across the river: the barren black sands, the empty paddies. Then she tilted her empty teacup towards Talia.

Talia saw a pattern in the leaves that startled her: fish shapes swimming between lines that looked like rice stalks. It gave her courage to ask her question, 'Do the fish press you for more life?'

'Of course.'

'But do they push you? Do they feel impossible, as though they're a wave you have to hold back? And how do you manage it, holding them back?' Talia tipped over her own teacup and righted it again. She looked inside. There was nothing but a clump of wet tea leaves. No magic to guide her. The only thing she had was her cursed talent and the rock skin she'd grown after saving Aikin. She held out her arms to the Kelp Companion. The skin had lost its raw, reddish appearance. Instead, it had the bleached look of dressed oak or ripened wheat or maybe it was the pale tones of polished rice.

'I'd noticed your hands and arms,' the Kelp Companion said. 'Does it work, your rock skin? I've not heard of a Companionari growing it.'

'If any had it, they'd have hidden it.'

The companion looked troubled, then sighed, 'Dust bush tea.'

'Yes,' Talia said, wondering whether the Kelp Mother was thinking of Fox.

'But can you rock sense?'

'I can feel people,' Talia said. 'I asked you about your fish because you feel different. More alive, more focused than your sorority. I thought you might be like me.'

The other woman laughed, 'I am like you. We're companions. But I'm about forty generations away from you. Read the poem. I don't have the answers, but it might help. And if you use that skin for anything, use it to watch Aikin.'

Talia and Aikin travelled for days, following the river out of Kelp province and into Eden, and from there along the towpath of Eden's inter-river canal to the Vagor. Talia had insisted they skirt the lock keepers' quaint and cosy cottages, denying herself rest. And Aikin was accommodating, almost too accommodating. It brought to mind the Kelp Companion's warning. But Talia didn't trust her luck with the riverhood's lock keepers, so she wore herself thin, keeping an eye on Aikin and a grip on her talent. It was a relief when she could hear, ahead of them, the roar of the conjunction of the Vagor and the Cava. It meant she would soon be free of him.

Now they rode in single file: Talia in front; Aikin following. They were quiet. Conversation had lapsed the night before and there seemed no paint in reviving it. The days and nights beside Eden's plants were dispiriting. The humid scent of greenery mocked the wintry air with a false promise of summer. Talia had picked a tomato when they'd first entered the province. The fruit was glossy red but rotten inside. She'd picked another when they slept their first night beside the canal's towpath. That one had been full of millipedes. And it was no better now. Bitter cucumbers. Peppers smothered in aphids and tomatoes with blackened hearts. She wished she was already in the port's hinterland. She longed to leave Eden behind.

A slapping sound brought her back to the present. Her horse was knee-deep in rice stalks. She groaned, glared at the rice over-running the tow path, and then braved a glance at the surrounding landscape. Not that she needed to look to know. Her trees were displacing Eden's tainted produce. She gathered herself, shut down the trees, but she let the rice run riot. At least it was edible and releasing was a relief. She glanced back, dreading Aikin's smirk, but he was oblivious. Nose in an open book, letting his horse follow hers.

It didn't matter, not really. But it rankled that she carried all the worry and unease and he was free to read. 'Put the book away,' she said, half regretting the words even as she spoke them. Engaging was a mistake. He lifted his gaze, a blank expression on his face. 'Put it away!'

He lowered the book without closing it, rested it on the pommel of his saddle. 'Why? It's not hurting you. I'm not doing anything wrong.'

'This isn't a pleasure trip,' she said, unable to keep the resentment from her voice.

He laughed, shook his head, lifted the book, resumed reading. Talia felt the same tangle of feelings she always felt around him: confusion, disappointment, and fury. She'd felt it on the train and in Kelp Manor's garden, but somehow it was worse the longer she spent in his company. The Kelp Companion's assertion that Aikin would dupe Talia, make her into a travelling companion, or best her, returned. The thought of it settled beneath Talia's breastbone, adding to her burdens. It felt sour, like indigestion; sour, like weakness. She should have turned away from him, but didn't.

Aikin spoke from behind the book. 'You'd like me to jump to attention, act like your domesticated pet, but I won't. I refuse to join you in your suffering,' he said, not bothering to look up from the page.

'That doesn't even make sense.'

Then he did look up. Gazed at her over the top of the book, smiled. 'Really? Here we are, riding together. The sun is out, and the day is pleasantly cool. We can hear the music of the two rivers making love as they flow into one another. We've food in our saddlebags. I'm reading and you're morose, verging on weepy.' He jiggled the book, waved it at her. 'Maybe I should read you something to comfort you or lift you up.'

'I don't want to hear anything from you.'

'But this is the greatest story ever written.'

'You said that about your other book. You said that about *The Book of Kinesis*.'

'And my assessment hasn't changed.'

Her back ached from twisting in her saddle, but she didn't turn away, just gripped the saddle's cantle for support.

Then she parsed what he'd said. The literal meaning. Somehow, he had *The Book of Kinesis*. He must have stolen it back from the portal tent. The sour feeling beneath her breastbone bit harder. That cursed book that had led to her downfall. She wanted to reach back and grab it, but had to turn away because her horse had ambled off the towpath. So she spoke without looking at him, 'You stole it back from the Berans? How did you get it out of the tent? Presumably, one of your lackeys did it.'

She heard him sigh, 'So, that's where it went. I wish I'd known. I would have stolen it or had someone steal it for me.' Her rock skin was becoming more attuned to her surrounds because she felt him bring the book back up in front of his face even though she was no longer facing him. It was a bit like catching movement in the corner of her eye. He spoke again from behind the book, 'I don't blame Mica for stealing it from the Oak library,' he said. 'One takes a book when one needs a book. At least, I do.'

She twisted around to look at him again. 'Have you been in my saddlebag? Did you take back the book the Kelp Companion gave me?'

'No. Your gift is right where you left it in your saddlebag.' Talia's horse resumed its drift off the path and she altered the pressure of her legs against its belly, bringing it back on track without turning away from Aikin. Aikin closed the book he was reading, stroked it. 'This is my bit of theft. Something I needed and they didn't. They weren't using it. Didn't even know it existed.'

Talia held out her hand. 'Whatever it is, give it to me.'

'Not a chance. And don't try telling me you'll kill me if I don't hand it over. We both know you won't. Besides, I won't help you with your poem if you take my book away.'

She dropped her hand and faced forward again. 'I don't need your help. It's just a poem that doesn't make much sense..'

'An important poem. A poem that might save you.'

She didn't look back, but she could rock sense him smirking at her. Then he was speaking again, 'You've been wondering whether I've had any more insights, but you're too proud to ask. Admit it.'

'No.'

'Well, I have. Didn't your parents tell you pride is a failing?'

Talia flicked her reins to put more space between them. She didn't need rock skin to know he hadn't finished; there was more he wanted to say. Well, she wouldn't help him. If he wanted to talk, he could do it without her prompts.

'I've been thinking about it,' he said. 'I can recite my latest translation.'

Against her better judgement, she turned around again. 'Don't bother. I'll translate it again, myself, when I get to port.'

'When you get a dictionary.' He put his book away, re-buckled his saddlebag and urged his horse forward. Then he was beside her, between her and the landscape. Her horse shifted over, moved closer to the river to accommodate its stable mate.

'There's no shame in using a dictionary.'

'Seriously,' he said, 'you need to uncover its secrets, hear it again and again until we find the answer. Because there's an answer in it somewhere... Or the promise of one.'

'Any answer you think is good, is probably evil.'

'Stupid girl. I told you: pride is a failing. Let me help you.'

'Thank you, but I said no.'

He gestured to the trees that had returned unnoticed, waved at the trunks threatening to hem them in. As she looked, they accelerated, cracking with the force of their growth.

'What's going to happen when we get to port? All those people and you exhausted? You might not care about me, but what if you kill someone?'

Talia pursed her lips, fought the fury. The trees swayed and popped. She hated him, but he was right. She clenched her fists. It helped sometimes: the distraction of nails biting into palms. Not this time. She let go, calmed herself the Companionari way. Then she knotted her reins and reached into her saddlebag for the book. It was a tiny thing. Not really a book at all. Just a couple of pages between cloth-covered boards. She opened it and moved to hand it over, but Aikin was already reciting:

> 'On a brutish Path
> A rank conception embeds
> A strange feral horse
>
> It gallops the waves
> Its hooves tear down the garden
> Nature is dismayed'

Talia couldn't help herself. 'I already know this. You already told me this, or something close to this. I don't see how it can help. The brutish path is the killing of the stone. The conception embedding? Presumably, that's the treatment taking hold. And the strange horse must be the crushed rock. And so on and so forth.'

'Just keep listening. Open your rock sense.'

She closed the book with a slap. 'No. If you know something just tell me.'

Aikin began reciting again:

> 'Under my soft skin
> The stallion hosts a seeded pouch
> Spewing endless fry'

'That's new,' he said. '*Fry*. My last translation of the Old Treaty used the word *oranges*. Clearly wrong, but confusing because oranges are produce. Then I thought of *fry*, which is an aquatic word. A better translation, I think. Baby sea horses,' he said. 'Fry. That's what they call them.'

'This isn't helping.'

'Just listen:'

> 'Fish pressed against fish
> Grasses tangled in grasses
> Kelp displacing kelp
>
> Beneath the vast sky
> I rail against the Turning
> Adulthood's burden
>
> The sky is silent—'

And then he interrupted himself, held up a finger for Talia's attention. 'Focus on this next bit. It's new.'

> 'I roll my galloping horse
> Try to end my life—'

'Well, thanks. Very helpful,' she said. 'Now you want me to kill myself? Great solution. I can assure you I won't be doing that before I toss you off the Stone Body.'

'Shush. This next bit's good. I remembered the word *light*, which is what I'd used before, can also mean *dirt*. Dirt makes the meaning pretty clear. Pay attention to this last part:'

> *'Dirt shatters my skin*
> *Sweeps my blood to the dance floor*
> *Music calms the beast'*

'Argh,' Talia said. 'First the story is some sort of horse-baby, then it's a seahorse, then the Kelp Companion's riding an actual horse and then she throws herself to the ground and rolls in the dirt?'

Aikin shrugged. 'More or less. No one ever claimed the first Kelp

Companion was a talented poet. Her metaphors drift. But I think it means you need to cut yourself and rub dirt into your wounds.'

Talia gave a bitter laugh, 'Again? You think I'd trust you to do that to me again?'

'Not me. Do it to yourself.'

'And what dirt? Not another rock child? I won't do that again.'

'We don't have any crushed rock children, thanks to you and your friends.'

'Thank the Back!'

'But I think it's just dirt. Just earth from the Stone Body,' Aikin said. 'Any dirt. Scour yourself. If it doesn't *calm the beast* at least you'll feel punished, and you'll stop being such poor company.'

She shook her head, stared at the ripening rice surround them. 'I won't hurt myself to please you.'

Then he moved. Lightning fast. He shoved her, pushed her off her horse with open hands, threw her from her saddle. She was airborne. Then she hit the sharp rocky edge of the path and bounced. Nothing stopped her as she slid across the gravel and over the lip of the Vagor's bank. She tumbled, rolled down, gathering speed. She bounced again on the rocks at the river's edge and then landed on her back in the water. No breath to cry out and then Aikin landed on top of her, almost knocking her senseless. She tried to push him off, but his attack was ferocious. Clawing at her skin and rubbing dirt and sand all over her. There wasn't even time to call the trees, but they came anyway. And the rice too. The trees surrounded them, clogging the river, shifting its course, leaving her and him on a bed of filthy festering rice.

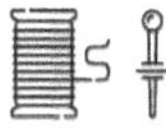

Aikin leapt out of the way as one of Talia's trees toppled onto the sodden tangle of rice stalks that was keeping them afloat. It fell with a muted splash that did nothing to stop them plunging into the water. He felt his foot contact Talia's head or shoulder as he scrambled. It was an accident, but he suspected he'd knocked her out because she wasn't moving, save for the movement of the current. Then again, she might have been injured before the tree fell ... but the trees had stopped growing. He looked up, smiled. Yes, they really had. Then again, maybe she was dead and that's why the trees were quiet?

He grabbed a hunk of her hair to stop her floating away. While there was no use saving her if she was already a corpse, he wouldn't know that until they were on land. He wanted her alive and cured. He needed a cure. They all needed a cure. If the portals proved unproductive, his method and his cure would be the undeniable solution. And Fox and Saury's twin-less appearance in Kelp suggested the portals were unreliable and his knowledge was going to be needed.

But first he had to get Talia to the bank, check her for signs of life.

He took a deep breath and pulled her with him, had to drag her under the floating trunk that was blocking their path. She was heavy, and the water fought him for control of her, but he kept a firm grip on her hair. He reached the riverbank and dragged her out of the water. Thank the Back, the trees had reworked the bank, otherwise he'd never have managed it. He dropped her to the ground and flopped down beside her, lay flat on his back.

She coughed, retched.

Not a corpse, then. He lifted a foot and half-kicked, half-rolled her onto her side. Probably a bit harsh, but giving her a couple of bruises was better than letting her stay on her back to inhale her own vomit. He rolled away from her, and the effort made him pant. The sky was vast, pale and empty, and the air was cold. He reminded himself that empty was good. No trees sprouting up around them. No rice tickling his fingers. He'd succeeded! And the noise of her vomiting up river water made it clear she was alive and likely to stay that way.

He realised he was shivering. Time to move, but before he could make himself do anything, his horse's head loomed above him, blocking his view of the sky. Then Talia's horse appeared beside it. Talia's animal sniffed him, snorted, and backed away. He caught his own horse's reins before it could do the same and, much to its displeasure, used them to pull himself upright.

'What happened?' Talia asked, her coughs subsiding.

Had she forgotten, then? Aikin felt a jolt of delight at the thought that she might have a concussion. 'I'm not sure.'

She sat up, which set off another bout of coughing. 'After you attacked me, I mean.' She glared at him. Her face was scratched and blotched, her hair tangled with rice stalks and muck. 'You really are a monster.'

He sighed. Everything would have been so much easier if she'd forgotten his attack. He shrugged, but didn't bother answering. Only fools wasted words on pointless conversations. He turned away, pulled his blanket from his saddlebag and rubbed himself down. Then he stripped and put on fresh clothes. He couldn't help noticing his hands. Chipped nails and ragged cuticles. And his ugly, useless rock skin still looked malformed. 'Well?' he spoke over his shoulder. 'It worked, didn't it? Hopefully, there's some talent left?' He turned to face her.

'I'm not...' she said, and a frown flicked across her face. 'They're gone... I can't feel the trees.'

His heart sank. It had worked too well. Next time he'd have to be more careful. Run a few experiments. Start small.

Talia put her hand to her chest as though her heart hurt. 'Wait. I think... I'm wrong. The trees are still there, but I feel all even and warm inside. And the landscape... It's hard to tell, but yes! It's still pushing me. Only it's softer. Like a cat pressing against your leg. And it isn't hard to stop a cat from knocking you over.'

Aikin smiled. 'So, it worked.'

'I'm not grateful,' Talia said.

But she was. He could tell. She didn't want to be but she couldn't help herself. Then her expression changed and she looked puzzled. 'I think someone's coming.'

He looked up. At first the path was empty, then a few moments later he caught sight of them. Soldiersisters riding towards them from the west. When they were close enough to make out, he saw there were four of them: two sharing the same horse and two riding solo. Aikin stilled his movements, let the moment unfold, thought of the words in *The Book of Kinesis*.

Leave room in your plans for the act of the Other. When the Other acts, your reaction will carry greater kinetic energy.

He thought of his new edition, rejoiced that it had remained in his saddlebag when he fell into the river. He'd have to revisit that passage. The wording had been different in the new volume, but he was yet to commit it to heart. What had it advised? Something about the possibilities offered by the Other's various intentions. Failing to recall the passage made his skin itch. But there was little he could do. And yet, even without the book's full guidance, he could see an opportunity when it rode towards him.

They were still some distance away, but Aikin knew the advice of his heart. Stand straight. Resist the urge to tidy your hair. Don't hide your ugly, ruined hands. Because the Author of the Future wouldn't fidget. And the Author of the Future wouldn't need anything beyond his own words.

Aikin found the right expression: a slight smile to convey a certainty that these sisters would obey him. Then his smile became genuine, reached his heart, as he recognised a face. One of the soldiersisters sharing the horse belonged to Whilomena. For a second, Aikin doubted himself, wasn't sure whether he could trust a Wheat soldier, a soldiersister who might have heard how Whilomena had humiliated him. But no, this woman wouldn't have heard. She was Aikin's to take and mould, which meant the other three would also be his.

'Master Aikin!' the woman shouted, recognising him.

Aikin nodded, reaching for her name and failing to find it. 'Soldier.'

'Violet Wheat,' she called out, letting go of the woman who was dinking her, giving Aikin a salute.

From the corner of his eye, Aikin saw Talia getting to her feet. Time to move. The Other had acted, and he needed to take control of the new situation before Talia got in his way, before the soldiersister came close enough for a concerned conversation. He mounted his horse and cantered off, leaving his wet clothes and Talia behind him. And she wouldn't catch up. Not without her horse. Because her horse was following him, tripping over its reins to keep up with him. How natural it all looked. How lucky he was that the path was flat and clear of trees. He had everything he needed to leave Talia behind now that he no longer needed her.

He pulled up in front of the soldiersisters. He tilted his head at Talia's horse. 'Can one of you catch that animal while Violet gives me her report?' He glanced at Violet. 'And make it concise because I'm in a hurry.' Aikin turned his head, just enough to keep Talia in his peripheral vision. She was on her feet, but groggy, making no move to follow him. Not yet.

The solider who'd been dinking Violet handed Violet the reins and slid from their shared mount to retrieve Talia's horse. Violet moved forward, easing herself over the cantle, slipping into the vacant seat of the saddle. She glanced down, shoved her feet into the stirrups. Then she met Aikin's gaze and began her report, 'We captured some rock children and a wanderer, but we lost them when a couple of Berans attacked us. We tracked them all the way to the Cava. Lost them when they hailed a barge. Our orders were to keep a low profile, so we held back, didn't let the barge see us. Then we turned east again and resumed our mission, searching for wanderers.'

A barge. A problem for this lot; an opportunity for Aikin. A path to New Lytalia. Another thought tickled. Could it be Whilomena's barge the idiots were avoiding? Perhaps this was his reward, the kinetic energy he'd been hoping for. If he could hail it, he might find her aboard. If not, he might use it to intercept her on her return journey, make her return the rock child she'd stolen. The stone would give him an advantage, might offer leverage in future negotiations. The thought rushed him. 'When was this?' he snapped.

A different soldier answered, 'Just now. You'd be able to hear the engine if it wasn't for the rivers.'

Aikin listened. There was a faint rumble. Probably just the rush of the waters, but maybe not. Out of the corner of his eye, he saw Talia take a step. Time to leave. He kicked his horse into a canter. 'Follow me!'

'What about the woman?' Violet called after him. 'Your companion?'

'Forget her! We have work to do.' He looked back and was relieved to see the soldiersisters were following. Behind them, Talia took a few more steps and then stopped, alone and bedraggled. She was too far back for him to see her expression, but he imagined the stupid girl was confused. Too confused to use her trees. That or she'd lost too much of her talent to block Aikin's path. Well, she could walk back to the last lock keeper or try to walk to the port. Neither option would hurt him. Or her. She might even use the time productively, learn to control her talent. Because the Stone Body needed all its companions, even difficult adolescents like Talia.

17

Aikin sat on his horse on the riverbank and watched the barge in front of him settle against its anchor. Whilomena stood on the deck, hands on hips, glaring at him. She was glaring, but she'd stopped the barge for him and that told him everything he needed to know. Yes, she'd abandoned him, hadn't cared about humiliating him, but that was when she'd decided she had no need of him. And now? Likely, she needed a fresh audience. Doubtless, she was sick of the one she had because she'd taken one look at Aikin and his entourage, and she'd yelled at the skipper to drop anchor. And Aikin had to admit it, he was pleased to see her too. She was a gorgeous woman even wearing a stupid costume that didn't flatter her. He felt the pull of her. He felt her reeling him in and he had to remind himself of his resolve: *Don't be the flapping shoe slapping the path, lamenting her. Don't let your heart call for her. You loved in error. Don't be stupid. Don't repeat your mistake. Walk up to her if you must, but walk your heart around her. Do what you have to do to get what you need. Keep clear of those corners where you sent her.* He was taking a liberty with the wording, but was sure Gideon Aries wouldn't object.

The breeze picked up, and Aikin's nose wrinkled. Eden's smell was overripe and made worse by the stench of rotting fruit that was wafting across the river from the Pike Companion's western bank. He sneezed and sneezed again. The port would also smell. It stank of salt and fish last time he'd visited and a place like that didn't change.

Whilomena cupped her hands around her mouth and called out to him, shouting as though the distance between them was vast, 'I'm sending a rowboat.'

'How delightful,' Aikin didn't raise his voice, but it still carried. 'I can hardly wait. But perhaps you could ask your skipper to send something more commodious. I'm loath to leave the horses.'

Whilomena looked behind her. 'Ogden! Master Oak wants his horses brought aboard. Have you got something that can ferry them across?'

A tall, rather brutal-looking woman appeared at the rail. Presumably, Ogden. The woman scowled at him, glared at his party, pursed her lips. Then she turned to Whilomena. When she spoke, her voice was rough and carried none of the respect the Wheat Companion normally attracted. If Ogden was the sort of company Whilomena was keeping, Aikin wasn't surprised his former lover had stopped to pick him up.

'We'd have to turn the stern about,' Ogden said. 'Tie up the barge, drop the loading ramp. Could be hours. Not sure you'd want that, taking all that time.'

Whilomena drew herself up. 'What are you suggesting? That I'm short of it? That I'm time poor?'

'Far be it from me,' Ogden said. 'I'm just a lowly riverhood skipper on your contract. But you've already changed our terms by taking people aboard. I have to think about the riverhood's reputation. Now you're wanting to take on five more. And horses to boot.'

'Just turn the barge and get on with it!'

Aikin caught sight of the skipper's expression as Ogden began issuing orders to the crew. More than irritation. Some sort of disgust. He wondered what Whilomena had done to set the skipper against her.

In Aikin's opinion, the manoeuvre took longer than was necessary. Ogden seemed unsatisfied with the barge's position and the keeler made endless minute adjustments. It was Aikin who suffered, not Whilomena. He really didn't want Talia to catch up with them, complicate things, and Ogden's delay was making that more and more likely. He found himself standing in his stirrups, twisting around, scanning the landscape. He hoped Talia was too sore from her tumble into the water to make much headway.

It was a relief when they led the horses up the ramp. Even more of a relief when the barge's engine shifted from its low idle to the rumbling purposeful percussion of full throttle. Aikin watched the riverbank recede and somehow the smells and the annoyances of the past few hours fell away. When Whilomena joined him at the rail and slipped her arm through his, he felt an unexpected and unwelcome gratitude.

She brought her head close to his, her breath warm against his ear. 'You followed me. How sweet. I admit, I was cross with you. But seeing you over there, calling out for my help...' She lifted a hand and caught up a lock of his hair with her index finger, tucked it behind his ear and he shivered. He told himself to pull away, but couldn't quite rouse himself. 'My cabin isn't all it could be,' she said, 'but perhaps there's room in my little bed for such a sweet little man.'

Aikin let go of the rail, forced himself to step away from her. 'It was kind of you to stop,' he said, 'but I wouldn't want to trouble you. I'll sleep on deck with the soldiersisters.'

Whilomena's expression froze. It was a good Companionari minute before she spoke, 'My soldiersisters sleep where I tell them to sleep, and they won't be sleeping with you.'

Aikin told himself to stop but couldn't catch the words before they fled his mouth, 'The days of sharing a bed are over. We are no longer engaged.'

'How quaint of you to worry about that. We slept together before our engagement. I'm sure we can repeat the practice, post-engagement.' She winked at him, reached out and cupped his face. 'There's a reason you followed me halfway across the Stone Body and I think I know what it is.'

He stiffened. 'I wanted to see what you were up to, hurrying to New Lytalia. Without me.'

'Hurrying? Hardly,' she said. 'Focused on higher matters, more like. You're the one who's rushing. You followed me because you can't resist me. When I reach New Lytalia, I'll be attending to something far more important than you. I'm on a spiritual quest. I'm taking the Komic Silence.'

'That,' he nodded, pulling away from her hand, 'yes. I'd heard about your quest.' Then he affected an expression of sudden recollection. 'Oh, that's right. I forgot. Not on your own. I believe your quest involves a moment of intimacy with one of *my* rock children.' He leant close, wanting her to feel something of the threat he could pose. 'A rock child you *stole* from me.'

She didn't cower. If anything, she looked affronted, as though he was to blame. 'I provided everything to get those rock children. Call it a fee for services. I provided the transport, moved the unwanted people, disposed of the inconvenient wanderers. I organised it. I paid for it. You owed me. I saw to it that you paid me. Simple as that.'

Aikin took stepped back, looked her up and down. 'I'm not entirely sure that red suits you. And I must say, you're ageing. Is that grey hair I see?'

Her hand went to her hair. 'Don't insult me Aikin or I might just toss you into the Cava. I believe it's quite turbulent with all the extra water from the Vagor. One wonders whether you'd survive.'

'I want my rock child back,' he said. 'You don't even know how to use it.'

'I do. You told me all about it. Endlessly. Tediously eloquent on the subject, if I recall.'

'You don't have the equipment or the knowhow.'

'Don't flatter yourself,' she said. 'I don't need you.'

'Where's the stone hidden? I want it back. Is it on the wharf? Or is it somewhere in your embassy?'

'You're so grasping,' she said, taking a step closer to him. 'I don't know why I didn't notice it before. It's unattractive. No one will want you. You're lucky I bother with you. Very well, you can have your stupid stone back when we get to port.' She gave him a self-satisfied look. 'I have plenty of my own now. And I've got something else that you might be interested in.'

Aikin opened his mouth, frowned, closed it again, and she laughed. 'Curious? You are, aren't you? You never could resist a surprise. I've found your ungrateful daughter. I was thinking of drowning her, but I haven't quite decided.'

'You've got Fox? Here? On the barge?'

Whilomena nodded. 'But not as you remember her.'

Aikin's heart raced and he wasn't sure why. Fox was nothing to him but the idea of Whilomena hurting her was intolerable. 'If you've hurt her...'

'Not at all. I'm keeping her safe, locked up with her sister and a wanderer, and his little, precious rock children. I'm full of possessions.'

'Then what's wrong with Fox?'

'Her rock skin has changed. It's quite revolting.'

Whilomena gave a long and florid description of some sort of monstrous transformation. He wouldn't have credited it but for his recollection of Mica's changed rock skin when he'd journeyed through a portal. And it was plausible that Fox had found a portal. Aikin recalled the library in Oak House and the clues he'd given her. 'So she's journeyed the Stone Body with a rock child. I need to see her. She might have a talent or a twin. There weren't any twins when you found them? There should have been. Take me to Fox.'

Whilomena held up her hand. 'No. She's my prisoner. I decide who sees her.'

'She's my daughter.'

'A daughter who ruined our lives.'

'A misguided, idealistic daughter,' Aikin said, surprised to hear himself defending Fox. Because Whilomena was right; Fox had ruined everything.

'I think I'll drown her,' Whilomena said. 'There! I've decided.'

Aikin stepped forward, came right up to the rail, put his face in Whilomena's face. 'Keep away from her.'

Whilomena lifted her hands. He thought she was going to slap him, but she pushed him. She shoved him against the rail, and he lost his balance and toppled over. He screamed without meaning to, and then the water knocked the wind out of him. When he surfaced she was standing there, alone. When he surfaced the second time, there were crew members and soldiersisters shouting and running. He caught the words *man overboard,* saw Whilomena turn away, and then someone threw him a lifeline.

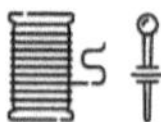

Fox had been the first to feel Aikin. He hadn't been on the barge then. On the riverbank: smug but anxious too, looking over his shoulder as though someone or something were following him. Then Saury had rock sensed him, faltered, glanced back at Fox, terror in her signature and fear on her face. Fox couldn't afford any reassuring words, not while they were still making their way through the barge's corridors. She'd waved Saury on with a quick flick of her fingers and tentacles.

Then the barge had stopped, turned about, headed for the riverbank, and the inevitable. Fox had known from the moment she felt him that Aikin would come aboard. All three of them had been frightened then because Aikin or Whilomena or someone else was just as likely to come below deck and find them. So they'd hidden in a closet during the embarkation. Somehow Fox wasn't scared of Aikin himself, but she was frightened of being recaptured and more determined than ever to get her sister and Peri away. Their luck had held. Probably the sight of the famous couple's reunion had kept the crew and the military sisters occupied, along with the business of loading the horses. Long enough anyway for the three of them to move. They'd crept onwards, slowly at first and then with more confidence, Peri still leading the way, following the call of his rock children. Above them, Aikin and Whilomena had strolled the length of the barge, oblivious to the Berans mirroring their progress below.

Peri's caution had deserted him when he reached the door of the foremost cabin. He'd thrown himself inside. By the time Fox and Saury reached the doorway, he had the stones in his hands and a grin on his face. The place was strewn with women's clothing. Expensive, wheat-coloured gowns. Fox had ducked her head at the oppressive sensation of Whilomena and Aikin standing right above them. Too close. So, they had moved across the corridor while they could, had entered the cabin opposite, and waited in silence.

'Can we go now?' Saury said.

Peri looked up, head tilted, arms loose. 'They're arguing. Angry. Really heated. Hang on! She's… She's pushed him.'

But Fox didn't need to be told. She'd felt the sharp shock of the push and Aikin's panic as he realised he was falling. There was a cry as he hit the water and she'd gasped as though it was her falling into the river. 'He'll probably be okay,' she whispered, surprised to find she'd spoken the thought aloud. 'I mean, he can swim. But the river—'

'This is our chance,' Peri said. 'We have to go!'

'Yes,' Fox said, but she didn't move and her grip on Saury's arm had tightened as she rock sensed the activity on deck. 'Oh! Okay. They've thrown him a line. They'll haul him in.' She found her heart was pounding. She forced herself to turn back to the others.

'I hope he drowns,' Saury said.

'No,' Fox said. 'Don't say that.'

Saury pulled away, dragged a chair from the desk to the porthole. Fox reached out with a tentacle and caught her. 'Wait, not yet!'

Saury turned to Peri.

'Maybe your sister's right,' he said. 'We've got to time this perfectly. Almost everyone is at the bow now. They're all looking at the water. If we jump, they'll see us. Sit tight a minute. There will be another chance when the drama subsides. That's when we'll go.'

Saury nodded and Fox felt her little sister give way. Fox let go and Saury sat down on the chair. The girl looked as though she was about to cry. Fox spoke, thinking to distract her, 'Well, at least Talia isn't with him. I can't feel her anywhere. Maybe she didn't betray us.' Peri raised an eyebrow and Fox explained about Talia's disappearance from Komey.

Then Peri held up his hand, stared into the distance. 'Okay. There you go. Won't be long now.'

Fox felt it too: Aikin was back on deck. 'The skipper's even more furious than before.'

'Good,' Peri said. 'She won't let this drag on. She'll get the crew back to work and then we can go.'

All three fell silent as they waited. Saury rested on the chair and the adults stood next to her. Above them, the heat of Aikin's anger burned. Then abruptly the riverhood and the soldiersisters surged as Aikin lunged at Whilomena.

'That's changed things,' Peri said. 'The Skipper's made some sort of decision. She's certain about something.'

Fox felt it too. They couldn't hear the words, but they all rock sensed the skipper waving her arms, directing people. The woman's conviction was running hard and sharp under her movements. The soldiersisters stepped back and most of the sailors moved off, walking toward their stations.

'I think she's arresting Whilomena and Aikin,' Saury said.

'No,' Fox said. 'Whilomena's soldiersisters wouldn't let that happen. And Aikin and Whilomena are upset with each other, but not with the skipper. And they're moving. I think she's going to bring them below deck for a stern talking to.' Fox looked at Peri. 'We should go!'

'We can't,' Peri said. 'There are still some soldiersisters at the rail.'

'But they're not looking downriver,' Fox said. 'They're watching Whilomena.'

'Not all of them,' Saury said. 'Some of them are looking at the water. And... And the rest of them are turning towards the water,' her voice was thick with despair. 'Now all of them are looking downriver.'

'It's because Whilomena has moved out of sight,' Fox said.

'They're gossiping,' Peri said. 'We'll have to wait them out.'

'Fretting about whether their precious, murderous Mother will be all right without them,' Fox said.

'Either way, we have to wait,' Peri said.

They waited, but Fox wasn't the only one with a sinking heart. She felt Peri and Saury's dismay and it matched her own. Then she voiced what they were all thinking, 'What if they come in here, into this room?' She looked at their surroundings, realisation dawning. It was a cabin, but it was also an office, a place of meetings, of dressing downs, of negotiations. 'They're coming here,' Fox said. 'We need to hide.'

'I want to go back in the water,' Saury's fear made her voice sound younger.

Fox scanned the room, but there was nowhere to hide. The desk was the only large object, and it wasn't big enough to shelter all of them. She wasted precious moments thinking about running, looking for another cabin, but she rock sensed their captors were already in the corridor with an escort of sailors. Whilomena was yelling at Aikin and Aikin was shouting at her: insult for insult. Then Fox heard Ogden's voice, telling them to shut up. A struggle broke out. Fox sensed a confusion of limbs.

'We have to go,' Fox said. 'No choice now. It's the river or nothing!' She felt Whilomena hit Aikin and Aikin push back. She was aware of Saury climbing onto the chair, of her sister's hurried movements, of the chair tipping over. Fox spun back, grabbed Saury with one hand to stop her from falling, and righting the chair with the other.

But it was already too late. The cabin door opened.

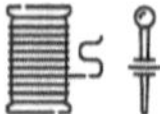

Fox stepped in front of Saury, tentacles fanned, knife already in her hand. Peri stood at her shoulder as Ogden took a couple of steps into the office. Fox watched the moment the skipper's feet caught up with her brain and she understood what she was seeing. Ogden stopped, stared, surprise on her grim face. But Fox had to give the other woman credit because she only paused for a fraction of a second. Her gaze flicked back to her three crew members ushering Whilomena and Aikin into the office. 'Hold them!'

'The Berans?' one asked.

'No. The Mother and her lover.'

Whilomena swore at the barge hand who tried to grab hold of her, slapped the woman's hand away, but Aikin stood still, watching. Then he opened his mouth to speak but didn't get a chance. A barge hand spun him about, grabbed hold of his arms and pinned them back. The other two barge hands already had a firm grip on Whilomena. The women were fast and efficient.

'And get that door shut,' Ogden snapped. 'We don't need anyone racing down here to make this office any more crowded than it is.'

The crew member nearest the door shut it with her foot.

'All right. Good,' Ogden said. 'Put Aikin and the Mother up against the wall. This needs sorting. The river comes first. And who are we?'

'The riverhood,' the barge hands answered.

'And by the Back,' Ogden said, 'no entitled trouble makers from Komey are going to sway us from our peaceful and orderly work.'

'Charming,' Aikin said. 'Laudable.' He sounded measured, but beneath the surface, Fox could feel her father was excited. That made her nervous, but she reminded herself he wasn't a physically powerful man. If he was excited, it just meant he thought he'd best everyone with his words.

Whilomena bit the hand of the woman who held her. The barge hand swore, but didn't let go, redoubling her grip. Her colleague pulled the companion's head away, held the Wheat Companion by her hair.

'Let me go!' Whilomena yelled. 'You should be catching the Berans!' Then she seemed to get her temper under control. When she spoke again, her tone was measured, 'They're my prisoners and I'm your passenger. I hold the contract.'

'Quiet,' Aikin said.

Somehow, Whilomena freed a hand and she slapped him and followed it up by spitting at him. Her spit landed on his already wet lapels and his disgust was so strong it almost hurt Fox's rock skin. Not just disgust. He wanted to hurt Whilomena, would have if he was free. Fox firmed her grip on her knife.

Then Ogden turned to Fox. Not a smile, face still stern, but the skipper's disposition wasn't threatening. She nodded toward Fox's tentacles. 'So, you got out of my hold. I thought you might. I'm glad you're still here, though. It's not safe on land. Apparently, there are soldiersisters roaming about all over the place.'

Whilomena renewed her efforts to free herself and then seemed to think better of it. She stood up a little straighter. 'Have you lost your mind, Skipper? Do I have to repeat myself? I'm your passenger, your contract. Me. And they are my prisoners.'

Ogden looked her up and down. Fox felt rather than saw the skipper's dislike. 'I didn't want to bring the Berans on deck because I didn't trust you. And I was right. Your soldiers attacked them. You imprisoned them. Then you threw a man overboard. That in itself voids the contract.'

Fox could feel Peri was about to speak. She shook her head, but it didn't stop him. 'And you, Skipper?' he said. 'You let them lock us up.'

Ogden sighed. 'A few days in the hold and we would have reached the port. Plenty of helping hands.'

Fox felt Saury's reaction to the skipper's words. The reference to helping hands was close to Bride's story and the girl's terror eased. Fox felt the hope in her sister's voice when she spoke, 'So, you're going to help us?'

Ogden rubbed her forehead, looked around the cabin as though she was seeking inspiration. 'Complicated. Lots of soldiersisters on board. I brought these two below deck to dress them down, warn them. I wasn't intending to take them into custody. Their military sisters will look for them. We're not soldiers; we're riverhood.'

'We're grateful,' Fox said.

'Gratitude is nice, but it won't save anyone's skin,' the skipper answered.

Whilomena eyed Ogden. 'Perhaps we should come to terms. Because you're right, my soldiersisters will wonder where I am. It's only a matter of time, but I'm compassionate.'

Aikin made a face, and Fox and Saury spoke at the same time: 'Don't trust her,' Fox said; 'She lies,' Saury said.

Fox took a step forward, lowered her knife. 'Please! All you need to do is return all the soldiersisters to the riverbank. Surely that's possible.'

Ogden stared at Fox, shook her head. 'Easier said than done. Besides, I can't be responsible for the damage they will do, the Berans they'll hurt. I plan to give them to the water guards when we reach the port.'

'Won't work,' Aikin said. 'Not a workable plan. You haven't thought things through. Too many variables. Find another way to be rid of them.'

'Whose side are you on?' Whilomena said.

'My own.'

The Wheat Companion looked as though she might spit at him

again, but she contained herself. Instead, she turned on Ogden. 'The Pike Companion is a great friend of mine. A great friend. She's on her way to the port right now. Walking with my sorority. I can help you. I'm the Wheat Companion. Release me. I'm in a forgiving mood. I'll double your fee, triple it.'

Fox took a step forward, knife still lowered, but ready to use it if she was forced to. 'Don't. Leave the soldiers on the riverbank without their weapons and horses. They won't be able to do much harm like that.'

Whilomena tried to talk over Fox, promising exclusive contracts, free wheat for life. Ogden told her to be quiet.

The skipper gave Fox a long look. Some of the gloom had returned to her grim-looking face. 'Easier said than done to get them off the barge. No blood on the deck. That's the riverhood code. And I'd very much like to know how to rid myself of so many military sisters without the deck getting wet.'

'I can tell you how,' Aikin said, sounding relaxed now and not a little smug.

Fox frowned. She could feel how delighted he was, so full of anticipation. 'You can't trust him either,' she told Ogden. 'He's dangerous.'

'But I can listen to him,' the skipper said.

Everyone looked at Aikin. Fox expected her father's suggestion would involve freeing him, using him as an intermediary. It didn't. Instead, he told Ogden to use him as a hostage. 'And the Wheat Companion too. Make it dramatic. Knives to throats. Plenty of threats of bloodshed. You look the part Ogden. You'd make an excellent pirate.'

'Are you insane?' Whilomena turned to him.

'On the contrary. I'm pragmatic and there's no need for all of this. I was travelling to New Lytalia. You were travelling to New Lytalia. This barge is travelling to New Lytalia. What's the problem?'

'The problem is, stupid,' Whilomena spat the word, 'we're prisoners.'

'So *now you care* about my status?' he sneered at her. 'You were quite happy to leave me in a cell in Komey and throw me overboard. Yet you expect me to believe you care about my fate.'

'You are insane,' Whilomena said.

'And you're stupid,' Aikin said.

Ogden turned to the barge hand who was standing idle. 'Two big knives. Go! Let's get those dreadful soldiersisters off our deck.'

18

The sailor yanked Mica forward and Mica tripped, almost pulling Cerulean down with him. The rock man yelped and set the air shimmering. Mica righted himself, reminded himself that he'd practised this. His hands were bound, but there was enough slack in the bindings for him to grab the rope. This time, when the sailor pulled him forward, he didn't lose his feet and nor did Cerulean. And he remembered to use his voice. He kept a stream of comforting reassurance and love flowing in Cerulean's direction.

'Shut up!' the sailor said. She didn't look back, just jerked the rope, pulling them toward the rail where the ship's crew stood in a line. None of the soldiersisters were in sight, but Mica could feel them. They were on the opposite side of the deck. He could sense their signatures. They were keeping out of the way, wanted nothing to do with the crime the sailors were about to commit. But Mica needed them closer. All the Companionaris had to be on the same side of the boat with their backs to the hatch when he and Cerulean went overboard. That was the only way the Berans could overrun the ship.

The ship's captain stood between Mica and the sea, silhouetted in front of the setting sun. She was in full uniform and she met

Mica's eye. Mica could feel her dismay, her uncertainty and shame, but she hid it well. He turned his head, looked over his shoulder at the military sisters on the other side of the boat. How to get them to come closer...

'You're part of this!' he called out. 'The Stone Body will remember you were here on this day. You can't hide. It will curse you if you don't come forward and witness this.'

'This has nothing to do with us,' the commander called back. 'The ocean is the oceanhood's business. They have their own ways. We're not on the Stone Body.'

'Please,' Mica said. 'I have a family. Please witness this and carry the story back to them.'

'You've plenty of witnesses,' the commander said, and she waved a hand at the sailors.

Mica felt some of the soldiersisters wavering. One or two took tentative steps toward him. Several craned their necks, glancing from Mica to the commander and back again. Mica renewed his appeal, careful now to keep his tone strong and respectful. 'The oceanhood aren't fit to witness this. They're our executioners. I don't blame you. You soldiersisters are as much victims as we are. If you do this one thing, you'll have my gratitude, our gratitude.'

A soldier stepped forward, but the commander turned on her. 'Not another step. No one moves.'

Mica was close to the rail now and he couldn't keep his dismay from flooding his signature. It was too late. The plan was going to fail. The Berans would emerge from the hatch and the military sisters would see them straight away. They'd kill his people. He and Cerulean would be sacrificed for nothing. And what if the slits in their rock skin weren't gills? They'd drown. All for nothing. He should never have come. He should have listened to the warning about unfamiliar stones and portals.

Mica realised he was struggling against the rope without meaning to. But it gave him an idea. If he could attempt an escape, make it look real, the soldiersisters might yet get involved? He tried to attract Cerulean's attention to warn him somehow, to reassure him, but couldn't catch the rock man's eye. Cerulean staring down at his harness, straining against it, walking backwards. Mica found himself being dragged away from the rail. The harnesses tightened, and the rock man muttered and cried, clawed at the ropes. Each cry compounded Mica's feeling of doom. Then the sailor yanked on the rope again, pulling them back toward to the rail. The air tightened, sharp and cold and brittle, and things spiralled.

Mica looked at the people in front of him and saw it happening, felt the rush of stone. Persica's fate befalling the ship. The sailor holding their rope staggered, her back bent, her hair salty white beneath her flat cap. She swayed, stared at her arthritic hands. And it wasn't just her. The ship captain's face was hollow and wrinkled and the crew's line was unsteady, hands gripping rails as sailors fell to their knees.

'Turned God save us!' the captain cried. Then she called out to the military sisters. 'Kill them! Kill them before they kill us.'

The sailors scattered, some running, others crawling as they attempted to get away. The captain ducked to avoid the soldiers' arrows, or maybe she'd fallen. Mica couldn't tell. Beneath Mica's feet, below deck, the Berans were panicking, pounding the hatch. Most of the military sisters' arrows were falling short, their hands too weak for the task, but some were getting close.

'Don't!' Mica shouted, holding his bound hands high above his head in surrender. But the sound was odd because it came from a mouth full of loose teeth. 'Wait!' he called out, and his words whistled. Then he dropped his hands and turned to Cerulean, stepped closer, put his forehead against his twin's. He told Cerulean to trust him. The chaos continued. Then an arrow hit Cerulean. It bounced off his rock skin, but the rock man screamed; a dreadful, terrified sound.

The sea churned as fish and weed began growing and dying. On deck and in the water, everything rushed. Mica felt a school of whales caught up in Cerulean's frenzy. They banged the ship as they flourished and died. Water slapped the hull, sending spray across the deck. Then the deck shuddered, cracking. People screamed.

The hatch opened. Aged and dying Berans crawled onto the deck.

There was no time left. They had to leave if anyone on board was going to survive. Mica turned, grabbed the rope connecting him to his twin. He pulled Cerulean to the rail, lifted his own bound hands, and dropped them over Cerulean's head, embracing him. The wanderer used their combined weight to pull them overboard. They fell, tumbling into the dark busy waters.

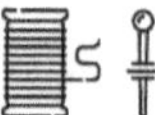

Mica woke face down in the ocean with the sun's heat on the back of his head. He jerked back, tried to right himself. The horror of it, of his face being in the water, flooded him, but he couldn't seem to lift himself. Then he realised he and Cerulean were still stuck in the embrace that had carried them off *The Crested Wave*. He looked down, saw his twin floating beneath him, eyes open, unblinking. Dead.

No, no, no!

Sorrow and regret hit Mica, but panic and the need to survive hit harder. He reared back as far as he could, flailed about, but his efforts did nothing to help. He and Cerulean were entangled and his struggles were making things worse. They were sinking. Mica shut his eyes, tried to prepare himself for death, thought of Fox, waited for the darkness to swallow him.

Nothing happened. Then Mica felt Cerulean move. Mica opened his eyes and met his twin's gaze, rock sensed strength and health, wondered how he'd mistaken life for death when life was so obvious. Cerulean blinked. Laughed. No sound, just an open smile and an eruption of bubbles.

A vision of their gills slid into Mica's mind, but he couldn't hold it. The certainty that he needed air was too strong. He kicked, frantic to reach the surface. Cerulean mimicked him and they bobbed up like corks. Mica coughed out the salty water, and then sucked in a huge and desperate breath of air, and another and another. And then, because they'd both stopped kicking, they sank.

Mica didn't know how to swim. Even if he could, his arms were bound around Cerulean making it impossible to stabilise his position on the ocean's surface, assuming he could reach it again. A part of him knew he didn't need to reach the air, not if he had gills, but his mind couldn't grasp the thought. His chest burnt with the effort of holding his breath. When he couldn't hold it in any longer, he exhaled a swathe of bubbles and then sucked in cold ocean. The shock of it stilled him and in the quiet, he felt a sucking sensation in his rock skin. Breathing. He was breathing. And, as his panic receded, he realised he could suck deeper when he needed to because his rock skin worked the water the way his lungs worked the air. Now it was his turn to laugh. No bubbles; nothing left in his lungs. But Cerulean gave him a grin. A toothy grin.

Teeth.

Mica ran his tongue around his mouth. Yes. They were back. And looking at Cerulean's youthful hair, he knew his twin had restored them, reversed the rush. The realisation filled Mica with hope.

He and Cerulean had begun drifting up again, the rope the sailor had used to pull them along the deck, trailing them.

If *The Crested Wave* was close enough, Cerulean's reversal would have worked for everyone. Mica might yet free his brothers and sisters. Then he remembered the plan. They needed to stick to the plan. No point going back to the ship until he and Cerulean had freed themselves. Abrade the ropes against rocks on the seabed. That was the plan. Mica frowned. But how did one move down on purpose? He tried to recall what he'd done when he hadn't meant to sink. He'd sunk when he'd lifted his knees. The movement had carried them down. He tried it now, lifting his legs and then extending them more slowly, more carefully. It worked. He repeated the movement, and Cerulean copied him.

They made their way, face-to-face, embraced, slipping, frog-like, to the bottom. With his feet on the ground, Mica lifted his arms over Cerulean's head, freeing them from their tight tumble into the ocean. They were connected still, harness to harness, but now they could move, turn about, walk away from each other. Cerulean danced a little jig, which stirred up the seabed and made it difficult for Mica to see the ocean floor. When the water cleared, his heart fell. There weren't any rocks. The ocean floor was a sandy desert. Worse still, when he looked up, extended his rock sense, he couldn't feel the ship. He stretched his rock sense to its limits, feeling the surface, and his heart sank. Nothing; there was nothing. Just endless ocean.

No help then. Not for the two of them and not for his fellow Berans. He would have spoken, said something reassuring to Cerulean, as much to reassure himself as his twin, but without air, there was no voice. No voice for him, but the ocean was full of sound, a strange cacophony of clicks and shudders, squeaks and thumps, and booming, bell-like tones. He turned around, looking for the source but the source was everything, everywhere: the rocking water, the fish, the sand.

Mica tried to think. Searching for *The Crested Wave* in the sea's vastness would be folly, but he had an inkling he could find his way back to the Stone Body. And once he was there, he might appeal for help, contact Willie at the Oak Embassy and organise a search party for survivors.

When he looked up this time, he searched for the sun. He found it behind his back, a white orb that rocked with the movement of the water. When he'd woken face down in the water, that sun had felt like a morning sun, the eastern sun. And the Stone Body lay to the east.

Mica faced the orb. He lifted one foot, then placed it on the sand before lifting the other. They would walk. It was slow, but they had no choice. At least with their lungs empty of air, remaining on the seabed wasn't too difficult.

Some time later, while the sun was still in the east, they came upon a rock shelf. Mica began by freeing his own hands, then Cerulean's. The rope dropped onto the seabed. Mica fingered the umbilical cord that connected them harness to harness. No, better they remain connected until they reached the shore.

With his hands free, Mica began to understand the water. He felt its weight in his rock skin, the life in it, the gusty push and pull of it. It was like walking through tall grass, like the way you could pull on the collective stalks to quicken your walk or push against them to hold you steady when the wind blew.

Mica tried a small hop and used his arms to augment it. Cerulean copied him. Soon, they were leaping, then they were kicking to lengthen their leaps. Sometimes the water surged and flung them apart or knocked them together and Mica was glad he'd kept their umbilical rope.

When the sun was overhead, they rested, waiting for it to move into the west. Periodically, he sighted along his upraised arm, trying to judge whether the sun had begun its descent, whether they could put their backs to the orb. Sometimes Cerulean mimicked Mica; sometimes the rock man ignored him, crouching in the sand and drawing swirls and lines and circles. Mica tried to make sense of the pictures his twin was creating, but the water swept them away.

When it was clear the sun was behind them, they continued their journey.

About two hours later, Mica rock sensed the Stone Body lipping the sea. The feel of it was so overwhelming he almost missed everything on it: the people moving about; the wharves and piers of what had to be New Lytalia. He rifled his memory for the location of Oak's embassy. South of the quay. He just hoped he would recognise it when he saw it.

He turned and gave Cerulean a smile, but the rock man wasn't looking. Then Mica felt it too: small shapes. Bundles of something in the water… Floating… Boats? Pleasure crafts? They were full of people. People who might have seen *The Crested Wave*.

With a renewed sense of urgency and hope, Mica half ran, half swam toward the boats. Later, afterwards, he wondered why the signatures ahead of him didn't give him pause, but they didn't. They were foggy, but familiar, but everything around him now felt foggy and familiar.

When they reached the first boat, he forgot he needed to cough up the sea before he could speak. His attempt at a greeting was a horrible gagging, vomiting splutter that seemed to terrify everyone on board. He grabbed the prow, pulled himself up to try again, and the people shrank back. Then an old man stood. He lifted his oar over his head and brought it down on Mica's hand. Mica lost his grip and fell back into the water with the memory of events on deck filling his senses.

Lifeboats. These were lifeboats and they were full of jumbled signatures that were familiar because these were people he knew: Companionari and Beranish. Familiar but wrong because they were old.

'It's okay!' Mica shouted, reaching for the prow for a second time. 'Cerulean can turn you back. We just need to reach the shore.'

The old man was on his knees now, leaning out over the water with both hands on his oar, waving it at Mica, pushing Mica away. The others huddled, moaning, crying out for Mica to show them mercy.

'I promise,' Mica tried again, 'Cerulean can fix you. Don't be frightened.'

No one listened. People began screaming, and the tiny boats rocked dangerously in the water.

'Go away!' the man with the oar yelled.

'Please,' another shouted. 'Have pity on us.'

Cerulean had caught up with Mica and his stone thoughts were jagged, painful, brittle. Mica turned and fled and Cerulean followed, the rock man's signature calming, ebbing, softening the further they went. The wanderer was aware there was someone behind them in the water. A woman had dived in after them. She was... Old, but familiar. But all of them were old and familiar.

He didn't stop. He and Cerulean needed sanctuary and time to complete their bonding process, but for now, there would be no running or half swimming. No rushing. Calm. Above all, they needed calm. Mica resumed his slow underwater walk, and Cerulean followed as they headed for the beach.

He'd find Willie. Willie would help rescue the survivors and that would give Mica time to work out what he and Cerulean should do next. And where they might find Fox and Patience and Saury. And how they might undo the damage they had done.

19

Talia stood on a flat piece of rock and looked around. Beside her, the Cava was broad, stretched wide by the inflow of the Vagor. She could see three provinces from where she stood. Eden beneath her feet. Briar across the river. And like a tongue reaching out to lap the conjunction of the rivers, the southern-most tip of Maize. Maize and Briar were busy. She could see people harvesting corn and across the river, people were cutting flowers. So normal, but vastly different from her journey to date. For too long, the world had felt empty. Not just felt. It had been empty. Kelp's people had clustered near the water's edge. Then Eden had been vacant apart from the lock keepers and then the soldiers. She supposed there was no point in Eden's Berans working the land when the produce was inedible, but their absence had been disturbing.

Talia looked north, from the flower cutters to the people harvesting corn, searching for any sign of Aikin and the soldiersisters. She used her nascent rock sense to supplement her sight. She mightn't recognise the soldiers if she saw them again, but she knew Aikin, and he wasn't in either field. Not in plain sight; not hiding.

She turned her attention downstream, but the Cava looked and felt empty, just fish and water and weed.

It wasn't a surprise. She'd watched Aikin ride away and hadn't seen him since, but she'd needed to be sure. She'd needed to look to convince herself that he was beyond her reach. She'd half expected she'd feel devastated at the confirmation that she'd failed in her role as his jailer. After all, she'd set herself one task, to contain him, and he'd escaped her custody. But instead of feeling guilty, she felt wonderfully free.

There was a choice now. She had a choice.

Her fate, escorting Aikin, had been thrust upon her but now that was over. So too was the imperative that she isolate herself to protect the world from her wild talent. What remained? She wasn't sure. Would she go to Rice Manor? She didn't think so. Rice had felt like a refuge, but she no longer needed it now she had control over her talent. Oak then? But that didn't feel right either. Perhaps one of the southern-most abandoned provinces would be the place to start afresh. Somewhere like Canis.

Talia stepped back and caught her heel on a ridge of rock. She sat down hard. The jolt brought tears to her eyes but she laughed. She'd been so busy looking for Aikin and thinking about her future, she hadn't watched her feet. She wiped away her tears. A little rice had sprouted between the rock plates, but just a fringe. The landscape still clamoured for her, pushed at her, but the gate within her was closed. It was astounding. Like a rebirth. Not even the cold weather nor the overcast sky could dampen her mood.

She stood up and this time she watched her step as she turned to walk downriver. Ahead of her, the world was empty again. She was half inclined to find a route across the Cava and join the flower cutters in their work, just for the company. It wasn't such a bad idea. She had to do something. The more she thought about it, the more she liked the thought. But getting across the Cava wasn't straightforward. Talia could swim, but she was tired and sore from Aikin's attack and the river was broad. Perhaps she could continue south and find a way across? There were structures downriver. She wasn't sufficiently adept with her rock skin to know whether she was sensing buildings or bridges or locks, but there were things downriver that weren't plants or trees, so she kept walking.

As the ground flattened, the river began to meander, slowing Talia's progress. By the end of the day, she almost regretted the decision to head south. She was hungry and tired and had seen no one at all. She told herself that she should be grateful there was no shortage of water, but it was cold comfort. And literally cold. It had been misty for hours and the ghostly damp had found its way to the roots of her hair and under her clothes. Her tunic and shirt were heavy with it, and they clung to her, chafing her skin. It was dark by the time she found what she'd promised herself would be the stone bridge. It wasn't. Instead, she stood before a cluster of long-abandoned buildings. Humble cottages that were populated by a poor selection of Eden's failing pumpkin vines.

She walked from building to building. There were five cottages. All were single room dwellings and none were habitable.

Talia stood in the doorway of the least worst cottage and couldn't help feeling lonely and a little hopeless. The walls might still be standing, but they were damp. And the roof beams had fallen in. Abandoned and unwanted; a bit like her, really. A tear trickled down her cheek and she snorted. Was her happiness at the sudden lifting of her talent's burdens so shallow that it couldn't last the day?

She spoke aloud, determined to chase away the self-pity, 'Be grateful for what you have. Make the best of it.'

She took a second look at the cottage in front of her and the world around her, but there was no escaping the fact her situation was miserable. The evening was dark, and the cottage was even darker. Clouds obscured the stars. The moon was too low to offer any light. And she was cold.

Talia closed her eyes, reminded herself to be strong, to value what she had, value what was in front of her. She opened her eyes and tried again. Now, when she looked, she saw the walls were solid.

That was something. And yes, the fallen beams and the scraggly pumpkin vines were cluttering up the usable space, and the open roof was letting in the mist, but she could fix all of that. Probably. It was worth a try.

She had avoided touching her talents since Aikin had forced the cure upon her, but she remembered the fringe of rice that had grown between the rocks when she'd fallen over. It had been small and delicate, proving she could be precise. That rice had squeezed past her control when she'd fallen. The trick would be to let go in tiny increments, try to shape the letting go instead of blasting the Stone Body.

Talia began by settling her emotions, then set to work. She used her rock sense to feel the fallen beams, to know them inside and out. When she had them in mind, she touched her abundance and drew it forward. She wrapped the beams in her attention, reducing them to humus, then to dust. When she'd finished, not even a splinter remained.

She leant against the door frame, tired but pleased. She turned to the tangle of vines in the cottage and rock sensed them. Despite her determination to remain optimistic, what she sensed left her feeling sad. Sad that such beautiful living things were so unwell. She didn't know whether her talent would work on a vine, but she half hoped it wouldn't. It didn't feel right, ending the vines' faltering life just because they were sick. She hesitated, wondered whether she could transplant one. Not in the dark, not without tools.

Talia bit the corner of her lip and thought. If... Perhaps she could work on the nearest one? There couldn't be any harm in trying. She could experiment, learn. She could try to push the vine to send a tendril out the door, then push the tendril to fruit and drop its seeds. That way, when she cleared the room, the vine's descendant could live on in its place.

She turned her attention to the closest stem. She explored it the way she'd explored the beams. That was the easy bit, but she didn't know it in the way she knew timber or rice. She and the vine didn't match. It almost felt as though the plant resisted her presence. She ignored the feeling and pushed her way inside. The hairy stems bristled and her skin itched even though she wasn't touching the plant physically. Talia withdrew and leant back against the door frame, thinking. She could push the vine. She could ignore the discomfort they both felt, but somehow that didn't feel right.

Talia licked her lips and tried again. This time, she positioned her attention just ahead of the tendril and called the vine, whispered to it with her talent. The tendril rustled and spun, stretched toward her. Although she didn't need to move, she moved. She took a step away from the door and called the vine. It followed her, new leaves emerging, everything shivering and shaking and stuttering as it traced the path of her backward footsteps. She led the tendrils deep into the landscape surrounding the cottage. Then she felt for the hidden shapes of the pumpkin vine's flowers and began whispering to them. They took shape beneath the moonless sky. Fruit swelled at the base of the flowers. She kept calling until pumpkin seeds rained to the ground. As they fell, she rock sensed the seeds and it seemed easy enough to untwist what was twisted and boost the parts that were healthy and right. Then, returning to the cottage, Talia whispered a goodbye to the vines and rotted them to dust.

She was tired now, but she hadn't quite finished. She looked around and rock sensed several acorns buried deep in the landscape. They were long dormant, but she woke six of the healthiest. Those, she grew into trees and then she harvested their acorns and carried them to the cottage, dropped them outside the stone walls and called on them to grow. She coaxed the trees into sprouting horizontal boughs, then called the boughs to lie across the tops of the walls, before detaching them from the trunks. Then she thatched the new beams with a shower of oak twigs.

She could have made a sturdy bed, could have woven a flax blanket, but she was too tired. Instead, she lay down on the earth and simply called to the trees to slip their branches through the doorway and wrap her in twigs and leaves to keep her warm.

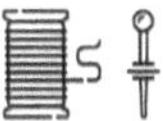

The next morning Talia stood and surveyed her work and couldn't help smiling. The oak twig thatch on the first cottage was a complete mess. Of course it was. She'd made it last night, in the dark when she was tired, when she didn't know what she was doing. Now, her roof work was more adept. It wasn't an exaggeration to describe it as joyful, beautiful even. Her most recent thatch was a swirl of floral patterns. She planned to rework the first cottage roof this afternoon, just as soon as she finished growing the espaliered oaks and corks that had already begun to ornament the exterior walls of each building. So, after lunch... And maybe after a rest. She had a mild headache. Too many complicated thoughts about how to make her espaliered oaks draw shadow patterns against the cottage walls without stressing the trees. She was being overly ambitious. Pretentious even. But she didn't care. This would be her new home. This place! And she'd make it as glorious as she wanted.

She'd woken before dawn and had been growing timber ever since. First beams and thatches for the roofs. Later, she'd worked on the interiors. Tables with curved legs, chairs with plaited backs, empty cupboards and empty beds. No mattresses, although she had a couple of ideas about that. She'd put nothing in the cupboards. Not yet. Wooden cups and plates would be easy enough, but she could do that later. When there was more time and there were more people. It was sad not having anyone with her to enjoy her new world, but that's why she'd restored more than one cottage. That was her new idea.

This place! This was her place. And she wouldn't be alone forever. People would come past on their way to somewhere else. Then they'd take a liking to her little hamlet. Like she had. This place, this bit of the Stone Body, felt good. Course, it would be complicated. She wasn't naïve. She'd need to come to some arrangement with Sorrel's sorority to remain in Eden, but Sorrel's people would let her stay. How could they not when she could help with their troubled crops? Maybe she'd choose an Edenic man to father a daughter. And she could trade with those who were passing through. Companionaris were nothing if not traders. Maybe she'd offer rice and pumpkins and other Edenic produce for fish hooks and cooking pots.

Talia paused for a moment, reached out to steady herself against her newest oak tree. She wondered whether she was unhinged. All these thoughts about making her own little world were odd; and yet they felt right. But she was tired, and she had been through a lot. It wouldn't hurt to rest and eat.

She closed off the last spurt of growth on the espaliered oak in front of her and headed for her camp fire. The soles of her feet hurt, which was stupid. She sat down too quickly, too hard, but the warmth from the fire's edge eased the pain in her feet. Thank the Back, yesterday's drizzle was gone, and the day was dry. Sharp with cold, but dry and the sky above her was clear: a wide, pale blue vista. She'd been lucky with the weather and lucky too with her find inside the furthest cottage. Three earthenware pots half buried under pumpkin vines. The best of the three now nestled in the coals, full to the brim with a mushy mix of pumpkin and rice. Her mouth watered.

She'd grown herself a spoon and two wooden oven gloves. She slipped on the gloves and lifted the pot from the coals, then shook them off and picked up the spoon. Her hand hovered over the food, but she stopped herself from dipping in. Too hot. She put down the spoon on the dirt and lay back. She'd wait a few minutes.

Talia woke some time later, stiff and sore, her mouth dry. She sat up and saw the coals were already turning to ash and the day had chilled. She shivered and put her hand to the side of the pot. It too was cold, but she was desperate to eat, so she picked up her spoon and tucked in. It would have tasted better if she'd had salt and pepper, but the meal was still wonderful and the ache in her head lifted.

After she'd finished eating, she rubbed her feet, wondering whether there was some connection between her soles and the Stone Body at the point where they touched. She would need to pay more attention to the possibility and it wouldn't hurt to slow down. Not just her racing thoughts, her work too. She reached over and put a little more wood on the fire and then lay back down. A flock of birds crossed overhead. Parley gulls. She imagined they were heading to their roost. It made her think about her own roost, her sleeping nest. She should make a proper bed and have a proper sleep. Because it wasn't just her feet that ached, her chest ached too, and her rock skin. Talia frowned. No, not her rock skin. The feeling in her arms was almost an ache, but not quite. Something was pressing against her new sense of her surrounds. Someone was coming.

Talia stood, rolled the stiffness from her shoulders. She was hungry again and thirsty, too tired to grow any more food, but the river could quench her thirst. And while she was there she could look and see who or what was coming her way.

She threw a few more logs onto the fire to keep it going, then walked toward the towpath, stretching her rock sense. Talia had assumed she'd been feeling the leading edge of a boat or a barge, but she soon realised she was wrong. Even to her unschooled rock sense, she recognised the feeling of people. People who felt as though they were in the water. She frowned, hurried her step. That couldn't be right because there was nothing surrounding them, nothing beneath them. And it didn't feel as though they were swimming, either. It made no sense. Anyone travelling the Cava would be in a barge or on a boat. So, they had to be on the land... Walking. Sometimes travellers walked. And walking made sense because these people felt exhausted. She smiled, nodded to herself. Her hamlet would have its first guests. If they were hungry, Talia would feed them. If they needed shelter, she would house them. She hurried the last little way to the towpath and looked north, but the path was empty. Likewise, the towpath on the opposite bank and the paths downriver. They had to be swimming. Must be. She sought her trees, stepped up to the edge of the bank, thinking about a bridge. She wanted a bridge, but was now the right moment? She was already exhausted. A jetty, then. Protect her strength; make only what was needed.

She stared upriver because she could feel them in that direction. They were close now, but she still couldn't see them. The structures she'd need began taking shape in her mind. Briefly she wondered whether some steps from the river to the towpath would be sufficient, but realised tired visitors couldn't be expected to swim to the bank. Not if they were as depleted as they felt.

She refocused her rock sense to check their position. She could tell there were three of them and, against all reason, they really weren't swimming. They were walking underwater. The thought sent a shiver down her spine, but she didn't let it stop her. She moved quickly, finding more acorns and growing trees. Soon, trees crowded the towpath, surrounding her, and she used her hands to help her picture the shapes she needed. She bent saplings over the river and speared their tips into the riverbed. Then she thickened those tips into solid posts and separated them from their parent branches.

Talia glanced upriver again, but still couldn't see anyone. She was glad they seemed to move so slowly because she was tired. She leant against the trunks behind her and kept going. Now, she grew beams to join the posts and then lay down planks, dovetailing them into the beams with a loud wooden clatter as they fell into place from the overhanging branches.

Talia pushed herself away from the trunks, stepped onto her new jetty. She had to grab the rails to stop herself from falling into the water. She felt sick now, almost ready to bring up her lunch, and the soles of her feet were agony.

She looked over her new structure and hesitated. It was a fine, good thing; well made. But it didn't seem to be enough, so she extended it. She made an arch in the middle and dragged herself up the arch to stand at the apex. For some reason, the smell from the opposite bank was terrible, but she couldn't work out whether she was sick or whether there was something bad in the air.

The visitors were closer now, and they *were* in the water, and they *were* walking. She'd felt it, but seeing it made it feel impossible.

And the feel of them... Awful. Wrong. Or maybe it was just her nausea that was messing with her rock sense. Talia bit her lip. The strangers felt like hunger and sorrow and fear. Then the feeling was on top of her as they came into view. They walked, step by slow step, three shadows beneath the water. Talia called out and one looked up. Talia's fingers dug deeper into the handrail. It was impossible, but it was Fox, walking underwater with no recognition on her face. Then Fox, if she was Fox, dropped her gaze to the riverbed and continued walking, her need still pressing against Talia's rock skin, making it ache. And she didn't stop. None of them did. Talia had forgotten the ladder!

The three of them passed under the arch and Talia realised what she should have realised from the beginning: it wasn't Fox. And the others wouldn't be any of the other Berans she knew. These were twins without their people. Talia's grip eased now that she could make sense of what she was seeing, but her worry didn't leave her. If Fox and the others weren't with their twins, then something had gone wrong.

Without knowing her plan, just feeling it, Talia called on the last of her reserves and began working her trees once more. She shook the ones growing beside the towpath until they flung their acorns in every direction, raining them down on the river, hundreds of them. Then Talia felt for the ones in front of the twins' path and she grew steps, steps that curled around and back and joined her jetty.

The twins ascended stairs. Fox's twin in front and, behind her, Saury's twin. Talia was pretty sure that last one looked like Patience. She racked her brain for a way to reach them, get them to notice her. What had Mica said? Welcome them and name them.

There was no time for anything considered. She had to be quick.

She pointed at Fox's twin, 'Welcome to the Stone Body. I name you Amber for the colour of Fox's hair.' The rock woman stopped and looked up, really looked. It wasn't recognition, but it was seeing. Talia felt the air tighten, didn't know whether it was for good or ill. All she knew was she needed to hurry. She pointed at Saury's twin. 'And you, you're welcome too. I name you…' Talia hesitated, reaching for a name, any name. Then she remembered the colour of the sea in Kelp and then she had it. 'Cyan… Cyanna! I name you Cyanna because the sound of it will make Saury smile.' Saury's twin stopped, looked up. The last twin was still oblivious. Talia held up her hand to call him to a halt, forgetting for a moment that it required words, not actions. He was almost on top of her when she spoke a welcome. But she didn't know what to call him. Some horse-related name, but what? He was so close Talia could smell the river on him. 'And you, you're also welcome.' The rock man cocked his head and Talia's heart raced. The air didn't feel right; everything smelt terrible, and she was beyond exhausted, ancient with fatigue. And she still hadn't thought of a name. Then she remembered a fourth story about a horse trainer. 'I name you Baylor for Patience's province and his love of horses.'

Baylor smiled, and the air eased.

'Welcome, all of you. Welcome to my home. There is a place for you here. I'll look after you. We'll find the others, but you're safe with me.'

20

Fox was grateful for the uneventful nature of life on the barge now that Ogden had reasserted control. Thankful for the food, for the time to recover her strength, for the slow changes in the landscape as they travelled downriver, and for the comfortable beds in their cabin. But none of it eased the sense that Fox should run, take Saury and Peri and run. And yet, there was no obvious danger.

Ogden had left the soldiersisters on the riverbank, horseless and weaponless, just as promised. She would have confiscated Fox's weapon too if it wasn't for a quick sleight of hand on Fox's part, and the loan of Saury's lace collar. It gave Fox comfort, feeling the knife wrapped in lace, hidden in her hair. But Ogden's sense of even handedness also extended to setting Whilomena and Aikin free. The two of them moved about the barge as though nothing untoward had happened. Fox abhorred Whilomena, but without her militia, the Wheat Mother was toothless. It was Aikin who disturbed Fox. She still didn't fear him physically, but she knew his ways and feared them.

Her father seemed to be everywhere, all the time. Talking. Making helpful suggestions. Aiding the crew in their work, displaying a disturbing talent for knots and rope. And when Fox wasn't watching him work, she was hearing him share just the right quote from *The Book of Kinesis*. That first night, he shared his insights with the cook. The next morning, he extended his reach to the mechanic, the barge hands, and Saury. Saury! Fox worried he'd infect them with his sincerity and his regretful but ruthless fanaticism. She was glad he no longer had the book itself. It was much safer in Komey, in Beranish hands, under Quartz's watchful eye. And then there was his laughter at mealtimes. It grated. He sat near enough to Ogden for the skipper to hear his jokes. Initially, Fox felt Ogden's careful reserve holding Aikin's charm at bay, but by the time the skipper was folding her napkin after that first breakfast, her grim face was almost easy under Aikin's seductive stories.

Worst of all was the feeling of Aikin's gaze on Fox's and the unasked questions it implied about her rock skin and the missing twins.

Fox relied on her rock sense to avoid her father, but on the afternoon of the second day the barge reached a lock and she found herself on the Edenic towpath, standing between Aikin and a barge hand, being instructed on how to close the paddles on the lock's lower gate. Aikin had convinced someone, likely Ogden, that Fox had a lifelong interest in the operation of locks.

'Why am I here?' she hissed when the barge hand disappeared to fetch a handle to work the lock's mechanism. 'You don't need me. Don't include me in your plans. Run off if you're running off.'

'Why would I run off? I told you yesterday, the barge is taking me where I want to go.'

'To New Lytalia?' The scepticism in Fox's voice sounded whiny and complaining, even to her own ears. 'Seriously? I don't believe a word you just said. You're such a liar!' She hadn't heard or felt the barge hand return, but Fox certainly felt the woman's censure and then made it worse by trying to explain, 'I'm sorry,' she turned to face the hand, 'but you don't know him. You can't believe a word he says. He murdered my friends.'

The woman's weather-worn face paled. 'Murder?'

'Friends who are miraculously still alive,' Aikin said, full of good cheer. 'For which, I'm grateful. I don't enjoy killing people.'

'But you do kill people,' Fox said, 'don't you?'

'Only when there's no other choice.'

The hand gave Aikin a wary look and put a little more distance between herself and Fox's father. Then the woman cleared her throat and resumed the lesson on operating locks, her voice stiff and forced, her accent suddenly thicker, 'So this here bottom paddle has to be closed so water don't run out, like. And then we's open top paddle and top water flows in. Gets high enough and we's bring in them barge.'

Fox looked past the woman to the top gate. Its wings were closed, pointing upriver, a chevron against the weight of the water. Her explanation finished, the barge woman bent and fitted her handle to the poppet-like device that controlled the bottom gate's paddle. She eyed Aikin and, reassured that he hadn't moved, gestured for Fox to take a turn at the handle.

Fox stepped up, took hold of it expecting it to be difficult. It wasn't. The poppet clicked as she wound it and she rock sensed an actual paddle turning underground, below their feet, closing, stopping the water running downriver. Then the barge hand led them to the top gate.

The three of them watched the water level rise in the lock. It wasn't companionable. Fox's feelings had settled somewhat, but she kept her rock sense open, alert to any tricks Aikin might have in mind. And the prickling in Fox's arms coming from the barge hand suggested the woman was even more wary than she was. Then, without warning, Aikin reached out and patted Fox's shoulder. 'See? I knew you'd find it interesting. I always know what you're going to like, and you like seeing how things work.'

Fox slipped out from under his hand and sensed a slight dimpling in his signature. It was only present for an instant, then somehow he transformed it into a burst of enthusiasm: happiness, pleasure, joy. Worse still, love. He actually seemed to love her. She hadn't known. It was only now her rock skin had matured that she could tell. Fox didn't know what to make of it and hated herself for caring, wished she could excise the part of her that hadn't wanted him to drown and still sought something from him. It was then that she noticed the air, some sort of sickening smell. For a moment, her nausea had her worried, but when she checked, the suppression was still holding her pregnancy quiescent.

'Pay attention Fox,' Aikin said. 'The hand wants your help again.'

Fox looked up and saw Aikin was right. The barge woman was poised, ready to lean her weight against the horizontal post that worked the nearest wing of the upper gate. The woman had kicked a couple of sickly looking tomato plants out of the way, clearing the towpath. For a moment, Fox supposed the split fruit had caused the taint in the air, with its blackened, weeping hearts. But when she sniffed the air, the tomatoes didn't seem to be the source.

The barge hand patted the post beneath her hands, recalling Fox. 'Help me push this'un.'

Fox hurried over to help. To her horror, Aikin came too, grinned at her, clamped his hands down beside hers.

'On three,' the barge hand cried. 'One... Two... Three!'

They pushed and Fox felt the gate move. It wasn't until a few moments later, she realised the barge hand and Aikin had stepped back. She was opening the first half of the gate on her own. She couldn't help smiling. It was so clever. So well designed.

With the Edenic side open, the barge hand led them over a walkway to the other bank to work the second wing.

Everything was so much worse. In the way of all the Stone Body's borders, the change was abrupt. On this side of the river, Briar's flowers carpeted the towpath. There were poppies and peonies, roses and daffodils, and too many other blooms to name. Beautiful, but the air was terrible. Evidently, the river's breeze had been protecting them. Now they were in the thick of a shocking stink.

Fox looked at the barge hand.

The woman shrugged. 'Happens sometimes. Growing things. Dying things. All sorts along river.'

'So it's normal?' Fox asked.

'Like as not,' the woman almost sounded cheerful, but her voice was tight and her actions belied her words. She practically threw open the second wing of the upper gate and didn't invite their help. And then she turned and hurried away, leaving them to follow.

Aikin put a hand on Fox's arm, as though he would hold her back, share his thoughts. She shook him off, ignoring his hunger to talk. Instead, she followed the barge hand, climbing the steps to the walkway.

'I'd hoped we might reconcile,' he spoke to her back. 'That we might speak.' The past pulled at her and Fox felt an urge to turn back, but she forced herself to keep walking. 'We should pool our knowledge,' he said. 'It would benefit the Stone Body.' When she remained silent, Aikin sighed and tucked his emotions away. He spoke again a moment or two later and his tone had lost its persuasive edge, 'You asked the barge hand about the smell, whether it's normal.'

Her steps slowed, but she didn't turn around. 'Yes.'

'You were right to be worried,' he said. 'Eden's failing. Anyone with eyes knows it's failing.'

'But the smell isn't from Eden—'

'Let me finish. It's connected. It's something worse than Eden. Not Briar, obviously. Their flowers are fine.' She turned, and he smiled and waved a hand at the bank behind them. 'Something further inland, I think. A calamity.'

Fox resumed walking. She wanted to hear what he meant, but she wanted the river's breeze to carry away the smell, so she didn't slow until she reached the midpoint on the walkway and could breathe again. She looked back. 'Okay? So? What are you saying?'

'What if it's your solution?'

'What do you mean?'

'We know the cost of creating companions my way. We don't

know the cost of using portals. And everything has a cost.' Fox didn't answer. She looked down at the barge, watched it moving beneath them as it eased its way into the lock and she thought about the lost twins, wondered whether they were a cost. Aikin was still talking, 'We should pool what we know. Tell me what happened in Kelp. Clearly, you found a portal and then things fell apart when you used it. You're alone and you shouldn't be. What happened to your twin and your sister's twin?' There was hunger in his question. Greediness. Her arms prickled with the intensity of it. He didn't want to help her, just extract her information. She started moving again. Better to keep silent, get back onto the barge, find Mica when she reached New Lytalia, assuming he'd made it to the port. Certainly, Aikin couldn't be trusted.

Behind her, Aikin started quoting from his murderous book:

The forest is full of song. And full of wings and beaks and scrabbling feet; and fur and snouts and claws. The Hunter dies when she falls for the music, when she fails to reach for her knife.

Fox told herself not to ask, but she asked: 'Meaning?'

He didn't answer immediately, but she heard his footsteps hurrying to catch up. Then he grabbed her, pulled her to a standstill and leant in, whispered in her ear. 'I'm a knife and you're about to be eaten. We all are. So what are you going to do? Push me away because you prefer to wander around listening to some pretty song about magical stones and portals?' He didn't wait for her to respond, just pushed past her. By the time she stopped shaking, he was walking along the Edenic bank with a bureaucratic stroll that suggested nothing worse than surveys and measures: nothing more alarming than the possible impost of taxes and tariffs. But her arm almost rang with the threat in his touch.

Aikin stepped onto the slow-moving barge. She heard him asking Ogden questions about the river as the skipper settled *The Meandering Queen* in the lock.

By the time she stepped back on deck, the barge was dropping down to meet the river. Fox went below. She stayed in the cabin, insisted Saury and Peri do the same. She wasn't sure how much risk there was in associating with Aikin or in breathing in the awful air on the western side of the Cava, but his story made her afraid.

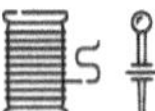

The barge passed through three more locks before the Cava wound its way west, heading for the sea. The further they travelled, the more the lingering undertone of rot eased, giving Fox some space to think. She'd been worrying about the twins since her conversation with Aikin. Her decision to flee Kelp no longer felt justified, and she longed to talk to someone about undoing it, looking for them. She had half a mind to share her thoughts with Peri, but not when Saury was listening. Her sister had been through enough without adding to her worries.

So, they sat, almost silent, in their cabin. Saury rested on a bunk, beneath the porthole, watching the night descend. Soon, her eyes were heavy and her breathing deepened. Fox motioned to Peri. He looked up questioningly and Fox pointed to Saury and then gestured to the cabin door. They stood up quietly and Fox led Peri into the corridor, closing the door behind her.

Fox opened her mouth to share her thoughts about searching for the twins, but found there was something more pressing she wanted to say, 'We need to leave the barge.'

'Good,' he said. 'Let's go. We should wake Saury.'

'I thought we should wait until we're closer and past the smell of rot.'

He shrugged. 'We're almost past it now. Besides, you're not sick. I'm not sick. Neither is Saury. And we'd best not wait.'

'It wasn't the smell itself that worried me.' Fox shook her head. 'It's the mystery behind it. I don't want us stepping into something we don't understand. Something that might hurt us.'

Peri frowned, leaned his bony back against the wall. 'I still think we should go. The port is a risky place for us. Berans aren't welcome at the best of times. And these aren't the best of times. The longer we wait, the more people will be around. More chance of being seen.'

It made sense, but the memory of the barge woman's anxiety about the smell emanating from the north, and Aikin's talk of a calamity, worried her. Her father had been using whatever means he had to frighten her into an alliance, quoting from his horrid book to convince her she needed him, but there'd been truth in some of the words he'd shared. There always was with Aikin. The portals were an unexplored forest and Aikin said forests were dangerous. 'Have you smelt anything like it before?'

Peri hesitated, 'Not exactly, but it's probably just decay.'

'I think something might have gone wrong in Persica.'

'In Persica? Why?'

'Two of their wanderers went into the portal before I did. We'd all agreed to keep back if we weren't bonded to our stones. One of the Persican wanderers said something about not being sure about the stone that was calling him. He left before anyone could stop him. He didn't seem able to help himself.'

Peri frowned and hesitated. 'Okay. I can see why that would worry you when we are so close to Persica. But we can trust the Stone Body.' He glanced at Fox, half hopeful; half worried. 'I'm sure it knows what it's doing.'

'Trouble is,' Fox said, 'I'm not so sure it's thinking of us. We're not living a fourth story. This is the real world.'

'But the rock man you told me about, Obsidian, you said he was good and kind, so what could go wrong?'

'*Good and kind* doesn't guarantee a happy ending. Besides, Obsidian was...' Fox looked up, rested the back of her head against the corridor wall, tried to work out what it was about Obsidian that worried her. 'He was... You could see how things might go wrong, accidentally. He understood some things, what he wanted and didn't want, but the rest...'

'And your twins?'

The question hurt. This was the core of her deep unease. 'I don't know. I wish I knew.' She should have put Saury somewhere safe and returned to Kelp to search for them. The decision to flee was reckless and selfish, like abandoning newborns. The feeling churned inside her, made her want to turn back. Fox realised she'd crossed her arms and unwound her tentacles. She was stroking her skin as though she was comforting a child. She laced her tentacles back around her wrists. The question was, should she turn back now or later? Impossible to know. She wondered why she'd never thought to use her rock skin to look for them. They could have followed her. She closed her eyes and opened her rock sense, searched the river.

She felt the barge and the people within it. Beyond the barge, she felt the water stoking the hull and the solid edges of the land. She pulled her rock sense away from the land, focused on the water. Fish and weed and rocks. Locks and more and more water... Then her senses frayed as she reached her limits. Not even a hint of the rock people. She should never have left them. But Kelp had been dangerous. Dangerous for her and Saury and the baby. She dropped her consciousness down to steady her feelings, felt the comforting quiescent presence of the baby: neither growing, nor fading.

Peri coughed. Fox opened her eyes and looked at him. 'Felt you looking,' he said. 'I can't feel them either. What were they like?'

'I never saw them...'

'But you felt them. Surely? When you first arrived? Before they disappeared? Was there something about them that worried you?'

'No. I should have stayed and searched for them, found a way.'

'Your signature is full of shame. But you felt them, and maybe there was something disturbing about them because I can sense you're relieved they aren't here.'

'That's not true.'

'It is.'

Fox groaned. Of course, he was right. 'They were... Well, obviously they were frightened.'

'And?'

'They felt volatile. Dangerous. But it's no excuse. I should never have left them.' As she spoke the words, she knew she spoke the truth. She had made a shocking, unforgivable error of judgement.

Peri said nothing, but Fox rock sensed he agreed with her assessment. When he spoke, his voice was kinder than she deserved, 'What you do now won't undo what you did then. But now also matters.'

'You think I should go back?'

'I can't answer that. It's your question.'

Fox thought about it. There was only one answer: 'I've come this far. I need to keep going for a bit longer, find Mica if I can, if he's in the port, and then I can go back to look for them.' It wasn't just her need to see Mica again. She needed someone with more experience with portals and rock people. While it was possible that he was still in Komey, she felt certain he would have been called and his call would have taken him to New Lytalia. And afterwards, after they'd spoken, she would go back and search for the twins. Her sister could stay with Willie in the Oak Embassy. Mica too, if he was needed in the port. But she would return to the rivers and try to undo the harm she'd done.

She turned to Peri. 'Thank you. You've given me a lot to think about. We should try to rest.'

'We should leave now,' he said.

She shook her head. 'We're too close to Persica. And if there's been trouble there, we should avoid it.'

'We'll be even closer when we're in port. Persica's territory almost reaches the Cava in some places.'

'But we'll have friends in port. We can get help and advice. We won't be alone.'

He nodded. Not happy, but resigned. She led the way back into the cabin and Peri followed. Fox crawled into the bed beside Saury as Peri made his way to his own bed.

The porthole was dark when Ogden woke them, whispering that the quay was close. The three Berans pulled on their tunics and tightened their belts. They'd abandoned their shoes during their swim in the Kelp River and there wasn't anything else to carry or fasten. They used their rock sense to hide the sound of their steps so that anyone who was awake would only hear the skipper's familiar tread and they'd be reassured all was well.

The deck was silent and the dawn air was cold, but the sky was opening.

'I love this part of the river,' Ogden spoke softly. 'We'll be at Pike's border in a few minutes and the scent will change. Pike smells like its port, but while we're here, it costs nothing to enjoy the Briar Companion's bounty. And thank the Back that stink has almost gone.'

Fox looked up. The sky had transitioned from dark purple to bright crimson. She should have asked Ogden earlier, but it was only now that the day was dawning and they were leaving that she thought to ask about the port's politics. 'Are they close?' Fox asked. 'The Briars and the Pikes?'

Ogden's signature almost laughed at the idea, but her expression remained grim. 'Have you met the Pike Companion?'

'I know her,' Fox said. 'Yes.'

'Then you know she could not be an easy neighbour.'

'And the Briar Companion?' Fox asked. 'I've not met her. I don't think she's often in Komey.'

Peri and Ogden spoke at the same time:

'Lovely,' Peri said.

'Different,' Ogden said. 'She visits her fields now and then, comes right down to the riverbank to check her flowers. So I've met her. Close to her Berans. A bit like your Oak Mother, but perhaps a little softer.'

'That wouldn't be difficult,' Fox said.

'The border is close now,' Ogden said. 'You need to go.'

Fox turned and looked downriver. There was a distinct line where the Briars' blooms ended and scrubby coastal grasses began, but here and there flowers were growing in clumps, intruding into

Pike's territory. In the distance, she could just make out the port. The sun had risen, turning the buildings gold. Even the humble fishing shacks looked magical.

'Off you go,' Ogden said. 'See you fetch up on the north bank. There aren't any buildings there, just scrub and trees. It's sheltered enough for you to walk all the way to the beach without being seen. Then, if you don't mind a swim, and I know two of you don't, swim out a bit before you cross the Cava's mouth. Then head to your embassy's boat ramp and keep your wits about you.'

21

Mica and Cerulean were in the shallows now, but still attached, harness to harness, via their umbilical rope. Step by step, they approached the beach. It should have been a happy moment for Mica, but he was consumed with worry for the survivors of *The Crested Wave*: whether they'd be all right; whether he'd find help for them in the port. And had all of them reached lifeboats? Perhaps some were still in the sea. As his head broke the surface, the chill winter air was so cold and intense, his scaly rock skin lifted in a mimicry of goosebumps. He felt breathless, exhausted, unsteady on his feet. He coughed, clearing the water from his lungs. Then his gills closed tight. Better. Still tired, but orientated to the airy world, capable of seeing and thinking. Cerulean seemed to manage the transition more easily.

It was then Mica caught sight of what was ahead of him... No, not what: *who*. A familiar and beloved figure was sitting on the beach, looking dazed. Against all odds, Quartz was sitting on the sand, rubbing his face and rolling his shoulders as though he'd taken a tumble. Mica's worry almost fell away at the sight of the old man, but then Cerulean halted abruptly, jerking Mica to a standstill.

The rock man was staring at the beach, a concentrated stillness in his expression. Mica followed his gaze and realised Quartz wasn't alone. Doubt was with him. The boy must have been lying on the sand, but he was upright now. Mica wanted to call out a greeting but didn't. Too worried about Cerulean's reactions. But he got his twin moving again and together they jogged forward, crashing through the waves, jumping the wavelets, Cerulean sharp and focused on the scene ahead.

Doubt raised an arm, flung it about as though Mica was blind and Mica put his finger to his lips, hoping the boy would get the message or rock sense the need to be careful. He must have, because he didn't shout, just hurried to Quartz and pointed at them, helping the old man onto his feet. Then, behind the pair, closer to the dunes, two more people rose from the sand, and now Mica understood Cerulean's intensity. The closest figure was Oria, but more importantly, the second figure was Oria's twin.

'Steady,' Mica spoke to Cerulean. 'Everything is going to be fine. They're friends. All of them. They must have just arrived.' He shook his head. As though his twin understood, could judge such things. Mica couldn't help recalling Obsidian and how different this would have been if he were here. He would have laughed or tousled Mica's hair, but Cerulean did none of those things and his jog slowed to a toy soldier march, his gaze fixed on Oria's twin.

Oria had her back to Mica, hadn't seen him, but even from the back, still inhabiting Promise's body, the wanderer had no trouble telling her apart from her twin. She stood, legs apart, her right fist on her hip. No doubt she thought someone needed bossing about, probably the poor rock woman in front of her. He'd seen Oria looking like that in Oak and Komey and too many other settings to mistake her, always looking as though she was planning a difficult parley with a fraught guest list. Her rock twin on the other hand was like sea grass in the wind. Fluid, full of movement, never mind she was standing still. Her face was turned to the sea and she seemed unaware of Oria's attention.

Mica moved closer to Cerulean and reached for his hand but

missed it as the rock man's march picked up pace. Never mind. This was perfect. Oria would use her authority to marshal the search party for the lifeboats and those still lost at sea. Everything would be all right; as right as it could be. Mica called out to Cerulean to slow down. He didn't want the rock man to startle Oria's twin. Cerulean didn't seem to hear him. The rock man strained at the rope that joined them and when they reached the shore, Mica had to run up the wet sand to keep up. And Cerulean looked odd. His hands were pressed together, palm to palm, fingers pointing down. Fingers splayed. There was something about it that felt unnatural. Mica gave the rock man his full attention. Cerulean's gaze was still fixed on the beach, on the rock woman, but he was moving slowly now. His twin gave a jagged intake of breath and Mica wondered whether this was Cerulean recognising his own kind, whether this was a prelude to a greeting. The rock man's signature sharpened and he came to a halt.

'Friends,' Mica said, feeling an edge in Cerulean's reaction. 'Our friends, all of them.'

Then Oria turned, caught sight of Mica and her signature bristled. 'You? I have half a mind to slap you. I told you to stop, you impetuous idiot! But you ran into the portal. Ran when you were told not to run. What were you thinking?'

'Well,' Quartz said, sounding surprisingly jolly, 'it seems there's no harm done. We're all here and we're all alive. That's one less worry. I wasn't sure. I thought Oria lost her grip on you and that's why we didn't see you when we awoke. Dumped you in the water, eh? Bet that was a shock.'

Mica frowned. So he *had* been followed into the portal. But time had treated them differently.

Oria turned to Quartz. 'And you didn't help. What were you thinking, chasing after me like that?' She rounded on Doubt. 'Or was that you? Did you grab hold of me?'

Doubt looked pleased with himself. 'Yes, because everyone knows that you're not meant to go on adventures on your own, Huntress. Not when you have friends.'

Oria's signature softened. 'You're an idiot boy with no business jumping into portals.'

Doubt turned to Mica, gave him a conspiratorial grin. 'Me and Quartz are here even though we didn't have stones. That's why we don't have twins. Oria carried us. It's a brilliant discovery. You don't need to walk from place to place ever again. You can go from Komey to New Lytalia as quick as a tree falling over on a windy day.' He looked back to Oria. 'We *are* in New Lytalia, aren't we? I thought we would be. Do you have a name for your twin? I could name her for you. I know lots of the best names for baby girls.'

'She's not a baby,' Oria snapped. 'And she's Laurel. Laurel Oak.'

Doubt made a face. 'Shouldn't she have some sort of fishy name? She was born on a beach and you've both got scales.' The boy pointed at Oria's arms and the old woman looked down, frowned at the new rock skin on Promise's arms. From where Mica stood, it was hard to be sure, but it looked like the skin Cerulean had gifted him, only a little more colourful. Then he realised Oria's twin was staring at Cerulean and she no longer seemed fluid. Instead, she seemed frozen, her hands pressed together, palm to palm, pointing at her feet, fingers splayed and straining.

'Who's that with you?' Quartz asked Mica.

Mica frowned, but before he could introduce Cerulean, Oria started talking again, 'At least we don't have to go searching for you,' she said. 'Thank the Back for neat stitches.'

That was when Mica realised Quartz was staring past Mica at something behind him. Mica turned. A woman, familiar but aged. Lupe. So, someone *had* jumped into the water after they fled the lifeboats. He'd been right.

Before he could lift a hand to greet her, he felt himself jerked forward. The rock man was moving again, his signature ripe with purpose. Mica felt himself being dragged across the gritty sand towards Laurel and picked up his pace. Cerulean's attention felt sharp as a hunter's, as driven as prey. It didn't feel right. It reminded Mica of the last moments on the ship's deck. He came level with his twin. A soft word from behind reminded Mica Lupe would help. But from the corner of his eye, he saw something bizarre and knew it might already be too late. Doubt was taller, and Oria and Laurel were more obviously pregnant. The rush! He couldn't let it happen again.

He reached out for his twin, remembering to use his voice, 'Slowly dearest Cerulean,' he crooned, resting a hand on his twin's shoulder. 'Steady Beloved.'

'Good work,' Lupe spoke quietly, her voice still some distance behind them.

The rock man seemed to listen. At least his hands relaxed, and the people on the beach were no longer ageing before Mica's eyes. He and Cerulean had reached the soft, dry sand now and the rock man rocked on his feet. For a moment the world was silent.

'Did I hear you correctly?' Quartz's voice was stiff with age and disapproval. 'Did you call your twin Cerulean?'

Mica nodded and began introducing everyone, careful to keep his voice warm and welcoming, 'This is Quartz,' Mica directed Cerulean's attention to the senior wanderer. 'And that's Doubt.' Then Mica gestured at the pair in front of them. 'And here are Oria and Laurel. And behind us is Lupe. You remember Lupe, don't you?' Cerulean didn't respond, so Mica let go of his twin's shoulder and reached out and took hold of his chin, gently turned his face. Cerulean gave Mica a blank look and pulled away, returning his attention to Laurel. The rock man's signature was full of anticipation and longing, but at least he'd stopped rocking. Mica gestured for Lupe to come closer.

Quartz was speaking again, oblivious to Mica's efforts to keep the tone soothing, 'Cerulean! When you told me that it was your schist that called you into the portal? Are you asking me to believe you named your schist Cerulean? This is your turquoise rock child, isn't it! You ignored the rules. You lied to me. And what about Saury and the others? If your foolishness has hurt them...'

'It hasn't. Not them, anyway. I haven't seen them,' Mica said, doing his level best to keep his voice even and his emotions in check.

'I've been here. For days. On a ship. With Lupe.' But Quartz's disapproval and his question about Fox's whereabouts made Mica's heart sink. A desperate worry seized him, but he couldn't afford that feeling. Not with Cerulean so reactive. He forced himself to let go of his guilt and his anxiety about Fox. He'd done what he'd done. Fox would take care of herself. And Saury. And Patience would help. Fox wouldn't be alone.

He thought he'd managed it, had settled himself and his twin, but then Cerulean let out a long chain of uneven clicks and a wave of rock thought hit Mica. He hadn't realised until now that rock thought had been missing from Cerulean's repertoire. Unlike Obsidian, his new twin hadn't pushed his thoughts at Mica. Was it a good sign that he was doing it now? Did it mean they'd bonded and Cerulean was trying to communicate? Quartz was talking, still asking questions. Mica held up his hand. 'Not now. Please don't. This is complicated enough.'

Quartz's signature tightened. He looked from Mica to Oria and Mica sensed Quartz was only now taking in the sight of Oria's rapidly advancing pregnancy. 'Stone Body save us,' he muttered. 'Not Persica again.' He took a step back, eyeing Cerulean, pulling Doubt away, pushing the boy behind him. Then he took another step back, gesturing for Oria to do the same. 'You didn't know your turquoise well,' he said, keeping his voice low and even. 'You weren't properly bonded and there's been a cost. Something's happening here. Another Persica. And what of the ship? Were our people aboard? Are they all right?'

'I... There was a rush, yes, but not a complete disaster. Bad, but not as bad as Persica. I think Acacia was right. Frightened rock twins overreact. There was an incident on the ship, but only because Cerulean was threatened. He's okay when there isn't a threat. He'll be okay now if we keep calm.'

Quartz continued walking backwards and he gestured for Oria to follow his example, move away from the rock twins. Oria was still ignoring him, glaring at Mica. When she spoke, she was careful not to scare the twins, but her meaning was full of judgement, 'I seem to remember Acacia was making the point that transformed rock children need known and trusted wanderers. You've acted true to form. Ignored advice. Put people at risk.'

Lupe came to rest at Cerulean's other shoulder. She didn't waste time acknowledging Mica. She ignored the conversation and focused on the rock man, whispering endearments. Cerulean didn't acknowledge her. He'd turned his head and was staring at the port. Mica followed his twin's gaze. There, in the distance, he could see the shipwreck survivors. They'd reached land and were making their uneven way along the beach to the wharf. It was a welcome sight, but they didn't seem to be the target of Cerulean's gaze. And yet there was no one else in his line of sight, neither Beran nor Companionari.

Mica turned to Laurel. Oria's twin mirrored Cerulean. She, too, was gazing at the port.

The air thickened, and in moments it felt as though something was coming alive. To Mica's eyes, nothing had changed, but to his rock skin the air between the two magical creatures felt lattice-like. An invisible web had sprung up between the pair.

'What are they doing?' Doubt asked. 'Should they be doing that?'

'I don't know,' Mica said. Cerulean hadn't moved, was still gazing at the port.

Oria spoke, 'Something's not right. This feels dangerous.'

Quartz cleared his throat but kept his voice low, 'Whatever they're doing, I think you should try to stop them. I'll get Doubt out of here.' He reached for the boy, but Doubt dodged away. Cerulean's signature sharpened and Mica did the only thing he could think of doing: he joined Lupe, began murmuring reassurances. For a moment, Mica thought it was working because Cerulean shifted, swung his head from right to left. But the movement was all wrong. It was sweeping, abrupt.

'Did you see that?' Doubt said. 'They moved at the same time. They're like birds. They're turning their heads like birds.'

'Courting,' Lupe said.

Oria put her hand to her mouth. 'Turned God, I think this is the start of some sort of dance.'

'They're not supposed to dance,' Doubt said. 'Remember. That was one of the things they're not supposed to do.'

'No, that was us. We weren't supposed to dance,' Quartz said. 'Not sure about rock people, but maybe they shouldn't.'

The twins turned their heads again, north to south. Now, there was no mistaking the ritual nature of the movement. The rock twins took a couple of steps toward each other.

'What should we do?' Oria called out to Mica.

Mica did the only thing he could think of. He grabbed the umbilical rope and held it taut. It didn't halt Cerulean, but Mica was ready to pull back if he needed to.

The rock people walked towards one another, Cerulean dragging Mica and Lupe in his wake; Oria trailing Laurel. Lupe's hand was still on Cerulean's arm and Mica rock sensed her increasing the pressure. It seemed to do something. Mica let go of the rope and put his hand back on Cerulean's other arm. Felt the rock man's signature attending to him, feeling him. 'Touch her,' he called out to Oria. 'But gently.'

Cerulean and Laurel were closer now. Step by slow step, the rock people came closer until they were face to face, toe to toe, with Oria, Lupe and Mica like nervous supplicants, hovering at their elbows. The rock creatures looked past each other, over each other's shoulder. Laurel gazed out to sea and Cerulean stared at the dunes beyond her. They reached for each other and clasped hands like a couple about to begin a country dance. Then, like dancers, they each freed a hand and reached for a partner that wasn't there, swept the air as though more rock people should be present and ready to join in.

'This is not good,' Oria said. 'We have to do something else to stop them.'

'Focus on calming thoughts,' Mica said.

'I am,' Oria snapped. 'We all are. It's not working.'

'Rock speak,' Quartz said. 'Quickly! Like you did in Komey when you called Fox.'

Behind him, in the water, Mica heard a flapping, splashing sound. He chanced a quick look, saw the bay was churning with life. Fish. Flashes of bellies and backs and fins: blacks, whites, pinks, greys, and browns. 'Hurry Mother Oak,' he said, using the title he'd spent Beranish and Companionari lives trying to destroy. 'Now! Please!' A crab scuttled over his foot and he jumped back, but somehow kept his hand on his twin.

Seconds later, he heard the Oak Companion speaking in his mind. A gentle whisper. There were some words, but very few. Somehow, Oria combined those words with an image of a quiet canyon surrounded by immovable rock. Mica felt easy again. Relaxed. He felt as though a beloved had reached for his hand and had pulled him down to sit and admire the world. There was no need to rush in life, there was time. He should wait, he should enjoy things as they were. Then it subsided, and he came back to himself and saw he was sitting on the sand. They all were. Even Laurel and Cerulean. Laurel was as fluid and easy as when he'd first seen her, her head resting on Oria's shoulder. And Oria's pregnancy had retreated, no longer close to term.

Mica spoke softly, 'Do you think it's over?'

'I don't know,' Oria said, 'but this feels better. Perhaps we're all right now.'

'Cerulean's feels like a dog after a long walk,' Lupe said. 'Laurel too. They're happy. Rested.'

'But we can't take them into port,' Quartz said. 'We don't know what sets them off. We don't know how to guide them.'

Mica looked toward the port, wondering what they should do. There were soldiersisters on the beach now, milling around the shipwreck survivors. He nodded in their direction and Oria followed his gaze. There seemed to be a lot of them, at least twenty. Mica's heart sank. They'd surrounded the Berans. He suspected they were about to re-enslave the survivors.

'We should get out of here before they spot us,' Lupe said. 'They'll interfere. Once they see we're Berans, they'll try to lock us up. Who knows what will happen then?'

Oria stood up and brushed the sand from her hands. 'Yes, we can't stay.'

But it was already too late. A couple of the soldiersisters were looking in their direction. Mica watched as they started up the beach. One gesticulated, pointing in their direction, calling out to the others. Mica thought the militia looked odd. He wasn't completely familiar with the Companionari military sisterhoods, but he could have sworn the sororities favoured sombre outfits. But there wasn't time to think it through. The surrounding air tingled as Laurel and Cerulean watched the soldiers hurried approach. The twins weren't in sync, not yet, but Mica could feel something imminent in their attention.

Laurel stood up and Mica got his first good look at her rock skin. He was right. It was like his. And he was pretty sure she and Oria had gills. He stood up too, and the others followed his example. 'We have to get out of here,' he directed his words at Oria. 'You, me, and our twins. Off the beach and out into the bay. The soldiers are far enough away for everyone else to run inland and escape, but the twins won't cope. We need to swim out and around, enter the embassy from the water gate.'

Oria looked stricken. 'But I can't swim.'

Mica tapped his rock skin and lifted his gills to draw her attention. 'You've got them too. You'll be fine.' Then he reached out and gave Doubt a quick shove. 'Go. Now!'

Doubt didn't need telling twice. He grabbed Quartz and pulled him towards the dunes. Lupe was already moving, heading in the same direction. Mica called out after her, knowing he could trust her good sense. 'They'll give up the chase when you disappear. They've got enough on their hands with those shipwreck survivors. Keep clear of anyone and everyone and we'll meet you at the embassy. Quartz knows the way.' Then he stepped forward and reached for

Oria's hand, hurrying her to the water. Laurel followed, her signature full of agitation. Likewise Cerulean, but Mica ignored them, along with the residual of the rush: the crabs and flashing fish. Getting away was all that mattered. Evidently, the twins agreed because the tingling sensation in the air subsided as Mica ran into the water with Oria's hand in his and the umbilical rope in the other. 'It's going to feel like drowning,' he called out to Oria, 'but listen to your rock skin. You'll be fine.'

Soon, the water was at their chins, and the waves were moving them like toys. Oria lost her footing, falling backwards. He didn't pull her out. He pulled her under.

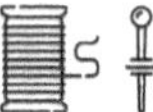

Despite Mica's confidence that all would be well once they were in the water, everything was confusion and panic. Somehow, he found himself tangled in the cloth rope that joined him to Cerulean. Then Oria hit him. She didn't mean to hit him, but instinct was a fierce thing. Only the twins seemed calm. He caught flashes of them staring at each other, locked in an exchange that seemed to exclude the world surrounding them. Mica didn't know whether to be grateful or frightened. It didn't matter which because it was all he could do to keep hold of Oria, stop her lifting her head above water and alerting the soldiersisters to their position. Because he could feel them nearby. The military sisters had waded into the water. They were searching.

The waves were keeping the rock twins apart, stopping them from commencing some sort of water dance with an unknown consequence. Mica hoped it was more than luck, that the Stone Body was on his side, but he put little faith in the notion. He took a firmer grip on Oria's hair. He couldn't do much more, too tangled up in Cerulean's rope to manage a gentler approach. The last thing Mica wanted to do was to frighten the Oak Companion, but it was better than being caught and manhandled by the soldiersisters, risking another rush of stone. Oria fought him with every bit of her being and almost got away, but he grabbed the back of her tunic and kept her down.

Then she stopped fighting and Mica felt a burst of something like laughter in her signature. He couldn't see whether it was safe to let go. The churning sand their struggle had tossed through the water, obscured almost everything. Then a patch cleared and he caught sight of the Oak Companion's rock skin. It was moving, a bright rainbow of articulated scales, with gills lifting and falling. He let go.

Oria brought her face close to his and he heard her speak, not her airy voice, her rock sending voice. It was strong and warm and intimate and contained just three words: *Thank you, Mica.* Then she spoke to the twins, rock sending a call to follow her, drawing Laurel to her side. The twins released each other's hands, drifted apart.

Oria took the lead now in all things. She gestured that Mica needed to unsnarl the umbilical rope that had twisted about his arms and legs, but she didn't wait. She took Laurel's hand and the rock woman acquiesced, even stroking the Oak Mother's hair. The obvious affection reminded Mica of Obsidian and all that he'd lost, but there wasn't time for grief or regret. Oria and Laurel were already moving, the Oak Companion's steps made graceful and languid by the weight of the water. Cerulean was following them, or trying to, straining at the end of the tangled rope. Mica began hopping about, unwinding the twists of plaited cloth from his legs. Once free, he followed, aware that things would only become more complicated once they reached their destination.

Oria didn't rock speak again. She led them across the mouth of the Cava without even glancing back to see that Mica was following. He liked to think she was silent because she was listening, as overawed as Mica by the underwater symphony surrounding them. The noise in the bay was louder than it had been when Mica and Cerulean were out in the open sea. Mica felt on the edge of something almost comprehensible, as though there was a language in the underlying hum: echoes of calls and responses, hoots and taps and knocks and drum rolls, bangs and rattles and clicks and clatters. Halfway across the river's mouth, it rained in the world above them. Mica heard it like a sound from home, like wind rushing through oak leaves in a gale. He made a promise to himself. After all this, when life on the Stone Body was plentiful again, he would return to the Oak camp and invite Fox to come with him and they'd pay proper attention to the Stone Body. Because he suspected there was much he'd missed, sounds and sights that would yet surprise him.

Some twenty minutes later, Oria turned toward the shore. They were beyond the quay now and had already passed several large buildings. Mica couldn't see past the water's surface, but boat ramps extended beneath the water and he'd rock sensed the shape of the buildings they belonged to. Each one was grand; each one bristling with ornamentation that told its story. Ornamental stone horns for Taurine's embassy, leaves worked into the plaster on Salix's home, painted wooden sheep horns for Mouflon's embassy, plaster berries for the Fraise Embassy, and now the stone acorns and leaves of Oak.

Still hidden by the water, Oria looked back and gave Mica a smile and a nod, her signature a mix of pride and relief. Laurel copied Oria's expression, but her affect was more playful. Cerulean strained at the rope, his signature an imperfect mimic of the rock woman's. Mica thought it felt like a game of emotional whispers, with a sentiment running from Oria to her twin and then to Cerulean. He gestured for Oria to hurry on and she turned away and started walking up the section of the boat ramp that was beneath the water. They had to stop to cough out the sea once their heads breached the surface. Mica hated the noise, scared it would attract unwanted attention. But when he looked around, the shoreline was empty.

In front of him, Oria swayed. She turned to him, her expression panicked, her lips turning blue. 'Keep coughing!' Mica said. 'It will close your gills.' Then she coughed and he felt her gills shut tight and she pulled in a deep breath of air. He glanced at the rock twins, but they seemed fine. They were staring at each other again, but the intensity of their earlier encounter was absent. Interesting the transition from gills to lungs was so easy for them. Mica took it as a reminder that they weren't human.

There was an external staircase running up the side of the embassy's northern wall. Steep stone steps, covered with loose sand. A pair of long abandoned sandals sat on the third step. Mica started towards the stairs, but Oria rock spoke, calling him back with a rock voice whisper: *Let's not take any chances. We should use the back entrance. Get undercover.*

She led them up the boat ramp, which entered the building via an arched tunnel. They didn't stop until they reached a locked metal gate. Beyond it was a cavernous room, filled with parked sailboats and stacked canoes.

'It's safe to talk now,' Oria said.

Mica stared at the gate in dismay. 'How are we going to get through this?'

Oria raised an eyebrow and walked over to the side of the tunnel. She reached for an ornate brass knob and gave it a pull. 'Doorbell. I had it installed when I was in my twenties. I used to holiday here. When my talent was so prodigious I could keep things growing from a distance.'

Mica wanted to remind her that her prodigious talent wasn't something she should be proud of, that it had been stolen, but he felt Cerulean becoming restive again. The rock man paced, and Mica suspected his own hostility to Oria was the cause. He made himself relax. He focused on the truth that the old woman was doing her best, was doing better than he would have expected. The tension in Cerulean's signature eased, and the four of them waited in silence. Some minutes later, in the distance, Mica heard footsteps and felt a familiar signature. Acacia was heading their way.

'Those uniforms looked wrong,' Oria said.

It took Mica a moment to realise what she was talking about. 'The soldiers on the beach?'

'Roses and peonies. Mother Briar's ridiculous motifs.'

'They were Briar's people? Why would the Pikes be using them? Do you think there's trouble in the port?'

Oria sniffed, 'Likely. Maybe something to do with Whilomena's slaving schemes. That's where you were, I take it?' She gave Mica a sharp look. 'On a slaving ship?'

He nodded, gave the briefest of explanations.

'I'll want a full report when there's time. Still, the Briar Mother's a fool to get involved here. And fancy dressing her militia like that. Embarrassing. I mean, every house likes to add a subtle touch on an epaulette, a reference to their bounty. An oak leaf, a fig, a horse.' Oria lifted her hand and tapped her own shoulder as though she needed to show where that sort of ornament might sit. 'But a riot of flowers? Ornament an entire uniform?'

There wasn't time for Mica to comment even if he had wanted to because Acacia arrived at the gate. The gold and silver needles in her lapels caught the light and there was a broad smile on her face.

Oria drew herself up. 'And what are you doing here?'

Acacia held up her hand to halt the lecture that was doubtless coming. 'I know, I know.' She bent and slipped a key into the padlock, giving the twins a curious look. 'Forgive me,' she said, opening the gate. 'It's a long story that won't please you. Suffice to say the sorority ran a little wild when you disappeared. Something of a coup. They announced Talia's ascension to Senior Companion—' Oria spluttered. 'But Talia's missing, so it's nominal. Then they appointed me as provisional ambassador to the Pike Borough. To get rid of me. But I came because I felt you might turn up. But where have you been? It's been days and days.'

Oria reached for Laurel's hand and led her past Acacia, past the canoes. She spoke to Acacia over her shoulder. 'I had hangers on. Quartz and Doubt. Stowaways. Think they slowed me down. Here now, so I'll thank you for a full report just as soon as we're settled in the sewing room.'

22

Aikin buttoned up his coat, straightened his collar and ran his fingers through his hair. He'd improved the situation with his jacket and trousers since his unexpected bath in the river, but there was a limit to what he'd been able to do with the brush and cloth he'd borrowed from the barge's keeler. His clothes had seen rough use and it showed. He was just thankful that his saddlebag hadn't gone into the water with him. If he'd had his new copy of *The Book of Kinesis* in his pocket when Whilomena pushed him in... Well, the world would be a poorer place.

He slipped his hand inside his jacket and felt the book beneath his shirt, bound to him with a strip of stolen canvas. Not safe, but there was no real alternative; he couldn't leave it on the barge, so it would have to do. At least it was close. He dropped his hand and smiled at his reflection. Satisfied, he turned away. Two quick steps and he was free of the cabin, glad to see the back of its cramped little world. His material needs were small, but his vocational imperative was vast.

Aikin climbed to the deck and felt the barge bump up against the quay and then settle as the crew berthed the vessel. Whilomena was about to disembark. He needed to hurry. The timing would be tricky.

Aikin didn't want to get too close because he didn't want to be associated with her, but he had to keep her in sight. He wanted his rock child back, and she'd lead him to it if she thought she'd shaken him off. Peri's stones were out of reach now, which made Aikin's missing rock child even more valuable. He planned to gift the Pike Companion its talents to buy his way into New Lytalian society. Or he'd give it to one of her daughters. The woman was a known contrarian, and he suspected she'd relish leading a move against Komey by supporting him.

He picked up his pace, leapt up the barge's steps. He caught sight of his hands on the timber rail. The nascent rock skin was still a shock. It was unconscious prejudice, finding his straw-coloured rock skin so ugly. He'd tried telling himself that he'd have liked it well enough if it worked, but knew that wasn't true. Aikin lifted his gaze, kept moving. He loved Berans, but a part of him didn't want to be one. He'd root that prejudice out later. It was beneath him, weak and cheap. But right now, he needed to concentrate. He needed to be alert, find the right sort of crack in the port's culture and ease in the correct wedge, one that would support his thinking. The port needed to look to him, revel in his recommendations. It would take time and luck, and likely getting that rock child back from Whilomena. From this moment on, each word and act mattered. Had to, for everyone's sake.

When he reached the deck, Whilomena was already descending the wobbly timber and rope walkway. She looked immaculate and overdressed. Ogden held her forearm. Anyone looking would mistake Ogden's touch for solicitous care, but Aikin could see that the skipper's large hand was as much a cuff as a support. Perhaps Ogden wanted to hand Whilomena over to the harbour mistress. The notion had Aikin looking up, had him seeing what he should have seen the minute he reached the deck.

Something was wrong in the port.

The quay was busy enough. Civilians and port workers bustled about and their voices were cheerful, but the port militia said it all.

Instead of the muted colours of Pike, the quay was alive with the colours of Briar, and Briar's flags fluttered above the warehouses and sheds. Aikin didn't need to ponder it. It was obvious. He began adjusting his thinking. No gifts for Lucia Pike. Forget her. There had been a coup. He'd be courting favour with the Briars. And that might be complicated. The Pike family had a hostile attitude towards Berans and Aikin had imagined that his rock child treatment would be warmly received. Who knew what the Briars' attitude would be? He would need to be careful. No wonder Ogden had such a tight grip on Whilomena. The skipper was trying to work out whether the riverhood needed to keep the Wheat Mother or let her go. If Ogden needed a bargaining chip, there was none better.

Aikin eased back behind a stack of crates.

The Wheat Companion had reached the bottom of the walkway. She still hadn't seen what was in front of her. Too busy looking over her shoulder, glaring at Ogden and trying to shake off the skipper's hand. Ogden ignored her, which added to Whilomena's outrage. She twisted under Ogden's grip, tried to peel the skippers fingers from her arm. When that didn't work; she unleashed a litany of threats. Her rising tone lifted heads. Several soldiers began moving toward the barge. Mainly sisters, but there were men in the ranks, too. More men than was usual in a profession dominated by women, and it was a man who looked to be in control, his hand on his ceremonial sword. In fact, all of them had their hands on their ceremonial swords.

Aikin stepped back into the shadows. The swords were ceremonial, but that didn't mean they couldn't do damage. His heart fluttered: fear, but excitement too. A cascade of kinetic energy was unfolding right before his eyes. He could use this. Maybe. But how?

Ogden's warning to Whilomena was a sharp hiss. It was enough to get her attention, but not enough to keep her quiet. She looked up, saw what everyone else had already seen, and it took less than three seconds for her to make things worse. She'd learnt nothing from their recent troubles. The woman would end up in another cell if she wasn't careful.

'What the Back!' Whilomena turned on the man who stood below her on the boardwalk, a corporal by the look of him. 'What are you doing roaming about the wharf? This isn't Briar! Get back to your embassy.'

The soldier didn't answer. He stood before them and he held out a plump hand to Ogden, ignoring Whilomena. 'Contract. Port pass.'

'I... Yes.' Ogden looked around, searching the deck for someone. 'They're... In my cabin.'

'Fetch them.'

Ogden didn't move, reluctant to let go of his troublesome passenger. Instead, the skipper craned her neck, but kept talking as she scanned the deck, 'My apologies Corporal. Normally, I bring them to the harbour mistress after the passengers have left.'

The man stretched out his hand again. 'Papers!'

'What gives you the right to bother my skipper?' Whilomena interrupted. 'Surely, Lucia didn't ask Rosey Briar to police the quay. Don't tell me that because I don't believe it for a minute. The idea is ridiculous!'

The man turned to Whilomena, looked her up and down. 'And you are?'

Whilomena drew herself up. Aikin had to admit she looked astounding. Hard to believe such a small woman could appear so large. 'Whilomena Wheat, the twenty-fifth Wheat Companion. Entitled to full diplomatic courtesy. You may escort me to my embassy if you insist, but my patience is wearing thin. I will not wait about like a dock navvy while you pore over scraps of paper.'

The soldier and Ogden spoke at once:

'The Wheat Companion?'

'The riverhood's contracts are not scrap—'

'Shut up!' Whilomena reached out with her free hand and pushed the corporal back. The man stumbled from the unexpectedness of it. The soldiers on the quay reacted as one. Five of them came at the barge at a run, swords out. And Aikin didn't need a background in armoury to see the swords weren't ceremonial.

Ogden released Whilomena. The skipper lifted her hands in surrender and retreated a few steps, backing up the walkway, motioning with her fingers to her crew to stay still.

The soldiers on the boardwalk had surrounded the Wheat Companion, had pulled her onto the wharf. For her part, Whilomena was red in the face, but she'd stopped talking. Must have dawned on her she was in trouble.

'Any other passengers?' the corporal asked.

Aikin felt as though time halted, as though the Stone Body was making room for his calculations. In an instant, he had the right passage from *The Book of Kinesis*:

Opportunity stands in your path, blowing kisses like a newly grown man. The woman who steps forward, meets Opportunity lip to lip. But ware its lustful promise. Once chosen, it always and immediately becomes a constraint.

Strangely, Aikin trusted Ogden. The woman wouldn't betray anyone on her barge. Aikin could hide if he wanted to. But Aikin wanted to embrace the future, didn't he? Meet the future face on. Did that mean setting a tone with the new mistress in New Lytalia? But if he chose her, the lure of the unexpected, he would have to live with his choice.

He stepped out of the shadows and rounded the corner of the crates at a leisurely pace, still undecided but curious. He was careful to do nothing that looked furtive. 'Good morning, Corporal. I am honoured and privileged to call myself a passenger on *The Meandering Queen*.' Aikin halted, bowed and then straightened up, continued walking towards the gangway. 'Our illustrious skipper was understandably hesitant to mention me. I am not, I am afraid, covered by a riverhood contract. The skipper took pity on me when she found me exhausted on Eden's riverbank.' Aikin put his hand on the rope guides and stepped onto the swaying walkway, easing past Ogden, giving the skipper a pat on the arm as he went. He turned his attention back to the corporal. 'The horses aboard are mine, but I would be grateful if you'd allow me to leave them here for the moment. My embassy has been closed for some years and might not be in a fit state to accommodate them.'

Aikin smiled at the corporal. The man didn't return the smile, but nor did he reject it. If anything, he looked puzzled. 'And you are?'

Aikin nodded. He delayed for a second or two, but kept nodding as though he would speak once he caught his breath. And he would. He just needed something, anything, to tell him how to frame himself. Should he be Oria's nephew? Or the head of the Department of Beranish Affairs? Perhaps he should be a nobody from Oak House? Then he spotted two Berans in the distance, two women! And he knew what to do because New Lytalia was a port known for its obsession with excluding them. 'I'm Master Oak, a manager in the Department of Beranish Affairs in Komey. I was heading to New Lytalia, personally, to urge the Pike Companion to lift her prohibition on Beranish women entering the port in the light of recent events on the Stone Body. I didn't realise she wasn't here. It's clear Lucia Pike isn't the companion I need to petition.'

Aikin didn't need his useless rock skin to feel everyone react. He was aware his lies would offend the rigidly upright skipper who knew Aikin was on no such mission, but Ogden would keep her mouth closed. Her imperative was protecting the riverhood and Aikin had done nothing to threaten that sisterhood. But lying in front of Whilomena was risky. And sure enough, the Wheat Companion began objecting, claiming Aikin was her jilted lover, and a known criminal who'd escaped custody. But the corporal was unmoved by Whilomena's long list of accusations.

Then Ogden spoke up from behind Aikin. 'I'll fetch that contract Corporal, and our port pass. I'll not comment on Master Aikin, but you should know that the Wheat Companion attacked him during the voyage. She had to be restrained. She is no friend to *The Meandering Queen* or the riverhood. As I said, I won't speak to Aikin's business in the port, but we brought those horses aboard when we picked him up. That much I can vouch for.'

Aikin felt the shift. The corporal relaxed. He gestured for his soldiers to take Whilomena away. They led her down the boardwalk, and she cursed them with every step. Let her keep it up. The angrier she was, the smoother Aikin's path would be. He turned and nodded to Ogden, acknowledging his debt to the riverhood, and then he stepped onto the wharf.

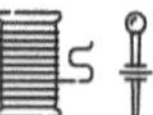

Aikin walked shoulder to shoulder with the corporal, itching to ask about what had happened, knowing he'd be a fool if he did. The answers would unfold and Aikin would be patient.

Ahead of them, Whilomena walked between two soldiersisters, stiff with indignation, but saying nothing. Ogden had remained on the barge. She'd produced her papers and had declined the corporal's invitation to visit Briar Manor. *Briar Manor*. Not embassy. If Aikin had needed confirmation that the coup had occurred, there it was. A manor was the seat of a companion's power in her province. Her house in Komey and her embassy in the port were footholds in other people's domains. The Briar Companion had expanded her territory, had claimed the port as the new centre of her province.

Ever courteous, the corporal ushered Aikin across the street that ran parallel to the water, careful not to lay a hand on him. Aikin took the courtesy as a good sign and allowed himself a curious look up and down the long line of shops. The produce was a little scarce, but there were flowers everywhere and plenty of Berans, men and women. Some of the Berans were old. Those ones sat on the footpath, resting their backs against shop façades. It was odd. All of it. Odd that the Rosey Briar allowed Beranish women in the port when tradition excluded them. Odd that she'd brought her camp's elderly with her. Perhaps her province had failed and the entire camp had to move? But the abundance of flowers suggested not. Something else then.

Aikin didn't have time to ponder what he'd seen because Whilomena had stopped at the foot of the road they were about to ascend. To all appearances she looked overwhelmed at the prospect of climbing the cobbled road, but Aikin knew it was pretence. The woman was fit. No doubt she was planning an escape. He wished she wouldn't. He'd made his choice to follow the militia to the new Briar Manor, but Whilomena's escape plan compelled him to reassess. If she fled, would he follow or would he chose the novelty of the coup? Choices were troubling because they mattered. Follow her or stay? He wasn't sure, which was an unfamiliar and uncomfortable position to be in.

Whilomena started up the hill with a deep, audible sigh. Some part of Aikin agreed. The houses and shops that lined the narrow street crowded out the winter sun. The route looked depressing, never mind the ostentatious presence of flowers.

Aikin pulled himself together, recalled the need for discipline. He stopped worrying, stopped staring, and started walking. With his eyes on the cobbles he saw enough: the new shop signs sporting floral motifs, the traders eyeing the soldiersisters, and Whilomena working her plan. The Wheat Companion moved slowly, stopping now and again to catch her breath. It was well done, and it was possible it might just work. When they'd started up the hill, she and her captors had been well ahead. Soon, Aikin and the corporal would overtake them. If they did, Whilomena would have one fewer soldier watching her when she grabbed some opportunity to break away and dash down a side street. She might succeed and Aikin might remain where he was, in which case Aikin would lose his chance to regain his rock child. Did his earlier decision still hold? Would he stay with the Briar militia?

Aikin found he'd decided. Perhaps he'd regret it later, but

curiosity won out. He would plunge into the Briars' new culture, find a place for himself in this future. As he and the corporal overtook Whilomena, Aikin focused on the man's chatter. The corporal was eloquent about the weather but he complained about having to live among buildings instead of being surrounded by fields of flowers. 'And so many people,' the corporal said. 'We're not used to crowds in Briar.'

'Fewer people here than in Komey.'

'I don't doubt that. This must seem very ordinary to you, coming from such a big city.'

'Not ordinary. Not really.' Aikin wanted to ask about the coup, but didn't. Instead, he asked about the sight that perplexed him. 'We don't see so many Berans in Komey and certainly women aren't often present in the city.' The corporal stiffened. If Berans were a sensitive topic, he would need to be careful, learn what he could. Best start by diffusing the tension with the man beside him. An honest excuse then. Always best to be honest when one could. 'Forgive my curiosity. As you know from our brief introduction on the boardwalk, Beranish Affairs has been my life. Clearly, their rights concern me.'

The corporal's shoulders relaxed. 'Ah yes, of course. That makes sense. The fact is, Briar has always had a large camp. Picking flowers... It takes a great many people.'

'And the older ones? They're no longer needed in the fields?'

The corporal shook his head, gave a slight laugh. 'No, those ones had some sort of calamity at sea. A ship that went down. They're not from Briar. None of them. They claim they're young.'

'They what?'

'You heard right. Claim they lived through a fourth story.' The corporal inclined his head toward Whilomena, and then lowered his voice to a whisper, 'They're blaming her. Said she stole them away from the Stone Body. Mother Briar will be very interested to hear she's turned up. You're lucky you're not with her. The Mother is furious with her.'

Aikin took a moment to watch a group of young Beranish women walk by. He might not be able to work with this new regime, but it was interesting. He increased his pace, put a bit more distance between himself and Whilomena. 'And these confused Berans,' he smiled at the corporal, 'the old ones, they think the Wheat Mother magicked them into old age?'

'No, no, no. Nothing like that. That part's nothing to do with her. We think they might have been so hungry and thirsty they halluci-nated. They say a pair of Beranish brothers appeared out of nowhere and put spells on everyone, made them old and frail.'

Aikin's skin prickled. 'Twins?'

'Then you've heard the tale?'

'Not exactly, but I might shed some light on it, help your dear Companion Mother. Would you be able to secure me an audience? I'm so looking forward to meeting her.'

'Most days she's running parleys. You'll speak to her if she wants to speak to you.'

Aikin nodded, and he and the corporal lapsed into silence. It was a relief. Aikin had almost too much to think about. His hand stroked the book, bound to his stomach. Twins doing harm. He knew some-thing about the harm rock people might do. They'd been no mention of it in the previous volume, but this one covered it and what he'd read was both disturbing and thrilling. He'd planned to share a few insights with the Pike Companion, but he'd not rush to share with the Briar Companion. She'd be sentimental about rock children because of her affection for Berans. The question was, would she be practical? Most companions were. If she was smart, she'd face up to his evidence. His method for generating talent was safer for all of them, Companionaris and Berans. The plague of old people in her port was evidence of that! But what to call the rapid ageing the new book spoke of? It needed a name, an alarming name. The Blight of Age? The Decrepitude Disaster? Accurate, but not frightening. Then he had it, the Age Plague. He smiled and immediately felt better about his decision to remain with the corporal.

Aikin wished his rock skin could tell him what was going on

behind him, track Whilomena's emotional signature. He wanted to be in exactly the right position when she made her escape. With his ugly, useless rock skin, he had to rely on his ears. Right now, she was chatting to her escorts. All sweetness; all charm. Periodically, she paused, her breath laboured. Then she'd start up again.

'… and my father said my pattern looked like foxgloves, not wheat ears and my mother said that was a compliment…' One of the soldiersisters mumbled something Aikin couldn't catch. 'Yellow, yes. Quite. And I didn't have the right detail.'

Aikin and the corporal passed another cluster of shops. These were coffee merchants and they'd painted frothy white arabica flowers on their front windows. Akin couldn't help admiring their approach. How very Companionari not to let a coup interfere with trade.

Then the street broadened, admitting more light. Aikin remembered this area from a past visit. The finance district. A group of Companionari traders and Briar officials stood, blocking their path. The group stood in front of a merchant bank, and everyone was arguing. Aikin knew Whilomena would use this moment. He looked back; couldn't stop himself. She'd bent down to retie her shoe. Her guards stood on either side, but they weren't watching her. They were looking at Aikin's corporal as he told the traders to clear the path. The traders shifted a pace or two, but continued arguing. Aikin's corporal started walking toward the group, but stopped when he realised Whilomena and her guards weren't following.

'Enough Mother Wheat!' he snapped. 'Mother Briar will want an account of what you're doing in port and whether it's true you've been abducting elderly Berans and sending them to Galea.'

Briefly, Whilomena looked startled by the inaccuracy of the accusation, but she quickly regained her hauteur. 'I very much doubt my business is any of her business,' her voice was loud and sharp, designed to carry. 'Last I heard, this was Pike territory.'

'Here, here!' a trader said. Others echoed the sentiment.

'And yet this is Port Briar,' the corporal said. 'Briar territory.'

A trader turned and spat on the cobbles at the corporal's feet. Someone else said something insulting about Rosey Briar's father. A Briar official near the door of the bank slapped the trader who had spoken. Aikin watched as a scuffle broke out. So obvious.

From the corner of Aikin's eye, he saw Whilomena's guards listening and watching. Whilomena took a step back. One step. She met Aikin's eye, waited a moment. There was a question in her gaze, an invitation. He didn't move. He wouldn't follow her, and he still wasn't quite sure why. But he wouldn't stop her escape despite his knowledge that he'd never see his rock child again. Aikin nodded, gave her a tiny signal with his chin, telling her to go. In front of Aikin, a trader punched a soldier and Whilomena's guards surged forward. Whilomena smiled as she walked backwards. Then she turned and ran, disappearing around a corner.

$$\odot \; \odot \; \bigcirc \; \bigcirc \; \bigcirc$$

23

Mica followed Acacia and Oria as they took the stone steps from the boat room to the house proper. The women were busy arranging everything between them, acting as if they knew best. Which was a joke. Life with rock twins was too chaotic for anyone to know anything.

'The kitchen then,' Acacia said to Oria.

Oria patted Acacia's shoulder. 'From what I hear, my Komey House cook was excellent with Obsidian. So yes, we can leave them with Willie and then parley in the sewing room. We need to talk about what Rosey Briar is up to for a start.'

Acacia sighed. 'I know what the Briar Companion is up to. I wish I didn't.' Then she looked back at Mica. 'That's what you said, wasn't it? That Willie was good with Obsidian?'

Mica cleared his throat, ready to explain that no one could make a rock twin do anything or stay anywhere, but then he shrugged, nodded. Why not? Maybe Willie had the touch that Mica lacked. Mica slowed his steps, realised he was close to tears at the thought of the pain and suffering he'd wrought on *The Crested Wave*. Ahead of him, Cerulean stirred, glanced back at Mica. The wanderer managed a reassuring smile and Cerulean relaxed, faced forward again.

Giving up was a cowardly impulse. He'd created this mess. He had a duty to teach the others about rock people, protect anyone he could protect. Mica opened his mouth to speak, but Acacia and Oria had already disappeared into the kitchen, were already out of earshot and the twins had come to a halt in the doorway, blocking Mica's path. They stood on the threshold, feet aligned, their signatures brimming with anticipation.

Mica reached up, put a hand to each of their shoulders, gentle as he could, fearing another outbreak, another rush. To his relief, Cerulean turned to look at him and Mica saw happiness on the rock man's face. And Mica rock sensed the source. Something simple and harmless, just a reaction to the delightful smell coming from the food cooking on the hob.

The twins moved, spilled into the room, no longer aligned. And Mica saw a familiar back working dough at a broad table that was dusted with flour. 'Willie! It's good to see you,' Mica said. 'And can I please have a serve of whatever's on the stove? I'm starving.'

They ate around a table still covered with sifted flour. They'd been too hungry to wait for Willie to clean up, so the bowls rested on the white powdery surface.

Cerulean and Laurel had no difficulty with the crockery or the utensils or the unfamiliar sensation of sitting at a table, but they were as restless as children. They rocked their stools, making galloping sounds on the stone floor, and laughed and clapped at the sound. Then, when Mica distracted them by running his finger through the flour, they turned their attention to the table, patting the flour, making clouds of it lift into the air. Oria reached out and clasped Laurel's arm to stop her, and Mica felt the rock woman's irritation. Yes, she was more like Obsidian than Cerulean, but that didn't mean she would obey Oria. And right now, her irritation felt like a prelude to a tantrum.

Mica cleared his throat, still careful to keep his words warm and easy as he spoke to Oria, 'Don't.' He shook his head. 'Use your rock sense. Laurel doesn't like you telling her what to do.'

'Children have to learn,' Oria said.

Mica continued shaking his head. 'No, she's not a child. And this isn't the time or the place. You want to teach her? Wait for Lupe. She'll show you how. She was brilliant with Cerulean.'

Oria looked from Mica to the mess on the table to Laurel. Laurel swirled her finger in the flour, then brought a little pile of flour to the table's edge, spilling some grains onto the floor. Oria pursed her lips, but said nothing.

'Why don't you show her how to draw?' Mica said. 'Bond with her.'

'You're hardly the one to talk about bonding,' Oria said.

Mica looked down at his food. He wasn't going to argue. It wouldn't help. He used a piece of bread to clean the last of the fish stew from the bowl, and Cerulean copied him. What would Lupe do if she were here? Mica knew the answer. Lupe would show Oria the right way.

Mica reached over his bowl and drew a fish in the flour. Cerulean cocked his head. The rock man put his finger in the flour as though he too would draw, but he didn't. He just moved his finger, displacing the flour. That's all. No shape. Nothing. He didn't get it. He wasn't connecting the flour fish to the fish he'd seen in the Komic Sea.

'I don't think that's enough of a drawing for Cerulean to see what you mean,' Acacia said.

'Hardly surprising,' Oria sniffed. 'Because it doesn't look like anything.'

Laurel had swept away most of the flour in front of Oria's bowl. The Oak Companion reached across the table and picked up Willie's sieve. She moved her bowl out of the way and refreshed the white canvas. She handed the sieve back to Willie. Then she held out her hand to Acacia. 'Give me one of your needles.'

Acacia glanced down and pulled a thick gold needle from her lapel and handed it over.

Oria began drawing. The Oak Companion had a quick hand. A

picture of the sea emerged from the undifferentiated flour, somehow suggestive of currents and movement. Then Oria started on the fish. Mica leant forward to watch, as did the others, including the twins. Then Oria's left hand moved, seemingly of its own accord. It snatched the needle from her right hand and took over the drawing.

'What...' Mica began.

'You're ambidextrous,' Willie said.

'Don't ask!' Oria's face flushed and Mica wasn't sure if it was embarrassment or fear. He rock sensed the woman could do little more than watch as her left hand drew four figures. She shrugged, but only her right shoulder moved. Then she sighed and laughed, a high harsh sound. 'I'm in someone else's body. Promise is... Well, I don't know where she is, but my left hand isn't always mine.'

Mica's rock skin scales lifted, and he shivered. 'This is Promise?'

Acacia pointed at the table. 'Look at what she's drawing.'

Mica wasn't sure what Acacia was seeing. He was too far away, but Oria's left hand was labouring over two of the figures, filling them with some sort of detail. He stood up and came around to stand behind Oria's back. Cerulean and Laurel joined him, and they leant forward, staring at the images.

Mica saw himself and Oria; empty outlines. But the rock people weren't the same. Each had a human outline, but within the outline was a multitude of creatures, picked out in grains of flour.

The air felt warm. Mica felt Cerulean move. His twin reached out and put a hand on his own figure. Then he lifted his hand and put it on his face, leaving a floury print.

'I think he's got it,' Acacia whispered. 'He knows the drawing is him. He's made the connection.'

Oria smiled, and some colour returned to her face. 'We've got a language. We can talk in a way they understand, and they can answer.'

'All well and good,' Willie whispered, 'but who is it we're talking to?'

M ica sat in a tapestry covered chair across from Oria in the embassy sewing room. The companion was already working on a bit of embroidery. Everyone was there. Well, not Lupe and the others who were yet to arrive, but the embassy household, including a valet and a kitchen hand, Willie, Acacia, and the twins. But not everyone was sitting in the sewing circle. Cerulean wouldn't sit. He walked the perimeter of the room, running his hand along the painted daisy chains decorating the walls, making a soft, whispering sound with his fingers. Laurel seemed more relaxed. She sat beside Oria, seemingly intent on Willie's account of the state of the embassy even though the words meant nothing to her. Mica's rock sense suggested her real interest was the piece of lace the cook had pulled out of the sewing basket.

'And you're telling me this is the only parley room that's usable?' Oria interrupted. 'In the entire building? I'm seem to remember there was a room upstairs...'

Acacia sighed, but didn't answer. The question wasn't new.

'The one with the leaking roof, yes,' Willie answered. 'As I explained: open to the sky. The building is in dire condition.'

'Well, I'll need a new parley bed if we're to continue using this room,' Oria said. Then she turned her attention back to Acacia. 'I'll grow timbers for the roof, but we'll need to send someone to Komey with an order for a new parley bed. I've never been good at growing joinery.' Acacia nodded and reached into her basket, examined her threads. Oria sighed, fidgeted. 'And tell them I want motifs of needles and threads and buttons in the carvings, not oak leaves. The bed will be stuck in the middle of a sewing room, so a sewing theme makes sense.' She looked up, watched Cerulean run his fingers along the daisies on the wall. 'And daisies, I suppose. Although flowers are an irritant under the circumstances, but it will look good coming off the barge, assuming the Briars are still in charge.'

Willie flattened the lace on his broad thighs, frowned at it. 'Not much doubt about that.'

Oria clapped her hands. 'Right then. Enough waffle. Welcome all. Welcome dear twins, dear Berans, and my precious household staff. We are here to decide how to care for our twins and how to manage life in the port.' She put down her lace and lifted her chin in Willie's direction. 'You're the spy. What have you found out?'

'The Briars claim there was a dispute on the quay and Rosey Briar stepped in to help Lucia Pike. Because the Pike Mother's away in Komey. A favour, apparently. Now, talk in the Taurine kitchen suggests the coup's been years in the making. And the Salixes... Well, they have a fish trap outlet on the docks and they say there's something troubling about the Briar's sisterhoods. A lot of men.'

Oria nodded. 'That's true. One glance at their militia and you see it. And the Taurines are right too. Those uniforms didn't happen overnight. Though they should have spared themselves the effort. They're awful.'

'But it doesn't matter,' Mica said. 'None of that matters. We have to find a safe place for the twins. Then we need to organise a search at sea.'

'Willie, tell them about Pike Manor,' Acacia said.

'Burnt down,' Willie said.

'The Back!' Oria said.

Laurel reached out for the lace Willie was holding, pulled it off his lap. It was a half-finished picture of thready-looking fish. The rock woman held it up, ran her finger over it, sniffed it, licked it, and then made a face at the musty, cottony taste.

'Thinks it's food,' Acacia said.

Oria huffed, 'Don't be silly. My twin isn't an idiot. Probably seeing what it's made of.' The companion took the lace from Laurel's hands and gave it back to Willie. He spread it on his knees again, then had to dry his fingers on the tail of his shirt. Oria dug about in her basket, pulled out a lace card, a lace cushion, some pins and a handful of bobbins loaded with coloured threads. The parley came to a halt as she showed Laurel how to set up the card and work the bobbins. Mica schooled himself to be patient. She was right to be taking the time to teach Laurel. It was the only way forward. But the wanderer felt so anxious he was having trouble remaining in his chair.

Laurel began working the bobbins with a soft clatter, and Acacia turned to Mica. 'I'm afraid I can't help with organising your search party, but the rest of the staff will help.' She glanced at Willie and the two others and they all nodded. Acacia turned to Oria to explain, 'I've a summons to present my credentials to Rosey Briar.'

It made sense, but Mica's anxiety was getting worse. It felt as though no one else was seeing the urgency. He unclenched his fists, forced himself to relax his hands on his thighs. 'We need a story cycle. I need one.'

Oria laughed 'I'm time rich, but the world feels extraordinarily time poor. We should make a plan and then get on with it.'

'I know, but that's exactly why we need a cycle,' Mica said. 'A cycle will help to get our thinking on the right track.'

Laurel had stopped moving the bobbins and was now rearranging the pins Oria had stuck into her card, making a nonsense of the card's pattern. Cerulean paused to watch and then he turned away. Instead of resuming his pacing, he picked up a chair and carried it to a patch of wall illuminated by the afternoon sun. He'd climbed up and ran his fingers across the wall, tapping the centre of each daisy.

'Will a story cycle help us with them?' Oria inclined her head, gesturing to the rock twins. 'Are they tameable? Can we domesticate them?'

'I told you, they are not beasts.'

'What are they then?'

'There is a story I know that might help. A fourth story.'

Laurel had wound some red thread up her arms and Oria reached over and tried to unwind it. The air tightened. The companion held up her hands in surrender and returned to her own work. 'Well, then.' She nodded. 'The four stories. Perhaps you're right. What will you talk about? The trouble in the port?'

'No. We need the Briars' story for that, their first-hand account, and we don't have it. I suggest we make the cycle of our transformation. Yours and mine.'

Cerulean climbed off his chair and came to sit in the middle of the sewing circle. He bent forward and began tracing the pattern on the rug: oak leaves and human figures and Beranish motifs. Mica was glad his twin didn't seem tempted to lick the rug.

'What's the point?' Oria said. 'We went through the Lacuna bell portal and you wound up on a ship and I wound up on the beach.'

'A cycle offers depth. Depth matters.'

Oria shrugged, returned to her embroidery, focused on her stitches. Mica felt her unspoken admission that he was right in the way she focused her attention. He admired her for trying.

'I am a wanderer,' he said, 'but that might be the only fixed point, the only thing I am certain about. I would have said *I am twenty-seven years old*, but I have learnt that my body might not always match my years. Today, in this iteration of my body, I have fish scales for rock skin and I might be a little older or a little younger than my twenty-seven years. Likewise, in the past I might have said *I hear the call of rock children* and I would have called them *living stones*, but I now know they are neither children nor stones.'

'But they're not people, are they?' Acacia said.

'No, I don't think they are,' Mica answered. 'That image Promise drew in the flour. Outlines of people, but something else inside.' He shivered and looked down at his twin. Cerulean had stopped playing with the rug. Now he was on all fours, moving from basket to basket, pulling out threads and bobbins. And Laurel too, was focused on the baskets. She'd discarded her lacework and was collecting pins. Mica waved at them. 'They have their own purpose.'

'Which we don't understand,' Oria said.

'Which we don't understand. So I am also bringing my confusion to the cycle. And my worry about Doubt and Quartz and Lupe, whether the Briars have caught them. And we still haven't heard from Fox and Saury and Patience. I wish I could walk out of the embassy and begin searching for all of them, but I'm responsible for the shipwreck. Cerulean and I can't go wandering until I can communicate with him or find some place safe for him to live, and at least attempt to find those survivors who might still be on the water.'

'True,' Oria said.

'So, I feel confused,' Mica said, 'and scared and impatient. And I feel compelled. This is my first story.' He paused a moment and then invited Oria to share the story of her journey through the Stone Body.

For a moment, she was silent, watching Laurel. The rock woman had moved, was standing up and poking pins into the wall as though it was a giant pricking card. She was using a pair of embroidery scissors to make the holes in the wall and was then pushing in the pins.

'The second story,' Oria said. 'Yes. In short, I followed you to the trench, to the portal's edge, to stop you. And Quartz and Doubt followed me. I grabbed you. I didn't even notice Promise's rock child, Laurel...' she corrected herself. 'Didn't notice her calling me. I fell. I lost my grip on you. I woke on the beach with Laurel and the two idiots who'd grabbed hold of me: Quartz and Doubt. My actions and the actions of idiots caused all this.' She waved at Cerulean and Laurel. 'And I include you as the greatest idiot.' She stared at Mica. 'But the Stone Body also acted on me. Surprised me with gills and fish scale rock skin and Laurel. So strange. And surprised me again with the twins' desire to dance.'

'Their desire felt purposeful,' Mica said. 'Maybe the cycle will help us see its meaning.'

'I hope you are right because these two are wild and dangerous and beyond our control.' She nodded to herself and turned her attention back to her lace. 'And they're ruining my sewing room wall. That is the second story. I hope it's good enough for you because that's all I have.'

Cerulean was up on the chair again and he was hanging bobbin pairs over pins as though he were a sewing sister working a giant pricking card. Laurel had fetched a second chair and had dragged it over to join him. She, too, was hanging bobbin pairs on pins. Mica wondered whether they would create some sort of lace pattern. Whatever they came up with, it would be an important piece of Beranish history.

He recalled himself to the cycle. 'This is the third story,' he began. 'I lay in the portal and the Stone Body pulled me into its womb. Time passed, but I didn't track it or know it. I don't know where my soul dwelt during that time. I believe it cleaved to Cerulean's soul like a baby on a father's back and Cerulean must have felt my worry about my people, the Beranish refugees, because he carried me to *The Crested Wave* where I should have done some good but I mainly did harm.'

'So, you were worrying about the refugees when you stepped into the trench?' Oria said.

'I was. I was worrying about them being transported and sold. And you, what were you thinking when you fell into the portal?'

'I had a memory of waves lapping New Lytalia's beach. Just a sentimental thought. No grand longing.'

'But it was enough for Laurel to carry you here. When I woke on *The Crested Wave,* I found myself with a twin who felt like a stranger. I've been thinking about that and comparing it to waking beside Obsidian.'

'And?'

'Cerulean didn't feel like kin.' He smiled at his twin, but the rock man didn't turn around. He and Laurel were too busy knotting threads, creating wild lace stitches like crazy moth-eaten drapes hanging against the daisy-painted wall. 'A little more like kin now, but still... We don't know each other.'

'And you think that's the difference?' Acacia said. 'A family bond?'

'Obsidian knew me like a brother, a true twin. He mirrored my behaviour, my habits.'

Willie grunted, nodding. 'Could see that. Obvious he loved you.'

'And Laurel was Promise's kin,' Oria said. 'So, I wouldn't feel quite right to her either.'

There was silence in the room other than the slight rattle of bobbins knocking against the wall. 'So, there is a fourth story I've been thinking about,' Mica said. 'It's one of the *world upside down* stories. They're always fantastical. I think it might... No. I'm forgetting myself. Tell the fourth story before you talk about its lessons.' He cleared his throat, started again, 'One day, Spring got a notion in its head that it wasn't getting the respect it deserved from the Stone Body, so it stayed away. When it came time for Spring to appear, it didn't arrive and none of the new plants so much as poked their noses out of the Stone Body's skin. And none of the new animals felt any desire to be born. Day after day the people cried from cold and hunger. Keeper pleaded and Wanderer walked, but Spring was haughty and wilful and refused to listen to tears, or words, or even the heartbeat drum of Wanderer's footsteps. The Camp grew hungry, Keeper's voice grew hoarse, and Wanderer's legs grew tired. Soon everyone lay down to die and before long there were as many cold bones on the Stone Body as there were hard rocks. The Stone Body felt worried. It felt sad. It saw that there was too much sorrow and death and it called on Spring to come home and do its duty, but Spring wouldn't come. The Stone Body brought Spring a beautiful warm wind to wear but Spring still didn't come. Then the Stone Body gave Spring a week of golden sunrises and sunsets, but Spring stayed away and Winter reigned. Soon the Stone Body was covered with a giant sheet of ice and out of hundreds, there were just thirty wanderers left to walk the world and carry rock children. When the Stone Body saw how few they were and how few were the last of their rock children, it yearned to act. Soon thirty became sixteen and still the Stone Body hesitated. Then sixteen became ten and ten became nine and nine became eight and when, finally, those eight stepped over Death's threshold and disappeared with their stones, the Stone Body was filled with grief. For pity's sake, for the sake of love, it turned the world upside down and made eight wanderers anew and eight twins to pair them.'

Oria's head snapped up. 'Finally. Some account of thresholds and earth and rebirth.'

Mica continued the story, 'As fast as an eye might blink, or a tongue might click, or a head might turn, or a clarion gull's wing might clap, or a toe might tap, the Stone Body made the rocks and wanderers dance a wild reel and from the dust of their feet rose a new creation of wing and leg and thrashing tail, of fibre, and water, and laughing fire. And the world tipped right side up with a roar and a flash and a shout. That is the fourth story.'

'And you didn't think to tell me this, tell anyone this, a little earlier? In the portal tent?'

'I did. We shared our tales, all of us, but it was hard to know which mattered and which didn't.'

Oria shook her head. 'Eight pairs of twins and a dance. How do we read it now?'

Mica knew how he read it. The beginning or the end. The twins could create either outcome, and just the thought of it made him anxious. 'It's too dangerous to try. They might do a beautiful job recreating the world and kill all of us in the process. Twins have a talent for death as well as life.'

'I think you're right,' Oria said. 'I wish Quartz was here. I'd value his advice. I expected he'd be here by now. I hope the Briars haven't captured him. I think we should accompany Acacia, see if our people are there and, if they are, demand their return. They can hardly deny me. A coup is a coup, but even coup leaders need trade to survive. Timber for boats. Timber for furniture. For houses...' She chewed her lip like a girl. 'So Mica? The plan? I think you and I should leave the search for any Berans still on the water to the embassy staff. A large purse will help. And after the visit to Briar Manor, before the day is over, you and I should set out with the twins for Persica. It's not far, and it's already rushed, so we can't do much harm. But first, Acacia and I must face Rosey Briar and get our people back.'

'And what about Fox and the others?' he asked. 'We have no idea where they are. Someone will have to look for them. Because we'll need their twins if we decide to create the eight. Theirs and three more. If a childhood thought brought you to the port, Fox's feelings have probably carried her to Kelp. Perhaps Cerulean and I should head for Kelp.'

Oria held up her hand. 'I sympathise, but no. We need to deal with the crisis in front of us, move Laurel and Cerulean to peaceful surrounds. Learn to communicate our needs before we look for more twins, before we choose our path. You and I will be responsible for that, taking over Persica, working with the twins we already know about. Quartz can take responsibility for the rest. So, we must deal with the Briars and find out if they have Quartz and the others. Diplomatically.'

'Then best I do the talking,' Acacia laughed. The twins hooted at the sound. At least, that's how it felt to Mica. As though Acacia's laughter set them off, but then they climbed down from their chairs, and Cerulean's rock thought felt as bright as light breaking through cloud.

'I think they want us to admire their work,' Willie said.

Mica and the rest of the parley left their seats and followed the cook over to the twins. The lace picture was wild and loose with none of the delicacy of Companionari lace, but it showed eight pairs of dancers who seemed to have wings and tails and feet. It sent shivers down Mica's spine, but he took it for a sign. They would trust the Stone Body. They would take the risk of assembling the eight.

24

The Cava River had felt like a sister or an aunt, like someone with open arms. Fox had planned to head straight to the northern bank and then to the beach as Ogden had advised, but once she was in the water, things changed. For the first time in her life as an adopted Companionari, she understood the urge to cherish time. Perhaps the Companionaris had perverted something that had begun as a virtue because here, near the river's mouth, time was a glorious thing that was worth valuing. It didn't lessen Fox's desire to find Mica or her sense of duty to help the Berans and the Companionaris adjust to the upside down world the Stone Body had created, but in the river she'd felt as though everything could wait.

Right from the moment they entered the Cava, the water had felt good. She and Saury had unravelled their suckered arms and Fox had tasted the river: mostly fresh, but there was a hint of bay and a more distant suggestion of ocean. The touch of salt in the estuary made all the difference. She'd arrived in the sea after passing through the portal, been born again into salty water. And the salt in the river felt the same. The feeling led Fox astray. Instead of helping Peri and heading for the north bank, she'd dawdled and let the river carry them. And she would have drifted out into the bay if it wasn't for Peri's signature. The skinny wanderer could swim, but he'd tired quickly, and soon felt cold in a way she and Saury didn't. Then he'd stopped kicking altogether and started sinking.

Fox swam over, used the strength of her tentacles to pull him back to the surface. A moment later Saury was at Peri's other side, helping. Together, they pulled him to the bank and dragged him from the water.

It was only now Fox realised how long they'd been in the river. The morning was well and truly established, and it was a winter's morning, a sharp wind, coming off the ocean, parley gulls dancing in the sky as they witnessed the world, the sun obscured by clouds. 'Fire,' she said, as much to remind herself as the others.

'We'll be noticed,' Saury said.

Fox looked up and down the river bank. There were no houses, no buildings on this side. There were some worn wooden jetties, but they were empty of boats. The Pikes controlled both sides of the river and she imagined locals used this bank to catch crabs, or maybe worms for bait. She could feel plenty of life beneath the ground. She wondered why the Pikes hadn't built here, then she looked down and saw the muddy sand and understood. It was a coastal swamp. You'd need prodigious talent to grow things in a place like this. And there wasn't any dry wood. She turned to the wanderer. 'Can you walk a little further? If we make it to the dunes, we can hide in the scrub, build a small fire.'

Peri grunted and got to his feet. It was a sign of his extreme exhaustion that he didn't quibble when Saury slipped under his arm to keep him upright.

Fox stood where she was a moment longer, biting her bottom lip, deep in thought. Her plan was stupid. They didn't have a flint. Maybe she could make a fire without a flint, but it would be difficult. Peri probably could, but he was in no fit state to do anything. He'd be lucky to make it to the dunes. And Saury was right. It was likely they'd be seen from the port. 'Wait.'

Saury halted, half-turned her head.

Fox gestured to a relatively dry and sheltered patch of land. 'Change of plan. You two sit down, try to keep warm. I'm going to steal a rowboat and we're heading straight for the embassy.'

'No fire?' Saury said.

'No fire,' Fox said.

Fox made quick work crossing back to the other side of the river. She stayed below the surface and ducked in and out of moorings. In the end, she had to swim a little way upriver, beyond the larger vessels designed for the open sea, to find the smaller rowboats. She chose a well-built rowboat and noted its location. She would return it before she made her way back to Kelp to search for the twins.

She used her knife to cut the thick mooring. Conscious that she mustn't be seen, she held the rope underwater as she cut. Even with her tentacles to hold her steady, the task wasn't easy. And it took much longer than she would have liked. Once she'd freed the boat, she didn't bother getting into it. It was easier and faster to stay underwater and lead it like you'd lead a reluctant dog, tugging it across the flow.

Fox brought the rowboat to the worn jetty nearest to where she'd left Saury and Peri. She was tired now. Worse still, she discovered she'd cut the rope too short to moor the boat. With no other choice, she heaved herself into the boat itself and wrapped her tentacles around the nearest post to keep the rowboat steady.

'Saury,' she called out, keeping her voice low. 'Bring Peri. I've got the boat, but I can't tie it up! Hurry.'

But neither Saury nor Peri answered. Then she felt them and understood what was wrong: solidersisters. Soldiers she'd been too preoccupied to notice. They had Saury and Peri and ... Quartz? And Doubt? Somehow they were there too. And there was another Beran with Quartz. Now she'd sensed them, Fox felt everything: the sharp hard grip of a soldier's hand on Saury's shoulder, the rope around her sister's hands constraining Saury's tentacles. And swamping everything her little sister's terror. Fox didn't think twice. She pulled herself out of the rowboat and threw herself onto the jetty, tentacles writhing. She landed with her knife already in her hand and she threw it. It hit the soldier.

The woman dropped with a sharp cry of pain, and Saury ran to Fox. With no other weapon, Fox pushed Saury towards the rowboat and launched herself at the other soldiers. She wrapped a tentacle around a neck, used her other hand to pull another soldier away from Quartz, had an idea the two of them might prevail. Then two more soldiers emerged from the scrub with their arrows notched and aimed at the Berans.

With a cry of despair, Fox let go, stood down. A soldier, a man, tied her hands, and bound her arms, and she let him. Another two caught Saury. They were trapped.

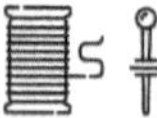

Talia woke with the realisation that her arms were uncomfortable. Empty. Almost painful, as though she'd been carrying something too heavy or lying in bed the wrong way and the waking had brought the pain to life. She rolled onto her back. She shouldn't be uncomfortable. It had been days since she'd solved the mattress problem by growing a wild flax crop. The mattress wasn't a mattress, more like a pile of flax, but it was comfortable. The bedding, less so, but it was adequate. Talia's blankets were coarse and lumpy and scratchy, and mainly constructed from knots. She shifted her shoulders, rubbed her upper arms, her fingers kneading her rock skin, bringing some relief to the ache but not the itch.

She'd dreamt that Sorrel was living in Talia's hamlet. The baby companion was tiny and hard to supervise. Too young to walk, but she'd scuttled about on hands and toes like a crab. Sorrel kept escaping and falling into the river. A restless night of saving the baby from drowning. Talia didn't need a story cycle to make sense of it. Improving the hamlet was tiring, but caring for the lonely twins was exhausting.

She sat up, heart racing, knowing exactly what was wrong. She couldn't feel them. Her arms felt empty because they really were empty. The Back! The Back! The Back! Why hadn't she woken when they left? The three of them must have wandered off in the night. They'd wandered before. They wandered around and around the hamlet, but never at night. Usually, they ended up in a line on the towpath, swaying as though they might erupt into song or step into a dance. It seemed to Talia that the river troubled them or called to them. The only thing keeping them in the hamlet was their attachment to her. Since she'd named them, they didn't seem to want to leave her despite their restlessness. Their unhappiness made the Cava clatter and the air shiver, and when that happened, Talia felt her rock skin prickle and mouth dry out and her bones ache. She'd called them back to the camp fire each time. She'd given them something to eat or set them to work, improving Eden's plants, and that soothed them. That and using their names and chatting to them.

But she'd been a fool. She'd felt them straying all day yesterday, finding them further and further along the towpath. She should have left with them, accompanied them. But she'd been so fixed on this being their new home, she hadn't seen things from their point of view.

Talia rolled out of bed, tripped on the wooden toys she'd made to distract the twins in the evenings, and then righted herself. It was still dark, but she could feel the morning reaching for the Stone Body. She tucked her hair behind her ears, her body still ajangle, and attempted to calm her racing heart as she rock sensed the cottage. Not a very successful effort because everything felt wrong. Talia put her hand on the nearest bed and, for the first time since she'd woken, she felt some relief. The bed was warm. They hadn't been gone long enough for the mattress to cool despite the chill in the air.

She still had her Komey clothes. A little worn and ragged, but patched and repaired using the sole needle that had survived the journey from the train and some thinner bits of the flax fibre she'd grown. But the clothes she'd worn when she left Komey weren't warm enough for the season, so she'd added a homemade cloak and warm pants to her wardrobe. Her clothes-making efforts were almost as poor as her blanket-making. Her loom had been fine, but her warp kept failing so weaving had proved impossible. Instead she made an ugly lace fabric in the style of her knotted blankets.

When she reached the river it was dark and still, with no sign that anyone, neither rock nor human, had entered its waters. The same unpleasant smell lingered in the air, but it seemed milder now, or perhaps she'd adjusted to it.

Talia stood on the bank, shivering, and called her acorns out of the ground. She fashioned a rowboat plank by plank and joint by joint. The urgency and effort made her head spin, but eventually it was done. She dragged it to the water and used the jetty to walk it further into the river. Then she stepped off and settled herself on the thwart. Her new boat began taking water almost immediately. The thing had seemed sound before she stepped into it, but with her weight inside it, it was no match for the Cava. She grabbed hold of the jetty and pulled herself out of the sinking boat and immediately lost control of it. With a sinking heart, she watched it slip away.

She stood on the jetty, her shoes wet, her stupid pants and cloak wet and heavy, her rowboat gone. Infuriatingly, her rowboat looked buoyant now. Without her weight, it bobbed happily as it headed downriver. Confounding! She'd made furniture that didn't collapse and had fashioned the jetty. She hadn't realised a rowboat would be so complicated.

Talia untied her wet cloak and rubbed her temples to ease her aching head. She wouldn't catch up with the twins on foot. If Fox were here, she would know what Talia had done wrong with the boat. But Fox wasn't here. Talia rubbed her face, tried to clear her mind for more useful thoughts. A raft. A raft was a simple thing, and she'd lash it together with a flax rope. If she used logs and made the raft big enough, it would hold her weight. Nothing complicated about that. Her stomach rumbled. No breakfast and the morning was cold, which made her hunger worse. She ignored it. She was losing time. With every minute she stood about, wondering what to do, the twins would be further away.

But a raft... A raft was doable.

Talia ran along the jetty, back onto the towpath, and pulled a handful of acorns from her pocket. She placed them in a line on the ground, at the very edge of the path, and stepped on them, then stepped back. Ten saplings sprang up in a neat line, cheek by jowl. She halted them at hip height. She'd rope them, then grow them a little higher and then rope them again.

The rope was harder to make. Flax was always harder than trees. Growing it wasn't too bad; making it fall apart into usable fibres was headache inducing. Headache on top of headache! But when it was done, she had an enormous pile of chilly fibres that she plaited into two long ropes.

Talia was faster now. Her hands hurt, her head hurt, and her body ached, but she ignored all that. She bound the trunks, loose enough for them to thicken as they grew. Then she released them, grew them taller and roped them again. Finally, she halted the trunks when they were tall enough to form a broad and stable plat-form. Then Talia secured the loose ends of the ropes to the jetty. She wouldn't let the raft float away like the rowboat had. Finally, she rotted the base of the trees, pulling on the ropes as she did so. The raft fell onto the Cava with a splash and Talia clambered aboard, heart racing, aware of how long her fumbled constructions had taken. She waited a moment, eyeing the oak logs, waiting for the raft to sink, ready to jump back onto the jetty. River water seeped between the trunks, but the raft remained afloat. Talia smiled and untied the first rope connecting the raft to the jetty and moved to the second. She hesitated. What if Fox and the others arrived in the hamlet looking for the twins? They wouldn't know what had happened.

Talia turned her attention back to the cottages. She concentrated on the closest one, on the espaliered oaks against the wall that faced the river. It was easier now, after so many days of working with those trees. She reshaped the branches, spelt out two words: *twins* and *downriver*. That would be enough. Hopefully. With that thought, she pushed off from the jetty. The river caught hold of the raft and spun her about. She'd forgotten to make oars, but it was too late. The current pulled the raft into the centre and swept her down the river. The smell of rot was stronger now, but still less unpleasant than when she'd first sensed it. Perhaps whatever was rotting had composted down. An hour or so later, the smell had almost disappeared. She couldn't help noticing the improved air coincided with Briar's landscape extending more deeply into the northern bank; a clue that it wasn't Briar that smelt. She called up her childhood knowledge of the provinces beyond Briar. Persica, Galliform and Dyr, the three stacked together like a pile of books nestled in the crook of the Stone Body's right arm. Dead deer or a mass death of Galliform's clucking and quacking bounty or maybe a problem with Persica's fruit. The port would know. If she and the twins made it that far. If she found the twins.

She began sensing the three rock people just before midday as the Cava ceased its meander and began arrowing towards New Lytalia. Half an hour later, she was close enough to the twins to know that they were indeed walking underwater. And hungry. And needy. Just like they were when she first met them.

Talia cursed herself for a fool. She'd not given a moment's thought to food. She should have brought something with her. Growing rice was useless if she couldn't cook it, and it wasn't as though she could explain that to the hungry twins. Her stomach rumbled and the ache in her head picked up again. And the landscape clamoured. Acorns and date pits were always present, but there were more of them now she was near the port. The Cava and its towpaths were the only roads to the port. People walked and rode its banks, as well as journeying on its waters. Talia could feel the places where seeds had fallen from sacks and pockets. Rice. Flax seeds. Pits of some fruit she didn't recognise. And everywhere… everywhere for miles and miles and miles there were rose seeds. Thousands of them. Beyond thousands. Millions. Calling her because of the Oak family's minor talent for roses: nudging Talia; pressing her. It wasn't like it had been in Komey. Aikin's cure was solid. The door to her talent was under her control, but the pressure was growing. She could even feel it on the top of her head. She looked up and saw why. An eagle overhead. Another minor talent. Further east, she sensed its chicks.

Talia clasped her hands together to stop them shaking. The feeling of the world hungry for her, wanting her, would be easier if she wasn't hungry and aching. She closed her eyes, dropped a slither of consciousness into her body and dissolved her fear and tension. She opened her eyes again, feeling bounded.

The Cava River was broader now, slower. The sea wasn't yet visible, but Talia could feel it. And the landscape had changed. There were flowers still, but they intermingled with the coastal grasses. She opened her rock sense. The twins filled her arms, enormous and needy and exhausted, but there was something else in the river. Struggling against the flow, just downriver from the twins, was a shape. She thought it was a woman in a boat. Talia's heart leapt at the thought it could be Fox. But it wasn't. Not Fox, but something about the person felt familiar.

Talia's pockets were empty of acorns, but she didn't need to be precise to deal with the twins now that she was so close. She felt along the banks. Date pits and acorns were easy enough to find. She ignored the date pits and concentrated on her true talent. She grew a quick and ragged forest on the towpath just downriver from the twins and shook its branches, casting acorns over the water. Then she grew tree trunk piles in the river, like two rows of teeth, separating the twins and the solitary woman. Next were steps and a deck for the jetty. Talia felt the woman's surprise, felt her lose what remained of her oars' rhythm. As the twins reached the steps and rose from the river and Talia's own raft slammed into the structure, she spared a thought for the solitary woman who had now dropped an oar. Downriver from the poor thing, Talia sent a tree branch from the towpath. Grew it over the river, lowered it into the water, curled it around the woman's rowboat. Then Talia lost track of everyone and everything because she needed to get off the raft.

She grabbed hold of a piling as the river ripped the raft away. Talia heard the woman shout, but could do nothing more than hope the stranger made it out of the river. Talia wrapped her legs around the piling and reached up for the jetty. She half pulled, half pushed herself higher. She got her chest over the deck edge and then a leg, and then she rolled to safety.

She lay on her back, on the deck, looking up and at the sky. She rock sensed the twins. They were on the towpath, watching the stranger. She sensed the shape of the woman, clambering onto the tree branch. Everyone was safe, so everything could wait. Talia's arms hurt, her back hurt, her shoulders hurt.

'You!' the venom in the woman's tone startled Talia from her rest. 'Of all the people! This is all your fault.'

Talia turned her head, ready to accept the blame for costing the woman her boat. But the stranger wasn't even looking in Talia's direction. And she wasn't a stranger. It was Whilomena, and she had an oar in one hand and was using it to keep her balance as she navigated her way over the broad back of the oak trunk, which leant over the river. The Wheat Companion was glaring at Amber. Grunting and cursing, she reached for the nearest upright branch and used it to help herself onto the towpath. Then everything fell into place in Talia's mind. Whilomena was yelling at Amber because she thought she was yelling at Fox.

'It's not—' Talia said, struggling to her feet. 'Wait!' In the seconds it took Talia to stand up and start moving again, Whilomena was running. The oar was above the Wheat Companion's head as she ran, ready to bring it down on Amber. 'Don't!' Talia called out, but Whilomena kept going. Then her footsteps slowed as Talia felt the air become brittle. Talia watched Whilomena's hair growing faster than her feet were running, and it was white as it left her scalp, and dark where it dragged on the path behind her.

'It's not Fox,' Talia cried, but her voice was too feeble to carry.

The Wheat Companion swung the oar and brought down, aiming for Amber's head, only it never reached Amber. Mid-swing, Whilomena seemed unable to support its weight. She dropped it and it bounced on the towpath, hitting Baylor's foot. There was a thud beside Talia. A bird, an eagle, lay on the jetty's deck. Not the healthy bird Talia had rock sensed early; the same bird, but old and dead, fallen from the sky.

Nothing made sense. The skin on Talia's arms was wrinkled and sagging, her hands were gnarled. She heard a more distant thud and rock sensed Whilomena falling. But Talia couldn't feel the other woman properly. Just a slumped shape. Because... Because she was dead. Whilomena was dead.

Talia rolled herself to the edge of the jetty's deck. She'd die too if she didn't get away. She tipped herself into the water. The river picked her up and swept her away. She called to her trees. Managed a ragged branch to keep her afloat. At first, she was nothing more than fear and clawed hands, a withered cheek on the rough bark and a weak heart full of dismay. The twins had killed Whilomena and nearly killed Talia. Then she gathered her herself. She was alive. And the twins? They'd been frightened. It wasn't their fault and they would need her help.

Talia lifted her head. She was already further away than she wanted to be. This wasn't good. She needed to get back and reassure them. Because her work wasn't over. Old or young, it didn't matter; Talia had to get out of the river and return to the twins and do what was right. Someone had to care for them, teach them until Fox and the others returned, and that someone was Talia.

Talia kicked her old, feeble legs. Slowly, she made her way

towards the bank. The slope to the towpath was relatively flat, and she dragged herself out of the river and onto her feet. Where could she take them? Anywhere so long as it was away from people, which meant away from the Cava River's traffic. Into the northern provinces then. The smell would help. It would keep others away. Dyr, Galliform or Persica? Didn't matter. Talia would find the source of the rot and make that their home.

25

ikin put a hand to his face and flinched. He examined his fingers. No blood, but he was certain he'd awaken tomorrow with a black eye. Worth it, though. The brawl had been quick and sharp, but he'd managed to aid the corporal.

The man in question sat across from him in the nursing sister's examination room, a junior sister stitching the gash on the soldier's arm. The corporal lifted his gaze. 'Thank you, Master Oak. Confusing for you, I'm sure. Knowing which side is in the right and which is in the wrong.'

Aikin quieted his breathing. This mattered. Not the rights and wrongs of the coup. That was trivial in the broader scheme of things. An opportunity perhaps. At worst, an inconvenience. No, this was Aikin's opportunity to talk about the twins, test out the best story about the risks the twins posed and hint that he might know a way to control them. He daren't touch *The Book of Kinesis,* still strapped securely beneath his shirt, but the thought of this edition's promises of magical dancers and callers had him itching to caress it. He'd keep his words vague, but the corporal's reactions would show Aikin what attitude to take before he came face to face with the Briar Companion. And thank the Back for the shipwrecked Berans. They were the entrée to the subject and all the evidence of danger he needed. Aikin just hoped no one had noticed his previous visit to the port because his proximity to Whilomena was a problem. He was probably safe enough. He'd been in the background, an anonymous Companionari man in Whilomena's entourage.

Aikin shrugged. 'Not that hard, really: knowing right from wrong. It's what you told me just before the fight broke out that clinched it.' Aikin smiled at the corporal's confused expression. 'The calamity at sea. You said the Wheat Companion was behind it—'

'Behind the Berans being on the water, yes.'

'I figure she couldn't have put that many Berans on a ship without the Pikes knowing. I don't know what's brought the Briar Companion to the port, but I'm not a fool. Mother Briar didn't come as a favour to the Pike Companion. But I do know the Pikes aren't on the side of right, not if they force Berans into exile.'

The nursing sister gave Aikin a look of approval. The corporal seemed less convinced. 'You make a good point. Not a word out of place. But your own story doesn't feel as solid.' The man returned his gaze to his wound and watched the sister tie off the last stitch. 'Would you care to revise it before I decide what to do with you?'

'You don't believe the skipper found me on the riverbank?'

'I don't believe your story about coming to the port to petition the Pike Companion on the matter of Beranish women entering the port.'

Aikin smiled. The man wasn't stupid. 'What gave me away?'

'Hard to believe you were unaware the Pike Companion was in Komey.'

'Ah. Yes. I see.'

'And Komey bureaucrats aren't known for their love of Berans.'

'You forget which department I work for.'

The nurse turned in her seat and dropped her instruments into the sink before turning back again. She picked up a bandage and began wrapping it around the corporal's arm.

'Well?' Aikin heard a warning in the corporal's tone.

'Families have secrets. The Oaks are no different.'

'No one has secrets when territory changes hands.'

'But duty remains,' Aikin said, 'and I have a duty to my family. I will speak with the Briar Companion.'

The corporal thanked the nurse and stood up, gestured for Aikin to follow him. He spoke as he walked out of the examination room and into the ward. 'You'll have to convince me to take you to her. You can wait in the cells or you can talk to me.'

Aikin looked around. The embassy's small hospital was full of soldiersisters and traders. Most looked well enough apart from grazes and bruises, but they were still arguing about the scuffle. He couldn't afford to be locked up with the port in such turmoil. Too much risk he'd be forgotten. He hurried his step until he was walking side by side with the corporal.

'Please call me Aikin.'

'You think that will warm me to you?'

Aikin smiled. 'I wish it were that easy. No. But I believe in the power of personal relationships. You've asked me to share my confidences. We should at least know each other's names.'

'That's fair. I'm Allium.' The man held out his hand as they continued walking and Aikin took it and shook it. 'Allium Briar. And now we know each other's names, what next?'

'If you're unhappy with what I feel at liberty to share with you, you can drop me at my embassy or lock me in a cell. The former is my preferred option.'

'Our cells are rather full, but I won't hesitate to lock you up.'

'Then I'll do my best to avoid inconveniencing your jailers.'

Allium gave Aikin a sharp look. 'You're pretty fragrant for a Komey bureaucrat. It's harvest time. Tell me your business.'

Aikin was silent for a moment. The truth, or part of it, was always best. 'I take it the port has been closed to river traffic until recently?'

'You promised answers, not questions.'

'Just trying to work out what news you've had from Komey.'

Allium led the way into some sort of anteroom and then stopped. He folded his arms and waited.

There was no point delaying, so Aikin began with the story of Mica and Obsidian, omitting his and Whilomena's actions, focusing on the portal and the rock child's transformation. Allium's eyes widened. 'We heard a rumour about people travelling through the Stone Body, wanderers talking about an end to the famine. A new treaty. We thought it was…' he hesitated, checking himself.

'A good moment for change?'

'You could say that. That's not an unreasonable inference. But you still haven't told me why you're here.'

It was an impossible to answer with a lie now that news was flowing between Komey and the port. 'I'm in disgrace. Sent to the port. I had some hope that I'd be allowed to live in my embassy, but exile to Galea was on the cards.'

Allium looked taken aback. 'What did you do?'

'That's something I might share with your companion, but I won't tell you. All you need to know is I understand what happened to those Berans at sea. It's a plague. It will happen again and again if anyone uses the portals without knowing what they're doing.'

'You said exile to Galea was on the cards. Past tense. It's no longer on the cards?'

'I love the Stone Body,' Aikin said, ignoring Allium's sceptical look. 'I feel a sense of duty to my family to protect their interests. And, like you, like all of us, I have a trader's heart. I want to remain here, where I was born, and I want the best for our world, but I won't give my knowledge away. I'll trade for my freedom and the betterment of the Oaks.'

'And what shall I say to our Mother? What are you putting on the table?'

'A method for controlling twins. A way to save us from a plague.'

Allium frowned. It wasn't disbelief. Aikin could tell. Allium was thinking, but there was some hesitation in his expression, some repugnance that made little sense. Aikin wasn't sure which part of his story was troubling the other man, but he sensed he'd need to be careful. Then Allium sighed, nodded. 'Very well. You'll have your audience. But I think Rosey will want to see you in private, away from the hall full of traders and soldiers. She's running her late morning parley right now, but I'll send word, requesting a meeting. In the meantime, we'll eat.'

Allium gestured for Aikin to follow, and he led them into the depths of the manor. Aikin felt relieved. The arrangement would give him time to prepare. A private audience suited him. Fewer people meant less chance that some fool would pipe up and tell tales about his previous visit or share some rumour from Komey about Aikin murdering Berans and crushing stones.

They passed the kitchen and a few steps later they entered a bustling dining room. Aikin had to force himself to keep moving because the sight that met him wasn't what he expected. The room was full of Briars; all the Briars. Companionari Briars and Beranish Briars sitting together as though there wasn't a difference between them. Thank the Back he'd seen this curious social arrangement before meeting the Mother. Aikin would need to be even more careful than he'd thought he needed to be. Describing the calamity as some sort of rock child induced plague wouldn't sit well with Berans who revered stones and Companionaris who loved Berans. He'd find something else to explain the acceleration. And he'd need to rephrase any discussion about his knowledge of the secret to controlling rock twins. The word *control* wouldn't do. Better to talk about companioning? No, that was too loaded. He'd speak of matching or something of the sort.

'This way,' Allium said, gesturing at a table with vacant seats.

Aikin smiled, a genuine smile, full of gratitude. 'Thank you. You don't know how welcome this is.'

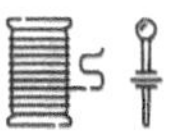

Mica accompanied Acacia and Oria as they walked to the Briars' former embassy and newly designated manor house. The Oak valet and the kitchen hand were two steps ahead, dressed as soldiersisters. Despite the household's best efforts to militarise the pair, they weren't impressive. Their uniforms fit well enough, but neither had the right posture. Willie might have done a better job if they'd dressed him up as a soldier, but the cook was looking after the twins. Laurel and Cerulean were still in the sewing room. Willie had distracted them from the departure by showering them with plates of delicacies. Even without the offer of food, Mica thought the rock twins might not have noticed everyone leaving. The pair had upended the sewing baskets, and when Mica had last seen them, they were laying out threads and buttons in lines, covering the carpet.

The road to Briar Manor was busy with soldiersisters and traders, the latter with signatures that were full of worry. But the closer they came to the manor, the more Berans they saw. Curious. Mica had visited New Lytalia in the past. The place was more hostile to Berans than Komey, and that was saying something. But today, the only looks his honey-coloured eyes and rock skin attracted were from the oldest of the Berans. The frail ones who felt so familiar there was little doubt about the reason for their fearful looks. They flinched as he passed. Oddly, it brought Mica some comfort. It meant more had survived the shipwreck than he had any right to hope.

Acacia walked behind Oak's pretend soldiers. Her white suit had a large oak leaf embroidered on the back and an acorn on her chest. Her confidence and deportment almost made up for the small size of their party, and Mica felt hopeful as they approached the open doors of the Briars' home. The trading hall was full and their approach was unnoticed except for the soldiersisters standing ceremonial guard on either side of the doorway. Mica glimpsed rows of parley chairs between a crowd of shifting backs and legs. A parley was in session.

The valet and kitchen hand halted outside the entrance. As agreed, the pair rapped their swords against their shields, managing a clatter, but not achieving the booming sound that should have triggered the spread of quiet within the room in front of them. Acacia stepped forward and announced their arrival, giving Oria and Mica their traditional titles and a few newly crafted honorifics, her voice loud and commanding:

'Make welcome Oria twenty-third Oak Companion, Head of the House of Oak, Mother to Oak Province, First Sister of the Oak sorority, Companion of the First Settlement, Leader of Trees, Adherent of the New Treaty, Stone Sister, Laurel Twin, Beneficiary of Promise Ahead, Apprentice Wanderer, Beranish Body, Follower of the Path, Admirer of the Back, Dedicant of the Turning.'

'Make welcome too, at the Mother's side, Mica, Penultimate Oak Wanderer, Partner in the New Treaty, Stone Brother, Cerulean Twin, Crafter of Cycles, Builder of Knowledge.'

'And I, Least Among Greats, Ambassador Acacia Oak, Leader of the Oak Embassy, Member of the Oak Sorority, Child of the Oak Mother, Follower of the Path, Reverent of the Back, Dedicant of the Turning.'

The words were impressive, but had no effect, other than producing a look of irritation on the faces of the soldiersisters standing on the cobbles. There was no jumping to attention, no readiness to clear of a ceremonial path for the guests, not even a hint that they were in fact responding to a summons.

Mica peered over Acacia's shoulder but couldn't make out more than he'd already gleaned. He opened his rock skin instead. There were Berans inside. A lot of them. He whispered the news to Oria and Oria tugged Acacia's sleeve until the ambassador bent her head to listen. When the Oak Companion spoke, she didn't bother lowering her voice, 'We can't stand about waiting for good manners to bloom. Make them lead us in. Give Rosey's soldiers something to do.'

Acacia nodded and then stepped forward and handed her paperwork to one of the soldiersisters. The woman looked displeased at the prospect of having to usher them into the crowded hall, but gestured for them to follow.

There were indeed scores of Berans within, and not just in the parley hall. Mica felt them scattered throughout the building. So surprising he almost missed the other signatures. Doubt and Lupe and Quartz were half expected, but the next person was a shock. Fox!

He stopped moving, his smile growing. He stood, grinning like a fool, until Oria reached back and pulled him forward.

'Fox is here. Can you feel her?'

Oria glanced at him but shook her head. 'What about Quartz and the others?'

'They're here too. Doubt and Quartz and Lupe. They're fine. And Saury is with Fox and another Beran. Peri. I know him. But I can't feel Patience.' Mica frowned, halted again, checked, then pulled Oria to a stop. 'Aikin's here too,' he said. 'Not in the hall, but somewhere in the building.' Then Mica's frown deepened as he felt for Whilomena's signature. 'But not the Wheat Companion. Aikin seems to be alone. We'll need to be careful. He may have poisoned the Briar Companion against us.'

Their party wove its way between the chairs and the overspill of people. It was like no other parley Mica had seen before. Nor Oria, if her signature was anything to go by. He felt her calculating, reassessing, disapproving. Mica caught snatches of the guests' conversation as they made their way to the front. Whispered exchanges and emotional signatures that suggested few in the parley room were relaxed. The place was volatile.

And then he caught sight of Fox. Soldiers surrounded her. She looked wet and dishevelled, and her hands were bound. Not just her hands. The bindings rose from her fingertips to her shoulders. She met his eye, and he felt the depth of her relief. He looked past Fox to Saury. The girl was scared but masking it. For a moment, Mica thought Saury's hands were also bound, but then her bindings unravelled, moved, and Mica rock sensed the shape of them. Tentacles. The strangest rock skin he'd ever seen. He turned his attention back to Fox and used his rock sense to probe the shapes underneath her bindings. Just like Saury's.

Their twins must have transformed their rock skin. But where were the rock people? He couldn't feel them in the hall. Hidden somewhere, perhaps? He just hoped it was somewhere safe because no twin would tolerate their human being treated as Fox was being treated, not without someone like Lupe to teach them.

In front of Mica, Acacia and Oria had come to a halt and he got his first look at Rosey Briar. The companion was young. Hard to believe she'd staged a coup because she sat on the edge of the parley bed like a child. There was something of Talia in her manner, something of the ill prepared and frightened woman pretending a role. Her sewing was resting on the bed beside her as she listened to an account of the treatment some injured soldier had received.

Mica turned his attention back to Fox and realised what he hadn't noticed before. The soldiersister standing beside Fox was supporting another, an injured colleague.

A fight then. And it looked as though Fox was being blamed.

The Briar Companion cleared her throat and turned to Fox, 'While I sympathise with your side of this story, we will have order in Port Briar. We do not tolerate attacks.'

Then Acacia started speaking, 'Forgive me. I know I'm interrupting—'

The companion turned to Acacia. 'Yes, and you mustn't interrupt. We must have one subject at a time. That's the best way for a parley to run.'

'Of course,' Acacia said. 'But if I may, I'm here responding to your summons—'

'And you must wait your turn.'

'Yes,' Acacia nodded. 'Quite right. But I am also here to announce—'

The Briar Companion shook her head, held up her hand, and Mica felt a wave of mild panic in the woman's signature. Impossible to believe she'd led a coup when a parley interjection could throw her off course. And there was something else in her signature. Rosey Briar was waiting for something. Maybe there was a more powerful family member involved, a background figure who interceded when Rosey felt out of her depth.

Oria stepped forward, pushing in front of Acacia into Rosey's line of sight. 'Our news is urgent and the girl you have in custody is my great-niece. Whatever's happened, I can vouch for her.'

The Briar Companion turned to Oria, and her expression softened. 'We are most pleased to see new Beranish friends in Port Briar. If you're this one's great-aunt,' the companion gestured to Fox, 'then you must also be from the Oak camp...' She hesitated, her forehead furrowing. 'Or perhaps you're part of her original family in Kelp? Never mind. I can see it's complicated and I look forward to hearing about your journey and your place on the Stone Body, but as I've explained to your great-niece, she can't go unpunished for disturbing the port's peace.'

'The Oaks will make good,' Oria said. 'But I must insist you release Fox because there are more pressing matters that we companions need to discuss.' Rosey looked Oria up and down, confusion on her face. And then Oria announced herself, claimed her status as the Oak Companion and began speaking of her miraculous rebirth, and of portals and twins. At first, the Briar Companion continued to look confused. Then, as Oria spoke of Aikin, describing him as a murderer who was in Rosey's building, the Briar Companion's confusion turned into outright panic. Her hands fluttered as she looked at her sorority for help. Then, spotting the woman she wanted, she waved one of her sisters forward. They began a whispered conversation.

Oria waited, and the room fell silent.

The sister left Rosey's side and hurried across the room, beginning a low conversation with a soldiersister. The soldiersister then spoke with another and that one with another. Mica felt the conversations as bursts of hurried concern that leapt from one Briar to the next until they reached a Beranish woman. The woman stood, overlooking the hall, on a balcony at the back of the room, an ocean of calm.

Mica's rock skin prickled. There was something strange about this place, these Briars. And it went well beyond this nervous young companion. If ever there was a world upside down, Briar Manor was it. The woman on the balcony, the Beran, she was in charge. Mica smiled. Help was at hand. At least he hoped so, and perhaps he could ease its path.

He stepped forward into Rosey Briar's line of sight. 'Your trading hall is busy,' he said, lifting his voice so that all would hear. 'No doubt you will sit many times today to deliberate the great causes that benefit the port and its people. Let's not disturb your work any longer. Fox is a Beran, so we Berans should deal with this problem in private: Oak, Kelp and Briar's Berans meeting in private. If you could allow that? If one or two of your wanderers could spare the time?'

Rosey glanced up at the balcony and Mica rock sensed a slight movement in the woman above them. Nothing much, just a nod. He turned his attention back to Rosey. For the first time since they'd arrived in the hall, the Briar Companion's signature was relaxed and she pressed her palm to her heart. 'Yes! That's it. That's what must happen. Pearl? Would you mind? No doubt you'll want Tanzanite too.'

Mica didn't need to hear their answers. The familiarity of her tone and the warmth in her voice spoke of a very unorthodox arrangement between Briar's Companionaris and its Berans.

26

Aikin reached for another piece of bread then hesitated. Didn't want Allium to think him greedy when there was hunger in the port. He'd noticed how modest and careful the plates surrounding him looked, how little food they carried. But he should have looked up instead of comparing plates. He was aware that another group of people had entered the dining room, but there'd been clusters of people coming and going since he'd arrived. If he'd had his wits about him, he would have felt the change in the atmosphere because Allium looked up and kept looking. Not Aikin. He sat there like a fool, thinking about his stomach, imagining himself anonymous. Didn't realise he was in trouble until hands grabbed him and pulled him off his chair. He stumbled, hit his elbow, then found his feet.

'Captain?' Allium said. 'Something wrong?'

The tallest of the three soldiersisters holding onto Aikin, let go, turned her attention to Allium. 'This one's charged with murder. His family wants him in their embassy's cells. His aunt's the companion.'

'His aunt? Sent a letter?'

'No, she's here. The Oak Companion's here in person.'

Aikin glanced at Allium to see whether there might be some luck, some angle he could use to reach the Briar Companion and keep himself out of Oria's clutches. The corporal looked worried, but his next few words weren't what Aikin expected, 'There's an actual Companionari companion here?' Allium said. 'In our port? And our... ah... our leader thinks we should do what the woman wants?'

'She does. Unusual circumstances. An unusual companion by the looks of her. Pearl is taking things in hand and Tanzanite's helping her manage the situation. They'll walk the Oak Mother back to her embassy. They'll talk.'

Aikin didn't need functioning rock skin to feel Allium's relief at the sound of Pearl's name. He'd never heard of the woman, but then again he knew little of the Briars, much less the personalities in their camp, and Pearl was a Beranish name. The Briar family didn't run a Komey department, had little presence in the city, so he didn't know the family or their habits.

'I can lend a hand,' Allium said. 'Look after Master Aikin for Pearl.'

The captain shook her head. 'We need you walking the streets. Rosey is fretting about riots. We need to reassure her.'

Aikin didn't have a moment to ponder the captain's overly familiar tone when speaking about the Briar Companion because the soldier began pulling him, hurrying him, steering him between the tables. A little rough. A little high-handed, but Aikin didn't resist. And he did his best to remain on his feet. Didn't want the woman to grapple him and touch the book strapped to his body. And he didn't bother speaking. Words wouldn't work. Not in this situation. Knowledge was the only currency that could free him. His only task now was to keep the book, the source of his knowledge, out of other people's hands. He'd hide it when he could. Until then, he'd wait for life to play out. The world offered a clever man endless chances. All a man had to do was pick the right one. In the meantime, the book would stay where it was and Aikin would keep his feet on the ground, and his eyes and ears open. The inevitability of another age plague meant he'd be free again soon. More importantly, he'd be ascendant because he had the answer to controlling the stone twins. Assuming he wasn't aged to dust before he had a chance to turn what he'd read into reality!

When the soldiersisters reached the dining hall doorway, the captain released him. She stared him in the eye as though a stern look could bind a person. 'Do I need to rope you?'

'No need for that.' Aikin smoothed his hair back. 'I'm sure my aunt and I can clear up our family quarrel without resorting to ropes or chains.' He gave the woman his most earnest gaze. She seemed to accept it because she turned away and neither she nor her sisters looked back to check that he followed.

Aikin spent a couple of minutes thinking about an escape. Not that he gave any serious thought to it, but he'd be a fool not to give it some consideration. But each time he glanced at a doorway or examined an open window, the captain's posture stiffened. Curious, because she had her back to him. It wasn't rock skin. Shouldn't be. She was Companionari. He tried to recall her eyes. Had they been an overly honey-brown or an unexpectedly golden-green? Such things weren't unheard of and tended to be managed with a daily dose of dust bust tea. Out in the more distant provinces, it wasn't unknown for sororities to take the treaty a little less seriously than they should. He wished he could look at her arms.

Ahead of Aikin, the captain rolled her shoulders under his scrutiny and he looked away, concentrated on other things. No need to let her know that he'd guessed her secret. Besides, as much as he hated being in custody, escape wasn't a serious option. Aikin needed to be in the thick of things to regain his power. It was the cells that he needed to avoid and he'd talk his way out of that problem once he arrived at the embassy.

He smiled at Oria when they came face to face in the street. And at Mica, who stood beside her. Aikin ignored the look of hatred on the man's face. Mica was an unwelcome presence in the port, but his hatred was to be expected. Old Quartz was there too, looking sour. And Fox. Aikin's feelings got the better of him as he looked at his daughter, a rush of warmth in his chest. She glared at him, but seemed more tired and sad than angry. Her sister, Saury, stood beside her and Doubt was on her other side. The children gave him fearful looks. But what could you expect from children? He'd hurt them and they didn't understand the bigger picture. But Fox did. Should. She liked to pretend hard choices weren't necessary. And that was disappointing because he'd brought her up to see the world as it was, not as she wanted it to be.

He looked away. He didn't look down, but he avoided the hostile gazes. It was a relief to fall into place between the three armed guards and to find himself at the rear of the party as Acacia led them on their way. The moment for challenge hadn't yet arrived.

There were three unfamiliar Berans in the party. Tanzanite was obvious. His name identified him as a wanderer and he walked beside Quartz, wearing a wanderer's cloak. Aikin heard them exchanging small talk, Quartz commenting on the noisy clarion gulls; Tanzanite insisting the correct name for the birds was storm gulls. Time wasters, both of them, but Aikin couldn't help filing away the different Beranish names for parley gulls. If he ever got back to Komey and the Oak library, he'd check the open dictionary of Beranish names, make sure the variations were listed.

And it was clear enough who Pearl was because she'd positioned herself alongside Oria. The two were so busy talking they were oblivious to their surrounds, with Acacia needing to prod them from time to time, and steer them around corners. The only other Beranish woman in the party was unfamiliar to Aikin. She was old, but carried herself like a younger woman. He wasn't sure how she fitted in. She held onto Mica's elbow. Not for support, more like a guiding hand, a hand of condescending familiarity. He wished he could hear everything everyone said, but he was too far behind. He could see Pearl and Tanzanite seemed animated, whereas the woman beside Mica seemed troubled.

Then they reached the embassy and Acacia brought everyone to a halt. The painted façade was flaking and curling. Someone had boarded up two of the uppermost windows. Aikin felt a rush of shame and then anger that Oria had let the family's property come to this. As though Oak was a failed province of no consequence.

Acacia opened the door and ushered them in. Fox and Peri and the children first, spilling into the wide foyer, then Mica and his ancient Beranish friend. Oria was still busy talking, bending the ears of both Pearl and Tanzanite as she walked in. Aikin was close enough now to catch a few words about her precious new treaty, '...so it would join Companionaris and Berans together. Intermarrying. No more children taken from families.'

There was a moment then. Something in Pearl and Tanzanite's body language that gave Aikin pause. He didn't feel it in his arms. They were still useless, but he shivered at the sight of the Briars' sudden stillness. Then they were moving again, smiling, nodding, as though nothing had just happened. The Briars had a secret.

Aikin and his guards entered last. Pearl glanced back at him and with a wave of her hand, gestured for the soldiersisters to station themselves near the door to prevent his escape. Oria didn't seem to notice that a Beran commanded Companionari soldiers, but Aikin saw it: the upside down chain of command.

Oria gave an almost silent clap of her hands, a virtual parley gesture. Aikin suspected his aunt was about to launch into a tedious and unnecessary welcome.

'Yes, well...' Oria smiled at everyone, her attention settling on Pearl. 'There is something we didn't want to mention earlier,' her voice was quiet, almost as though the embassy contained sleeping children. 'We told you about recent events...'

'Obsidian and the portals, yes,' Pearl said.

Oria gestured for Pearl to lower her voice. 'Yes, and the changes in Komey, but there's more. We're not alone here. You'll need to be careful not to disturb them, but Mica and I have twins and—'

'Here?' Aikin asked. 'Twins, plural? More than one?'

Oria glared at him, a stubborn expression on her face. She didn't answer. She turned to Fox and told her to take the children upstairs. Aikin interrupted again. 'How many? Do they dance?' he asked.

Oria and Mica and Quartz gave each other knowing looks. It was answer enough. 'So they've danced. Or tried to. How many are here? Two? Four? Have you separated them?'

'No. They wouldn't tolerate being separated,' Oria said.

'But how many?'

'Two.'

'Then you'll need my help,' Aikin said.

'You?' Mica said. 'Your help?'

The old Beranish woman beside Mica touched the wanderer's shoulder. 'If this Companionari man knows something that will help us, we—'

'No!' Mica shook his head.

Fox stood on the stairs, listening, looking confused. Before she could ask what was going on, Mica was talking again. Not to Aikin; to the woman beside him. 'You don't understand, Lupe,' he said. 'Aikin murdered people and killed rock children.'

Lupe tuned to Aikin, gave him a long, penetrating look. Then she refocused on Mica. 'I'm not saying it doesn't matter, but you know as well as I do we can't control them.'

'With your help we might,' Mica sounded desperate. 'Cerulean listens to you. You—'

Lupe gestured towards herself. 'And look what he did to me. And the others. People are dead and dying.'

'What's she talking about?' Pearl asked Oria. 'What haven't you told us? Why would we need a murderer's help?'

Oria gave Aikin a disgusted glance, then turned back to Pearl. 'I'm afraid we need all the help we can get. The rock twins can end the famine, but they're unpredictable. Dangerous. Sometimes they're volatile. And we don't know why or when or what triggers it. And we don't know if Aikin's claims are a ruse. But I don't think we can ignore his offer to help.'

'What exactly is so dangerous about rock people being volatile?' Tanzanite asked.

Aikin cleared his throat. He'd need to be careful, but his moment had arrived. He kept his face neutral, projected a bureaucratic matter-of-factness into his voice, 'A stone twin on its own can cause a...' Aikin stopped, caught himself before he could utter the phrase *age plague*. It wouldn't do with these stone-loving people. He tried again, 'A problem.'

'What sort of problem?' Fox asked.

Aikin looked from Mica to Lupe, from Quartz to Oria, and back to Fox. 'An ageing problem that amplifies when there are two of them.' He turned back to Mica. 'Will you tell her more, or shall I? I gather she hasn't seen what we've seen, what I've read about.'

'There's a rush of life,' Mica said.

'Well, that's one way of putting it,' Lupe said. 'I'd call it a rush of age, and Cerulean did this to me when he didn't have another stone creature beside him.'

Oria took a deep breath and directed her words to Fox, 'After you left Komey we had news from Persica. It was destroyed. A whole province died when those twins arrived. Killed their own wanderers too. At least, that's what we've assumed because we've no sign of them.'

'Everyone died?' Pearl said.

'Likely it was a dance,' Aikin said, ignoring Pearl. 'An unmanaged dance.'

'What do you mean?' Peri asked him.

'Even numbers dance,' Aikin said. 'And when they dance, they can work miracles, but they can also destroy. And the bigger the reel, the more hazardous the dance.' It was more complicated than that, but Aikin wasn't in the business of giving away knowledge. He'd say what needed to be said to convince them he was important and nothing more. 'Point is, the two rock people you have in the embassy need to be separated.'

'But we don't know for sure there was a dance in Persica,' Oria said.

'Only that there were two of them and everyone died,' Quartz pointed out. 'Evidence enough.'

Aikin saw Fox started to speak and then stop. Then she tried again. 'I... I left my twin in the ocean. Do you think...'

'I did too,' Saury said. 'And Patience died.'

'We left three twins in the water,' Fox said. 'We couldn't find them and we had to flee. Pace, our father, he was trying to kill us.'

Aikin felt an unexpected need to reassure her. 'Three won't dance, but they're still dangerous. If they're in the ocean, they might not do too much harm. They'll probably be all right.' He turned back to Oria. 'But you're going to need my help with your two. You'd best show me where they are.'

Quartz was frowning. 'I can't feel them.'

Then everyone was hurrying from the foyer, following Oria.

Aikin was the last to enter the funny little sewing room. The place was empty of stone twins, but on the wall opposite, a strange lace curtain rolled in the breeze from the open window, a picture of a dance. Then Aikin looked down. On the floor, unnoticed, edges trampled beneath feet, was another image, this one wrought in buttons and coloured thread. Aikin recognised it: the Caller, the leader of the dance. The role Aikin sought for himself. In the picture, the figure had an avian aspect with its long upholstery needle legs, its thready body, and its toggle button nose. Aikin bent down and swept the image away before anyone else could see it. He smiled. Here he was, short and neat-nosed, nothing like the figure in the twins' picture. But he would be the Caller. He would control the dance and rule the Stone Body.

'They've gone,' Oria whispered. 'Where the Back have they gone?'

Aikin's smile broadened. Regaining his power would be easier than expected.

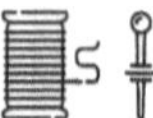

Fox leant out the window of the embassy sewing room. Fruitless, but she looked up and down the hill, searching for any sign of Laurel and Cerulean. The news of the Persican calamity and all it implied had shaken her. The people aged to dust. And she'd abandoned all three twins without a thought of what harm they might do. The Back knew what had happened to Kelp's camp and everyone in the manor house. She had to go back, try to fix things if she could, if it wasn't too late.

Across the cobbled road, three ancient-looking Berans shared a small piece of bread in the weak sunshine. She wondered whether these were some of the prematurely aged or simply more of the Berans the Briars had brought to the port.

She could hear snatches of conversation in the room behind her.

'... door to door.'

'... could be anywhere. Anywhere!'

'... gone inland.'

'Back and Path.'

'The river is just...'

'... must tell Rosey...'

Someone touched Fox's shoulder, and she pulled her head back into the room. Mica stood behind her. She turned, and he wrapped his arms around her, pulled her close. In a rush, she told him she needed to leave, head back to Kelp, and why. The relief was physical: an unknotting of her stomach, a tingle on the back of her neck. She held Mica close and stroked his back with her tentacles, rock sensed his reluctant agreement.

Oria was already issuing orders. 'We find them. We take them to Persica where they can't do much harm, if any. We leave the coordination of everything else to the Briars.' She turned to Pearl. 'The new treaty. Explanations about the twins. Managing Komey. All of that is up to you now, Mother Briar.' Fox saw the other woman flinch at the title, and Oria laughed, 'I'm no fool, Pearl. Rosey Briar isn't the Briar Companion. You are.'

Pearl looked troubled, but when she spoke, her words confirmed the truth. 'Briar has always done things differently. Camp and manor are as one: in marriage and management of our province. The companionship talent moves where it will. In this generation, it rests with me. I'd be grateful if you kept the truth within these walls.'

Oria looked at Aikin, and he shrugged. Fox saw a look of mild amusement on his face. 'Depends. I might keep her confidence and then again, I might not.'

Fox couldn't help herself. 'For once, can't you behave like a decent person? All of this is worse because of you. You don't have to squeeze personal advantage from every single thing. You've already won. We're going to be beholden to you if it's true that you know how to manage stone twins. Isn't that enough?'

Aikin looked uncomfortable. He didn't do more than shrug, but Fox felt him give way.

'I assume no one wants to waste time arguing about who should coordinate the search?' Oria said. When no one argued, she continued issuing orders, breaking them into pairs, including the children in her arrangements.

Mica brought up the survivors of the shipwreck, those who might still be on the water, and asked Pearl to add that search to her list of tasks. She agreed to send out some boats.

'I can organise supplies and a barge for transporting the twins once we find them,' Tanzanite said.

'Then use Ogden,' Aikin said. 'She hates me but she's not scared of strange looking Berans, so she won't mind transporting them.'

'Helping strange looking Berans?' Oria asked.

'She helped Fox and Saury despite their tentacles. Preferred them to me.'

'Good.' Then Oria turned to Tanzanite. 'Then speak to Ogden.' Then she looked at everyone else in the room, gave her last instructions. 'If you find Laurel or Cerulean, don't startle them. You'll need Mica and me to approach them, so send for us.'

Oria was careful to pair the Companionaris with Berans. *Eyes and rock skin complementing each other* was how she put it. Fox was sorry not to be paired with Mica after such a long separation, but searching alongside Acacia was almost as good. Together, they walked the foreshore north of the Cava, Acacia watching for footprints on the sand; Fox rock sensing the water. They talked as they walked, not chatter, just sharing what had happened to each of them in the other's absence. Acacia spoke of visiting Lark and Lark's slow conversion to Fox's cause and the impact it was having on Komey's other adoptees. Fox told Acacia about her journey. Soon though, they fell silent. Fox sensed she wasn't the only one who felt they were wasting precious time on a fruitless search.

'How far should we go?' Acacia asked.

Fox halted. 'And why would they walk this way? We're wasting time.'

'But we don't know what they'd do.'

The breeze played with the ends of Fox's hair and she turned to Acacia, an idea bringing a smile to her face. 'But maybe we do.'

'Tell me.'

Fox's smile widened. 'He thinks he's so clever.'

'Who?'

'Aikin. He thinks he's keeping all his secrets, but he lets things slip because he can't help boasting.' Fox turned toward the port, started walking back as she spoke, 'He kept talking about them dancing, about the risk of bigger reels, as though the dance is some sort of drive. I don't think he realised he'd implied that. What if Cerulean and Laurel are trying to find my three? Why else would Cerulean and Laurel leave Mica and Oria? They wouldn't leave unless something stronger was pulling them away. Obsidian never wanted to leave Mica. Never! So, I think they must have caught the scent of my twins, or the feel of them.'

'All the way from Kelp?' Acacia was following Fox, but she sounded sceptical.

Fox didn't need to argue; the idea had become a certainty. She started running, called out over her shoulder. 'Our twins must have followed Saury and me. I don't think they're in Kelp. I think they're much closer. And I think Cerulean and Laurel are heading upriver to meet them.'

Acacia caught up with Fox, and her voice was breathless when she spoke, 'That's a lot of maybes, but perhaps you're right.'

Fox picked up her pace. 'I am.'

They ran and, when they could no longer run, they jogged. They didn't stop until Fox came to a halt on the apex of the footbridge across the Cava. She leant over the rail, catching her breath, half hoping Laurel and Cerulean would be visible. Acacia came to rest beside her, and they scanned the river for the twins.

'They're not here,' Fox said. 'We're too late. They must be further upriver.'

'Then let's head back to the embassy and gather the others,' Acacia said, and she stepped away from the rail.

Fox shook her head. 'I'm not going back.'

'What do you mean?'

'You go. Get the others,' Fox said. 'Follow me on the barge. I'm going to swim.'

'But you'll be faster on the barge. It won't take long to gather everyone.'

'I'm not waiting. I'm done with waiting.' And before Acacia could stop her, Fox gripped the rail with her tentacles, pulled herself up and over, and she dived into the river.

27

Talia rubbed her lower back to ease the pain radiating from her hips, realised what she'd just done, and laughed at the caricature she made. A gesture of old age and a humourless laugh, but laughter was better than self-pity. She shook her head and stood up straight, willing herself to find the reserves of youth she hoped still existed somewhere in her body. It worked. A bit. Well, the stretching helped, but this decision to take the twins inland was easier said than done. She was stiff in the morning and tired in the evening and slow during the day. And shepherding the stone twins was a challenge because they wanted to return to their original path, and Talia doubted that would change. The poor things were still full of longing and seeking, a hunger for someone or something. Probably looking for Fox and Saury and Patience.

Talia looked around the campsite she'd created the night before. She'd grown a simple shelter, so they hadn't been too cold, but they hadn't eaten and everyone was hungry. Without her clay pot, cooking was impossible, and they'd lost their access to fish when they walked away from the river. Talia hoped they'd find somewhere more hospitable and soon.

Amber and Cyanna were sitting on the ground, playing with

320

leaves and pebbles, making patterns in the dirt. Baylor stood beneath one of Talia's date palms, looking up. He glanced over his shoulder at Talia and then turned his attention back to the tree, cupping his hands. Unlike many of the twins' wants and needs, this one was easy to interpret. Talia focused on the bunch of dates hanging above his head and hurried them along. The fruit fell like rain and Baylor squealed with pleasure, catching dates and stuffing them into his mouth. Soon, all three twins were beneath the palm tree and Talia joined them, catching dates, filling their bellies with fruit. It almost felt satisfying. But the distraction didn't last long. The twins grew restless. First, Baylor dropped a handful of uneaten dates on the ground, then Amber paused her chewing to sniff the air.

Talia didn't wait. She knew what would happen. They would remember the river and they'd leave if she didn't act quickly. She called out their names, using the singsong voice she would have used for a child. They turned back to her, responded with clicks and croons and she felt the warmth of their regard in her arms. As she led the way further inland, she shifted to something between a skip and a hop, finding a childhood song to suit her rhythm. They followed, forgetting the river for now. If only she were her correct bodily age, she'd manage this better. But it worked. They kept following. Perhaps it would get easier when they were further from the Cava, but she doubted it. They could neither see nor hear the river, and as for smelling it, the rotting fecund smell Talia was chasing had obliterated the scent of water. But the twins didn't seem to need ordinary human senses to know where they were and where they wanted to go. And they wanted to go back. But they followed her as she led them deeper inland. And Talia was fairly certain she knew where they would end up.

Yesterday morning, she'd spotted a pear tree. By the end of that day, peach and nectarine trees had joined the pears. It meant she was in Persica and Persica seemed to be the heart of the smell because the fruit was inedible, rotting on the ground, knee deep around the trunks. The trees looked sick: skeleton branches and troubled fruit. Talia consoled herself with the thought that the empty landscape and the sickly trees meant the people had left. A failed province didn't keep its people. And when they reached the manor, if it was empty, Talia would grow a wall of oak trees to contain the twins. The four of them would live out their lives inside the manor and its gardens, cooking rice and dates until they worked out what else they could do. The consolation didn't last long. Soon they were passing human bones and, after that, an empty Beranish camp.

A while later, they caught sight of Persica Manor. Silent and still; no sign of its household. The skeleton trees covered the ground haphazardly, trunks still surrounded by rotten fruit. Even the garden paths were obstructed by trees. The place made Talia shiver. This was no ordinary provincial failure. She wondered if her three followers had done this, if they'd been here before they'd taken to the river. Impossible to know, but even if they'd caused the disaster in Persica, she couldn't waver.

She began growing her fence as soon as she felt they were close enough to the manor. It was a challenge, juggling the need to concentrate on singing to the twins with the need to shape her fence. She was lucky the twins liked games. Anything approximating a proper game would have required too much concentration, but she got them to hold hands. Then, each time they needed to break the chain to avoid a tree, they all clapped. It was simple enough for Talia to manage, but she was footsore and tired by the time they reached the manor house.

Talia led the twins into the kitchen pantry and locked them in. It wasn't ideal, but the food would distract them and the fence had to be finished and she was running out of energy. She stood with her back against the pantry door, uncertain about whether she'd done the right thing because the air felt tight and cold and the door handle rattled as they tried to get out. For a moment, the air continued to tighten, then the sounds within the pantry shifted as the twins noticed where they were and began exploring. Talia sighed with relief. If she wasn't too long, they'd tolerate being shut in. Even so, her feet felt heavier and her heart seemed to work harder as she walked back to the front of the manor. Older. She felt older. Not by much, but she didn't have room for much.

Her fence was just a semi-circle still, the open edges visible in her peripheral vision, the Persican landscape wide open in front of her. She sat down on the verandah to take the pressure off her swollen feet, leant her back against the wall of the manor and resumed her work with the trees.

Her efforts were haphazard now and, as the fence grew, it was no longer growing in an elegant line. Trunks sprouted around objects and took ugly shortcuts. As the two ends drew together, Talia abandoned the curve and grew the open ends together in a straight line. But she did it. She closed the fence.

She lay down on the cold, tessellated tiles. Her heart was pounding, a thudding, rattling sensation, and she was too tired to worry about anything. She slept or lost consciousness. She wasn't sure which. But she came back into the world with a sensation of the air warming up and a thudding that she thought was her poor aged heart. Only it wasn't. It was fruit ripening on trees and then falling to the ground. She opened her eyes to find two Berans crouching beside her.

'I'm sorry,' she said. 'Back forgive me. I thought you'd all left.'

Then she realised her mistake, saw what was obvious. They wore wanderer's cloaks, but they weren't ordinary men. They were rock twins, grubby and torn and wary. The pair had twigs and leaves in their hair and the dried remains of what looked like fruit all over them. She sat up and smiled at them, but her heart sank. They'd done this. The poor things hadn't understood, and they'd killed everyone in the province. Thank the Back for her fence. She just hoped it wouldn't occur to them to destroy it.

'Hello twins,' she said, and her tongue was slow and thick with fear, her voice thin, but she tried to project some warmth and reassurance into her tone. 'Welcome,' she said. Then, somehow, she found a steadier part of herself that let her gain a bit of control. 'You'll need names.'

She took the hand of the nearest twin, a golden-eyed man with thick curly hair. He didn't pull away, but she could feel his alarm. This would need to be quick and simple or she'd lose them. 'I'm naming you Pear because I can see a pear tree right behind you.' She smiled and withdrew her hand. She reached over and touched the second. Couldn't do more than reach the back of his hand. His skin shivered under her touch. This one was younger, his eyes lighter, more silvery. 'And you are...' She looked behind him, but the garden offered nothing but pear trees and weeds. Then she had a thought. 'I'm naming you Freestone because it's the best type of summer fruit. Welcome to this life. You are loved and wanted.' It was a lie, and she hoped their rock skin didn't tell them it was a lie. She sighed. They would know. Of course they would know. 'You *are* wanted, but forgive me because I am frightened. I think... I think it's time you met the others and then everything might start feeling better.'

Talia held out her hands. The twins backed away, but she waited. After a few moments, Freestone touched her index finger. She smiled at him, nodded, praised him. Then Pear stepped closer. She turned her hands over, held them out palm up, and when their hands met hers, Talia clasped them. Then she pulled herself to her feet and found her feet no longer ached because the air was warmer and looser and the twins in front of her were smiling. She wasn't back to her normal self, wasn't inhabiting the body of a girl who'd just reached womanhood, but she was no longer a crone.

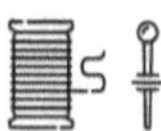

Mica untied the horses from the barge's hitching rail and gathered their leads. Getting the animals off the barge wasn't his job, but Ogden was moving too slowly and as for the rest of them... Their endless talk about whether they'd let Aikin disembark and whether he should be bound was driving Mica crazy. There was no time for argument. Fox was on her own. And the unknown situation in Persica wasn't the only risk. If she caught up with Laurel and Cerulean, anything might happen. The twins didn't know her and they might kill her. Unintentionally, but dead was dead. The image of Oria and her rebirth came to mind, but it was little comfort. Mica put a hand to his chest to soothe his racing heart, but the movement startled the horses. He shushed them and took a firmer grip on their reins.

He led the horses down the ramp and onto the riverbank. The animals leapt onto dry land as though they were jumping a fence and almost overran him. He managed to keep in front of their hooves, but had to run up the slope to do it. He was on top of Fox's footprints now, and he could see Laurel and Cerulean's prints, too. Mica had rock sensed the twins and Fox from the barge. All the Berans had. But now he was on the land, he was surprised to sense that others had passed this way. A little too faded for Mica to know for sure, but there was something familiar about them. Maybe Fox's missing twins and someone else, but it was hard to tell. He would have asked Quartz, but there wasn't time to waste and it didn't matter. Well, only mattered in terms of who should ride alongside Mica because there weren't enough horses for everyone. Only five, and Mica was definitely going to be on one of them.

He turned around, looked at everyone standing about on the riverbank. Saury would have to come if, indeed, her twin had passed this way. And Peri had spoken to Mica at the start of the journey about trying to bond with Patience's orphaned twin if they came across him. So Peri would need a horse. The same was true of Oria because of Laurel. That was four horses spoken for. And he'd need Lupe for her expertise.

Mica called out the names and held out the reins. His chosen people were quick to respond, but so was everyone else. Doubt especially. Insisting he should come.

Mica shook his head. The boy didn't enjoy hearing what Mica needed to say, but it had to be said. '... you don't need a horse, Doubt. You can walk. This is going to be dangerous and you're not essential.'

Doubt's gaze didn't waver. 'Everything on the Stone Body can be dangerous,' he said, echoing one of Mica's own refrains, 'but we all play a part. And maybe I am essential.'

'I said no.'

'But that's not fair! I want to help.'

'He can ride with me,' Oria said. 'I'll look after him.'

Mica wanted to argue, remind Oria that Mica's decisions about Doubt were none of her business, but Fox was alone in a province with an unknown number of stone people. He didn't have time for this. He shrugged and hoped he wouldn't regret it. He consoled himself with the memory of Doubt on the beach with Laurel and Cerulean. At least, the boy hadn't made the situation worse. Mica gave Oria the reins, and she led the horse away and mounted up, gesturing for Doubt to join her.

Mica handed over the other three horses to Peri, Lupe, and Saury.

'You should take a few more Berans with you,' Quartz said. 'You're forgetting Persica's twins. If you come across them, you'll need Berans to bond with them. Put Saury behind you, and that's one more horse that's available.' Quartz didn't wait for Mica's answer. The old wanderer turned to Tanzanite and Pearl. 'Either of you... One of you... Take Saury's mount.'

The pair looked at each other and had a quick discussion, then Tanzanite stepped forward and Saury gave him her horse.

Quartz was speaking again, talking to Lupe, 'And, if you don't mind... I think I'm light enough for your horse to carry me behind you, which should mean we have everyone we need. Even if it's not everyone we want,' he said, looking regretfully at those they were leaving behind. Pearl gave Quartz an approving smile, and as she did,

Mica smelt something lovely overwhelming the fruity rot in the air. Hundreds of daffodils and hyacinths were spouting and flowering in the surrounding landscape. 'Perhaps I was wrong about who we need,' Quartz laughed.

'No,' Pearl said. 'You were right. Take Tanzanite and go. We won't be far behind.'

Mica held out his hand for Saury, lifting her up and setting her behind him.

'Wait,' Aikin said. 'I'm coming. You need me.'

Mica opened his mouth to deny it, but closed it again. He sighed, nodded. If Aikin had knowledge, it was true they might need it.

'I'll take him with me,' Peri offered.

'It will be hard on the horses,' Saury said, 'carrying so many grown-ups.'

'We'll keep an eye on them, go slowly,' Oria said, 'but it is still faster than walking.'

Mica turned his horse and moved off. He opened his rock sense, feeling for Fox, and caught something. 'She's not too far ahead,' he called out. Then he turned to speak to Saury where she sat behind him, high up against the cantle. 'When we reach Fox, if everything is all right, we can dismount and walk. I'll make sure we don't over-work the horses.'

They rode inland and soon began passing trees knee deep in dead fruit. The smell was strong now that they'd left Pearl's flowers behind, but not intolerable. To Mica's relief, they caught up with Fox about two hours later. She was standing in a clearing ringed with date palms and oak trees. In the middle were the remains of a fire and beyond the fire, a lean-to made from living trees.

Oria was already off her horse and striding towards Fox before Mica had a chance to dismount. 'I can see Talia's hand in this camp-site,' she called out to Fox. 'So, where is she? By the Back, I'll have words for her, leaving Komey with no explanation.'

'Not here,' Fox said, turning to Mica, giving him a quick smile. It wasn't much, but he could feel the depth of her relief at his arrival. 'I only just got here.' She turned back to her aunt. 'There's no one else around, so we'd best keep going. I was just about to leave.'

Aikin slipped from his seat behind Peri and landed on the ground. He walked over to the shelter, looked it up and down. From the pride in his signature, a Beran could be mistaken for thinking he'd made it himself. 'So this is where my little Talia fetched up after we parted. Interesting.'

Saury dismounted from behind Mica, and Mica followed her example. He patted the horse's neck in thanks, glad to see it hadn't broken a sweat.

Then Quartz dismounted and held out his hand for Lupe, and Mica rock sensed Fox's dismay at the delay unfolding before her. Lupe was still suffering from her sudden ageing, and she moved slowly. Once she had both feet on the ground, she halted, examining the dirt. Quartz joined her and Mica felt them stretching their senses, feeling for the shape of the signatures that had passed by. 'Cerulean and Laurel,' she said, 'but there are others too.' She looked at Quartz. 'Do you know them? I don't recognise them.'

'Talia, yes,' Quartz said. 'And three more.'

'Three?' Fox said and Mica rock sensed her excitement.

'Three rock people,' Quartz said.

Fox walked over to the old man and hugged him. When she finally let go, she looked down and Mica felt her struggling to feel what Quartz had sensed, what Mica could sense. 'I was following footprints,' Fox said, 'and I thought I could rock sense someone I knew. It felt like Talia, but I wasn't sure. I could tell there were others with her. I thought it was just Cerulean and Laurel. But you're certain?'

Quartz gestured at the ground. 'Definitely Laurel and Ceru—'

'About the missing twins?' Fox repeated.

'One certainly feels like you,' Saury told Fox.

'Yes,' Quartz agreed. 'And one like you, Saury. And the third resembles Patience. So yes, all the missing twins. We're on the right track. There are five of them ahead of us. Separate groups, but all heading for Persica Manor.'

Fox closed her eyes, and Mica rock sensed tears beneath her lids. When she opened them again, her smile was broad. 'Then let's get going.' She didn't wait for the others to agree. She led the way, walked out of the clearing and everyone followed.

Mica thought it should have been a happy moment, but Aikin's signature worried him. The murderer exited the clearing at Oria's side, his signature full of avarice and excitement. The news about Fox's twins had pleased him, and the why of it troubled Mica. There was no doubt in Mica's mind that Aikin had a secret plan, probably several plans, that posed a danger to everyone. Mica wished he could interrogate the man, but there was no point. Aikin's responses couldn't be trusted. But Mica would watch him. Right now, he looked harmless, but Mica wasn't fooled so he handed his horse's reins to Saury and hurried his step, caught up with Oria and Aikin. Not too close, but close enough to act if he needed to.

'... so I gather Talia helped you escape.' Oria's autocratic tone had returned, and she gave her nephew a withering look. 'I must say, I'm disappointed.'

'In me?' Aikin said. 'You shouldn't be. I'm blameless.'

Then, before Mica had time to act, something happened and it wasn't Aikin who disturbed the peace. It was Oria. She shoved Aikin, then looked down at her left arm and blushed. 'I'm sorry. I should have—'

Aikin laughed. 'Getting impetuous in your old age. Well, I suppose I should say, *apology accepted.*'

Oria glared at him and then turned her attention back to her arm. She took a deep breath, shook her head, looked away. 'Yes, well, we're all full of surprises and not all of them are good. And while I continue to be disappointed by you, Nephew, I'd expected better from Talia. I can't believe I gave her a second chance. The Back knows I tried, but she turned out to be a foolish, foolish young woman, undeserving of her talent. The only consolation is, she doesn't seem to be causing too much damage out here.'

'You needn't worry about your trees, Aunt,' Aikin said. 'I solved that problem. I told you, I'm useful. Talia has control over her talent. And I gave it to her. You should thank me.'

Oria snorted, and several others objected loudly. For a moment, the signatures surrounding Mica were so incensed, he worried that someone might emulate Oria and hurt Aikin, but he kept his mouth shut and the threat of violence eased. 'Well,' Oria sniffed, 'you might be useful, but it doesn't change my judgement of you. You're never to be trusted again, and nor is that girl.'

Evidently, Fox had been listening because she'd dropped back and now she began objecting to Oria's analysis. 'We don't actually know what happened, why Talia left Komey. But I think she's looking after the twins. And if she is, we all owe her a debt. Me especially.'

'She was definitely with them in the clearing,' Quartz called out from behind them. 'That says something. That shelter wasn't for just one person.'

Oria sighed, but acknowledged the point and asked Aikin to account for Talia's role in his escape.

'No point asking him anything,' Tanzanite said. 'You can't trust someone like him to speak the truth.'

Mica agreed and his rock sense told him that Oria did too, but she had a complex relationship with Aikin, a family history. Perhaps it meant she would know his truth from his lies.

'You're all mistaken,' Aikin said. 'Except maybe Fox. Ask yourselves: Who banished me in the first place? It was Talia! Fox was there. Ask her. And so were you, Mica.' Aikin caught Mica's eye. 'It was Talia. So why would she help me escape?'

Mica held Aikin's gaze. 'Who knows what lies you told her?'

'Tsk,' Aikin grunted, turning away. 'Talia blames me for ruining her life. Despises me. And by the way, you're all wrong. I didn't escape. My well-meaning supporters abducted me. And ever since, I have made every effort to reach the port.' He spoke to Fox now. 'You know that. You were on the barge with me, heading to the port. You heard me say I wanted to go to New Lytalia. And that's exactly where I went. And I'm only in Persica because I'm needed.'

Now it was Tanzanite who snorted. 'You blackmailed your way here.'

'A little harsh, but I admit I did what I could to be included. But that doesn't change the fact that in every case I have submitted myself to the authority of the presiding companion.'

The party fell silent again. Fox dropped back and had a quiet conversation with Saury. Mica could feel her reassuring her little sister. He took his cue from Fox and gave his attention to Doubt. Both children were still experiencing the aftermath of Aikin and Whilomena's violence. Aikin's boasts weren't easy for them to hear.

A little while later, Fox overtook Mica. He thought she wanted to speak with him, but she just patted his shoulder as she passed him by and it was clear she was once more focused on the search for the twins. The party spread out as Fox moved ahead and the children and Quartz and Lupe began falling behind. Mica retraced his steps to check on them, and when he realised they were all exhausted, he helped them mount up. The smell of rot was growing stronger and all of them were tiring.

It was late in the afternoon when Mica rock sensed the manor and the landscape started to change. At first, it was the appearance of formal orchards. Later, they passed packing sheds and shelters. No living people anywhere, but there were bones on the ground, human and animal. Everyone was uneasy, but no one spoke. Then the Beranish camp came into view, and that hurt. More bones and the horrible sound of loose canvas flapping in the wind. A short while later, Mica rock sensed something different, something foreign. Ahead, between them and the more distant manor, was a seemingly endless line of oak trees. Freshly grown. Too close to one another to be natural.

'A fence,' Quartz said. 'Veer right,' he called out to Fox, 'And look for a gap. There's a gap.'

'I can feel it,' Fox called back, picking up her pace.

Quartz urged his horse past Mica and caught up with Fox, lifting her up to sit behind him. The pair cantered off, heading right. Mica lost sight of them as they disappeared into a thick grove of fruit trees. Just ahead he felt Oria struggling to rock sense what was obvious to everyone else. Then she found it. 'Oh yes! I can feel it. And it's broken. Or has it just fallen down?'

'It's broken,' Doubt said.

'Probably Cerulean and Laurel,' Mica said. 'Trying to get to inside.'

'Why would they break a fence?' Doubt asked.

'Compelled,' Aikin said. 'So, we should hurry. I should be on horseback—'

'You can walk,' Mica said.

'You're a fool, Wanderer!' Aikin snapped, and Mica felt an unexpected sincerity in the man's signature. 'I told you. I need to be there when they dance. At least Talia knows they're dangerous—'

'That's not fair. Obsidian wasn't—'

'So you keep saying, but he was. Utterly dangerous! They all are. Make no mistake about it. Talia must have seen what they can do. Or felt it. And she's tried to fix things. Her fence is a very earnest effort to protect us. Simplistic, but that's what she's like. You, on the other hand, are living in a fantasy world.'

Then, before Mica had to deny the danger he could feel in his bones, the fence came into view. For the most part, there was no light, no space, between the trunks. The trees looked united in a cause, woody arms reaching around one another's shoulders. Except where it had been flattened. 'If Cerulean and Laurel did this,' Lupe said, 'they must be strongly drawn to the others.' She looked at Mica, a worried expression on her face. 'And it must be a mighty powerful pull because they've pushed it, snapped it.'

Fox stood beside Quartz in the gap, her tentacles unwrapping and then re-wrapping around her wrists. 'And this time, when Aikin spoke, no one denied him: 'They're longing to dance,' Aikin said. 'And that, my friends, is why you need me.'

28

Aikin picked his way over the fallen trees lining the gap in Talia's fence. Tanzanite and Mica had moved some of the timber to clear a path for the horses, but Aikin was trying to keep his distance. The ride on the first part of the journey had been excruciating. He'd not wanted Peri to feel the book strapped beneath his shirt, so he'd held himself away from the other man, clutching the back of the saddle, hoping there was enough distracting Peri from wondering what Aikin was hiding. Because surely the man rock sensed the book. But the wanderer hadn't said a word. Dismounting had been a relief, and everything had been easier once they were walking.

Yet Aikin didn't imagine he was safe. His book wouldn't escape Beranish attention forever. He concentrated on his feet as he made his way over the damp trunks. He needed to get into the manor and hide the book. And if that didn't happen? Well, he'd think of a stop-gap. He crossed several logs without incident, then the clattering sound of a flock of parley gulls distracted him and the wind caught him and he lost his balance. He fell and yelped as his foot slipped between two trunks. Pain shot through his ankle.

Peri reached over and caught his arm, eased him back onto his feet. Aikin shook the wanderer off, but it was too late. The bindings that held the book to his body were already loose from the journey, and now the book slipped. Aikin clutched at it, hugged it, managed to keep it under his shirt. Succeeded, but evidently the Berans had rock sensed his panic and its source because they turned. All of them. Like predators catching sight of movement.

'What have you got there?' Quartz asked.

'Nothing,' Aikin said, gritting his teeth against the pain, hurrying the last few steps to solid ground.

Quartz huffed. 'You're hiding a book. Obviously. Why are you hiding a book?'

Aikin hobbled deeper into the gardens. He should have made up something clever. Or something distracting and pointless and boring. Instead, in his desperation, he limped away from them, gripped by some stupid notion of dropping the book, kicking it under the pile of rotting fruit beneath the tree ahead of him.

The wind buffeted him, but he kept going, unable to stop himself. It pushed him and pulled him, worrying the trees, throwing itself against Talia's fence. The landscape creaked and moaned with high pitch cries. The parley gulls circled overhead. The incessant clapping of their wings set off a thrumming in his ears. Aikin concentrated on the tree. He felt terrible, nauseated from the smell and the pain, and burdened by a lingering thought that he should have fled with Whilomena. Ahead of him, blackened and shrivelled pears clung to the leafless branches. With his luck, the rotten fruit would fall on him, make his travel-worn clothes even filthier.

So much self-pity! It wouldn't do. He lifted his head. He was tired and hungry and out of sorts. Yes, but that was no excuse. Not for an Author of the Future. Then his ankle gave way as he reached the tree and he caught himself against the thin trunk. A chorus erupted above him and he looked up. The fruit was moving! He recoiled, stumbled, dropped the book.

'It's just fruit bats,' Mica laughed. 'You're scaring them.'

'You're making a spectacle of yourself,' Oria sounded affronted. 'Pull yourself together!'

Above Aikin, the bats resettled, but their unease had spread through the garden. The world was alive with high-pitched calls, loud enough to drown out the gulls. Hundreds of bats. Maybe thousands. And their sharp smell tangled with the rotting fruit and Aikin gagged. He would have laughed if he could have, because his gagging had given him the perfect idea. He coughed again, this time on purpose. He dropped to all fours. Half sheltered by the tree's thin trunk, half sheltered by his own body, he shoved *The Book of Kinesis* under the pile of decomposing fruit. With his back to the others, he stuck a finger down his throat, brought up his last meal. Then he gritted his teeth and stuck his hands in his vomit. He stood up and reeled away from the tree, a genuine grunt of pain escaping his lips. If nothing else, the smell would keep the others away from his book's fetid hiding place and away from his person.

But dear, stupid Fox came to his side and took his elbow. She leant her head away from the smell, but kept hold of him, announced she needed to get him inside. Her fingers were sharp and hard where she gripped him, and her strange tentacles looked uneasy. He didn't need rock skin to sense her conflict: her dislike of him, her compassion, her lingering sense of filial duty.

Mica walked over. He reached out to take Aikin's other elbow and then hesitated. 'Wait a minute. Why did you dump your book? Did you think you'd hidden it?' The wanderer turned to the others. 'Feel him. He's smug.' Then he turned back, examined Aikin's face. 'Why are you smug? We all felt it.' When Aikin didn't answer, Mica spoke to Quartz. 'Something's wrong. This isn't what it seems.'

'Never is with him,' Fox said. 'But criticise him when we're inside. He's sick.'

Aikin resumed his limping progress with Fox beside him, but Mica didn't follow. Aikin willed the others to come, to take Fox's advice and save their questions. He could come back for the book later. The decomposing fruit would damage the cover, but hopefully the interior would survive the experience.

Then Quartz told Fox to wait. 'Sick or not sick, we need to look at that book.'

For a moment, Aikin considered lying, telling them it was a volume of Dabid Harwood's nostalgic poetry that he was planning to take to Galea. But they'd check. The truth then. Or part of it. He shook off Fox's hand and looked back. He waved his arm at the pear tree. 'A sentimental weakness on my part. But help yourselves, if you must. You won't want it. But don't destroy it, I beg you. It's part of our history.'

Mica walked to the pear tree and the fruit bats stirred once more. He used a stick to draw the book from the muck. He picked it up, careless of the stains on the cover. Aikin saw his sharp intake of breath, heard the revulsion in his voice. '*The Book of Kinesis*. But this isn't the same copy.' He looked up at Aikin. 'Where did this come from?'

Aikin shrugged. 'Kelp's library.'

Saury took a couple of steps towards Mica. 'He must have stolen it. The Kelp Companion wouldn't have given it to him. She wouldn't lend a book to someone like him. To a murderer.'

Aikin addressed his words to Mica, 'Keep it. Put it in Persica's library. Send it back to Kelp. Whatever takes your fancy. I wanted it, but I don't need it.' And it was almost true. Aikin had read it again and again, and he knew it inside out. He'd mourn if they destroyed it, but all that really mattered was that these people should not read it, not find out how to control the future.

Mica snapped the book shut. He gave Aikin a look of deep loathing and headed for the manor. The book was in his hand; his hand was at his side.

Luck.

Luck would carry a man a long way and, despite his ankle, despite being surrounded by enemies, Aikin felt luck touch him. They hadn't seen that the book was different, and they wouldn't.

Mica thought this was just another copy. And because he and everyone else found the book repugnant, they wouldn't examine it. They wouldn't read about the power of the Caller so Aikin could still win.

Everyone resumed walking. Only Oria had paused, stopped to regrow Talia's fence. This time it had a stile. Presumably, she wanted to make life easier for Acacia and Pearl and the others who were following.

Aikin turned away, trailing the others. He needed to keep his wits about him. In his mind, he turned the pages of *The Book of Kinesis*. Saw again what had been missing in Komey's volume: the scribbled, scarcely-literate warning:

The birth of twins signifys riske. If they are stone, kill them. Cover their earthy burows and distroy their Berrans camp. If you dont, all may be lost. If they Danse, pray to the Back the Callers vision prevails.

Written by a Kelp Mother. Perhaps. Maybe the very first, she of the bad, horse-themed poetry. Or perhaps a Kelp daughter, for the penmanship was childish. Beneath the warning, the unknown scribe had copied out a story, *The Caller's Wedding*. A classic fourth story title, but the tone of what followed wasn't right for a fourth story. But Aikin had smiled when he read it. Superficially, it was a creation myth, but in reality, it was a manual. The dance steps for four wedding reels. Reels with the power to make or remake the world.

The Paired Reel promised to fix a damaged patch of land; the Quadrille, a region; the Hexad, something bigger; and the Octet, the entire Stone Body. And Aikin had seen the lace picture, so he knew which set of instructions he needed. He would call the dance, he would rule over the result.

The Octet has eight beats, and each is a quaver.

Clap eight bars: a parley call, a clarion call; name it what you will. Knowing the Stone Body, the Caller owns the path and the destination.

Now, the dance begins.

The world turns in a circle, sixteen beats leftward to gather the past, sixteen rightward to set the future.

Eight stone creatures and eight real people: thirty-two feet slide from side to side in the setting step, furrowing the ground for eight bars.

Now your pairs drill the earth for thirty-two bars, dancing a spinning step. Call rock twin to face human twin, in a double-handed hold.

Aikin knew this, knew the forms. Any Companionari who'd grown up in a great house would. A reel was a reel even if the wording, with all its *furrowing* and *drilling*, was atypical. But the next bit was a puzzle...

And then the caller drops the seed with a cry or a sigh or a gust of wind for thirty-two bars.

That bit was perplexing. He had no idea what constituted *a cry* or *a sigh*. A gust of wind might be a gust of wind, but perhaps it was something else entirely? He'd hoped to have more time. He'd thought about working his way through the Persican Library once they reached the manor, but he suspected he wouldn't have the opportunity. As a last resort, he'd simply have to make a plea to the Stone Body when he reached that point in the dance and hope for the best. A literal plea. Because, surely, some sort of magic was at play and had to be summoned. And he'd read enough fourth stories to know how to form a traditional plea. Then all he'd need to do would be to finish calling the dance:

Thirty-two feet firm the seed for eight bars. Rock twin laced with human twin, turning about.

The rain comes! Dancers take turns to shelter beneath arched arms.

Eight spokes turn the Great Wheel for sixteen bars, widdershins then deasil.

The world is renewed and remade.

Aikin smiled and hurried his painful step as the front of the empty manor house came into view. He recognised it: the underlying dance. The Komic Reel. A Circle, a Set, a Two-handed Spin, followed by a Galean Turn, then an Arch, and finally the Plough's New Wheel. He'd danced at balls, had even called it upon occasion. If he was right, if he succeeded and had the luxury of writing his account of these times, he'd rename the dance, call it *Aikin's Reel* or if that was a little too egocentric, perhaps *The Bachelor Bureaucrat* would suffice.

Ahead of him, emerging from the manor's hedged garden, he saw something that brought an even bigger smile to his face. Well, well, well. He needn't worry about Mica reading his book because there wouldn't be time. Talia was walking towards them, horribly aged, her long grey hair whipping in the wind. And beside her were not three and not five, but seven stone twins. And where there were seven, the Stone Body would surely provide an eighth.

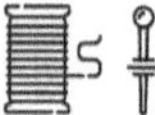

Fox followed Aikin's gaze and caught sight of Talia's approach. The three missing twins were beside her and behind them walked Mica and Oria's twins and two others. Fox's twin looked up, caught sight of Fox. A small frown, a moment of puzzled surprise, flitted across her face and she tilted her head. Fox smiled, and her twin smiled back.

The cold vanished.

The first few moments of warm air felt good, a relief. Then Fox had a slipping, shrinking sensation and she realised her grip on her pregnancy had faltered. She reached down, using the full force of her internal awareness to renew the suppression. But she couldn't seem to catch hold of her unborn daughter as the pregnancy receded, morphing the fetus back to an embryo. Fox shut her eyes, bent over, held on tight, willing her daughter to stay. She was aware that Talia was singing. A nursery rhyme of all things! It was too cruel. Then she felt... No, heard Oria. As though Oria was inside Fox's mind. Only this wasn't anything like Oria's shouted voice in the parley in Komey. This was soft thoughts of lapping water and cooling shade. Then the heat faded from the wind as the rush subsided.

Rock thought, and it had saved them. Fox opened her eyes and realised Oria wasn't the only one trying to help. Talia's nursery rhyme wasn't a taunt. She'd been trying to calm the twins.

Fox breathed again, felt for her daughter. The pregnancy was intact, but it had slipped back. It felt as though months had been undone, but her daughter was still there, and that was all that mattered. Fox looked at Oria. The Oak Companion stood on the path looking ashen, her belly smaller. Her left hand cradled her stomach, but she used her other to wave off Fox's concern. 'I'm fine, I'm fine.'

Fox looked around, checking the others. Saury had somehow made it to Fox's side without Fox noticing, but nothing else had changed. The horses' coats were gleaming, no sign of the distance they'd travelled or the weights they'd carried. Lupe stood near Quartz and Mica, holding Doubt's hand. Peri and Tanzanite were near the horses. Fox turned about, scanning for Aikin and was unnerved to find him just a step or two behind her, no sign of his injured ankle. Her tentacles unlaced and Saury's mirrored hers, readying for action.

'No need to be like that,' Aikin said. 'You looked as though you needed help. I would have helped.'

'She doesn't need you,' Saury said.

Aikin held up his hands, took a few steps back. Then Lupe called out to them. Her voice was gentle, but firm, 'All that can wait. Fox, Saury, Peri... Greet your twins. Mica, you too. Move slowly.' She waved them forward. 'Show your twins there's nothing to worry about. Watch how Mica does it. You too, Oak Mother,' she said, gesturing for the Oak Companion to follow Mica's example.

Fox turned her back on Aikin and found her twin was still watching her, head tilted. The rock woman's signature was full of cautious longing. Fox smiled and took a couple of slow steps, watching how Mica moved. She felt Saury half a pace behind her, also matching Mica's movements. 'Good,' Lupe said. 'Use your voices. Confident, warm welcomes.'

'Hello twin,' Fox said. She kept her fear in check, and her guilt and shame. It wasn't easy. Even without the memory of the rush threatening her pregnancy, the wind still buffeted them, and the feeling of Aikin's gaze upon her back made the world even more volatile. But Fox managed it, settled her emotions, smiled, kept her eyes on the face of the stone woman in front of her.

'Songs... Skipping...' Talia said. 'That sort of thing seems to help. And I named them. I know I shouldn't have, but it made them easier to manage. Saury, yours is Cyanna. Blue for Kelp's ocean. I didn't know what you'd want. I wasn't sure...'

'It's a good name for her,' Saury said. Saury moved ahead of Fox, held out her hand to her twin and Cyanna took it, examined it, and then clutched it, lacing their matching tentacles. Then the stone girl pulled Saury close and sniffed her, a smile of deep recognition and pleasure breaking across her face. Saury spoke a welcome, the sound slightly muffled by her twin's embrace.

Talia gestured at Fox's twin. 'Yours is Amber for your eyes. Not even the right shade, but I was in a hurry. And Patience's twin is Baylor. Where's Patience? I thought he'd be with you.'

Unnoticed, Amber had reached out to Fox and to Fox's shame, she flinched at the stone woman's touch. Fox forced herself to hold still, let Amber run her fingers and tentacles across her face.

'Use your voice,' Lupe reminded Fox.

'Welcome Amber,' Fox said, her voice husky. 'Welcome to the Stone Body, to this life.'

'Patience is dead,' Saury answered Talia.

Fox rock sensed the prick of tears in her sister's eyes and the wind sharpened, tossing Talia's ridiculously long grey hair, flapping Fox's tunic, and stirring the bats who resumed their high-pitched chitter.

'Talia,' Lupe said, keeping her voice low, 'hum a little tune. Something they know. Not too loud, just a background sound. And Peri, someone else can look after those horses. You're needed. Give them to Doubt. Introduce yourself to Baylor. Be kind. You know more about his loss than he does. Remember, he's alone and probably a little frightened.'

'A twin shouldn't stay alone,' Aikin said, his voice uncomfortably close to Fox's back, 'and a wanderer is an excellent substitute.'

Fox wondered what her adopted father knew, and how he knew it, then reminded herself to focus on what was important: the twins. Amber seemed to be content, exploring Fox, running fingers and tentacles down Fox's arms, but Cyanna was unnerved by Saury's distress. 'Think of something good,' Fox murmured to Saury. 'Don't think of Patience dying. Think of him and Sousette and how happy they were around their horses.'

Amber stepped even closer, took Fox's head in her hands and turned it so that they were nose to nose.

'Mimic her touch,' Lupe said. 'Mimic when it's positive. You're making a conversation with your bodies.'

Fox reached up and held Amber's head, careful to keep her fingers and tentacles gentle. The stone woman felt good, fresh and curious, and warm to Fox's rock skin. But there was an edge that reminded Fox of the horses, a wild thread running deep in her signature. The orchard had fallen silent again. The gulls had disappeared or were resting or napping on the trees' bare limbs. The bats, too, were quiet. Only Talia's humming remained. And the wind, gentler now but still creaking the trees.

'Amber seems to like you, Fox,' Aikin sounded pleased, 'despite the separation, which is interesting.' Fox didn't look around, but her father was too close for comfort. Then she rock sensed him shifting his attention as he scanned the scene. 'And Baylor looks at ease with Peri. What's your next move Lupe? The Persican twins will need your attention.'

Lupe didn't answer, but Fox sensed her motioning to Quartz and Tanzanite, holding out her hand for the reins Tanzanite was still clutching. Amber released Fox, and Fox took a step back, looked around.

'Names?' Lupe asked Talia. 'Have you named the last two?'

Talia stopped humming, dipped her head as she caught her breath. 'The older one is is Pear. The other is Freestone. But I think we should get all of them back inside. There is too much going on out here, and I don't know the last two twins at all. They turned up yesterday. By themselves. Food helps. They're always calm around food.' She turned to Fox, doing her best to keep her long hair out of her mouth as the wind picked up again, tossing it across her face. 'Please. I really think we should go inside.' She ducked her head and resumed humming, signalling for Fox and the others to start walking.

Fox took Amber's hand and started leading her towards the manor. She had half an ear on Quartz and Tanzanite, still greeting their new twins, half an eye on Talia. Then the wind gusted up, whipping Talia's hair above her head. Talia's humming faltered. Fox pulled the lace collar from her own much shorter hair and held it out to the other woman. Talia took it, fingered it. She frowned. 'Too beautiful. I don't know if I should.'

'Give her the other one,' Saury said, catching up to Fox.

Fox pulled the tattered lace from her pocket and handed it to Talia. She rock sensed Aikin. Very close now.

Talia held the tattered collar up to the sky, then lifted the other one. 'Dance patterns.'

Fox's rock skin prickled, electric with foreknowledge that this was a pattern that mattered. Aikin's endless talk of the dance. Was the Stone Body gesturing? Was there a way to keep Aikin out of the dance?

'Lark Mallow made them,' Fox said, her response automatic as she worried at the meaning of the collars. 'Always encouraging me to be more careful with my appearance.'

Aikin pushed his way past Fox and Saury, ignoring the twins. He held out his hand to Talia. 'Show me.'

'Don't,' Fox said. But Talia had already shifted so he could see.

'They are too pretty to be hair ties,' Talia said. 'I think Lark's embroidered the Komic Reel; the steps for it.'

There was a frisson in her father's signature, and Fox's stomach clenched.

'We ruined that one when we escaped,' Saury pointed at the damaged collar, 'so you can't really see the whole pattern.'

Fox reached for the collars, but Aikin was faster. He grabbed them. Fox caught his hand with a tentacle, wrapped another around his wrist. 'Give them back!'

Then everything happened in a rush. Aikin slapped at Fox's hand, then punched it. Fox gasped and let go, and he shoved her away. The air sharpened. Seven twins clattered and clicked and Fox felt an unpleasant press of sharp rock thought. A grove of oaks erupted from the soil, dislodging fruit trees as Talia lost control. Then Oria rock spoke. No images this time, but a nursery rhyme. The oaks sank back into the soil and the twins settled.

'You mustn't do that,' Lupe said to Aikin. 'You'll kill us.'

'Let him have the collars,' Talia said. 'I don't need them.'

Fox glanced at Oria. The companion looked exhausted and strained, so Fox nodded. Against her better judgement, she lowered her hands, coiled her tentacles, and stepped away from Aikin.

The wind kept blowing and the gulls were back, flocking, riding currents. Talia was humming something soothing. Fox did her best to join in. Soon, most of the party was humming. The twins were calmer, but not at ease.

'We should get inside,' Talia repeated. 'Something's bothering them.'

'I can smell Pearl's flowers in the wind,' Tanzanite said. 'She's nearby.' Then he turned to Lupe. 'The flowers might help. I'll ask Pearl to grow something soothing.'

Then Fox realised Quartz was holding up his hand, pointing to the east where a man was approaching. At first, Fox thought she was looking at one of Pearl's people. Then everything shifted. The twins turned their heads, moved as one and Fox's humming died. Saury's too. Then Talia's singing faded, and the twins turned their heads again, looking at nothing, seeing nothing.

Aikin laughed. And he clapped his hands. Loudly. Actually clapped his hands as though upsetting the stone twins didn't matter.

'Stop that,' Lupe said. 'Don't.'

'The eighth twin sparks the Octet!' Aikin said, and he lifted a foot off the ground and twirled, laughed. He clapped his hands again, harder this time. Louder. And the twins reacted. The noise didn't break the spell, didn't stop the approach of the eighth twin, but they flinched. 'If you want to live,' he was shouting now, 'you'd best do exactly what I tell you as I renew the world.'

A movement caught Fox's eye. The Oak Companion was in trouble, battling with herself. Her left hand seemed to want to join Aikin in clapping. It kept swinging, aiming for Oria's right hand, which Oria was holding out of the way. The companion grunted, hid her right hand behind her back, but her left hand reached behind, slapped the right hand. 'Stop it,' Oria hissed at her shoulder.

'It's Promise,' Fox said. 'Maybe she knows what she's doing.'

'Oh, it's Promise all right,' Oria snapped. 'And I'm not about to let a dead woman decide my fate.'

'Don't be a fool,' Quartz said. 'Let her rule. You know nothing of this. Whatever's left of her recognises it.'

In the brief time Fox had stopped paying attention, the twins had moved. They'd formed two lines and were facing each other. Baylor stood at the end, watching the eighth twin, waiting for him. Toes tapped; the air sharpened.

'I know what to do,' Aikin was calm now, earnest. 'I can lead this and it must be led.'

'Don't listen to him,' Talia said. 'We all know what this is. The collars showed us. It's the Komic Reel. Has to be. Why else would he snatch them out of my hands? We don't need him. I can call the reel.'

'Agreed,' Fox said, and no one argued.

'Do we join in? Do we dance?' Oria asked.

'Who knows?' Talia said. 'But we'd best be ready if it looks as though they want us to. Those who are bonded should be close.'

There was confusion then as everyone ran to their twin. Some people arrived at the end of the twins' lines, extending them. Others hovered near their twins, some on the right and some on the left.

'I'll call it as soon as the eight twin reaches the line,' Talia said. 'Just find your place and I'll call it.'

'To the left!' Aikin's voice was full of calm. 'Each of you needs to move to your twin's left.' Some of the Berans glanced at Talia, but they listened to Aikin. And yet, when everyone found their place, including the last twin, it was obvious they were one person short. The eighth twin needed a partner. Aikin spun on his heel to face Talia, waved for her to step in.

'But I'm Companionari.'

'With rock dust in your veins,' Aikin said. 'Just get on with it!'

'Lupe should do it,' Quartz said.

'Or Doubt,' Oria said.

'I'm an excellent dancer!' Doubt said. 'I can dance.'

'No!' Aikin said. 'Talia dances. I want her dancing.'

'Don't listen to him,' Talia said. 'You can't trust him.'

'Idiot!' Aikin shouted at her, and the sound rippled through the twins. He turned to Oria. 'Because she resents me, she'll kill everyone. I'm the only one who knows the beat and I'll let you die if you don't include her.'

People began arguing, but Oria's voice rose above the rest. 'Stop. Anyone with rock skin knows he's sincere. We've no choice. We can deal with him later.' She waved Talia forward. 'You. Quick. Step in beside the eighth.'

As soon as Talia found her place, Aikin started clapping and humming, opening the reel. A familiar tune, but faster, much faster. The wind picked up speed, thickened. Bats chittered; gulls called out. Fox looked down, positioning her feet, readying for the dance. Lizards and crickets skittered through the grass, and a field mouse ran over her toes.

'Here we go!' Aikin cried. 'Dancers together. And... The World Turns a Circle!'

Fox saw it, the whole of the dance, as though the collars were floating in front of her, undamaged. She caught Oria's eye and nodded. They moved. Fox and Oria danced backwards and the Berans followed their lead. The world was about to turn.

348

29

Halfway through the dance, Talia lifted her head and saw the air was full of parley gulls. So thick above her they blocked the light, so close she felt the wisps of air displaced by their wings. She heard the call of the horses beyond the circle of dancers, felt them pawing the earth; and Doubt, straining to hold onto the reins, and Lupe reaching to help him.

Her rock skin shivered. Too many signatures for such a newborn sense to cope with. The world felt dangerous. Or maybe it was the feeling of change. She wasn't sure which. Her arms and her back tingled. She braced herself against another rush of age, but when she glanced down to where her hands clasped the eighth twin's hands, nothing had changed. Not a rush then; no dancing to her death.

'The Caller drops the seed...' Aikin said, for the first time sounding uncertain. Then the next few words came in a rush: 'With a cry! Or a sigh, or a gust of wind.'

Talia felt it: he didn't know. The man didn't know what he was doing!

She caught Fox's eye, gave her a querying look, but Fox shook her head. She didn't know either. Talia held her breath, waited for some sort of instruction from someone, anyone. Nothing. She rock sensed everyone waiting. Aikin continued clapping the frantic beat, but said nothing. Then Talia spied Oria. The Oak Companion's left arm had broken away from the two-handed spin. She still held onto Laurel with her right hand, but her left seemed to be simultaneously reaching for the next stone twin and trying to drag Oria backwards. The companion caught Talia's gaze, licked her lips, motioned her head at her errant arm and raised an eyebrow. Talia ducked her head. Best follow the fragment that was Promise. Whatever was left of her appeared to know this step.

Oria led the way, and they all followed, re-forming the circle. Talia expected this was another Turn About the World. Only, it wasn't. When Oria moved leftward, her left arm pushed back. Then the Oak Companion tried moving rightward, but this time her left arm pulled her so she couldn't move in that direction either. So, they stood in the circle, all sixteen of them, holding hands, dancing on the spot to Aikin's frantic beat, with no idea what they were doing. Not Aikin; not any of them. The dance was being led by a ghost.

Then something changed. The sound of the gulls' wings flapping in the thickened air intensified. Talia looked up. A mass of grey birds was circling overhead, moving so fast their black markings and long red beaks made lines, like meteors in a feathery sky. As they flew, they drifted lower like a thick cloud descending. Lower and lower. Their savage cries pushed the thickened air down so that it sighed. When they were a hand span over the ground, they hovered. Above them, within the circle, the air felt light and still. Talia could hear Aikin clapping, but it was a distant, muffled sound.

'Parley gulls,' Talia spoke the name to herself, but her voice carried.

'Witan birds,' Peri said. 'Because they witness the Stone Body, know its past and future.'

'Storm gulls riding the wind,' Tanzanite said.

Quartz was smiling, and when he spoke, he was a little breathless from the dance. 'And in Oak we call them clarion gulls, because they call. I believe we've found the Caller. It isn't Aikin. The flock is the Caller.'

'*A cry or a sigh or a gust of wind,*' Saury said.

'And probably the tasselled edges of those collars were parley gulls,' Talia said, 'with their feathers spread wide.'

'That's it then,' Peri said. 'But didn't Aikin call out something about seed? That part is still missing.'

'Maybe it's coming,' Fox said. And then she smiled. 'One thing is for sure, Aikin isn't controlling this. We're in a fourth story and the Stone Body is working its magic.'

'Shush,' Oria warned. 'We need him to keep clapping.'

'He can't hear us,' Fox said. 'It's different inside the circle. We're here but not here. Can't you feel it?'

'Yes,' Talia said, 'but what do we do now?'

Fox had been watching their feet, keeping the beat, but now she looked up. 'Thirty-two bars, that's what he said. I think we're more than halfway through. We've got to keep dancing.'

'But what then?' Talia asked.

But there was no need for an answer because it was obvious. They would continue the reel.

A few more beats and Aikin's claps became louder. Talia realised she could hear him and he'd resumed humming ... or had been humming all along, but now she could hear him. The gulls were lifting, leaving the ground covered in feathers. As the birds rose, the wind of their passage flattened the dancers' tunics and trousers, and Talia's long hair streamed out behind her. When the gulls were once again above their heads, Aikin called the Galean Turn. The circle broke apart and the Berans and Companionaris and stone twins plaited arms to dance the turn, and their feet pressed the feathers into the ground.

Talia felt Aikin's confidence, his pleasure, his conceit, and was glad his rock skin didn't work. It meant he knew nothing of their own signatures, full of joy as they danced.

'The Arch Protects Against The Rain,' Aikin said, a slight giggle in his voice. The dancers didn't hesitate. They formed the arch, and each pair took their turn to dance its length. Talia looked up when she reached the end, saw an actual cloud had descended, felt mist against her skin. Not exactly rain, but water in the air and on the ground.

'Eight spokes for The Plough's New Wheel!' Aikin called. 'Eight bars widdershins; then eight deasil.' They didn't need Aikin's call to know what to do. Oria and Laurel led the way, and the arch broke apart. The dancers formed the wheel and Talia found herself at the outer end of a spoke, moving faster than seemed possible.

From the corner of her eye, two steps into the reel's right-wise rotation, Talia passed the horses. The animals were pulling back, staining against Lupe and Doubt as the pair struggled to hold them. Talia almost lost her step. She glanced down, focused on her feet. Then everything slowed. It was as though she was standing still. A ladybug climbed onto a stalk in front of her left foot. She tried to jump over it, but her legs felt leaden. Who knew what would happen if she crushed it. She forced herself to jump. Up and over the ladybug, and her feet were racing once more.

Then it happened, a click, a change in the air. It was fast, like a branch cracking and falling, like lightning hitting dry grass and a flame igniting, like snow sliding at the beginning of an avalanche. One moment there was only that taste of strangeness in the dance's timing, and then there was nothing but change. The dancers surrounding her fluttered, their shapes shifted, and abruptly they were grassy creatures, dancing scarecrows. Talia's legs were bundles of straw, held together with vines. Her feet were ridiculous: handfuls of hazelnuts caught in a spider web net.

She looked out, hoping for help, saw trees bent under a wind she couldn't feel, saw Doubt, Lupe and some others huddled as the gale stripped petals from flowers and bats from trees. Only Aikin stood. Clapping and laughing.

The dancers shifted again. Now they were people once more, but with iridescent skin. Another step and Talia was one of sixteen dancing cairns with feathered crests. She tried to calm her racing heart, told herself they would survive. Then she was a dancing fruit tree, then a fish, then a bird. Talia danced, and danced, and lived every combination imaginable: magpies with the faces of lizards, fish with wings, flowers with voices, swirls of dust with hooves and tails... She closed her eyes against the blur of change, heart racing.

No. It wasn't right to miss this. Whatever this was, Talia would trust the Stone Body, embrace the change. And if she was wrong, and this was Aikin's doing, she would face it. She opened her eyes, but now the change was too fast to follow. Just glimpses: snakes with the faces of dogs, bats and leaves; water shaped like grass; clattering, beady-eyed ants, and on and on. Then Aikin clapped louder, and they steadied. Now they were horses with reptilian scales and long sinuous tails. Then the clapping stopped.

The air surrounding Talia sighed. She shivered. A ripple of change ran through her and she resumed her human shape. The world felt quiet. It was still cold, still a little damp, but the pear trees surrounding them were studded with blossom buds. Everything smelt fresh.

'Look at the twins,' Fox said, her voice little more than a whisper.

Talia turned. There were only eight dancers remaining because the stone twins had held the change and were no longer human. They had thick, powerful back legs; dark leathery wings tipped with scarlet talons; scaled bodies with long muscular tails and human arms; and their faces suggested both lizards and horses.

'Chimaera,' Talia said.

'Or maybe these are the Stone Body's dragons,' Mica said.

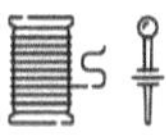

A ikin stumbled back at the sight of the creatures emerging from the disintegrating dance. This wasn't right. Or was it? He swallowed, cleared his throat, stared at the monstrosities in front of him.

But what had he expected? Some sylvan scene where he pranced about, telling everyone what to do? He drew a long breath of damp air, knowing that bit was true. He had expected exactly that. A vanity; a childish fantasy. Beneath him. And, consequently, he was a fool. He huffed, laughed at himself. This, this in front of him, this was transformative change. By nature, a true transformation should be unpredictable.

'Hey,' he called out, and the sound was little more than a puff of air. No one heard him, not even the latecomers who'd climbed the stile and now stood near Lupe and Doubt. Not surprising no one had looked up. A pathetic effort at taking command, gathering his minions. He snorted. It didn't matter how monstrous the stone twins looked or how surprised he was to see them, they were his. By the Back, he was the Caller! And *The Book of Kinesis* had promised the Caller's vision prevailed. He hadn't known this was what he wanted, but it must have been. His psyche had created it so it was his to command.

His hands ached from all the clapping. He stuffed them into his pockets for comfort, then took them out again. The cold air stung his reddened, pummelled skin. He'd had to pound his hands together to be heard against the wind. At least the wind was gone now. The orchard was still, and the world smelt good.

Aikin squared his shoulders, lifted his head, and strode to the dancers. He was glad to see Fox was unaltered. Likewise, the others. Completely ordinary. He examined himself and was relieved to find he was unchanged. Even his useless rock skin was unchanged.

He looked up again. Oria had caught sight of him, had the nerve to glare at him, as though he'd created the chimeric monsters on purpose. Well, he supposed he had some unconscious purpose. He almost flinched under her gaze, but held himself straight.

'You!' his aunt said. 'Stay right where you are.'

He ignored her, began circumnavigating the dancers and the monsters, ready now to examine his creatures. He'd heard Mica call them dragons. Aikin supposed they were. What were dragons, if not an unlikely assembly of power and speed and flight? Mythic, supposedly. Until now. All eight shared a basic similarity of form, but he could tell one from another. Fox's twin dwarfed her. The dragon's scales mimicked the curling pattern of Fox's tentacles and there were gills on the side of the creature's neck. A glance at his aunt's dragon was enough to confirm that one wore scales that matched her rock skin.

'Get away,' Oria hissed. 'We don't know what we're dealing with. I don't want you provoking them.'

He stopped, took an exaggerated step back. 'Here Aunt? Is that better?' Mica looked up; Fox too. And then Lupe and Acacia and the others turned to watch him. He grinned and took another step back. 'Or perhaps here? Is that far enough?' Then he spun about and strode away, heading for Persica Manor. He walked a good long way before turning back again. Now, everyone was watching, and the chimeras and horses had pricked their ears. 'It won't matter where I stand,' he called out, meeting Oria's hostile stare. Then he filled his lungs, raised his voice, ready to fill the orchard with his claim: 'I am in charge. The Caller's vision prevails. I command all of you to come!'

Nothing happened. No one moved. And then Saury laughed. 'The birds called the dance. They did it. You didn't.'

'What?' Aikin said.

'The flock called the dance,' Quartz said. 'Clarion gulls. Fly all over the Stone Body, so they see it all. It's the flock's vision that prevails.'

Aikin licked his lips, stammered a protest. But instinctively, he knew it was true. He'd heard enough fourth stories about those storm-riding birds, witnessing the Stone Body to see how well they fit into this particular story. And how poorly he fit. He turned, stomach cold and churning. He needed to get away. Away from this disaster. Find somewhere he could breathe. He walked toward the manor, and then walking became running. He made it halfway to the house when he heard a leathery slap of wings and felt the downward draft of a monster's flight. Then he was airborne. Laurel. Of course it was his aunt's beast. And she deposited him at Oria's feet.

Saury was still laughing.

'Shut up!' Aikin spat. 'By the Back. Shut. Up.'

Saury's laugh became a fit of giggles as she struggled to contain it.

Quartz gave the child an approving smile. 'I think you've earned your adult name. Saury Laughed. A beautiful sound on a beautiful day.'

Aikin shivered. The day was cold and miserable. And yet, when he looked around, he knew what Quartz meant because the monsters had remade the Stone Body. The fruit trees were in leaf again, but that wasn't it. The world around him was different. It was as though the Companionari talents had been tossed into the air and had come down like rain. There were all sorts of trees and grasses and flowers and edible plants, and the ground rustled with the movement of animals. He shivered again. If he was an author of this future, he was an incompetent one. Because this wasn't the future he'd envisaged. This was a world where he was unnecessary.

30

Fox looked at the blank sheet of notepaper in front of her, and hesitated. She tapped her pen against the edge of her desk and jiggled her foot. She knew what she wanted to say, but using pen and paper to say it didn't feel right. This shouldn't be just another in a long line of letters to Lark. She put down her pen and swivelled in her seat, uncertain about the best approach. The gift needed to reach Lark, and Lark needed to know Fox's gratitude was sincere. A conservative approach then, because Lark was a conservative woman? Fox knew the traditional procedure well enough. The youngest member of the giver's sorority delivered the letter and the gift. The receiver read the letter, then accepted the gift. Bowed and opened it. Fox smiled at the image. It was charming, but there wouldn't be much of that going on now the sororities had disintegrated, which left Fox wondering how to manage the process.

Take the gift herself? Just knock on the front door?

No, because Lark *was* a traditionalist, and she and her house deserved something ceremonial and beautiful. This gift needed to be emblematic of the future and the past.

Fox sighed, looked at the package on the bed that contained the collars. She'd laundered the lace collars herself, under the critical eye of the Mistress of the Laundry. When they were dry, she'd pressed them and wrapped them in rice paper decorated with stylised cotton plants. That part was right. Lark would like the paper and so would her household. Fox had found the paper in Oria's study. She'd taken it, hadn't asked permission because Oria and Talia were in the provinces, and these days no one knew who was in charge in Oak House. Mica had laughed when Fox had fretted about taking the paper without permission. Told her she should call a parley if she was really worried about who should authorise its release. Not as much a joke as it should have been. The new Beranish and Companionari parleys were chewing over everything in excruciating detail.

Fox stood up and walked over to the bed. She bent down and picked up Lark's gift. Maybe delivering it herself would be better? She could drop it off on her way out of Komey. Then she could speak her words, woman to woman instead of trying to capture everything in writing. Fox looked at her leather satchel, packed with clothes and ready to go, imagined stuffing the precious parcel into the front pocket. She clicked her tongue. A terrible idea that would undo the gratitude and reverence she felt. No, she had a better idea. Fox would lead a procession on foot that included anyone and everyone. It would delay the provincial survey by a day or two, but now they'd experienced the rush of stone, had travelled though portals, and had flown on the back of dragon twins, slow and fast had different meanings.

She found Mica in the trading hall, mid-parley. He was sitting beside Acacia on a newly installed parley bed in the chilly hall. The doors were open to let the dragon twins come and go as they pleased. Most of the timber had been moved outside, and what remained was pushed to the edge of the hall. Fox was just glad the dragons showed no ability to breathe fire because they were as capricious and opaque as ever and the trading room was a tinder box. Today, Fox's twin was nowhere to be seen, nor was Cerulean, but Cyanna was curled asleep in front of the parley bed and the guests had pulled their straight-backed chairs close to catch her radiant warmth.

'... we can't agree to that,' the speaker, a former sorority member, glared at the woman sitting beside her.

Her neighbour, a gardener by the look of her, drew herself up. 'The New Treaty is quite clear that—'

'We've been through this already,' a junior housekeeper interrupted. 'We need to adjourn the question of re-allocating suites and bedsits. We're not getting anywhere.'

A house bureaucrat stood up and waved some papers. 'Which is exactly why we should build a new wing, extend Oak House. We've got the timber. It's sitting outside in the weather. It will be silver by the time you lot see sense.'

A young Beranish woman shook her head, 'As I've already pointed out to you, the ownership of the timber is in dispute. The camp milled it and hauled it, and it was grown with stolen powers, and yet you want to use it to build Companionari bedrooms. I say no. And if we walk down to the camp and hold the parley there, where it should be held, I'm confident the camp will also say no too.'

The man gave her an affronted look. 'I never suggested building exclusively for Companionaris. Anyone can live in Oak House so long as they are part of the broader Oak family.'

'Why just the Oaks?' a woman asked. 'Shouldn't anyone be able to sleep in a comfortable room?'

'Why not be comfortable under canvas?' a Beranish man said. 'It's the Stone Body's way, the natural way.'

Fox caught Mica's eye, made a scissors cutting thread movement. Mica turned and nudged Acacia, drew her attention to Fox, and Fox made a sewing gesture. Acacia turned back to the parley guests, patted the needles on her lapel, and cleared her throat. She clapped her hands. 'One of our dancers wants to speak.'

The bureaucrat who'd advocated extending Oak House looked around, caught sight of Fox and scowled. 'Not more important than the future of the house.'

'You're right about that,' Acacia said, 'but you're aware Fox and some of the other dancers and their dragon twins are leaving. You and I have endless time. We're rich in it, but they're not.' Life on the Stone Body was changing, but Fox rock sensed the depth of the bureaucrat's pleasure at Acacia's complement. The dancers, for all their importance, were time poor and the bureaucrat supposed them too ignorant to hide it.

He gave Fox a patronising smile, then turned his attention back to Acacia. 'Of course, let her speak. She's in a hurry, which can't be easy.' He shrugged. 'Not that I'd know much about that. The bureaucracy is a slow vocation.'

Fox spoke about the collars, reminded everyone about the role they'd played in the Persica Reel. 'The sewing circles could have restored the damaged one, but it's a historic artefact.'

'We should keep it in Oak House,' someone insisted.

'It should be kept in the portal tent, in the camp,' someone else said.

'Lark worked the lace,' Fox said. 'Gave it to me to teach me a lesson. I was trying to persuade her to abandon the past. I was angry about the killing and the lies and the theft, and the way I'd been used.' Fox wiped her eyes, surprised that speaking the truth could bring the pain so close, so quickly.

'You were right to be angry,' Mica said.

Several people murmured their agreement and Fox heard a staccato patter as someone clapped the beat of the Persica Reel. She smiled. 'Angry, yes. But Lark was right too. About her life suiting her, about her choices being none of my business. I want to return the lace and thank her. We should let her decide what to do with what she created. The thing is, I'd like you to accompany me. All of you, and anyone else you care to bring along. In honour of Lark.'

The sun was out the next morning as the procession made its way from Oak House to Mallow House. It had none of the formality of a traditional Komey procession. There was no companion leading them and there were as many Berans present as Companionaris.

Lark must have heard of Fox's plans because she met them at the gate, cotton bolls bobbing in the ornamental fields on either side of her. She was dressed in a formal tunic and wore lace gloves, her lapels bristled with threaded needles.

Fox halted in front of her and bowed, held out the gift.

'Returning my lace, I hear,' Lark said, but she accepted the package. She turned it over in her hands, smoothed the wrapping paper. Slowly, and with great care, Lark pulled on the longer of the two ribbon tails. The bow unravelled and Lark handed it off to the sewing sister beside her. 'This paper is familiar,' Lark said. 'The twenty-first Mallow Companion's brushwork, if I'm not mistaken. I will look it up in the record of gifts between our houses. I'll let you know.'

'I suppose that means you'll write to me,' Fox said, 'because I'm leaving this afternoon.'

'Ah,' Lark smiled, 'you have me cornered. All those letters you've written...'

'Unanswered,' Fox said.

'Perfect words do not foster a warm and deep conversation. And your words were always too perfect.'

Fox opened her mouth to protest, closed it again. She was here to honour Lark, not to argue.

Lark turned the gift over and pulled back the folded edges of the paper to reveal the collars. She snorted, nostrils flaring at the sight of the damage. She lifted the worst affected collar, held it up. 'Well... I'd heard you'd damaged them, but this one is unrecognisable.'

'I used it to sheathe my knife.'

'A knife?' Lark's mouth thinned. 'Was that really necessary? Lace and knives do not belong together.'

'But in this instance—' Fox stopped, checked herself. 'You're right and I apologise, but your lace saved lives. More than that, your pattern heralded the Persica Reel and the role of the gulls. It is part of the story of the Stone Body's renewal.' Fox looked at the surrounding landscape and Lark followed her gaze. The cotton was thick and healthy, but it was the exuberant verges beside the path that held their attention. The plants were healthy and diverse, and there were herbs and flowers in the mix, some that hadn't been seen for generations.

Lark sighed, returned her attention to the collars, lay the more damaged one on top of the other, ran her finger over the broken threads. 'Well... In this instance, lace joined knife for good purpose.' Then she stood up straight and returned Fox's bow, only Lark's was longer, slower and deeper. Then she took Fox's hand. 'Thank you for the gift. I will journal about its meaning, discuss it with the Mallow Companion. We are sisters of a sort, Fox, you and I. I don't dispute that. And I am glad to see you standing in front of me. Letters don't always suffice, you see. A letter might change things, but a body speaking words matters more. Take this as my advice: be present and courageous on your tour of the provinces.' Then she looked Fox up and down. 'But that doesn't mean you should completely ignore convention. You still look dishevelled.' Lark reached out and straightened Fox's lapel. The motion pulled her sleeve back and Fox saw nascent rock skin growing on Lark's arms.

Fox shivered at the sight. So, Lark had abandoned her dust bush tea. The world really was changing.

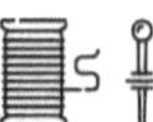

Talia rock spoke as she walked toward Yarrow. Nothing too complicated. She'd been practising, but was yet to master Oria's technique. She rock whispered a rhyme about birds flying west, combined it with an image of the Komic Sea. Her dragon twin, the eighth dancer, held his head high and away from her, signalling his uncertainty. But he sent images of rock-shaped waves. They were making progress. Talia wasn't convinced he understood, but knew it would be easier to communicate when she was on his back. At least he was no longer tightening the air whenever she stepped near. She rested a hand on his patterned scales. Rambling flowers. It didn't suit his personality, but he'd picked up the imagery from Pearl's presence in the orchard at the end of the dance. Evidently, Talia was a poor match. She shouldn't have let Aikin push her into the dance. She should have known better...

'Stop that,' she spoke aloud.

Behind her, Aikin protested he'd done nothing wrong, was doing nothing wrong.

She sighed, shook her head, but didn't immediately turn around to explain. It was difficult being close to him, and she dreaded the intimacy of the journey ahead. She took a moment, composed herself, then looked back, reminding herself to be compassionate. He looked diminished, bound and guarded, standing on the quay. 'Not you,' she said. 'I wasn't speaking to you.'

Even bound and gagged, he frightened her. And the thought of him riding behind her, arms around her, was abhorrent. But her feelings didn't matter. She'd be safe enough. They would be over the sea. If he knocked her off Yarrow, they'd both fall, and he was too selfish to do that.

She moved closer to Yarrow, lent against him, stroked his neck, felt his comforting heat. Yarrow bent his head and sniffed her hair. It seemed to reassure him because the air surrounding them relaxed. Talia reached up and rubbed the poll between his ears, and he brought his head lower still, enjoying the sensation. Then she lent in, cupped his tufted ear, whispered into it, simultaneously sharing images of maps and the flight ahead: 'We're going to carry him. We don't like him, but we can't burden a crew with him and he can't remain on the Stone Body.'

Aikin coughed. 'I can hear you, you know. And what are we waiting for if you're so anxious to be rid of me?'

'You're eager to see the motherland.'

'Not how I'd put it, but eager to be somewhere where I'm not covered in ropes and chains.'

She looked him over. 'I don't see any chains.'

He shrugged. 'Ropes then.'

Talia turned away again and tapped Yarrow's shoulder. The dragon lowered himself. There was no saddle, but his shoulder plates would cup their thighs. She climbed on, took a deep breath and gestured to the guards to bring Aikin forward. They unbound him, lifted him up and set him down behind her.

'Hold onto me,' she said.

He clutched her tunic, seemingly as reluctant to embrace her as she was to be embraced. 'What if I get tired? What if I pass out?'

'If I can stay awake, you can too.' Then Talia rock spoke, sharing an image with Yarrow of the dragon taking flight with his two passengers. Yarrow responded, lifting into the air, and Aikin yelped and grabbed hold of her.

Aikin had to speak into her ear to be heard, 'So, you're really going to do this? Banish me?' For a moment, he fell silent, and she rock sensed his sorrow and fear. When he spoke again, Yarrow had gained speed, and the wind whipped at his words. 'I always wanted to see Galea, but not like this. Please Talia, don't do it. There's no need. Drop me off somewhere remote on the Stone Body. It's not too late. No one need know. Please.'

Talia didn't answer. She leant into Yarrow and urged him forward. For a moment, she wondered whether Aikin would let go, give up on life, allow himself to tumble into the waves, but he wrapped his arms around her and leant forward.

Talia looked down, watched Port Briar fall away, and soon there was nothing in front of them nor behind them apart from the vast magnificence of the Komic Sea.

JOIN MY READING COMMUNITY

Thank you for reading *The Rush of Stone.*
If you enjoyed the book, please consider joining my reading community. You'll be the first to know about new releases, including the release of *The Stone Caller*, sequel to *The Rush of Stone*.
Visit www.torroxburgh.com/join
When you join my reading community, you'll receive a free ebook short story: *The Tidings.*

About The Tidings
When a man is found dead in a quiet Australian town, Detective Senior Constable Romy DuBois finds an unlikely ally in her investigation - a territorial magpie who can speak to her in perfect Old Birdic. As they investigate a string of cockatoo murders and a human death, they discover that justice comes in many forms, and some crimes can only be solved when two species work together. But in a world where humans and birds see justice differently, can there ever truly be a perfect resolution?
The Tidings is a darkly humorous murder mystery that blends natural and human law, told through the sharp eyes of Australia's most vigilant bird.

PLEASE LEAVE A REVIEW

Enjoyed this book? Your opinion can make all the difference.
Your review can help other readers find their next book. Writing a
review helps everyone, including me.
Please share your thoughts online. Whether it's a review at your
favourite bookstore or on your reading app, or a quick post on social
media, there is a beautiful wisdom of crowds when readers speak
directly to readers.
Thank you.

ACKNOWLEDGMENTS

I'm grateful to readers of Book 1, who pressed me to write *The Rush of Stone*. It took far too many years, but their persistence worked. I'd also like to thank my family who supported me to return to writing, and Georgette Kavelas and Ari Roxburgh for chasing my typos.

I am also grateful to Midnight Voss for her developmental edit, to Beauregard Furu for proofing the manuscript, to Stuart Bache for the cover, and to Patrick and Robert at Bigger On The Inside Media for website and graphic design support.

My thanks to my colleague, June Wilson for our deep discussions about plots and writing.

Finally, I'd like to thank Norma and Lindsay Rose, the Falkiner-Rose family, and Leslie Falkiner-Rose for their hospitality in hosting the Retreaters on our periodic writing sojourns on the Mornington Peninsula.

BOOKS BY TOR ROXBURGH

Tor Roxburgh is an emerging epic fantasy author with over 30 years of professional writing experience. She has published 17 works across speculative fiction, young adult novels, non-fiction, and short stories. A multidisciplinary creator, she exhibits artwork internationally and co-hosts *OK Smart-Ass*, a technology podcast. Her love of crafting worlds extends beyond the page – when not writing or creating art, she can be found reupholstering furniture, tiling floors or building stone walls.

EPIC FANTASY

The Light Heart of Stone
The Rush of Stone

SHORT STORIES

The Tidings (enjoy reading the ebook for free by joining Tor's email list at www.torroxburgh.com/join or read the story in print in the *Who Sleuthed It?* anthology)
The Boudicca Society (read the story in print in the *And Then...* anthology)

You can listen to *Ok Smart-Ass* via your favourite podcasting service or at www.oksmartass.com.

Tor's books and stories have been published by William Heinemann Australia, Pan Macmillan, Pan UK, Australian Consolidated Press, Greenhouse Publications, The Federation Press, Curious Crow Books (her own imprint), and Clan Destine Press.

Tor's digital home is www.torroxburgh.com and her online socials include Instagram at *torroxburghwrites,* and Facebook and TikTok at *torwriting*.

Recalling The Events Of Book 1

1 Mica and Fox conceived a child. Afterwards, Mica's obsidian rock child refused to remain with Fox.

2 Oria touched Promise's body and was transformed into a young Beranish woman.

3 Aikin organised a skirmish in an effort to steal Malachite's rock children. Fox saved Aikin's life.

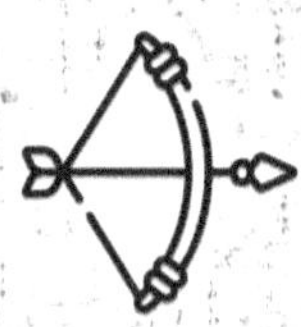

4 Fox left Komey to save the Oak sorority from Mica. Doubt and Oria entered Mica's tent, and came upon Fox.

5 Mica's obsidian rock child called him into Promise's grave. He lay down and lost consciousness.

6 Mica awoke in Komey. Beside him sat a twin, a rock man. He named his twin Obsidian.

7 Whilomena and Aikin murdered Beranish refugees and stole their rock children.

8 Aikin used a Galean device to crush the stolen rock children, and a scalpel to create new companions.

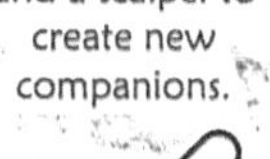
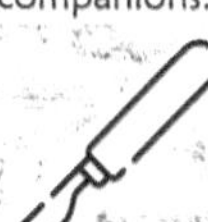

9 Whilomena and Aikin poisoned Komey's Beranish visitors. Obsidian died saving lives.

Then Fox examined her canvas map.

A Galean History Of The Stone Body

1. The Galean colonists arrived on the Stone Body 1118 years ago.

2. More colonists followed.

3. The Stone Body experienced famine.

4. Galeans and Berans died during the Treaty Wars.

5. An anonymous Galean wrote The Book of Kinesis (Promise's era).

6. The first Galean talent affected horses. The Galean settlers renamed themselves the Companionaris.

7. Fifteen years after they arrived, the Companionaris signed a treaty with the Berans.

8. Provincial boundaries were drawn three years later.

9. Now, 1118 years later, famine returns.